PRAISE FOR

THE PEARL OF KUWAIT

"With the innocent voice of Cody, [Paine] reaches something closer to *Huckleberry Finn*, a kind of clear-eyed naivete that stumbles on cultural insights without any self-consciousness or political correctness." —*The Christian Science Monitor*

"Sometimes comic, sometimes brutal . . . A straight-ahead adventure tale." —*Los Angeles Times*

"A tour de force: Mark Twain meets Joseph Heller." —*The Newark Star-Ledger*

"*The Pearl of Kuwait* [does] an awesome job at making us alternately grin at and grieve over the Desert Storm combat experience— but mostly grin. . . . Following in the bootprints of war comedies like *Catch-22*, *M*A*S*H* and *Three Kings*, Paine's debut novel convinces us that war is not only hell, it's funny as hell." —*January Magazine*

"This year's soothsayer award . . . has to go to Tom Paine, who taps into the Zeitgeist with *The Pearl of Kuwait*. This novel has it all: Baghdad, bad-boy U.S. Marines, the first gulf war and even a Kuwaiti princess." —*The Kansas City Star*

THE PEARL
OF KUWAIT

ALSO BY TOM PAINE

Scar Vegas and Other Stories

THE PEARL
OF KUWAIT

TOM PAINE

ci AD

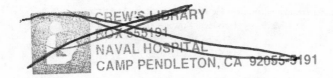
A HARVEST BOOK • *HARCOURT, INC.*

ORLANDO AUSTIN SAN DIEGO NEW YORK TORONTO LONDON

www.HarcourtBooks.com

This is a work of fiction. Names, characters, places, organizations,
and events are the products of the author's imagination or
are used fictitiously, and any resemblance to actual persons,
living or dead, events, or locales is entirely coincidental.

Library of Congress Cataloging-in-Publication Data
Paine, Tom.
The pearl of Kuwait/Tom Paine.—1st ed.
p.   cm.
ISBN 0-15-100518-4
ISBN 0-15-602898-0 (pbk.)
1. Americans—Kuwait—Fiction. 2. Vietnamese Americans—Fiction.
3. Marines—Fiction. 4. Kuwait—Fiction.   I. Title.
PS3566.A342 P43 2003
813'.54—dc21   2002151856

Text set in Spectrum MT
Designed by Cathy Riggs

Printed in the United States of America
First Harvest edition 2003
A C E G I K J H F D B

Do not let them have imagination,
it is enough to carry ammunition.
——RUPERT BROOKE

THE PEARL
OF KUWAIT

CHAPTER 1

All marines serve a six-month tour at sea at least once in their hitch as marines, and Tommy Trang and me were stationed together as Force Recon marines with another eight hundred marines on the amphibious assault ship USS *Inchon* in the Persian Gulf. Three months before the Gulf War and we were off the coast of Bahrain. We were chilling on our racks down within the *Inchon,* and I was telling Trang again about how like one time I had come in to check on him when he was in Walter Reed Hospital—he had been 'injured' during some advanced reconnaissance training at Quantico—and found a full colonel from the U.S. Rangers in there in dress uniform with all sorts of combat medals from Vietnam, and how the old dude was holding Trang's hand and crying like you have never seen a man cry, and how this was one combat-hardened old warrior dude and how he started banging his fist on his heart. I was telling Trang this again as it was curious stuff, but also thinking it might prompt him to open up about his Vietnamese past, as all he had been willing to admit as truth to date was that he was born in Vietnam in like 1974, that his father was a U.S. marine, and that he had been brought up in Trenton by his Vietnamese mother until she died and he joined the marines with faked papers at sixteen. If you asked him for more data, he'd just parrot his name, rank, and serial number with a grin. But then one day, with an even huger grin than usual, he let on his *real* last name wasn't even Trang, and that in Vietnamese Trang was like a girl's 'flower' name like Rose. It turned out Trang had enlisted under his dead mother's first name, to like win some honor for her.

Tommy Trang's favorite book was *Winners of the Congressional Medal of Honor,* and he stuck his grinning face in it every day for an hour, like others read the Bible. The more he read that book of mostly dead war heroes like Smedly Butler and Herman "Hard Head" Hanneken, who had earned their country's highest military honor for valor, the more bummed Trang was that we were like just steaming in circles around the Persian Gulf. He was just totally confident about his warrior skills, Tommy Trang. More than any other marine of my experience, Trang was hungry for trigger time so he could perform some heroics. Most marines wrote him off as a cocky gook, but as a surfer I got a kick out of his stoked vibe of superiority. Sometimes I'd see him just sitting on his rack spinning an empty M16 shell casing in his fingers like he was waiting for the call to arms. It looked like a real old bronze shell casing, kind of crushed like someone stomped on it. All Trang would tell me about the shell casing in those early days was that it came from like the Vietnam War.

Anyway, one day Trang just tossed the book of soldier heroes across the room with a hardcore groan and kicked upwards into the rack above, where I was sitting on my Cordell surfboard— without the fins—and reading. The board had general approval all around from my fellow marines, as it had a killer Stars and Stripes painted on it topside. Anyway, Trang said, "Tell me something cool, Carmichael." One thing about our being serious comrades-in-arms, over time the immigrant Tommy Trang started to talk like *me* some, using words like *dude* and *cool* and *like.*

"Trang, like what?"

"Like what you reading up there?"

"A guidebook about Kuwait."

"So tell me about Kuwait, dude."

So I told Trang about Kuwait. I told Trang the Kuwaitis were so loaded they like could buy most of America. I told him they were so loaded because 500 million years ago these like *amoebas* died and fell to the bottom of the sea, and this layer of dead *amoebas* got pushed down underground and became a layer of limestone geologists call 'Arab-D,' and this limestone was like a sponge full of *oil.* Trang wasn't into amoebas, or oil, and told me to tell him some cooler stuff. So I told him the shoreline around here was once called the 'Pirate Coast,' and that Arab pirates used to attack British ships from the islands and inlets roundabouts and slit the throat of all the infidels on board yelling praises for Allah, and that the Brits had to mount expeditions from Bombay against these pirates, and pretty much took over the place in 1839. It was a lousy old guidebook, but Trang made me read everything there was about the throat-slitting pirates, and every time I stopped he kicked the bottom of my rack. I remember I had stopped again as there was nothing *more* about Arab pirates, and when I continued I read, *In the days before oil, Kuwait was known for its pearl traders . . .*

Tommy Trang's freckled semi-Asian face emerged over the upper bunk, and his green-yellow cat eyes were like glowing, and he asked to see *exactly* where it said about the *pearls* in the guidebook. After a while I got to know, when Trang's cat eyes were glowing and his rock jaw jutting, *watch out!* I put my finger on the section and handed over the book, and then Tommy Trang read to *me*— kind of slowly and with some accent so you could tell the powerful dude wasn't born in America—about the major beds of pearls off Kuwait. In the days before oil there were ten thousand divers off the coast of Kuwait bringing up pearls. Trang jumped off his rack and read about the old pearl-trading days in the Kingdom of Kuwait. He was totally stoked about the historical pearls of Kuwait, but not out of like *historical interest.* It was Trang's opinion that the country of Kuwait was so loaded that they didn't give a damn about pearls anymore, so for fifty years or more those fat clams had sat down there on the bottom of the Persian Gulf, greedily hanging on to pearls as big as Trang's fist. That's what I got for the next week: Trang shaking his clenched fist in my face and saying *this big, man, pearls this big.*

Tommy Trang didn't keep his vision of monster pearls to himself. One time I came in and found him shaking an empty duffel bag in front of Captain Pitovik and saying how they could *fill one of these bags* in an hour with the biggest pearls. Captain Pitovik was a grizzled helicopter pilot with some serious gambling debts, and Trang told me later Pitovik was good to go, he'd drop us in the waters off Kuwait at night in our scuba gear, and extract us a few hours later for a cut of the pearl action. Trang was talking about 'utilizing' a helicopter from the Marine Corps for our own private pearl-salvaging operation off Kuwait, and if we were caught we'd be in Leavenworth for ten years banging rocks.

Captain Pitovik came to me privately to assure me he'd drop us and extract us up as part of some other operation, and so no one would ever be the wiser. And then a black marine sergeant dude who called himself Mr. Slick got right in my face and said he was replacing me on Operation Bigass Pearl—as this Mr. Slick called it—as Tommy Trang said *I didn't have the balls* for this walk in the park. This Mr. Slick kept calling me 'Sunny,' which was a nick-name slapped on me by some marines on account of my being a blond surfer from Huntington Beach, California, and generally having a stoked 'good-to-go' vibe at all times and under all cir-cumstances. Anyway, after the visit from Mr. Slick—who was an A-OK dude if you got past the ghetto gangster act—I went to Trang and told him I was in, and so we slapped each other five and shouted the Marine Corps seal call of *oooraah!*, and scrounged up some excellent maps of the waters off Kuwait, and sat down to make it a *mission.* We picked a drop, adjusted our schedules over the next few days to fit in with Pitovik's flight plans, and figured what stuff to snag from the scuba locker. Mr. Slick pulled back and agreed to stay on the helo, when it was clear we needed another guy up in the rotor, and we promised him his quarter share of pearls anyway.

Nobody really questioned if the beds of ancient pearls were still in the waters off Kuwait, and if they were there, maybe the clams weren't sitting in the waters smack off the beaches in front of the skyscrapers of downtown Kuwait City, waiting for two teenage scuba-diving reconnaissance marines to shovel them up into mesh bags. The night before the operation neither of us slept, and Trang went on and on about how if it worked out, this was just the sort of stuff we'd tell stories about when we were old dudes, and then Trang changed his mind and said he was never going to be an old dude in a VA hospital telling stories, but wanted to keep rolling the dice as hard and fast as he could until they came up snake eyes, and he slapped his shoulder tattoo which said DIE A HERO. Anyway, I pointed out to Trang we weren't *fighting*, or *dying* with any luck, but trying to get our asses tossed into the brig for the sake of a bunch of pearls mentioned in an old Kuwaiti guidebook. I said there wasn't even any *honor* in it, and Trang looked bummed when I said this, as I guess he figured I had a point.

The actual trip to the jump zone was like a *party.* Captain Pitovik brought along a couple of his gambling buddies who hammered beers and slapped our backs and told us we were two crazy-ass leatherneck marines from like the heroic days of yore, and said they just wanted a pearl each as a souvenir. One of them said this was the sort of legendary stuff they experienced when *they* joined the marines, and they were proud Trang, Slick, and me were not worried about our long-term careers in the Marine Corps like so many other zipper-head marines nowadays. It was kind of cool having these old officers so into Trang, as to be totally honest I got the vibe that your average marine had Trang pegged as a nutcase. I guess because Trang was always fired up with schemes like this pearl operation, or generally tossing off an attitude that he was like the greatest warrior in the history of the Marine Corps. Add to Trang's cocky attitude that he was a 'semi-gook,' and reminded some marines about how we lost the war in Vietnam just by his grinning *face,* and what I am saying is that I was like his only good friend in the Corps.

Anyway, that night the helicopter *whoop-whoop-whooped* with us over the black waters of the gulf. Looking back, we could see the lights of the USS *Inchon* retreating, and ahead, the skyscrapers of downtown Kuwait coming at us *fast.* The door to the helo was open and the warm air whistled by, and Trang and I were dressed in our black scuba gear with tanks on our back and mesh bags and flashlights in our hands, and I wanted to call the thing off, but then

I got punched in the gut with the sure knowledge I was like meant to hang with this excellent dude Tommy Trang, even if it meant risking Leavenworth. Captain Pitovik said we were over the release point, and he hovered. The office towers of downtown Kuwait were a couple of football fields away.

As I jumped from the helicopter I looked up and saw the flames of the Kuwaiti oil fields pluming in the distance, and then I shot down under the piss-warm waters of the Persian Gulf in a tunnel of frothing bubbles. It is strange to think, but as I swam back up to the surface I thought: *I am born! I am alive!* It was like at that moment I was on my surfboard and looking down the vertical face of some legendary liquid mountain like the seventy-foot waves at Maverick's. So I broke the surface with a shout and swam over to Tommy Trang when he popped up and I was just so totally stoked I started slapping his back, and he slapped mine as I guess he was feeling a similar power stoke, and we raised our fists together and pumped the Arab night air and yelled his tattooed motto, *DIE A HERO!*

When we dove down kicking our flippers to the bottom of the gulf we found it was pretty barren. We swam along together shining our beams right and left, but it was muddy and barren as the moon, not a damn clam. I shined my light on Trang's mask, and he shook his head and pointed off into the black gulf waters, and we'd kick hard onwards, but we found nothing in an hour to report except a big desalination intake pipe, and a busted-up fish trap made of like woven palm tree stuff. Soon after we swam through this like white cloud of fish eggs or something, and then we saw this massive spaghetti highway of oil pipes. Finally I tapped Trang with the flashlight, and pointed to my watch, and motioned back to the pick-up point with my thumb, and Trang shook his head and *swam off.*

And Trang started swimming fast, like he was trying to dump me. I whipped after him, until finally I grabbed his ankle and yanked him back pulling off a flipper, and jerked my thumb backwards toward the pick-up point. Trang nodded, and his cat eyes were glowing in his mask, and I let him go, and *damn if he doesn't keep heading off away from the pick-up point with only one flipper,* so then I grabbed him again, and this time I didn't let go, but just kicked like a bastard until we broke the surface. What do you do when your buddy wants to screw up so bad?

I yanked off his mask, and my own, and started yelling how we *had to get back for the Pitovik's pickup.* He yelled like a total maniac how we had to keep looking for the *pearls,* how they were probably out in deeper water, how there was plenty of air and time, and then Trang tried to shove off me and swim away. I didn't let go of his mask hanging around his neck, and Trang and me started to wrestle and curse each other there in the Persian Gulf, and I told him he *was* a crazy gook just like the other marines all said and why the hell was I his friend anyway, and he slugged me in my nose so hard it rocked me back in the water and told me he didn't ask me to be his damn *friend,* so I slugged with a roundhouse that clipped his ear and told him, *screw it, man, I ain't your friend, then,* and he slugged me right in the mouth and knocked a front tooth right back to my tonsils, where it bounced like a pinball and I damn near choked on it and the blood.

I remember Trang shaking me like a dog and telling me to *shut the fuck up* because I was gurgling and yelling about the tooth. As I might or might not have said, Tommy Trang didn't swear—it was one of some secret set of ten personal 'rules for warrior greatness' he followed along with doing five hundred sit-ups or push-ups every day—so hearing Trang swear I went dead in the water and then I heard it too. Someone was *singing* out there in the dark across the rippling waters of the Persian Gulf, and without another word we both started to stroke quietly toward the beautiful voice. It was a young woman's voice singing in Arabic and we were pulled to it like by a massive body magnet. We were able to barely see the dark outline of a funny-looking Arab rowboat of some sort, and in it a little figure dressed in black outlined against the quarter-moon night.

Then the figure ceased with the singing like she heard us frogmen coming, and there was a wooden scratching sound and we could see this figure shoving something off the bow. There was a splash, and then a real awful Arabic cry that daggered right into your heart. We both started sprinting toward the rowboat, and as we sprinted the big splash came as she went over the side, and we yanked down our masks and dove, with me shining a light ahead as Trang swam like a torpedo in the funnel of light. We came on the now naked little Arab chick—she must have tossed off her robe at the last second—about thirty feet down, kicking hard for the surface with her free leg, the other leg tied by a yellow polystyrene rope to something heavy below dragging her down. Trang had his knife out, and was trying to both saw through this rope and kick with her for the surface from below. I tried without luck to shove my bubbling mouthpiece into her mouth, at the same time I kicked and pulled her upwards by the armpit, and then the Arab chick just sort of sagged into deadweight.

Trang yanked the final strands of the rope apart and we drove her hard to the surface. I held her head above the waters while Trang flopped in the dinghy and then dragged her aboard. There was no way I could get in the dinghy too, so I just sort of treaded water and held the dive light so Trang could see what the hell he was doing, and he announced the naked Arab chick had a pulse but wasn't breathing, and I said to start CPR, and with his like palm supporting he gently bent her neck back. Her lips opened, and Trang lowered his head and just as he pressed his lips to hers her eyes snapped open and locked on Trang and then she started gagging up seawater. Anyway, that kiss—if you can call CPR a kiss— was like the real beginning of all the adventures in Arabia for Trang and me.

Right after this sort of 'kiss of life' Trang laid on the suicidal Arab girl, a huge Kuwaiti navy ship blinded us with a monster searchlight. We yelled and waved our arms and told them to cut that thing off, but they just burned it into us as they brought that bow damn near over us. Then like one of them threw us a ring buoy, even though the ship was now like five feet away, and the idiot sailor hit me in the head with it—and it felt like it was made of solid wood.

So the Arab sailors snatched the naked little chick right away, and ushered us roughly down inside the huge ship to this like room with wall-to-wall white shag carpeting like you'd see in 1970s America, and in the corner was like a serious golden throne. The

Arab sailor dudes left us in there without a word, so Trang like right away hops up on the throne. He looks around like he's thinking what to do next now that he's King of Kuwait.

"You look good up there," I said. "Say something."

"Let's party," said Trang.

"Roger that," I said.

"Let's teach these crazy Arab dudes to party," said Trang.

I looked around at our situation but said, "Roger that, Trang."

Tommy Trang like pointed right then to the white shag carpet, and then I saw that I was leaving a trail of blood. It was dripping from my scalp and nose, down my wet suit and onto the floor. I was also bleeding from my mouth from Trang knocking out the tooth earlier in the evening, but had been swallowing the blood, and licking the hole with my tongue. Right then this like Kuwaiti officer comes in. Trang starts jiving the dude from the throne like, *Hey man, I'm your new king. Let's party!*

The Kuwaiti officer is like a doctor and starts to deal with my nose which he says is broken. When he finishes with screwing my nose back on and has it taped, he deals with my head wound. He has a little leather doctor bag, and I see him get out the needle and thread. Trang comes over to watch the doctor sew me up. I don't know, maybe it was because my man Trang was watching, but when the Kuwaiti doctor takes out the needle, I tell him, *no, man, I don't need that novocaine, I'm a U.S. marine, Semper Fi!* Doctor Kuwaiti says nothing, just gives me this cool Arab shrug that seems to say he figured I didn't need the freeze, as clearly I was one tough U.S. marine. If I had to do it again I might have opted for the needle, if my man Trang hadn't been looking on. Trang had the doc look at my mouth, and when I opened up the doc started laughing—I guess at the gap in the front of my mouth. He tapped my guts, and I said *no dude, I spit the tooth out.* He shrugged again at my mouth and said, *Inshallah.* It was the first time we heard this phrase we were to hear so much over here in Arab-land, which boiled down to, *God Wills It.* I wasn't sure *God Willed* my tooth getting knocked out, if he hadn't been my *main man,* I might have rightly blamed Trang. The Arabs were big into *inshallahing* just about every obvious screwup.

No one came to see us after the Kuwaiti doc left, and the door to the room turned out to be locked. Trang was clearly curious about what was going to go down next in our young warrior lives—and he gave off the vibe he figured it was all going to be cool. Trang *always* thought the *next thing* was going to be totally cool—he always had his arms wide open to his golden future. Anyway, when the navy ship docked in downtown Kuwait, we were escorted off inside a crowd of like twelve Arab sailors, less apparently because they thought we were going to try to bust a move and escape, but more to like for some reason keep our presence a secret from anyone onshore. Somebody would have had hawk eyes to spot us, because like ten feet off the ship surrounded by all these Arab dudes, we were shoved into a golden Jaguar with tinted windows.

There were four of us crammed in the backseat, with me and Trang in the middle back, and the driver and a silent dude in the front, and all were in the local robes. Nobody said a word, but the driver kept leering in the rearview mirror at me, and as we pulled up to the Sheraton's back door he said in lousy English, *"You see her big tits, the crazy little Princess?"* Smash! The Arab dude in the passenger seat clocked him across the jaw with his left fist, and the driver's head bounced off the side window of the Jaguar and cracked it into a spiderweb.

Tommy Trang mouthed with a huge grin: *Princess?*

Then the door to the hotel room flew open and this monster like forty-year-old Arab dude in a full foreign military outfit with all the ribbons and medals is blocking the doorway. He like takes in us two teenage fools bouncing on the bed, and looks serious as hell and I was thinking: *no medals for me and the Trangster.* But then he sees the case of Heineken, and softly shuts the door behind him. He goes to the case, takes a bottle in hand, and whips it around. You would have thought he was smashing the bottle to smithereens, but he just clipped off the top on the wall near the shitter. It was snapped off so there was a broke glass top, and he like tips that sucker in the air a couple of inches over his fat lips and *glug, glug, glug, gone!*

So he was one of us, it seemed. Trang like finally put on the local robe and some boots that were just like marine boots, and hustled to the case and flipped him another Heineken, and he like twisted off the top in his teeth, even though Heinekens are not twist off. Once again, here was a sign this Arab Military Monster dude was A-OK, and more, that maybe our futures were still bright. So then we settled into some idle chitchat, which we were to come to learn was the Arab way and gave us all a chance to pound some more beers. We like talked about the weather in Kuwait, which as you might expect was like the weather in L.A., except hotter. There is not a lot to say about the weather in Kuwait, but we hammered a couple more beers agreeing it was *hot in Arabia.*

Your Arab is not really one for holding his booze. Maybe that's because they don't get much practice partying with old Allah eye-balling, but they tend to shed their civilization skin after a couple of pops, and reveal what is beating in their big, crazy hearts, *and it can go either way.* But this big dude was in a thumbs-up mood, right away he gets to singing the praises of America, and Americans, and American girls. Mostly the American girls, and we agreed they were some of the best in the world, but then he kept hinting American girls were all sluts, but to be civil we steered clear of this topic and got back to the weather in Kuwait. I for one was wondering about now if Mr. Arab Military Dude was going to get around to business, but then he settled his bulk into the couch to talk about stewardesses he had screwed and monster parties he had attended in Dallas. He had slept with a Dallas Cowboys cheerleader, and said she was the best despite tits of air, and how he watched her on satellite at home and how it still made him hard as a sword under his robes. He imitated her pom-pom dance, and to see this big Arab Military Dude high-stepping *was* pretty funny.

And then Trang motions to me and said, "This dude here is from Dallas."

Arab dude says, "This is true? I know many oilmen in Dallas."

Trang says, "Carmichael's family is in oil."

Arab dude said, "I must know your father!"

I don't know if he meant he wanted to know my father, or he was sure he *knew* my father from the international rich-dude oil circles. The only oil my father 'knew' was when he changed it under his old Chevy in Huntington Beach, California—and even then, on any given week, my father was lucky he could *afford* the quarts of oil. He was a boozer, my father. But anyway, one thing was sure, as a supposed oil-rich Texan I was now a golden boy. Arab Military Dude starts slapping me on the back and telling me *we must talk about doing a deal.* So then he says *you two are my friends!* And how friendship means the world to an Arab, and he damn near weeps as he embraces us one after the other. And then he looks around fiercely and says, *We are brothers! Your enemies are my enemies!*

Still, we didn't know this Arab Military Dude's story—like he could have just drifted into our hotel room *by accident.* But we weren't going to call him on it, as in our present screwy situation, Trang and me were in need of some Arab 'brothers' who thought 'our enemies were his enemies.' So Trang and me just kept partying hard with the big dude, and finally he got tired of talking tits and ass, and jumps his bulk up off the couch and says, "You saved the life of the Princess Lulu!"

So there it was!

The massive Arab dude was here on *official royal business,* sent by the King of Kuwait to invite us to like a royal reception that night at the local castle *in our honor!* And he introduces himself as Colonel Fawwaz, and says the Kuwaiti Kingdom is in our debt and will award us a medal for heroism. What we didn't catch right then was that this Arab Military Dude 'Colonel Fawwaz' was Colonel Fawwaz Abdul Aziz *Al Saud,* and that he was a *Saudi* military dude, and that he was of the *Saudi* Royal Family, and that he was *Princess Lulu's fiancé!* None of that was clear to us, because these Arabs spend so much time talking tits and weather as a way of avoiding any discussion of *the factual stuff that matters to an American!*

Trang was pretty stoked about the Kuwaiti medal for heroism. I think he was imagining how the medal would look on his Marine Corps Dress Blues. Colonel Fawwaz looks around our hotel room after the buzz of the announcement wore off like he was real deflated, and slaps his arm around my shoulder, and tells me we must all have *fun until the party!* Colonel Fawwaz was a dude, as we were to come to know too well, with a real short attention span and a real like obsession with *fun* as like a way of life. Next thing we know Colonel Fawwaz has us downstairs in the lobby of the hotel, and then in the back of a Rolls Royce with tinted windows. Trang and I are sitting on either side of big Colonel Fawwaz, and Trang leans across the foreign dude's gut to slap me five about us riding in a Rolls Royce. Colonel Fawwaz wants to slap us both five, and we do that, in the spirit of international brotherhood. There was a real feeling of partying brotherhood in that Rolls Royce that afternoon, and it is too bad what came down the pike later.

We were traveling in the Rolls Royce, which was cool, but you had to take pleasure from that, and not look outside. Kuwait was mostly ugly sand-colored concrete houses, some dolled up like birthday cakes—but still ugly as hell. You join the military as a poor man's way to see the world, and then find out much of the world is *plug ugly* compared to America. I was glad when we got past the last ring road and out into the desert. Of course the desert wasn't the pretty sand dunes like in the movies, it was mostly gravel plains, but still, it was some *open space.* I right away started looking for the Bedouin cruising on their camels, but there were none to be seen, and I was getting kind of bored, when Colonel Fawwaz says we are almost at the races.

Trang and me both figured Colonel Fawwaz was talking car races, but he was talking *camels*. We got out of the Rolls to walk around a bunch of camels in this velvet-rope enclosure. Most of the camels looked the same to me, but Colonel Fawwaz pointed to a leg here, and a chest there, and pointed to the different coloring of some, and talked about who sired who and from where—he was big into the Syrian camels and some white ones called *mugathirs*—and he told us he would place bets for me and Tommy Trang, which was good as the bets were running like 10 G's a pop. Then all these kids get out of a fancy silver bus with tinted windows, the kind a rock and roll band would ride on, and all the kids looked like fourteen or so, and like that Somalian waiter at the Sheraton they are clearly foreigners, and all dressed up in their colorful monkey suits. Colonel Fawwaz pointed to his favorite jockey among the kids and said the little kid's name was Ali and he was from Bangladesh. Even from afar you could see this kid Ali was sort of a pretty boy, and he was getting a lot of attention from the Arab dudes.

Trang said right away, "Got any Kuwaiti jockeys?"

Colonel Fawwaz thought this was a good joke, and slapped Tommy Trang on the back. But then he saw Trang was serious and said, "No, no, my good friend. All the Kuwaiti boys are too heavy, and besides, what Kuwaiti mother would risk them on such a dangerous sport? Sometimes these foreign boys are very badly hurt, perhaps they will be today."

Colonel Fawwaz gave Trang a sideways glance I caught, like maybe my man Trang was a little slow to ask such a stupid question. And then Trang glanced at me, like what sort of *Arab country was it that every kid was either too fat, or too afraid to get hurt to ride a camel,* which you would think would be like their *national sport?*

Trang and me like look on as Colonel Fawwaz and I guess the owner of the camel—who the colonel said was a *sheik,* which was cool as he was my first *sheik*—help the Bangladeshi kid Ali on his camel. The trainer then like dragged the camel up to the starting line with all the other foreign kids on camels. Colonel Fawwaz points out an oil well in the distance—the race course was straight

out to this oil well. I was about to settle back into the Rolls Royce—
my head was aching a bit from the stitches and other abuse, to be
honest—when Trang spins around and says to Colonel Fawwaz
with a bigger grin than usual, "Carmichael here is a *cowboy* from
Texas."

Colonel Fawwaz spins around and says, "A Marlboro man? I
thought you were a son of oil?"

Trang says, "His family has all those oil wells like you Arabs, but
Carmichael thinks watching oil get pumped is boring, and likes to
spend his time on the family ranch as a cowboy. He's won some
rodeos too."

That was so Trang, to make up this stuff about me being a *cowboy*. As you will see, Trang was a huge fan of slinging shit for the
kick he got out of seeing some stick. Trang didn't look like he was
a chain yanker, but like that was his genius: under the blank semi-
Asian face was a sort of secret poker player who was never totally
satisfied unless he was doubling down, doubling his bets or just saying some dubious shit to double the trouble. It was kind of weird,
really. It didn't look like there was much going on under his face
most of the time, and then, *bang,* he'd pop up with some totally
crazy stuff like that I was a *cowboy.*

Anyway, Colonel Fawwaz was pretty baked from the booze,
and he was back in a thumbs-up mood. He started calling a lot of
Kuwaiti Royals around and telling them, as far as I could tell, that
I was like a Rich Son of oil, a U.S. Marine Military Hero *and a Cowboy
from Texas to boot.* The Kuwaitis made much of this, and wanted to
know why I was a U.S. marine if I was so rich, and Tommy Trang
told them I got in trouble *with two sluts with big tits back in Texas.* The
Kuwaitis enjoyed this and it made me even more of an excellent
dude in their eyes, as they were suckers for a little talk about American sluts with big tits. So then Trang says he'd bet the good men of
Kuwait that if they put *me* on a camel, *I'd make those foreign jockeys eat
camel dust.*

Colonel Fawwaz was excited about bringing something new to
the camel races. In two shakes I was on a big yellow camel. The
Kuwaitis sent one of the little jockeys off to sit in a Rolls Royce.

Then Colonel Fawwaz was handed a M16 by some official dude, and he fired off a burst into the sky, and *the race was on!* Except my camel just sat there, with me kicking in my heels for all I was worth. The other jockeys were well ahead of me in a big pack heading for the oil well, and the Kuwaitis were yelling and laughing and calling *Cowboy! Cowboy!* They were a good-humored lot of guys, and I guess it was pretty funny, but as I was in the race and a U.S. marine, *I did want to win!*

I was whacking away at the camel, although I was pretty soon surrounded by a crowd of Kuwaiti men, all giving me advice in Arabic and English at the top of their lungs, between laughter. Those Kuwaiti men really knew how to laugh, that's one thing I liked about them. Right then Tommy Trang pushes through and grabs the like halter of the camel and yanks at it. Damn if that camel didn't take *a few steps forward.* And then Trang stops, and so does the camel. So Trang yanks again, the camel moves, and Trang starts *running,* and the camel starts to lope along. The knot of Kuwaiti men are left behind us, and we are out in the desert, a football field behind the pack in the race.

Those Kuwaiti men were not left behind for long. Their thing was to follow the race across the desert, leaning out of the windows of their foreign cars to scream at their camels, or just to enjoy the race from their air-conditioned vehicles. I was trying to get Trang's attention over all the cars beeping around us, and all the crazy Arabs leaning out their car windows and yelling encouragement at me and Trang. My man Trang is like waving his fist in the air and yelling, *"Hiyah! Hiyah!"* which is Arab for "Giddyap! Giddyap!" I am like dying from laughter up in the saddle, but did think Trang would stop running with the camel when the joke got thin, but that was stupid of me.

The oil well was a couple of miles away. The desert sun was cooking the sand at like a hundred degrees plus. Trang kept running, the camel kept following him, and the Kuwaitis in their expensive vehicles rolled all around us, screaming out their windows in Arabic and English. Trang never looked up at me, but just kept pounding harder and harder across the sand in his boots. I saw some of the foreign jockeys in the pack way ahead look back at this crazy guy chasing them on foot, and *one of them was so surprised he fell to the sand!* We never really even caught up with the main group of camels and jockeys. The clear leader of the pack ahead was the kid from Bangladesh, Ali. From afar you would have seen a little boy on a camel, chased by a bunch of other little kids on camels, and then way back behind them all a charging dude in the local robe running flat out, followed by a camel with a stocky guy, followed by dozens of honking vehicles filled with screaming Arabs.

That Ali could really whip a camel and won the race a hundred yards ahead of the rest of the camel pack. Trang put the pedal down when we were the last camel still out there running in the desert sun and the sweat was just shaking off his crew-cut head. We ended up crossing the finish line—a long red velvet rope tied between the bumpers of two Range Rovers—like ten minutes after the winner Ali. But the funny thing was *you would have thought my man Trang had won the race.* The Arabs spun their vehicles—they had followed and cheered us on the whole way—to a stop in the sand and gravel, jumped out of their vehicles, and tackled him. When you could see him again he was held up in the air by dozens of hands. They kind of paraded him around the oil well doing a sort of Bedouin war chant. The Arabs then stopped and like tossed him up and down in the air. I went over and shook little Ali the kid from Bangladesh's hand, as he seemed both relieved he wasn't going to get an ass-whooping for losing, and miffed no one noticed he won the race!

Just about every Arab there had to have a private moment with Tommy Trang. The Arabs were like ten-year-old boys, they really were tickled by Trang's desert run. Nobody there looked at him like he was a head case like in the Marines, or tried to play shrink and ask *why the hell do you do this crazy shit?* The Arabs were interested in *what* Trang did not *why* he did it: they had a hunger for a story to amuse their friends about the time the crazy American soldier ran the camel all the way to the oil well.

Tommy Trang was sucking down bottled water as fast as he could swallow. You could see his Adam's apple leaping around, and then it dawned on me that Trang *looked really down.* And a minute later came the answer, because Trang hops on a Mercedes limousine and says, *"Double or nothing against Ali back to the starting line."* Some of the Arabs let out a whoop, and then Trang's announcement of a race *with him on foot against Ali on his camel* is translated, and then all of the Arabs are screaming and ululating—that crazy thing they do with their tongues. One fat sheik was against the race because he thought Trang would die in the heat. He came up and looked in Trang's burning cat eyes, and then announced *he was cool with it too!* All the Arabs cheered—I guess because this fat Arab was a really cranky guy, who never liked anything or anyone. But he waved a big roll around, and I took it he was laying 10K on Trang—I guess just to show he liked a guy like Trang with two big crazy golden nuggets hanging between his legs. And the betting took off like crazy, with Colonel Fawwaz in charge from the top of his Rolls— I guess because he had brought my man Trang. And then I see Trang like toss his water bottle up in the sky, and he strips off the local robe. The betting is going crazy, and Trang stands there *naked* except for his boots—there were *some* limits to his craziness. By the way, I could tell a lot of the Arabs were commenting on the size of Trang's *personal equipment.* I guess they thought most Asians—or even semi-Asians—had little dicks.

Trang starts motioning to all the Arabs like *bring it on!* And one Arab gets it and shakes a carbonated-water bottle and holds his thumb over it and sprays Trang. So all the Arabs start to shake their water, and if they didn't have a bottle, yelled at their drivers or servants to bring one from their coolers. And Trang was like in such a spray I couldn't see him, but then someone fired off a volley from an M16, and he breaks from the cloud and heads off naked into the desert except for those big black boots. Little Ali didn't look too worried and was barely whipping his camel, I guess figuring Trang would be dead in the sand before the race was over. I reached down and touched the desert, *and man was it hot!*

I was on top of Colonel Fawwaz's Rolls Royce, and we were Trang's support vehicle. I did my best, standing on the roof, to keep Trang in some sort of a spray. Somebody inside kept handing me up bottles—they had tossed cases in the backseat—and I'd shake them and spray Trang. The other Arabs were leaning on their horns the whole way. Trang glanced up at me after a half mile or so, and gave me a huge grin, like *is this the most excellent experience of your young life?* And I grinned back at him and pumped my fist madly in the sky. Few get to live the extreme life like me and Trang in the last twenty-four, and it was all due to Trang. With every pump of my fist it was like I was going to crack the sky! My whole body was like shaking with this electrical buzzing!

Ali of Bangladesh was sort of trotting that camel just ahead of us—he was clearly not racing to win. And after another mile Trang was starting to slow some, and then he started to run from side to side like a drunken sailor. He was trying to guzzle water as he ran, but it mostly ended up on his face, as I think he was by now pretty totally zonked from the scorching sun. I started yelling to him to stop this craziness and get in the Rolls, but he ignored me or couldn't hear me, and when he looked in my direction I made the cutting sign across my neck, to signal *enough is enough man!* And right then from up on his camel little Ali waved to Trang in a joking way as if to say *faster, faster, you can do it!* And as Ali was waving, his camel just slammed on the brakes. The camel snapped his front knees and dropped his head to the ground all in one smooth camel motion, and little Ali the Bangladeshi jockey went ass over heels onto the desert sands.

There were cheers and horns and whoops and curses from the caravan of foreign automobiles. Trang tried to stop by Ali's side where he lay flat on his back on the desert sands, but Arabs were out of their cars and almost grabbing Trang by the arms as they pushed him forward towards the finish line. Trang stumbled forward, and at the finish line just fell to his knees and then lay back on the hot sands. The Arabs scooped him up and shoved him in the back of a Range Rover, and dozens of Arabs shook bottles of Perrier and water and sprayed him for all he was worth, while at the same time jabbering in Arabic and settling up the bets in a huge crowd behind the Range Rover.

I finally got them to shut the rear door of the Range Rover and crank up the air-conditioning to near-arctic conditions. Trang took deep gulps of the cold air as it reached him in the rear. And then he instructed me to drive him over to where the kid Ali fell off his camel and hit the sand. So I got in the driver's seat and drove away, and the Arabs all just sauntered along behind in this clot of robes, as if we were the center of the world. So we get out there to Ali, and then I see what is going on. The Arab owner of the camel had Ali the Bangladeshi jockey spread-eagled against his Jaguar, and he had the kid naked-ass, and was whipping him like a bastard. A lot of Arabs were into watching this whipping, and I got the weird vibe some of them were into it because Ali was such a pretty boy, and they were getting off seeing his small brown ass striped red. Anyway, Trang was like out of the Range Rover, and he just grabbed that whip on the backstroke and ripped it right out of the hands of that crazed Arab.

Trang was like holding the whip aloft and the Arab was pushing him backwards and screaming. Then the Arab takes a handgun out and points it at Tommy Trang's head. Everything is quiet for a second in the desert. I move forward like to get involved, and am grabbed by a dozen Arab hands. And that was when Colonel Fawwaz steps in between Trang and the pissed Arab. The Arab lowers the gun. But the pissed Arab starts storming in a circle, and then he marches over and empties the pistol into the losing camel's head. It was a semiautomatic, and was empty before the camel hit the ground.

Killing the camel seemed to chill the crazed Arab enough that Colonel Fawwaz was able to march him into the desert for a conference. Ali the Bangladeshi jockey had his arms locked onto one of Trang's naked legs. The Arabs let go of me, and I went up and handed Trang a water bottle. We both looked down at Ali and Trang said, "The kid's shaking like a dog on my leg."

Colonel Fawwaz came back and tried to take me and Trang off for a conference, but then saw Ali wasn't letting go of Trang's leg and said, "You see, we are brothers. I have taken care of this little problem of the slave."

Trang and me both looked down at Ali the Bangladeshi.

Colonel Fawwaz was full of good cheer. "You have made Sheik

Abdul very angry, but then I have explained certain things to him. And as a tribute to my long friendship with his family, he has agreed to let me buy for you this boy for the cost of his losses in the race."

"He's a slave?" said Trang. "A *slave?*"

Colonel Fawwaz smiled and said, "Not officially, of course. We have no slaves. But in fact, the boy is a slave, as were his parents. And I give him to you, Private Trang, as a small present for the rescue from the gulf of a certain important girl."

Trang shot right back, "So if he's mine, I can free him?"

Colonel Fawwaz frowned and said, "That is your *right*. But think of the boy before you take this action." And Colonel Fawwaz said something to the boy Ali, but the boy apparently spoke English which seemed to surprise Colonel Fawwaz, and the boy said, "I am the slave of Private Trang and no other."

We batted this slave problem around for a while there in the desert, but there was no way around it, no matter how much brain grease was applied: *to help the kid we had to take him on, at least for now.* Trang made it clear to the kid he was no longer a slave, but like a free kid, who could hang with us until we could figure out the best road to his future. My man Trang also decided for some unknown reason to make a kind of recruitment speech to the Bangladeshi kid about *the joys of being an American marine ready to die for Liberty and Democracy and Freedom,* and I won't repeat it here as it is pretty basic stuff and even for a marine a bit *much,* but the pretty kid Ali ate it all up like he was *starving* for this sort of apple-pie talk.

I was pretty impressed by the stoking energy Trang put into his speech about this basic American Mom-and-Apple-Pie stuff that would make some cynical civilians roll their eyes, but it was also weird hearing it from him. I didn't know Trang's past yet exactly, but I'd wager he was born into a unbelievably scrappy situation over there in Vietnam in the 1970s as a half-breed. But he was waving the flag in front of little Ali the Bangladeshi slave-boy's eyes so hard his arm was about to fall off.

Colonel Fawwaz interrupted Trang's speech to say it was time to head off to our audience with the Emir of Kuwait at Dasman

Palace. I will say Colonel Fawwaz looked more than a little *pissed* about some of what Tommy Trang was laying so thick on the former slave-boy Ali. I figured that was why Saudi Arabia like kept a strict limit on American tourists in nonwar years. They didn't want a bunch of freaky Tommy Trangs spouting a lot of solid gold American virtues to the in-the-dark towelheads.

The boy Ali hopped in the front passenger seat of the Rolls Royce and said as Tommy Trang and I got in the back, *You will take me to America?* Ali said it in this sweet high-pitched way, as clearly the kid's voice hadn't even broke yet.

And I'll tell you right now, when this was all over little Ali from Bangladesh did finally get his wish after some major-league hassles, and eventually dumped Allah and became one crazy flag-waving U.S. marine just burning to get back to old Arabia and kick some ass for American-style freedom.

CHAPTER 3

We're back at the Sheraton in Kuwait City, and little Ali from Bangladesh is assisting Trang and me into our own Marine Corps dress blue uniforms. It is time to go meet the Emir of Kuwait and like get our medals for rescuing the princess. I asked Colonel Fawwaz how our uniforms got here from the USS *Inchon,* and Colonel Fawwaz twirled his finger over his head like a helicopter. "They land on top of this hotel," said Colonel Fawwaz. I looked at Trang, and he slapped me five, as we both figured the Marine Corps wasn't pissed at us, if they were heloing in our dress blues. Trang nodded at me in a significant way that said he always knew it was all going to be cool with the Marine Corps. I don't know where he got his confidence in his personal military future, but it was like always present and accounted for!

So we were as high as you could get without stimulants after the news that we were maybe not AWOL from the Marine Corps, and I have to admit it was very cool to have little Ali acting like our butler. He was everywhere at once—brushing, ironing, shining brass. We were hustled down to the lobby, and a caravan of Mercedes limousines with tinted windows showed up, one for Trang and little Ali, and one for me, one for Colonel Fawwaz, and I guess the others were there just for show. They had flags like for diplomats on the hood, and flashing red lights.

It was not as much fun to be alone in the limousine, and the driver was closed off to me by a tinted window. I tapped on his window to like do the *friendly American thing* and chew the fat. So this driver, he like raises his eyebrows at me when the window is down, and not in a friendly way. He looks like an Arab hit man, but I've made the move to chat him up, so I ask him how he likes being a limousine driver for royals in Kuwait. He barely speaks English, but he knows I'm American as he keeps nodding back at me and sort of smiling with the question word, *America?* I'm thinking he's happy about me being American, so point to myself and say: *America, man, yes!* and kind of slap him on the shoulder, but he moves his shoulder away like I burned him, and starts going on in Arabic fast and hard, and it's clear he's *real pissed.*

We pulled up to what I guess was the Dasman Palace with that limousine driver working himself into a lather of Arabic, and I like let myself out of the limousine and think about giving up my *how-the-hell-are-ya* American way, but then say to myself, *screw that, I gotta be me!* If I'm a friendly American and the Arab locals have a problem with that, well, *they can just go to hell!* Anyway, the problem was the limousine driver stepped out of the limousine and started yelling at me and banging on the hood of the limousine for emphasis. And I'm willing to ignore him in a spirit of international brotherhood, but then he starts giving me the finger. So I get *that* without translation, and head off around the limousine to do some international relations, when little Ali grabs my arm and like drags me off to the side and explains the limousine driver is like going on about his *deep hatred for the State of Israel and Jews in general, and how he wants to like drop a nuclear bomb on the country of Israel.* The limousine driver is chopping the air with his hand as he gets back in his car, and then he speeds away leaving a track of rubber.

"Arabs hate Jews," says Ali quietly.

"You got that right," I said. "That dude's out of his tree."

I like prayed right then that whoever was in charge steer me clear of lunatic Arabs like that limousine dude, but this Israel craziness ran through most all the Arabs, as will be clear in a minute. Anyway, the Dasman Palace looked like it belonged in a movie like

Lawrence of Arabia. The palace wasn't very big, but it was like clay or something that made it kind of yellow and lumpy. Kuwaiti soldiers snapped to attention as I stepped inside with Ali and I snapped a salute right back like I was used to this sort of pomp and circumstance. It was real quiet inside the palace, and me and Trang and Ali were left standing by this mosaic fountain when Colonel Fawwaz mumbled something and slipped away. It was so quiet that I wondered if the emir and his clan were sleeping, or we had come on the wrong day, or they were giving the ribbons to someone else for some other heroism. The palace was lit by these hissing high-pressure kerosene lamps, and it seemed as we stood there waiting for the emir to wake up from siesta that the sun set, and the whole room was all shadows, and I swear I saw shadowy figures moving from behind these arches, and then I heard girls laughing from behind these screens, and then I was stoked and forgot about the crazy Anti-Jew Limo-Dude, *because it was like we were in old Arabia!*

Maybe the emir and his people wanted us to feel like we were in old Arabia before we got onto the ceremony, and if that's the case it was the right move, because it got us feeling all magical and honored and ancient. Colonel Fawwaz comes back in and motions me aside, and the look on his face was like someone had died, and I thought *we're back in the frying pan.* But he says he forgot to ask me a simple question, and because I am from America he must ask, although he hopes it is not an insult if it is not so—but unless I answer this question we cannot go on with the ceremony. I'm like, *Lay it on me, Colonel,* and he whispers, "Are you a Jew?"

Colonel Fawwaz looked so concerned his bushy black mustache was quivering and as I had just had the run-in with the Limo Driver Jew-Hater I was like stunned for a second, and Trang saw the look and came over and said, "What's going down, Carmichael?"

"The colonel here," I said, "wants to know if I'm a Jew."

Colonel Fawwaz looks at Trang and says with a hearty chuckle, *"We know YOU are not a Jew, Private Trang."*

And Trang as always never missed a beat, as he snapped back, "You sure, big man?"

And Colonel Fawwaz looked confused and says, "There are no *Asian* Jews!"

And Trang says, "But I'm only *half* Vietnamese. My father was American."

So the colonel almost whispers, "Are you a Jew, Private Trang?"

Trang looks up at the ceiling as if for the answer. He looks at me with a crazy grin, and then shoots back at the colonel, "My father was a Jewish marine in Vietnam."

You would have thought Colonel Fawwaz was shot between the eyes. He staggered away from us mumbling about how he must *consult with this and that Kuwaiti honcho about this new news about the heroes.* So we are once again standing in the lobby breathing the ancient vibe, but now it isn't as appealing a vibe, it seems more than a little *nasty.* Little Ali gets in Trang's face and says, "You joke with the colonel?" And Trang leans over and slaps the little jockey five and says, "Yeah, Ali, I make a joke with the big Arab dude." Little did we know at the time this one *joke* was going to like hound our marine asses right up to our last days in Arabia.

Anyway, Ali gives the finger to the shadows and says, "I *hate* the Saudis. They are bad rich men. You must joke with them more, Private Trang."

So Trang got this look on his face that he was thinking hard, and next thing I know he's moving out in the direction Colonel Fawwaz slipped away. Trang was like a bloodhound for trouble. Give him a sniff of shit going down, and he's that old hound baying down the trail for all he's worth. I followed down the hall with Ali. We go down this hall all covered with more random mosaics, and at the end of the hall are these serious gold doors covered with jewels. They have these two black dudes in robes and swords stationed outside, who are looking fierce, and when Trang comes up to the door they lower their swords in front of the door. These guys were great!

I was back feeling this good ancient vibe again like I was in the movies, and it dawned on me, given this was Arabia, maybe these big black guys were guarding a harem, and if I was right, *these black dudes had no balls!* I like suggested this to Trang, and he started cracking up, and Ali laughed, and then our little jockey must have translated my idea to the black dudes, because one of them like swung his sword around until the tip was about to prick my neck. And little Ali starts letting loose with a lot of angry Arabic. For a little jockey he could really holler, and then the big golden doors slowly swung open.

The emir is like on a throne with his wife next to him on her throne. The emir said one word, and the dude with his sword on my neck is like knocked down by some other robed black dudes and kind of dragged away. And then the emir is standing and motioning for us to come forward. Tommy Trang like walks right up onto the royal platform and there is a groan from all the robed dudes in the room, but the emir kind of *waves for them to shut up.* Trang like takes the emir's hand and gives him a shake like *how the hell are you, Emir?* Trang could do a simple thing like, a handshake in a way that said *AMERICAN* in capital letters, that said, *You may be the emir, but to me you are just a dude in robes, and that's cool, and as long as you don't screw with me, I'm pleased to party with you.*

Me and Ali stayed down off the platform, and there was this total silence when Trang and the emir turned around to face the crowd of robed dudes. I was thinking even then, *Tommy Trang is a natural king!* Anyway, the emir clapped his hands, and some like little foreign guys ran out and started singing a song, and Ali told me it was all about the royal lineage, about why the emir was the emir, given who slept with who in Kuwait going back to like the Early Camel Ages.

Trang came down and stood by my side while we listened to this Arabic jabber, and I like looked up at the serious chandeliers that looked like they were made of real diamonds. And it was getting kind of boring, as this was sex that happened long ago, and then there was some more fanfare, and suddenly from out of some curtains comes this Chick in Royal Robes, and her face is covered at first, but then she pulls down the covering, and I see it *is the chick we rescued from the gulf!* The emir urgently motions for her to raise the face rag, but she just shakes her head at him.

You got to figure she hadn't looked her best out there in the Persian Gulf as she was comatose and vomiting, but man, *now she looked hot!* She had oversized blue bedroom eyes with this burning and un-blinking look. She was sort of sucking on her soft lower lip as she looked at Trang. As far as her perfect little Arab body—and she was pretty much on the *small* side generally—she was mightily stacked! I glanced at Trang and he looked like his knees were about to buckle. He was never the same dude after looking into the burning and un-blinking blue eyes of that little Kuwaiti princess right then. I nodded like *I know what you mean man,* because Lulu of Kuwait was like hyp-notic, if you looked at her eyes you *like couldn't look away.* I mean you just wanted *to look and look and look.* You look at some things in life, and you say, *Got it! Seen it!* And eyes are just eyes! But these *Lulu of Kuwait eyes* you just never wanted to let out of your sight!

I kind of think all the other robed dudes in the room were thinking the same. Because everyone was staring at her like they were hypnotized. The lineage singers were checking her out, and little Ali was like mumbling prayers by my side. I said to a robed dude by my side, "That is one fine-looking girl!" And the Arab dude like gives me a sour look. And so I said to another robed Arab, "That Princess Lulu is the prettiest thing I've ever seen!" This time I got a sour look and a finger wag. Ali whispered to me, "Private Carmichael, you are risking the evil eye in naming her beauty." Apparently you don't go calling *a babe a babe in Arabia,* or else you might *bring some nastiness on said babe.* So to test this out I said to the cranky first Arab, "She is pretty fucking ugly." And he agreed with this, and gave me a sort of nod of approval, like *now I was hip to the Arab way.*

Anyway, the emir was trying to get the woman I figured was the queen to help Princess Lulu to cover her face, and the queen wasn't having much luck either. The queen would put up the face rag, and Lulu would yank it down again when the queen walked back to her throne. So the emir blew this off, and tried to get the attention of everyone by clapping his hands, and that kind of snapped the mood, and he said to us marines, "By the wisdom of Allah, you two were chosen to rescue Princess Lulu, daughter of my favorite brother, and beloved of all the Kingdom of Kuwait. For this you will have a rich reward."

So then the emir looked into the crowd, and out from behind some robed Arabs came big Colonel Fawwaz. He was kind of hiding back there for some reason. I had the sense, given our generally positive reception from the emir thus far, that old Colonel Fawwaz hadn't told the emir about Trang saying he was a *half-Jew.* And then the crowd of Arabs kind of parted, and I saw *why he was in the back of the room.* There were these big heavy royal curtains back there, and I saw the eyes of a girl peek out from behind one for a second. And I'll tell you: *one glance at that girl-behind-the-curtain's eyes told me she was mighty pissed about something.*

No one but me was looking at the girl in the curtains, because a golden tray just covered with jewels was being rolled in by some big black, robed dudes. There was like a pyramid of money in the center of the tray, and more necklaces and golden stuff was draped all over the cash. The Emir of Kuwait was now getting really flowery in Arabic, and I guess was telling us all about how great Colonel Fawwaz was generally, and the colonel was looking pretty proud by his side. I like still wasn't getting the total picture, and then when the cash and jewels made it to the front of the room, Colonel Fawwaz kind of took over, and started to tell everyone how great were me and Trang, and how *thanks to Allah we had rescued his fiancée, who had fallen in the water by accident.*

So there it was! Colonel Fawwaz of Saudi Arabia was *engaged to be married to Princess Lulu of Kuwait.* It didn't take a rocket scientist to figure out sixteen-year-old Princess Lulu wasn't too excited about marrying the forty-something colonel, given her recent 'accidental fall' into the Persian Gulf. And so I looked closer at the liquid eyes of Princess Lulu, which were still locked on Trang, but were still oddly not blinking, and her look was reminding me of something—and then it dawned on me: *that's the look of someone stoned out of their freakin' head!* But because I guess she wasn't a stoner, I decided someone had her seriously medicated!

Colonel Fawwaz told us that he and the Royal House of Kuwait were offering us these jewels and cash as a small thank-you for rescuing Princess Lulu from her recent tumble in the gulf. And I have to admit, that got my attention focused, and for a second I forgot about the Doped-Up Princess and the Girl Behind the Curtain. I had kind of guessed the cash and jewels were for me and Trang, but when Colonel Fawwaz said it was really true, well, *I was kind of shocked.*

And I was more shocked when Trang fired right back at the emir, "Thanks Emir, *but I don't want the money or the jewels.*" The whole Arab scene stiffened and kind of looked at me, and so I said kind of quietly, "I'll accept my half." That relaxed them a bit, but they still didn't know what to do about *Trang.* I knew the guy was poor as hell, and was pretty surprised he'd passed on the jewels and cash. And the emir started like sputtering like, "What then—you must name it—and if it is possible under Allah, you shall have it—for such is the love for Princess Lulu in the kingdom—you must name your reward ..."

So my man Tommy Trang, he snaps right back with: "Emir, I want to marry Princess Lulu of Kuwait." I think this marriage thing just sort of jumped out of his mouth right then—like he had no control over his tongue. Like the thing about being a Jew, it was just *said.* Some might argue Trang was into Princess Lulu like he was into the pearls—for the cash and adventure—but later I figured out something real deep inside Trang just *knew* Princess Lulu was like slated to be his number-one love, and the thing that really blew me away over the long haul was Trang was *right.*

Anyway, no one said anything when Trang announced he wanted to marry Princess Lulu. I thought I heard the jewels on the tray kind of shivering. The emir looked around like someone was going to tell him *what the hell was going on in his rich little kingdom.* Colonel Fawwaz didn't look confused: he looked like he wanted to *kill* Trang. Princess Lulu of Kuwait had stood up and taken two steps toward Trang like she was getting yanked by a big magnet, but then she suddenly dropped in a heap, and that broke the mood, and everyone scrambled to help her to her feet.

So the emir suddenly started talking to Trang like it was just the two of them, and he started going on about how *Princess Lulu had been engaged since she was nine to marry Colonel Fawwaz of Saudi Arabia,* and everyone was pleased as punch by the planned match between

two *fine royal families,* and that the wedding, although delayed because the princess fell by accident in the Persian Gulf, was still
going down in a few months . . .

And that was when the girl back in the curtain began to *ululate,*
which was the local word for screaming like your tongue is on fire.
But no one knew the girl was there behind the curtain, and it
looked like the curtain itself, or the whole wall, or some spirit just
over on that side of the room, was letting loose with some real
bloodcurdling cries. And the Arabs looked kind of scared stiff for a
second, until one of the black dudes dragged out this girl from behind the curtain. And that was when I caught Colonel Fawwaz
looking at the girl just like Tommy Trang had been looking at
Princess Lulu earlier.

Then Princess Lulu lets out a cry, and sort of makes her
drugged way over to the girl and *then the two are like hugging and crying
and carrying on like it's the end of the world.* They were both teenagers
really, and were crying and wailing in each other's arms until it
started to seem a little silly. And Ali has been talking to the local
Arabs in the crowd, and reports back to me and Trang that the girl
behind the curtain, now in the arms of the princess, is *the Palestinian
maid of Princess Lulu,* and that *she is the real passion of Colonel Fawwaz.* And
suddenly the maid slumps from the arms of the princess to the
floor, and is writhing her body like a snake, and it was pretty impressive, and kind of sexy in a weird way, if you didn't know she was
doing it out of grief. I like figured this was some sort of physical way
the Arab chicks had to *ululate,* but the damn thing was, looking at
her you couldn't help thinking what she'd be like in bed *with all that
hip action!* And then Princess Lulu like flopped down over her, like a
wrestler's move, to try and pin her to the floor, and of course she
too is weeping and carrying on, but she just can't stop that squirming maid!

I like look around the room, and all the Arab dudes are like in
a big circle around these two, and the emir is the only one moving:
he's trying to get the attention of like the black dudes with the
swords, but I guess they *had* balls, as they couldn't take their eyes off
that howling, hip-grinding maid! She was really mad with a broken

heart! It was kind of beautiful, if you think about it, and the Colonel Fawwaz was a sort of lucky dude if this passion was directed at him, I guess, other than that she was probably pretty high-maintenance and like difficult when she doesn't get her way.

I noticed she kept ululating the same sound, kind of like *oom arba wa arbaeen!! Oom arba wa arbaeen!* Some Arab next to me saw my lips moving over these sounds and he like leaned in and said, "Mother forty-four," which was real cryptic, but cool. I like leaned in and said into Trang's ear, "Mother forty-four," and he glanced at me, and I saw he was not in a mood for horsing around. He had his eyes still on Princess Lulu, who was now hanging on to just one wrist of the maid. She had that wrist pinned good, but the rest of the maid was like a fish on the deck.

Curious thing that happened next was the maid started slapping her own pussy with her free hand and shrieking, *"Oom arba wa arbaeen!!"* She was really whacking at herself, and all I could think at the time was that this was some secret Arab chick way of saying like MY PUSSY IS REAL SAD!! I saw some of the robed Arabs were starting to smirk as she swatted herself, and then the princess like flips up the maid's robe and sticks her head under there, looking for all the world like she is going to give her maid *some female pleasure*. Her head is like rolling back and forth under the robe, and now some of the black guard dudes are like pulling at the legs of the princess, so she is kind of upside down, and her robe falls to her waist. She is wearing this white lingerie number that was cut like a thong bikini, which was kind of a surprise. And then the princess is finally ripped out from under the robe of the maid, and she sort of staggers to her feet, and turns to the emir with her closed fist out. Then she like smiles, flips her hand open, and says, *"Oom arba wa arbaeen,"* and there is something in her hand that looks like a *centipede*. And I move closer along with everyone else, and see the emir kind of crack a smile, and it *is a centipede in her hand!* And so like Ali pulls me down so he can say in my ear, "The maid has a centipede up her leg. Women here think a centipede can enter the skin and go to the brain and make a person mad!"

So there you had it: a *centipede*! But of course solving the *centipede thing* didn't change the basic situation, and if the Arab Chicks' Feelings ran as deep and wild over love as they just had over the damn centipede, I figured the *emir better let these Arab Girls have their way!* Had I been asked, I might have helped the emir, as to an American, it would seem pretty easy to straighten this all out: Colonel Fawwaz elopes to Vegas with the maid on the next Air Arabia flight, and Princess Lulu marries Private Trang when she is a little older, less medicated, and like more *legal.*

So I am like wondering if anyone else is seeing the easy American answer, when Princess Lulu breaks away from her maid. She wipes her crying eyes with her robe, and then walks over to Tommy Trang with some cool dignity. She like takes Trang's hand and opens his palm. She places a pearl in his hand, and closes his fingers around it. Then she leans forward and whispers for a long while in his ear, filling Trang in on how she *was sure he had been sent by Allah to rescue her from the forced marriage situation.* So from the get-go, Princess Lulu had Trang marked as her one and only. I didn't have any trouble with that at the time, as she was in a tough situation, and probably grasping at straws.

But it turned out I was wrong to have doubts about her love for Trang. Princess Lulu turned out to really *believe* Trang was slated by Allah to be her one and only, and she was not the sort of chick to hand Captain Shakespear's ancient pearl over to just any old half-Vietnamese U.S. marine showing up in Kuwait. Because that was the thing: the pearl Lulu gave Trang once belonged to some historical British warrior named Captain Shakespear. And Princess Lulu had insisted to Trang she was like a *descendant* of this Captain Shakespear's royal Kuwaiti lover from back in like 1910. She said when this Captain Shakespear died as a hero on some place called the Plains of Jarrab in Arabia, the pearl was found after the battle sewn into his vest, and returned to the captain's royal Kuwaiti lover, who gave it to her royal daughter, and so on that pearl traveled through these like daughters of Arabia until the pearl came into the hot hands of sixteen-year-old Princess Lulu.

So right away you get the idea Princess Lulu was a fast talker, as she whispered all this curious stuff about Captain Shakespear and the pearl to Trang while the rest of us just stared at them with our mouths kind of hanging open. But I guess after a while it started to piss off Colonel Fawwaz to see his sexy young fiancée nibbling on Trang's ear at length, because I see him whisper something in the emir's ear, and then the emir like turns almost purple, and then *everyone* was kicked out of the room with a lot of hysterical scream-ing in Arabic like we carried the bubonic plague or something, and the jewels and cash were whisked away never to be seen again, and me and Trang were shot out of Kuwait like from a cannon.

CHAPTER 4

So a few months after this the crazy dictator Saddam Hussein invaded the rich little Kingdom of Kuwait, and me and Tommy Trang and our elite platoon of U.S. Marine reconnaissance warriors were detached from the USS *Inchon* and sent to Saudi Arabia. The air was so dry in Saudi Arabia that our hands cracked, and Trang was able to whistle through his nose "The Star-spangled Banner" and other patriotic songs. There were only some marine units and army paratroopers scattered along the Persian Gulf coastline in those early days of Desert Shield. If Saddam had wanted he could have rolled right over us and taken over Saudi Arabia as easily as he took over Kuwait, and me and Trang would have had to *fight to the death.* Trang said he imagined us standing there alone in the desert as the Iraqi hordes bore down on us, just like old Captain Shakespear stood solo in his pith helmet as some psycho desert dudes on camels called the Rasheed bore down waving their swords.

You might wonder how Trang and me knew this 'Rasheed-waving-their-swords' stuff about Captain Shakespear, and the answer is we had ordered a book from the MWR—Moral Warfare & Recreation—office in al-Jubail on the heroic British warrior written by a dude named H.V. F. Winstone, and took turns reading it to each other. The marine sergeant at MWR was kind of way into digging up this one and only book on Captain Shakespear. It turned out this Captain Shakespear was a friend of Abdul Aziz the founder of Saudi Arabia and was famous in Arabia for directing cannons for Abdul Aziz in a big battle against this tribe the Rasheed. Captain Shakespear's job in the battle was to like use the cannons to hold back the Rasheed cavalry, but in the middle of the battle all Abdul Aziz's fighters just suddenly boogied from the battle on their camels, but old Captain Shakespear in his pith helmet *didn't flee* even though he was standing there solo on the sands, just took out his revolver and fired on the screaming Rasheed cavalry as they bore down on him waving their swords. Trang said that Captain Shakespear had titanium stones hanging between his legs!

Anyway, the book by H. V. F. Winstone said the Rasheeds stripped Captain Shakespear of all but his vest, and gave his pith helmet to the Turks who used it to prove the Saudis were working with the infidels. That was how his servant found his body later, near naked in the blooded sand. There was actually no mention in the book of any pearl. I mean Princess Lulu did give Tommy Trang a huge pearl, and told him it belonged to Captain Shakespear, given to him by his royal Kuwaiti lover of yore. But was there really a historical pearl at all? Who knows? I know Trang got a stoking buzz out of Princess Lulu carrying on that *their* Gulf War romance was a sort of second chance for those tragic international lovers of yore to escape the blood-thirsty, sword-waving Rasheed cavalry bearing down, so to speak.

Old Captain Shakespear in the pith helmet standing firm against the Rasheed cavalry unto death had been talked about a lot by Trang and me for most of the three months since we rescued Princess Lulu from the warm waters of the gulf. As we were finally in a war I thought Trang and me might talk about something else, but to be honest, other than the possibility Saddam might invade Saudi Arabia and we'd have to fight the Iraqi Hordes, things were quiet, and no stories developed that were as good as the stuff that happened when we went looking for pearls in the Persian Gulf and bumped into a suicidal sixteen-year-old babe princess named Lulu. I guess that was the whole problem with the *official* Persian Gulf War for Trang and me: from start to finish it was generally *boring*. It is important to understand how bored were Trang and me with this war, and how we spent a lot of time talking about how we would have liked to have been by Captain Shakespear's side as the Rasheed cavalry bore down waving their swords. When we talked about this historical moment, we'd slap each other on our tattoos and yell out, *"Die a hero!"* It was what we did in those early days, my man Trang and me. I guess I didn't mention that I had a DIE A HERO tattoo too. Tommy Trang inked it into my shoulder one night before the war with like a needle and some ink and a lot of beer.

Anyway, as we figured the *present situation,* it ran like this: when the Iraqis blew across the border to take over Kuwait, the whole Royal Kuwaiti Family scooted to the Saudi border as fast as their stretch limos could carry them. So Trang figured Princess Lulu was somewhere in Saudi Arabia with all the other royal Kuwaitis. We heard the Saudis were putting them up in unbelievable style at various local desert palaces. We were pleased the chicks in the Royal Kuwaiti Family were probably safe and sound in Saudi Arabia and hanging around a blue pool at a local Saudi palace. But as warriors, Trang and me were not too impressed with the male royal Kuwaitis blowing town in their limos along with the royal ladies. Because Trang and me figured real royalty would have *fought to the death* to Defend their Country from the Iraqi Hordes. Trang reasoned if you blow town in your limousines with the ladies, and know you are leaving behind all your other nonroyal Kuwaiti females and children and the like to suffer bad under the hands of the Psycho Iraqi Barbarians, well then you lose the right to be considered royal. Trang and me talked a lot about this, and we took a dim view of the Male Royal Kuwaitis as a result. But then one day we heard a rumor about this one son of the Emir of Kuwait who stayed behind and stood on the steps of the palace and fought the Iraqi Hordes pretty much solo! This Kuwaiti Prince refused to hit the road to Saudi with the cruise control on and Donna Summer on the CD and scotch shaking in hand mumbling prayers from the Koran, and opted to *fight to the death* on the steps of the palace. So Trang said this dead Kuwaiti Royal Dude was a true modern Son of Captain Shakespear at Jarrab hanging tough in the face of the Rasheed cavalry. Trang said if the prince had lived we could have been like the Three Musketeers or something.

Anyway, I was talking about the situation in the early days of Desert Shield. You might think I might comment on the WAR situation, but there is little to *say* about that, we were just sitting around watching the troop build-up in the desert! Try and tell an interesting story about troop-and-supply *logistics!* The situation I'm talking about is the whereabouts and marriage status of Princess Lulu. Ever since we were removed from Kuwait by helo back to the USS *Inchon,* my man Trang had talked about little else! We figured she was somewhere behind us in the interior of Saudi Arabia, and we figured they'd rush the wedding since Princess Lulu had proven she would rather die than marry old Colonel Fawwaz, and it is best from the old-fashioned Arab viewpoint to get those sort of sixteen-year-old suicidal girls married before they can elope with a infidel guy like Private Trang.

In the face of obvious facts, Trang was sure that *somehow* he was going to rescue Princess Lulu from a forced marriage to Colonel Fawwaz, or from death, if she was to try that alternative before the wedding. Anyway, if you looked close at Trang during these early days of Desert Shield, you could see some signs that at some level even *he* had his small doubts. It seemed for inspection he couldn't get a shine on his boots any better than a monkey—one visiting major whispered to him that he could have done a better job with his boots shoving them up his own ass. And his cammies went to hell, and his cover looked like he had sat on it, and his M16 rifle had rust on the flash suppressor that showed he wasn't loving it the way a marine was trained to at all times. I tried to pick up his slack and acted a bit like his mother, tucking in his rack, and giving his military goods what attention I could spare while keeping my own stuff in order. And then Trang got a nasty case of trench mouth that wouldn't go away, and if he breathed on you, it would have made you puke. Some of the guys in the recon platoon started to leave toothbrushes on his pillow, and one joker left a note that said, BEFORE YOU KISS THE ARAB PRINCESS, BRUSH YOUR TEETH, MARINE.

The cool thing about Trang was that he snapped back. It was like his whole Trangness digested looking like hell wasn't going to help, and he just cracked that downer mood like a chick coming out of an egg and focused on the life around him again with all his energies. Not that he went AWOL at that point to rescue the princess, but he got back to being *my man Private Tommy Trang, U.S. marine!* As you will see about Trang, he *always* snapped back into shape and was good to go, no matter how grim the situation. But most marines were like that! Unlike the civilian population, we didn't put up with guys who crapped out under pressure.

Anyway, our position was like on this road that ran from Kuwait to Saudi Arabia along the Persian Gulf coastline. At first we were in charge of a large stretch of the Saudi coastline, but then they moved in these navy SEALs and gave them a piece of the beach near like al-Mishaab. Navy SEALs do what reconnaissance marines do, but spend a bit more time in wet suits. But recon marines—we who sneak behind enemy lines—and navy SEALs have some mission overlap, and some tension can develop as the SEALs can be arrogant and showboats. This new SEAL team assigned part of our former territory made a big show of guarding their perimeter all the time and spoke of their perimeter like it was the Great Wall of China, when it was just rolls of concertina wire. They patrolled the coastline of their perimeter in these cool jet boats night and day. One day I found Trang standing at our edge of the perimeter staring into the SEAL zone, and this bug-eyed SEAL was getting all pissed at him and telling him how their perimeter was impenetrable, and Trang just stared at him without saying a word, a fierce grin on his face. As I said, Trang had a sort of locked opinion of his own military greatness, and had a little trouble with direct challenges to this viewpoint.

That night I kicked upwards, and Trang was gone from his rack. I knew what he was up to, and went out to look for him, and followed his tracks to the shore. I saw by marks on the sand he had put on his scuba gear and flippers. Even at night the showboat SEALs were roaring back and forth in front of their perimeter on their jet boats like Saddam was about to try a beach landing at any second. So I went back to the rack and hoped he didn't get shot, and next morning my captain was like in my face waving a note, with the SEAL lieutenant next to him sporting *a real purple face.* The

note from Trang said: SEALS—GOT YOUR BOAT—TRANG, USMC. So the
SEAL lieutenant makes a big show of calling his commander in the
rear, and suddenly the SEAL lieutenant is saying, *"Aye, aye, sir. It
does prove we have a permeable perimeter, yes it does, sir. And I will have my
men thank Private Trang for the heads up about this situation. Aye, aye, sir, Private Trang has done the navy a service . . ."*

Anyway, it all worked out more or less, since the SEALs mostly
took the heat for Trang's craziness. Captain Pettigrew chewed
Trang out for form's sake, and then sent Trang and me to Dhahran
to get the day's issue of crypto fills so we could scramble our radio
transmissions. Tommy Trang thought this was excellent, as once in
Dhahran he figured he could sneak around and try to get some information on the whereabouts of Princess Lulu. Trang was, as the
old saying goes, always making lemonade out of lemons.

So we headed off on Captain Pettigrew's errand, and like drove
around Dhahran looking for some random Arab we could pigeonhole about Princess Lulu. And after a couple of hours we are getting
kind of discouraged, as everyone was either in their air-conditioned
cars or trucks, or inside behind the concrete walls. How do you contact a princess in a closed country like Saudi? And Trang was frustrated, and banging on the steering wheel of the Humvee, and soon
after that started trying to pigeonhole Arabs in their vehicles at
stoplights about *where the Kuwaiti royals were put up in the Saudi palaces.*
He didn't get anywhere with that approach, so we just kept driving.
And then we see this young Arab woman by the side of the road *getting whacked with sticks by like a band of old dudes in robes.* There is a Toyota
with an open door, and we figured she must have got caught driving—we knew that was verboten: no ladies behind the wheel in
Saudi-land.

Tommy Trang damn near runs down the pack of old Arab
dudes with the sticks. He was really in a bad mood. We hadn't eaten
all day, and been scanning Dhahran in the roaster heat of the Arab
day for hours. Trang was like out of the car, and he started grabbing
sticks from the old dudes right and left and throwing them or
breaking them over his knee. Some of the dudes with sticks still in

hand started whacking him, so I waded in and started grabbing sticks too. Soon we have most of the sticks cracked or tossed, and Trang and some old bearded Arab dude are going nose to nose, each yelling in their own language. So then the Saudi police come barging in, and Trang tries to reason with them, but they only speak Arabic and grab me and Trang and toss us in a police truck with our hands shackled. So next thing I know me and Trang are in the basement of like this Saudi prison, and Trang is acting kind of crazy and demanding to make a call to *Princess Lulu of Kuwait.* I thought we ought to be calling Captain Pettigrew, but Trang came to Riyadh to find Princess Lulu, and he was going to stick with his *mission!*

So who should stick his fat face into this little window in our prison door but big old Colonel Fawwaz. I guess someone knew Colonel Fawwaz was the fiancé of Princess Lulu of Kuwait, and put the word to him that there was a U.S. marine yelling that he wanted to talk to his woman. So then the prison door opens, and Colonel Fawwaz comes in and the guard puts a stool down for him to sit on and sets up a table so I guess we could have tea. The guard shuts the door, and Colonel Fawwaz slowly pours the tea and motions for us to like sit on the floor in front of him. We keep standing, and he shrugs in this Arabic way. Colonel Fawwaz is back in an upbeat mood, and sort of riffs about how once in Riyadh you were not allowed to be heard singing, or have flowerpots on your windowsill, that you couldn't even laugh in your house without worrying about one of these Saudi Samurai barging in and dancing a stick on your head.

"So things are better now," I said.

Colonel Fawwaz looked at me like I was a genius for this, and nodded like his head was coming off. "Slow change, but all for the good!"

Trang took a cup of tea and said, "Yeah, well, Colonel, glad to hear you boys allow flowerpots. But it is crazy to let these old guys whack a woman."

"Of course not!" said Colonel Fawwaz. "You never hurt a woman! Unless, of course, she has broken the law."

"No," said Trang. "Never."

As I said, Colonel Fawwaz came in pretty jolly, and when Trang let the topic drop for a minute he tried to talk us up on the hot weather and American sluts. This got him so jolly he stood up, yelled for the guard, and ushered us out of the cell and out into his limousine. But then we saw as we drove along some more of these stick dudes on a street corner, and Colonel Fawwaz and Trang got back into wrestling over *the right to whack chicks with sticks,* and then the colonel called him a *dirty Jew* and ordered a screeching U-turn and brought us back to the prison. He marched us back to our cell and personally clanged the iron door shut.

So then a few hours later our Captain Pettigrew showed up, with some other Marine Corps officers from the JAG. As we walked out of the prison Captain Pettigrew said like he was really pissed, "I hope you know I'm missing the quarterfinals of the Mixed-Doubles Coalition Volleyball Tournament." We looked at him, and he winked at us as he placed us in the back of the black Suburban with tinted windows. He got in the passenger seat and said to Trang, "So I hear you stopped the religious police from hitting some Saudi lady?"

"I stopped them," said Trang. "They were really whacking her."

"Didn't you go to our Arab culture lectures?"

You could see Captain Pettigrew was saying this kind of sarcastically, like he was already on the side of Tommy Trang. He got a funny look from the JAG guy, so Captain Pettigrew said with more seriousness, "This is a different culture, Private Trang. We have to work with the Saudis to accomplish our Joint Task."

"I don't know," said Trang. "Tough to work with people who beat their ladies with sticks for driving a Toyota. You sure that's part of a culture?"

"Private Trang," said the JAG officer, "you have to repress your natural instincts here for our greater cause."

"So we let the chick-beaters slide," said Trang. "Are you saying beating women is okay because Saddam is a psycho?"

There was silence in the Suburban. Then the JAG officer said, "You boys are in the old hot water. If the Saudis press the issue, you two will be up on charges and sent home with a dishonorable discharge, or worse."

Trang looked shocked. "My Marine Corps would discharge me for keeping a woman from getting whacked upside the head with sticks?" No one said anything, and Trang said sounding totally bummed, "If that's really true, I'll AWOL from this organization before it can discharge me."

When we got into the JAG office, where I guess we were going to wait for the Saudi response to the incident, we found a sheik standing in the main lobby. There were majors and colonels standing around him, and public-affairs officers. We all go into this room, and everyone looks real serious, *and then they all look at the sheik.* That dude comes over and stands in front of me and Trang, and then he takes Trang by the shoulders and kisses him on both cheeks. He speaks good English and starts thanking us *for helping his wife.* He says she's young, and was educated in the United States, and has radical new ideas like that she can drive a car, but he loves her anyway, and is grateful to us.

So we're cool. Everyone in the room seems real pleased, as I guess this was a real important sheik oil-wise. But then, in the midst of the like general good cheer, Trang pipes up to the sheik: "So you're getting me off?"

The sheik is feeling good, and says, "In this case you are lucky, Private Thomas Trang. But I suggest you do not try this rescue again, because next time she might not be married to a sheik."

The sheik nods and smiles at everyone like he has said something pretty profound, and there is like a ton of general appreciation expressed from the American officers for the sheik's goodwill and wisdom. But then as the sheik is taking a bow and starting to head out, Trang pipes up again: "Well, if that's the way it is, then charge me. I don't want to get off just because this sheik is letting it slide." But no one really listens to Trang, or they try not to, and me and Captain Pettigrew like grab Trang by the arms and pull him out of the room and down the hall and out of the building as he sputters and fumes like he still wants to get into it with the sheik. And then he remembers why he came to Dhahran and starts kicking himself for not quizzing the sheik about the whereabouts of Princess Lulu.

So we finally head back to our platoon with Captain Pettigrew. And all the way back the captain is telling Trang to stay out of trouble from now on. But the curious thing was you could tell Captain Pettigrew's *heart* wasn't really in his lecture. I mean it was clear he was secretly getting a *kick* out of Trang's crazy doings. Anyway, Tommy Trang promised the captain to like keep a low profile. So Trang and me took to hanging out at the edges of our camp. And one day there showed up just outside our camp a random refrigerated truck.

So to pass time, Trang and me went and talked to the Arab drivers of the truck to like find out why they were sitting in their air-conditioned, refrigerated truck up here near the border, and as best we could tell they were told to just take the supplies somewhere *away from the docks* that were overloaded and congested with the masssive swamp of supplies coming in for this war, and everywhere they went they found supply trucks unloading, and soldiers kept waving them forward with their supplies, until they gave up and just kept driving and ended up in our camp up near the Kuwaiti border. The Arab drivers didn't see the humor in the situation, and were kind of fuming, and as it was a refrigerated truck, Trang asked if we could open the rear and just kind of sit in the cold air.

It was the best feeling, just sitting there with our bodies washed by a cloud of cool vapor. Trang and me slapped each other five and yelled out, "Die a hero!," which was said with some humor, as we were not *fighting or dying* but cooling our marine asses in a truck full of Perrier that had no place to go up near the front of a war. Trang and me discussed why the hell they would send Perrier to soldiers in the middle of a deadly war with a psycho like Saddam, and I agreed there was something weird about it, but we were glad for the cool air on our bodies.

And then the Arab truck drivers were standing there behind the truck and glaring at us. We invited them to chill out. These

Arab dudes didn't know a simple pleasure like cold air, and shook their heads. Then they like started walking away. I guess they were going home, and to hell with the trucks and the Perrier. We go around and get up in the seats of the truck, and the passenger-seat floor is filled with plastic jugs of some sort of *Arabic Water*. Trang and me discussed why the Arabs would carry water in plastic jugs when they had a truckful of French Perrier, and came up with a lot of theories like that Arabs were not into bubbles in their water, but none really made a lot of sense. The bottom line was Trang and me were discovering these Arab Folk were *way different* than us Americans, and it was kind of a bummer, because your basic American attitude is: *Hey, you're a towelhead, and hot on this dude Allah, but we can still party together, right?* And not only wasn't this friendly *let's party* American approach working, but we were wondering if deep down all these Arabs really hated us generally.

After a while this sort of talk got us down, and we were quiet together listening to some Arabic music on the truck radio. Then it was clear *that* was getting us down too, and so Trang turned it off and we sat in silence. And this like wave of loneliness for *America* came on us hard. We were both feeling this loneliness, and both stared straight ahead out the window of the truck.

Then this camel walked up to the truck and looked at us, and they are some ugly creatures! Then I swear it like backed up to take a huge piss, and it was as if the camel was saying in camel Arabic: *I piss on you infidel boys!* But Trang was thinking, I guess, and he like grabbed one of those jugs of Arabic water, because it was close at hand, and hops out of the cab of the truck. And he goes up to the camel, and the camel gives him a suspicious look, but then when he sees Trang unscrew the top of the water he starts to look a little friendlier. And I am sitting in the truck and starting to laugh, because it was just so Trang and so totally American to break the downer mood, and try and do something *crazy and good,* like giving a camel some water. So I am getting a real positive vibe, and start to hammer on the horns of the truck, and this brings out some marines from where they are back lying on their racks listening to their Walkmans, and some of the marines start to wander over just as Trang lifts the bottle of water to the mouth of the quivering, greedy lips of that camel.

That was one thirsty camel, and he just sucked at that bottle like it was the last water in Saudi Arabia. And I see all the marines standing around sort of give Trang a cheer, as it is clear to them this is a *crazy but decent* gesture, and then this AP photographer comes running up with cameras bouncing off his knees, and he starts shooting like a madman, and has Trang hold the bottle up again to the camel's lips. Maybe you saw that photo in the newspapers back home of the GI standing in the desert giving water to a camel. Trang really made the photographer's day, as I guess he had taken all the photos he could of soldiers in their racks listening to their Walkmans, or of jets going over in the sky. It was a pretty boring war for the photographers too.

Marines are like giving Trang a high five, mostly because they thought the photo would make the newspapers. The photographer is trying to take down Trang's name and where he was from, and Trang was giving him a hard time, and saying he was *just this gook dude from America.* This is pissing off the photographer, but then the camel wanted to lick Trang's ear. The cameraman backs off from scribbling to get a photo of Trang and the camel as friends, and that was when the camel *bit* Trang's ear. He must have taken off the whole earlobe, because the blood was really spurting. And you know what? The AP photographer pretty much just walked away. I guess he only wanted *happy photos* for the folks on the home front. And that was when the camel started to get *weird.* It started leaping around like a bronco. First it went on its hind legs, and then on its back legs, and it was spinning and kicking and crying out like you would have thought someone had sliced off its balls. Marines are like backing off all around, but Trang is down on one knee, holding his ear under the crazy leaping camel. Just as I start to run toward Trang he catches a flying camel hoof in the skull. And right then the camel leaps on all four legs straight up in the air like fifty thousand volts had shot through him, and when he comes down his legs crumble beneath him and he lands in this big pile of camel hair, and it is clear this camel is *D-E-A-D*.

I like ran to Trang. He is out cold. I starting yelling for a corpsman, as I can't find his pulse at first, and it doesn't look good. And right then this army private—he must have been here on some random duty—this army private starts waving the near-empty jug of Arabic Water under my nose. I swat it away and yell at him to call a corpsman, but he's in my face yelling something. And that was when my brain registered the funny smell of that Arabic Water, and I hear what the army private is saying to me. He's yelling, "Gasoline, man! Asshole gave the camel *gasoline!*"

I like stand up. "Hey man," I said. "My friend's out cold here."

"But he gave him *gasoline,* man!" said the private. "The asshole *killed* the goddamn camel!"

So I like start pointing at Trang. "And maybe the camel killed *him!*"

But the private was one of those 'dog-with-a-bone' dudes who won't let it go, and he says, "The stupid asshole! Gave him gasoline! What a stupid *shit!*"

"Hey," I said. "He's my *friend,* all right?"

But that private was on a roll. He starts making fun of my calling him my *friend* in a lisp, like we are queer, and then he starts asking me, like he's really interested, "What is he anyway, a *gook*? Is he a *gook*? Huh?" And then an interesting thing happened. I could feel my arm going back. You know when your brain sends that signal to your arm and your arm jolts backward into a cock. But just as my brain sent the message, the private is swung around and a fist the size of a frozen chicken flies through the air. One big smash, and the private is down on the sand twitching and rolling and holding his face.

I never told you this, but back when Trang and me were at the School of Infantry at Camp Pendelton together there was this like blanket party set up to smash up the 'gook' Trang, and when the lights came on things had reversed and Trang had this massive Southern boy pinned to the rack by his neck. That Southern boy was Private Euclid Krebes, and after completion of the School of Infantry we three were sent direct to recon, as they were short of guys in those days. We all landed in the same recon platoon, but I don't think Krebes had said one friendly word to either of us since the School of Infantry given that bit of negative history—*but here he was grinning sheepish at me and shaking out his fist like he had hurt his fingers with his mighty punch!* And then he like drops to his knees next to my man Trang, and he whips off his T-shirt and starts holding it against the head wound like a compress, which is what I should have been doing all this time, as Trang's head was bleeding pretty good. He gestures to me to hold the compress, and then he says he's going to round up a corpsman, and he hoofs off and while he's gone Trang comes back to life. One of the marines hands him a bottle of Perrier, and he looks at it and cracks up and slugs it back. Trang drank the whole bottle down and then tossed it aside into the sand.

Trang had to go to the hospital in Dharhan as he had a concussion and some swelling of the brain. He had stitches on his head, and he lost his earlobe totally. I was still missing a front tooth from where Trang knocked it clean out when we fought in the Persian Gulf just before we heard Princess Lulu singing in the dark. The Navy had made me this fake front tooth. But over time it had gotten looser and looser, and just before I went to visit Trang in the hospital I just yanked it out and made a big point of giving Trang a smile that showed off the missing-tooth hole. I don't know why I wanted Trang to see I had the missing-tooth hole, but it sure cracked up my man Trang. Something about that missing-tooth hole made him real happy. Right away he made me feel where the camel hoof had left a permanent dent in his skull, and his missing earlobe. He like reached out from his hospital bed and started punching me pretty hard in the shoulder where I had the DIE A HERO tattoo. Then Trang made me punch him in the shoulder where he had the same DIE A HERO tattoo. We kept whacking away at each other's shoulders like crazy-ass marines until a doctor passing by came in and told us to knock it off, so then we high-fived each other. So I sat down and looked at Trang, with his missing *ear-*

lobe and shaved head with stitches where the camel kicked in his skull, and then I felt my own missing tooth with my tongue and my broken nose and thought with a primal stoke: *We are two crazy-ass marines at war!*

So I told Trang about how that redheaded redneck Euclid Krebes had knocked the army private out so badly that the army private was *also* in the hospital. I said Euclid Krebes might be in some hot water for his massive punch, but that Captain Pettigrew was trying to make it right. We both agreed Captain Pettigrew was turning out to be an A-OK dude. Trang was real surprised by the fact that the redneck had knocked out the army private *for him,* and said that when he got back to the platoon, he'd go thank him in person. Trang then got real serious, and said he had to think about this Euclid Krebes thing, so I sat down in a chair and said nothing. Trang asked me a couple of times to describe the look on Euclid Krebes' face after he punched out the army dude, and all I could say was that Krebes was *grinning,* like he was real happy. Trang said that what Euclid Krebes had done was like the coolest thing anyone had ever done for him, and this kind of bummed me out. Before I left the hospital room Trang said in a whisper, "You know, Carmichael, I was sure this like *dead camel* was a sign that I should like chill out. But this Euclid Krebes punch you tell me about—I may have to *rethink* chilling." And right then Trang opens his palm above the sheets, and inside is the pearl that Princess Lulu gave him. And Trang just stares into that pearl like it is a little crystal ball and he can see the future, and so he is clearly deep in his own world now, so I nod and slip out of the hospital room.

So a day later Trang is supposed to be sent back to the platoon from the hospital. He didn't show up, so Captain Pettigrew told me to go find him. The captain said *if* I found Trang, my new mission was to keep an eye on Trang generally.

"Keep an eye on him, sir?"

"Keep him out of trouble," said the captain.

"Sir," I said. "Yes, sir. I am to keep Trang out of trouble."

I repeated the order, as it was a strange order. You don't usually send one marine to watch another in that way. I was glad for the mission, as Trang was my main man, but it was an unusual show of *consideration* on the part of Captain Pettigrew. But there was some sort of mysterious bond there between the captain and Trang. And I wondered if it wasn't the same sort of mysterious bond that made Euclid Krebes the redneck knock out the army private. It was like there was this underground river of support for Trang, and I wondered where this river was flowing?

So I hitched to Dhahran and found Tommy Trang hanging out in the cafeteria of the hospital. He was just chowing down on cakes and stuff, and said he just wanted to do some hard thinking. So I asked Trang if he had any deep thoughts, and Trang said, yeah, he was still going to be one of the greatest warriors in the history of the Marine Corps, end of story. As I have pointed out a few times now, Trang had no problem with his personal confidence level. So then Trang stood up like he was at attention, and I took that to mean we were heading back to our platoon.

We hitched a ride with an army major by the name of Klein. All the way there this Major Klein made me tell the story of 'Tommy Trang Rescuing the Suicidal Kuwaiti Princess', and he really got a kick out of it, in particular when I told how Trang had told Colonel Fawwaz he was a *Vietnamese American Jew.* Major Klein acted like he had never heard anything so *funny,* and kept making me repeat the words *Vietnamese American Jew,* and every time I said it he slapped the steering wheel and laughed so hard he started coughing and tears came into his eyes. Trang wasn't laughing at all, and when Major Klein got out to take a piss in the sands, I nudged him and said, "What's up, man?" And when he turned to look at me, he looked so grim, and I *just knew he was totally thinking about Princess Lulu.* What I didn't know was that Princess Lulu had like *infected* him back in Kuwait, and he was just going to get sicker and sicker over her *memory.* It is a rare dude that gets seriously infected by a babe, and usually such dudes are not jarhead marines. I'm not even sure *Trang* knew he was that sort of dude—I think it was sort of news to him.

Anyway, as we are getting out of the Humvee with Captain Pettigrew back at our camp at al-Mishaab, our platoon's sergeant runs up and informs us we are to *saddle up ASAP.* It sounds like the real thing. Apparently the Iraqis are on the move, and we are to get picked up in a big bird and be brought up to the Kuwaiti border to try and slow them down. As I said, at this point in Desert Shield, there were few heavy assets in position to stop the Iraqis if they wanted to roll over Saudi Arabia in their tanks. And we barely have time to grab our packs before a big helo drops down and sucks us all up into its belly. We're all putting on desert face paint.

I look over at Trang and he is slapping his shoulder where the tattoo is that says: DIE A HERO. I give him the thumbs-up. After all the endless training we are finally going to be put to warrior use! The helo drops down into one position up on the Saudi border, and the ramp drops, but there are already army assets on the ground, so we go back up in the air. We go around in circles, and get a lot of conflicting rumors, and then suddenly we drop down from the sky like an avenging angel, and the rear drops, and Trang lets out this *war cry* so the whole platoon sort of stops to stare at him, but then we are all whooping and charging out of that bird *like we are taking the beaches at Normandy!* We scatter into a defensive perimeter with maximum excitement!

The big helo takes off, and as it does a couple of our guys blow off some rounds to salute it! And then we all blow off a few rounds, but Captain Pettigrew is really pissed and screaming for fire control, and we all settle down, as it was a pretty unprofessional display for an elite team of marines. So we lay out there in a half circle in the sands facing Kuwait, and Captain Pettigrew made a beautiful speech as the sun set that we were here to stop maybe an Iraqi brigade, and that we had been ordered to hold out to the last man to slow the Iraqi advance, and that we were not unlike the defenders of the Alamo. That historical reference got our people stoked, and not one showed a flicker of fear! We were trained and ready to *die a hero!* All the men had their ears and eyes trained toward Kuwait. Once, a sort of tremor ran through all the men, but it was a lizard out there at the edge of darkness. And it was right then, as we waited for the attack side by side in the sand, Trang took out that old M16 shell casing he said was from Vietnam and commenced spinning it in his fingers. And right then he opened up a little about his past and whispered to me, "My mother always got me a Christmas tree."

I whispered, "When you were a kid in Vietnam?"

Trang shook his head and whispered, "No, Carmichael."

"So you grew up mostly over here?"

"Since I was like six years old."

"Did you get adopted or something?"

"No way," whispered Trang. "You ever heard of the Vietnamese boat people?"

I whispered to Trang I hadn't heard about this.

"We got out of Vietnam with about two hundred others on this piece-of-crap boat," whispered Trang. "And then the boat sank in the South China Sea. Most of them couldn't swim. My mom and me got picked up by this Libyan tanker and taken to Taiwan. On account of my being clearly the son of an American soldier, they let me and my mom into America. She was so happy when she saw the Golden Gate Bridge she cried all over me."

On account of her crying about making it to America, I stupidly decided in a flash she must have had a good feeling about Trang's father, and maybe tried to track him down. That was stupid of me, but I whispered, "So did she try and track down your father in the States?"

Trang didn't look at me but ahead into the darkness, and whispered, "She was raped, Carmichael. She was raped by a squad of U.S. marines and hung up in a tree by her ankles. My grandfather was killed in the same attack on the village. My mom was like twelve and had to look at her grandfather's shot-up body from upside down in the tree until somebody cut her down a few days later. She never walked well. It messed with her ankles, hanging from the tree."

"Whoa, man. Sorry, man. Why the *hell* would she ever want to come to *America* after that? And why would *you* ever want to join the *marines*?"

Trang turned to me, and man, he looked fierce. He looked kind of let down too, like he had been over this stuff before a hundred times and expected *I* at least wouldn't have asked such a totally stupid question. Trang whispered, "Get this straight in your head, man. *America* didn't rape her. And the *Marine Corps* didn't rape her."

And because my man Trang was down on me, I didn't know what to say, so I blurted out, "So where is she now?"

"She died last year in Trenton, Jersey. You know what she wanted to have in her coffin with her six feet under?"

I shook my head, but I was guessing maybe a picture of her boy Tommy. But Trang whispered, "She wanted an American flag, man. I folded one up myself, put it in her hands, and then the dude and I closed the casket."

I didn't know what to say when our whispered conversation got to this point, with Trang closing the casket on his mother holding the flag. Trang didn't say anything for a while and went back to spinning the M16 shell casing. Then he tossed me the shell casing and said, "The round from that casing was fired by the marines during the attack on my mother's village. My mother kept it all the years since the war, and gave it to me before she died." It was spooky holding the crushed shell casing from that nasty war, and I was pretty okay with handing it right back. But Trang said he wanted me to like *keep* the casing, and that as brothers-in-arms we *were surely going to fire some hot rounds for freedom.* He said with a quiet laugh I was the only person who knew he was a bastard son of the United States Marine Corps.

During the night I heard some marines writing last letters and I guess pinning them inside their cammie blouses. We were pretty sure the attack was coming at dawn, as Captain Pettigrew said that was the Iraqi way. By noon the next day we had begun to get pretty parched, as we were operating with just a couple of canteens each, and that was gone fast, even as we tried to make it last. We were under strict radio silence, but Captain Pettigrew broke it late that afternoon when some of the men sat up and just sat with their heads hanging in the sun. It took a few hours, but we got picked up by a bird, and in the helo found out we had been dropped off in the wrong place, and anyway the mission was a false alarm— Saddam had not budged from Kuwait.

Then as we are approaching our position on the al-Mishaab coast the helo pilot comes on and tells us to lock and load: he says our al-Mishaab position has been overrun by Iraqis. He says this with a laugh, and we are all confused. The captain goes up to look out the pilot's window to see what we are facing, and comes back with a downer look on his face. He tells us not to worry, but to keep our fingers on our triggers just the same, until we can scope out the situation.

When the ramp on the helo dropped and hit the sand, we see a couple dozen Iraqis running at us waving their hands. They stopped halfway up when they saw all our lowered M16s. For a second we stood facing each other, and then Captain Pettigrew walks in front of us and down the ramp saying, "These Iraqi guys want to surrender." Captain Pettigrew is shaking his head, and the Iraqis part to let him pass, and then they turn to follow him—I guess they figured it was best to follow our leader. So we walked out of the back of the helo and watched the dozen skinny, dirty Iraqis following our captain like a pack of dogs across our camp.

It turned out there were Iraqis in all our bunkers and mess hall and so on, they had gone through our personal items looking for food, but some of them were stealing stuff too. We rounded them all up and got them on their asses a way off from camp and tried to find some of the personal belongings of our men. I said to Trang at one point, "What do you think?"

"These must be the cowards, Carmichael. The *real* fighters are still over there."

CHAPTER 5

A week later Captain Pettigrew ordered us into this one big air-conditioned room we had in a mobile trailer. We didn't get to sit in there much, so that much was fine with the men — excellent cool air! But then Captain Pettigrew said, "Men, I have been instructed to give you a lecture, and the lecture is called 'Understanding Your Iraqi.'" There was a general groan in the room, and Captain Pettigrew shook his head and like told us to listen up and he'd try and make it as painless as possible. So Captain Pettigrew proceeded to just drone on and on about how Saddam Hussein and these crazy dudes the *Baathists* came to power in Iraq by killing everyone right and left. And Corporal Micholski suddenly said so everyone could hear, "Man, what I'd do for a cold *bath* right now."

This got a good laugh, but Captain Pettigrew tried to hammer on about Saddam and these nasty Baathists, and someone else said louder, "Man, I'm a *Baathist*. No man, I'm a *Jacuzzist!*"

Corporal Michaels yelled, "Maybe Saddam invaded Kuwait to like *take a cold bath*, man."

There was loud agreement that we U.S. marines were all *Baathists of the Cold Water Desert Sect.* You would think this might have ended the lecture, but this is when Captain Pettigrew took a strange turn. He like seemed pleased the men were joking around about being *Baathists,* and said this: "Suppose that's what a Baathist was:

someone who liked a good bath. And you men clearly like cold baths, and so does the average Iraqi soldier, I'd wager. So in that sense we're all Baathists, aren't we? In that sense, you and the average Iraqi soldier could have some common ground, do you see?"

No marine of Third Platoon could *see.*

There was silence and the humor evaporated. Captain Pettigrew was up there hanging, and you would have thought he'd pull back from the edge, but he stumbled onwards and said, "All I'm asking is for you not to demonize the individual Iraqi soldier. The average Iraqi soldier is a human being just like you who"—and here you could see Captain Pettigrew trying to circle back and tie it all together but having some trouble—"who likes a good cold bath just like you men." And then Captain Pettigrew said something that even he looked confused about when it came out of his mouth: "What I want is for you men to feel there is a fellow human in the Iraqi out there in the trenches."

There was total silence. I don't think any of the men had known there was such a *chaplain* hidden in their captain. I had the sense that even Captain Pettigrew was surprised he had a chaplain hidden inside, but war changes people in all sorts of ways. From then on Pettigrew was known behind his back as *Captain Chaplain.*

After a full minute of chair shifting and silence, Private Trang raised his hand and said, "Sir, a question?"

Captain Pettigrew looked rescued and said, "Yes, Private Trang."

"Sir, why do you want us to *feel* for the Iraqi soldiers? I've heard they're raping and torturing and killing women and children with power drills and jumper cables over there in Kuwait. Shouldn't we be *feeling something* for those women and children? What I'm feeling is I want to do something for the women and children left behind in Kuwait."

There was general loud agreement with Private Trang. Marines started banging on their desks to show their approval. Corporal Krebes raised his hand and stood up and said, "Sir, when are we going to chase these *evil bastards* out of Kuwait? We're good to go *right now!* I say let loose the *Dogs of War!* Let's take a big bite out of Saddam's *ass.*"

If the reconnaissance marines in that trailer had gotten permission, we would have all charged into Kuwait right then and fought to the death like Captain Shakespear. But Captain Pettigrew suddenly went to the door and brought in this Air Force officer, who like started explaining to us what his planes were going to be up to in a few days when the air war commenced. He said there were hundreds of thousands of Iraqis massed across the border, and that they were going to drop bombs from B-52s and A-10s on their bunkers, *but that the goal at this point was not really to kill Iraqis.*

Trang raised his hand, but the Air Force officer waved him off and said, "I repeat: *the goal is not to kill Iraqis in large numbers.* If we wanted to kill Iraqis, we'd load the planes with lots of antipersonnel munitions and they'd reduce the Iraqi soldiers to hamburger. But we're just going to drop *regular* bombs, and most of the time, they'll just make a lot of noise and make a crater in the desert. We want to *scare* Iraqis."

My man Trang raised his hand again, and said when the Air Force dude looked at him, "Sir, you want to *scare* Iraqis?"

The Air Force officer looked at Trang hard and said, "We're trying to send a *message*. We want to say: We don't have anything against you *personally,* Mr. Ali Baba Iraqi in the trenches. But we, America, are angry like the gods. So we will throw thunderbolts down to show our displeasure until you vacate from Kuwait."

You could see Trang was getting kind of fired up, and his hand jammed into the air again. The Air Force officer asked if there were any questions and ignored Trang's flagging hand. He was about to step down when Corporal Krebes stood up and said, "Sir, I think Private Trang has a *question.*"

So the Air Force officer nodded at Trang, who jumped up and said, "Easy question, sir. When do you expect we marines will see some action on the ground?"

That Air Force officer shook his head, and said as if Trang would be *glad* to hear it, "Truth is, marine, if all goes well with the air war as we expect, there may not even be a ground war."

Trang shook his head like he had water in his ears and said, "Sir, are you saying I *may not get* to fight the Iraqis?"

"That's what I'm saying, private. This is a new kind of war, and with any luck, we won't need your services."

"Sir, are you saying I may not get to fight to free Kuwait?"

"That's what I'm saying, soldier."

"Sir, pardon me, sir. But that's unacceptable."

"Excuse me, private?"

"I said that's *unacceptable,* sir."

"Careful, private."

"*Unacceptable,* sir."

Corporal Krebes right then let out a huge Marine Corps seal call of, *"Oooraah!"* in support of Private Trang, who was still standing and staring down the Air Force officer. The other men started to chant, *"Oooraah! Oooraah! Oooraah!"* until Captain Pettigrew snapped out of his fog and stood and glared at us. When we were quiet, he like escorted the Air Force officer out of the room.

For a few days my man Trang was in a daze. The air war started, and Trang wouldn't even come out of the barracks to look at this massive and continual flyover of jets. It was one of the most unforgettable things I have ever seen, and I prayed for those pilots. It was like History in the Sky. It was like being witness to D day at Normandy. I was so stoked I was out there on the sands waving a T-shirt at our pilots as they flew over until some of the marines started to look at me funny. But Trang was stuck on the idea that the pilots had taken *his* war away from him, and from then on he had like a real dislike of planes and pilots. He seemed to want to pretend the air war wasn't happening, that the modern age wasn't even happening, and that was a little over the edge, in my opinion. Add to the mix that he was sure Princess Lulu was either married or dead by suicide, and you can understand my man Trang was in a sketchy state of mind. He felt he had lost out on both love and war.

Trang was ready to *rescue* Princess Lulu, and he was ready to *save* Kuwait. He had *massive energy* ready to devote to either cause. And that powerful energy was sort of bottled up inside him, and it had nowhere to go for the present. He wasn't being asked to be a Captain Shakespear, and he had no information on the whereabouts of Princess Lulu. It was my belief that if the Military Powers had given

Private Trang a *death-or-glory* mission right now, he would have made them proud, and he would have been seen as one *Gung-Ho American Marine.* But because he didn't get that *heroic mission,* people thought what he did *next* confirmed the general belief he was a head case.

I saw my man Trang the next day dragging his metal rack and mattress through the main street of our camp. He was dragging it behind him, and leaving two scratch marks on the pavement. I tried to ask him what he was up to, but he shook his head like he wasn't in a mood for talking. And then he bent his trajectory down the road, and I saw he was aiming for our HQ. It was this cinder-block building where Captain Pettigrew had his office. No one was in there, and my man Trang pulled his bunk through the screen door, and then motioned to me to pick up the end and lift it over the three wooden steps. So I lifted up the end and helped Trang bring his cot into Captain Pettigrew's office. I was like saying, *Trang, you can't be in here, man. This is like off limits.* But the thing was, Trang wasn't really stopping in Captain Pettigrew's office, he like kept dragging his rack right into Captain Pettigrew's *head.* It was a pretty spacious head, about half the size of the captain's office, and there was room for the rack. Trang like nodded at me and then went and got his gear. While he was gone I like used the head, as we enlisted guys used these cat trenches in the sand outside of camp and so a real shitter was kind of a luxury, and as I sat on the throne I wondered if Trang was heading for a Section Eight discharge.

Trang came back in, and he started pinning up all these topographical maps of Kuwait on the walls of the head. I saw he had drawn all sort of lines and figures all over them, like he had been mapping his way into Kuwait for some time. It seemed kind of useless to argue with Trang about not camping in the captain's head, but I tried once or twice anyway, and then just sat on his bunk, waiting for the return of Captain Pettigrew. And then I heard the screen door slam, and knew the captain was in his office. And then Captain Pettigrew banged into the head, and *I swear he never really even blinked.* That was what I found so amazing about Captain Pettigrew: he was like the most *unflappable* dude I have ever met in my life. He took it all in stride, and seemed to get a kick out of the *weirdest shit life has to offer.* So I guess he was the ideal officer for Private Trang. Because Captain Pettigrew took in Trang's rack in his head, and the maps of Kuwait on the wall, and believe it or not, he totally nailed Trang's like *thought process.* I personally had little idea why Trang was in Captain Pettigrew's head. But listen to what Captain Pettigrew said after a glance at the situation: *"Closer to the action here, Trang?"*

Trang looked over from his maps and nodding said, "Exactly, sir."

"Sure the stink won't get you?"

"No sir," said Trang.

"Carry on," said Captain Pettigrew. And he left us alone in the head again. And then I heard him quietly cracking up out there in his office. And I went to the door of the head and like listened to him on the phone, and heard him say to someone, maybe another officer somewhere in the Gulf War, these words: . . . *unsurpassed entertainment value* . . . So I guess Captain Pettigrew was into Trang's weirdness because it gave him something to talk about with his officer friends.

I found it hard to believe Captain Pettigrew was going to let Trang stay in the head, and was thinking he was just letting Trang do his thing, *to see what Trang would do next, because it would make a good story in a boring war.* But I figured it was all going to be over in a few days, because Captain Pettigrew might find it *amusing* to let Trang ride, but the captain couldn't have an enlisted dude living in his head if a superior officer came to visit the camp. And like two days later word came a colonel was coming by to see Captain Pettigrew. And I was in there when Captain Pettigrew came to give Trang *the word.* The captain was playing it like he and Trang were on the same page, that it was all pretty funny, but the joke was over. But it was clear Trang wasn't seeing his actions as *humorous,* so Captain Pettigrew shifted gears and said, "I understand your need to be closer to the action, Trang. But you know your own hootch isn't that far from HQ."

"I know, sir," said Trang. "But I like it here."

"Trang," said Captain Pettigrew. "It was funny, and I get your point, but the bottom line is you can't live in here. That's the bottom line. I've got Colonel Waters coming at fourteen hundred, and he might not understand your need to be close to the action."

Trang nodded and started to gather his gear. Captain Pettigrew looked at me with this satisfied look of *You just have to reason with Trang*. He said to me, "Carmichael, you help Trang pack up his gear and get this rack out of here." I was kind of surprised Trang had folded his tent, so to speak, so easily. And then I saw Trang look up at the ceiling of the head and start to like *talk to himself about what Chesty Puller would do*. In case you don't know, Chesty Puller was like this legendary marine hero. Anyway, I knew talking to yourself out loud means you are one step from certifiable, and I started to worry, and right then Trang says to me, "I can move my own gear, man." I wanted to help, but Trang made it clear he wanted me to leave the head. So I went back to my rack and lay there thinking, and then sat right up, because I *just knew what my man Trang was up to!* And I hustled down the road, and sure enough, there he was, up on the *roof* of Captain Pettigrew's cinder-block office. He had his rack up there, and his gear, and he was just sitting on the roof looking down at me.

This was like more of a *public situation*.

And marines from our platoon started to gather around and laugh. And Captain Pettigrew came from down at the motor pool, and he sauntered up the street, and was like shaking his head and at first he was laughing too. I could hear him saying to himself: *Entertainment value! Wait till I tell the other officers!* I like looked at my watch, and it was 1330, so there was only thirty minutes to get Trang off the roof of HQ before the arrival of Colonel Waters. And Captain Pettigrew came and stood next to me and said, "I thought you were going back to your own hootch, Trang?"

"Sir, you ordered me out of the head."

"Well, you can't live up there, Trang."

"Sir, I want to be near HQ."

Captain Pettigrew sort of turned to the men around him, like they were an audience, and jokingly asked, "So Trang, do you have some demands?"

"Yes, sir."

The men started to laugh at this game, and Captain Pettigrew said, "Go ahead, Trang, what would it take to get you off the roof of HQ?"

"It's very simple, sir."

"Spell it out, Trang."

"Sir, I need a mission."

"We all do, Trang."

"You don't understand, sir. I need a *real* mission. I want to go after Saddam."

"Our time will come, Trang."

"Sir, send me into Kuwait. The Saddam dude is raping women and we're playing *volleyball.* It makes me sick, sir."

Captain Pettigrew lost his grin for a second, I guess because he felt the same way as Trang. Come to think of it, I think we *all* wanted to go after Saddam, and we *all* knew Kuwaiti women and children were dying over there. So Trang's joke was not a joke, and Captain Pettigrew was silent and serious, and kind of looked *longingly* toward Kuwait for a second. A bunch of the marines around me looked in that direction too, as if we could hear the cries of the women and children. It was like being a fireman and watching a house burn, and doing *nothing.*

Trang in the middle of this serious silence yelled out, "Sir, send me on a mission! There are women getting raped over there!"

Captain Pettigrew looked at his watch, and I guess he realized Colonel Waters was like on his way to his camp. And suddenly he lost his sense of humor about the whole thing. He snapped at Trang, "Enough is enough. Get down from there, Private Trang." There was no debate in his tone, but Trang just sat there until Captain Pettigrew sent some of the guys up to drag him down.

After the rooftop protest ended badly, Tommy Trang ceased with the weird stuff. I am not a shrink, but the guy just like changed in a fundamental way. You didn't see him dragging his rack down to HQ to be closer to the action anymore. And the mood of the whole platoon sank some generally. People were suddenly not as into killing time playing volleyball. It got to the point where some marines came to Trang like as a joke and said they wanted him *to go back to the old crazy Trang.* And Trang just told them to tell the captain that *he wanted to be sent to Kuwait to take down Saddam.* They laughed, but Trang just stared at them like he was dead serious, which made them laugh harder, because I guess they thought this was a glimmer of their crazy old Trang. But for now the crazy old Trang was dead and buried. I tried to talk to him about it, but all he said was, *Tell Captain Pettigrew to send me to fucking Kuwait, man.* It was like only the second time I had heard Trang *swear,* so you can take that as an indication of how upset he was in like a deep way.

Krebes was meanwhile walking around camp talking about HUBRIS, which I thought was a military acronym for like a new weapon system or maybe a cousin vehicle to the humvee. Krebes was upset by Trang's new mood, and didn't fill me in on HUBRIS, just kept muttering about it under his breath, and like when some of the other men heard about HUBRIS and asked me about it, I like told them it was a secret experimental weapon system that our platoon was slated to acquire soon and this seriously elevated the spirits in the platoon, as soldiers love new war toys, and it was probably an *honor* to be chosen, and indicated we might be using it in some real action soon. Krebes finally came down to earth when he overheard talk about HUBRIS, and he came to me and said HUBRIS wasn't a damn weapon system but just a Greek word for like *a huge egomaniacal state of mind* not unlike that of Thomas Trang thinking he could go into Kuwait and take down Saddam *solo.* Krebes added that people with HUBRIS always got killed in the end.

The platoon was generally pretty let down to learn HUBRIS was not a top-secret weapon system, but just an old Greek word for like Trang's *personal instability.* The whole HUBRIS thing let the cat out of the bag that Private Euclid Krebes was not just a tobacco-spitting redneck, but a *weird genius who knew Greek,* and everyone started calling him Dr. Krebes and asking him to *say something in Greek.* And Krebes looked pretty down, as I guess his acting like a redneck had always let him be treated as just one of the guys in the past, and now he was treated like Trang as sort of a freak. So Krebes as a result spent a lot of time following Trang and me around, and we all became friends. It turned out he really was some sort of weird genius. He was like picking up Arabic in his free time. He would read or see something and it would be locked in that big brain of his. And he literally had a huge head and had to like cut a slit in the rear of his cover to make it fit—as if there was extra room for files in his skull.

Anyway, one evening we three were sitting around shooting the shit, and suddenly we three see the lights of some vehicle in the distance barreling toward our camp. Krebes had just completed writing KNIGHTS WITHOUT A FIGHT in the sand with his M16 when we saw this vehicle. Me and Trang and Krebes look at the words and give each other a nod like *there it is,* and then raise our eyes to the oncoming vehicle. It was a limousine. It slowly slid to a halt before us three, and the tinted passenger window slides down, and this voice from within says, "Private Carmichael." I kind of recognized the Arab voice, and then I see the face with these dead black eyes in the window, and it is old Colonel Fawwaz!

Colonel Fawwaz was kind of rude to Trang, he just kind of nodded to him. Then he turned his big face to me and said, "Care to go for a pleasure ride?" And I'm like *no thanks,* on account of his rudeness to Trang and to Krebes too, who was sitting there and who the colonel ignored also. But Trang like says, "Go with him man," and as Colonel Fawwaz's face slips back in the limousine to answer some question from his driver, Trang whispers to me in a stoked way, *"You go with him, and find out the status of Princess Lulu."* So I now have like this *mission,* and the limousine door is opened by the driver, and I'm like, "I can't just go without asking Captain Petti-grew." So Krebes is sent off on the double by the Saudi colonel to get Captain Pettigrew, and when he shows up Colonel Fawwaz goes off for a walk with him, and when they come back I am like cleared to hang with Colonel Fawwaz for as long as the big Saudi dude needs me for his *special mission.*

So then we are in the limousine, and the colonel calls me Cowboy, which he made up on the spot and said like we were *old buddies*. And he hands me a drink of Jack Daniels on ice, and puts some Donna Summer on the cassette player, and starts wagging his finger at me telling me *I should of told him of my important father long ago*. I take a sip of Jack, and like say, *yessir, I should of told you*. But I have no idea what the hell he is talking about. And he rattles on about how now he knows I am *that* son of *that* Carmichael from *that certain city* in Texas. And it is all *wink, wink, nudge, nudge,* and a good laugh was had by we two *about my hiding that I was that Rich Son of Texas Oil!* I am like not as good as Trang about surfing a wave of shit, but for the *good of the mission* of finding out about Princess Lulu from the big drunk Saudi colonel I do what I can, and it was kind of easy, but still, at first I wasn't all that comfortable with all the *lying*.

I guess because I wasn't a good liar, our like conversation came to an end. He had been telling me about his time at Oxford, and had the idea somehow that his *imaginary* Cody Carmichael the rich Son of Oil from Texas had dropped out of Yale to join the marines, and that this imaginary Cody Carmichael had known the colonel's brother Abdul at Yale, and that me and Abdul had hammered back the beers and chased American sluts together. His brother Abdul had told Colonel Fawwaz I was A-OK, and so Colonel Fawwaz had decided to let the *past be past* and take me away from the war for a few hours. This was all totally nuts, but I decided to go with it for the sake of, as I said, *finding out more about Princess Lulu for my man Trang.*

Plus, it was getting interesting. I was a couple of drinks into it now, and Colonel Fawwaz slapped me on the shoulder and told me we would have *fun!* I don't know about his idea of *fun,* because the first stop wasn't much *fun!* We pulled in front of this like huge old-looking concrete building, and from the animal-looking Arab guards at the door, I was wondering *if I had been tricked and was being sent to a nasty prison or something on account of what happened in Kuwait.* We walked past the guards and into a courtyard. I was almost running to keep up with the big Colonel Fawwaz. And then he braked his bulk in the middle of the courtyard and clapped his hands and yelled in Arabic. Strange, but right then I was thinking about the earth erupting with like *fiery gas plumes*. Maybe it was kind of the nasty vibe of the place was giving me a *walking nightmare*. Colonel Fawwaz squeezed me on the shoulder and said he had promised his brother from Yale to keep an eye on me while I was in the gulf.

And right then these huge metal doors opened, and in march guards in robes, and behind them come these like four black dudes. I mean they were not Arab, but black, like real African looking. And they looked bug-eyed scared, and I would have been too, as right behind them comes this huge mother of an Arab waving a big scimitar. That's what Colonel Fawwaz called it, a *scimitar.* The black dudes are like dropped to their knees, and then their heads are pushed down. And then I hear something overhead, and I look up and it is these gallery windows sliding open. And there are all these dozens of Saudis like gaping out through these windows. And when I looked down again at the black dudes, one of them like locked eyes on me, like as if to say, *man, this is 1990, they don't cut off heads in 1990!*

I like take a deep breath, and was thinking *what to do!* when some official little midget dude starts reading this long riff, I guess on their crimes, from this scroll thing that looked real ancient. Then Colonel Fawwaz gets a sly look from the official dude, and the colonel nods, and the official dude nods, and like the dude with the scimitar pokes it into the first black guy's back, and like just as his back snaps upwards in pain, *whoosh,* that scimitar had his head bouncing on the floor. The other black guys start like moving out on their knees like chickens running, but Mr. Scimitar went into swishing action, and *Whoosh! Whoosh! Whoosh!* off go all the heads rolling around on the concrete floor.

And I shit you not, right then Colonel Fawwaz like looks at his watch and says: *these official duties take so much time.* And when we rush back in the limousine Colonel Fawwaz slugs back his whiskey and pours us both a couple, and then kind of snuggles his massive back into the seat with a cozy sigh. And all I can do is slug a straight drink back and say: *What did they do?* And the colonel is reading some papers and looks up as if surprised and says: "They? They are rapists."

"Who did they rape?"

"They have tried to rape some Saudi women."

"They tried?"

"Luckily, they were caught."

Colonel Fawwaz made it clear he wanted me to ask no more questions, and shoved some papers in my hands. He said it was a recent speech by President Mubarak of Egypt about the war and that he had tried to get our General Schwarzkopf interested in it, and had translated it personally from the Arabic at great pains, but that our general had shown no interest at all. From what I could gather this brush-off from General Schwarzkopf was really bugging Colonel Fawwaz, and he started hammering drinks and rattling on about *Showing Respect for Arabia and Arabs!* Which led him as we drove into some historical territory. It suddenly became real upsetting that I had never heard of these Saudi dudes of ancient times called the *Ikhwan*. They were like some seriously whacked-out but important religious dudes, as far as I could tell, because Colonel Fawwaz was *cranked up* I didn't know about the *Ikhwan*. So I'm feeling short-tempered on account of seeing the decapitations, and am like, "Hey, Colonel Fawwaz, tell me about the *Mormons*. We've all got our religious nuts." But Colonel Fawwaz didn't get the point about the Mormons, except when I said the Mormons had the option of a lot of wives, which kind of calmed him down and turned him on as he was imagining like a harem of blond-haired blue-eyed American sluts. But once he lost his erection, he got back on the topic of the *Ikhwan,* who were these ancient camel-hoppers who would cover their face rather than be looked on by an *infidel.*

Colonel Fawwaz put down his drink and covered his fat face with his hands and turned to me and said through his fingers, "You, Cowboy, you are the *infidel.* You see?"

I wasn't sure I liked being called an *infidel.* Say what you will about the Mormons, the few I'd met going door-to-door in California were always extremely friendly guys, and not one ever covered his face rather than look at me or insulted me and called me an *asshole,* which is what *infidel* sounded like the way Colonel Fawwaz said it. I was thinking on these things, and Colonel Fawwaz lowered his hands and slapped me on the knee and said, "Cowboy, why do I go on like this? I am certainly not *Ikhwan!*"

"That's cool," I said. "I'm not Mormon. Can we drop the God thing?"

"The God *thing*?" said Colonel Fawwaz.

"You know," I said. "Let's just chill on the *God thing*, cease and desist that conversation, if you see what I mean."

And here Colonel Fawwaz sat up his bulk and slapping his chest with a thud yelled out, *"Never! I am a slave of Allah the Most Merciful!"*

I was thinking *yeah, yeah.* Allah the Most Merciful who slays some black dudes *whish, whish* without a trial. It just really was becoming *clear* we as Americans were in bed with some crazy Arab mothers just off their camels civilization-wise, and it was becoming harder to keep on a party face. I was wondering if deep down they were secretly all these Ikhwan dudes who hated us Americans on sight. But Trang had sent me on a mission to help scout out the Princess Lulu situation, so I bit my tongue about old Allah the Most Merciful for the moment.

Next thing I know the limousine is screeching to a halt in front of another concrete monster of a building. It still had those big construction bins outside, and it turned out this new and additional Ministry of Defense building was like finished last week. Colonel Fawwaz said he had been in charge of the construction, and patted a concrete column like it was slapped up by his own soft hands. He whisked into this concrete building and punched the top-floor button of a chrome elevator and said, "Soon this building will be full of the personnel of battle!"

Since the battle was already *on* from the American point of view, I was thinking, *Take your time, Colonel.* So we go into this huge empty room full of boxed Apple computers, and he waved his arm and said, "The nerve center of my command post!" *Crazy, that's what it all was!* So we march past this one lonely Arab dude with an operational Apple, and he's playing war games with a Black Hawk helicopter. I mean he's playing war *games,* like kids play back home in the States. Colonel Fawwaz watches the game, and then pats the Arab dude on the shoulder like he's *hot on the job,* and then we find this guard in front of a room in the rear, and the dude like stumbles up and salutes. Colonel Fawwaz opens the door on this bachelor-pad room, with wet bar and big-screen TV, and says, "I have built these quarters, as there will be many late nights of work during the war, and perhaps I will catch forty winks here."

And then from the back comes a chick's laugh. And Fawwaz like calls out, and she comes sliding out from the back in high heels and this slinky number riding up her ass. She's got a paint-by-number makeup job, but then she smiles and I recognize her as the Palestinian Maid of Princess Lulu, the Girl Behind the Curtain, the One with the Centipede in her Private Parts, and the *rumored great love of Colonel Fawwaz.* I like am thinking, *Now we're getting closer to the news on Princess Lulu!*

So the maid comes and takes my hand and leads me to the couch as Colonel Fawwaz goes and puts a Jets game on the big-screen TV. And as I look at her, I suddenly have the feeling I totally know her from somewhere, and then it hits me where: *the beach!* The maid is now featuring some dyed blond hair, and she has big Chiclet teeth that are sparkling white, and these like gleaming cocoa-golden eyes that seemed to telegraph: *let's just party!* She looks totally athletic and trim too, like she was way into fitness—her stomach, of which I caught a glimpse later when she was shot up, was like brown paper over her stomach muscles. Her tits rode so high I'd have to say they were fake. It turned out the colonel had bought the tits for her, but that didn't dent the strong vibe I had that she could easily have been a real popular surfer chick back at Huntington Beach. She was all about bubbling laughter, that maid, and making sure all present had a good time in the here and now. I was like half ready to grab her and make a dash for the door and try and hop a transport back to the Pacific, to transplant us both back onto the beach, as she was bringing back potent memories of my mellow life as a surfer. But then I remembered my *mission,* so the first quiet words out of my mouth were, "So, where is Princess Lulu?"

But that maid just ignored my question and batted her eyes and said, "You do not know my name? Should we not be introduced?"

She's playing it like she's the hostess, and that I am being rude with the direct questions. So as the colonel goes to make a drink, I stick out my hand and say quietly, "Cody Carmichael, U.S. marine, great to meet you. So where's the princess?"

And she takes my hand in a kittenish way that was very sexy and says, "I am Leila. Do you know you are very handsome? Is your hair bleached so blond?" So as I get into how I was a surfer back in Huntington Beach, she starts rubbing my crew cut with her fingers, and that like drove intelligent thoughts right out of my ears with a decompression *pop* you could almost hear, and she has one of those knowing chick looks, like she knows she's the first girl who has touched me in a long time. And Colonel Fawwaz comes over right then and as he hands me a drink says with enthusiasm, "Let's go to Cairo!" And the maid Leila sneaks a kiss of my hand and purrs, "Yes, we will go to Cairo, Fawwaz."

Right then there is a serious distant honking. And Colonel Fawwaz takes out a cell phone and goes to the window. He jams it open and sticks his head out and starts yelling into the cell phone. And Leila the maid almost falls into my lap to whisper, "It is Fawwaz's mother. There was a SCUD attack. His mother always comes by the Defense Ministry after every attack to see her boy Fawwaz is safe. And it is not enough to hear him on the cell phone, she must see his face."

I am like looking at Colonel Fawwaz when he pulls his head back in from the window like as to say, *your mother comes by to check on you?* And he says, "See? In Saudi Arabia it is all about family!" But he pretty much pushes me out of the office and into the elevator and out into the limousine. To go outside Leila the maid throws a robe over her sexy self, and then tears it off again with a laugh when we are in the limousine, and straddles Colonel Fawwaz's lap and starts chewing on his big lips. I have to put up with her squirming in a lap dance all over him until we stop at a huge gate and the door opens, and in hops another chick in a black robe with a giggle. And then when the door of the limousine opens I hear American jets thundering overhead, and I think about our pilots putting their lives on the line while I party with these yo-yos. The new chick of course throws off her robe, and she's in a halter top and Levi's and is pretty in a fist-faced sort of way that is kind of like a lousy version of Princess Lulu. The 'robe over the sexy clothes' was kind of a fun game in a way, even if it felt kind of *high-schoolish,* but it did give you a buzz when the girls tossed off their robes.

The more I looked at the fist-faced chick the more she looked like Princess Lulu. But I'd have to say what she *mostly* looked like was: a *ghost.* First of all, she was pale as hell. But it wasn't white pale, but almost *clear* pale. She applied red lipstick and eyeliner with a strong hand, but it was like she was trying to circle her eyes and mouth to prove they were there at all. She kept blinking and biting her nails, and when she touched me her hands were cold. She tried to be perky and flipped her frizzed-out hair when Colonel Fawwaz looked over, but it was a weak effort. She was broken, is what I'm saying—and I still think about her over there in Arabia, and hope she worked it out and found some happiness. As we would come to know all too well, Arabia was really rough on chicks.

Anyway, mostly in the early part of this car ride my natural focus was on Leila the maid, who was giving me the sparky eye like to say *I'd rather be with you* while she chewed on the ear of Colonel Fawwaz, who had his eyes closed and was just enjoying the hip grind. Colonel Fawwaz told me in snatches when he came up for a breath how he had stopped off the day before to see some Egyptian troops and the gist of his effort at their camp was to tell them *to write their mothers back in Egypt.* Apparently Colonel Fawwaz had gotten word that some mother in Egypt was not getting letters from her son. He repeated again to me that "In Saudi Arabia we are all about *family!*"

I guess because I had my eyes on Leila, I also ended up taking a closer look at Colonel Fawwaz. And I kept looking at the gold watch on his thick wrist. It was like choking with diamonds of course, but what was weird was that it looked like it was cutting off circulation to his large sausage fingers. I mean, he wore that watch so tight, you could sometimes see these dark red lines angry on his skin where watch met wrist. And that got me thinking how—and I'm no tailor here—but it was like the colonel wore his uniform a few sizes too small on his big grizzly bear of a body, and he kind of cinched in his belt on his gut so much you hoped it was made of strong webbing. And as I was sitting there, I began to think about the colonel's eyes in terms of all this tightness. And it was like the colonel dude's *skull* was too tight: those eyes were seriously bugging out. Later on I'd wonder if he wore his Koran thing too tight too, for a guy who seemed at heart a born party-boy.

As we pull into an airport I feel a hand reaching over my crotch, and it is the lousy Princess Lulu look-alike, and she smiles at me like, *You want me to do that more,* but when she smiled she looked kind of less pretty, and I like yelled out, "The Airport!" like I had never seen one before. I mean I was horny, but not *that* horny— and I felt kind of bad for her too, on account of her like dead spirit. Still, I didn't want to be too rude to her, and also figured she might know something about Princess Lulu, and this was my *mission.*

It turns out we are at the airfield at King Khalid Military City, and when we stepped out of the limousine and looked at the sky you could see circling stacked in the sky all these American C-141 cargo planes. I chatted with an American sergeant, and he said they were usually backed up, but that for the last fifteen minutes no one had been allowed to land on one of the main runways so a Saudi prince could get his personal jet in the air. We were waiting to board the jet because Colonel Fawwaz had run off when the limousine stopped to where some American freight was being unloaded into some trucks. He was waving his arms over there, officers were called, and some wooden crates were opened with crowbars, and he ran back to us with a lobster in each hand. "These lobsters are for your officers," said Colonel Fawwaz. "They are from your state of Maine."

Colonel Fawwaz thought it was pretty funny to push the lobsters into the faces of the two ladies. When we climbed into his jet, he put each lobster in a seat and tried to buckle them in as they wiggled their many legs in the air. When we were in the air he held them up and said the lobsters were to be called "GEORGE BUSH" and "SADDAM HUSSEIN". When we reached altitude, Colonel

Fawwaz held George Bush up with his claws near the controls as if he was flying the jet. The pilot and the maid Leila and Princess Hayat—that was the name of the ghost chick who looked like Princess Lulu—made like this was *the funniest thing they had ever seen,* and then they all hit the bar for refills.

Colonel Fawwaz was one of those guys who liked to surf a joke long after the wave was gone, and he got a Magic Marker and put a big *G* for *George* and *S* for *Saddam* on the backs of the two lobsters, and then made the girls help him make a fight ring on the floor with some pillows. And then he pulled off the bands from the claws and dropped the lobsters into his ring. I guess he expected them to fight to the death. But they just stood there clacking their claws a bit and waving their antennae, like as to say, *just take me back to Maine, man.*

Colonel Fawwaz started to get pissed the lobsters wouldn't fight, and so he tried to drop little liquor bottles on the head of Saddam the lobster—I guess to piss the lobster Saddam into fighting—but he couldn't hit the lobster, and he started to look kind of down and angry, and I slipped away to talk to the pilot. There was no copilot, so I got to sit there and look at Cairo in the distance. There was a yelling behind me, and I looked back to see Colonel Fawwaz holding apart the maid Leila and the princess Hayat. He had them both by the arm, and they were screeching at each other. I like glanced at the pilot, and he was looking at Cairo but then said under his breath, "One is a servant and the mistress of the colonel, and the other is the half sister of the colonel's Kuwaiti fiancée. So there is anger between them."

I took a look back again, and that princess Hayat really *did* look like Princess Lulu. And then I remembered my mission was to find out for Trang the whereabouts and marriage status of Princess Lulu, so I said to the pilot, "So Colonel Fawwaz has not married Princess Lulu yet?"

"You know the Kuwaiti princess?"

"I've met her."

"I have heard she is crazy. They say she was raised by the Bedouin and it has made her wild. They say she cares more to be in the desert than for any human person or any money. The emir spoiled her after the death of her parents. Allah said to guide a woman with a strong hand or she will surely become a prostitute."

I tried to get more out of the pilot, as I was curious about this stuff about Princess Lulu being raised by the Bedouin and 'loving the desert more than any person or any money', but he had shut down. There was a limousine waiting for us at the Cairo airport, and Princess Lulu's half sister Princess Hayat sat on my lap and gave looks of hatred at the maid Leila, who sat on Colonel Fawwaz's lap and mouthed things back at her when Colonel Fawwaz wasn't looking. Colonel Fawwaz was in a slump most of the ride, but cheered up when we got to what he said was the *Best Nightclub in Cairo, with Many Saudi Friends!* There were dozens of limos lined up outside the Cairo Hilton—which was situated right on the Nile river—and the girls put on their party faces, and we all trooped in-side. When we got a seat on a couch, Princess Hayat told me the maid Leila was essentially a servant *who was paid to serve the colonel sex-ually,* and that the maid Leila was a fool if she thought the colonel *could or would* marry her when he was engaged to Princess Lulu. I asked casually how the real Princess Lulu was doing, and Princess Hayat looked around like a spy and said *not now.*

Soon the Colonel Fawwaz and I were at the bar. He made me drink a martini, and made me admire this really ugly Egyptian belly dancer shimmying up there on the stage. All the towelheads in the audience were digging the fat lady, and Colonel Fawwaz indicated your basic Arab liked 'em plump and kind of sloppy. The colonel liked a tight body like us Westerners, and went on a riff about how having Arab chicks wear a blanket all the time made them like less interested in keeping in shape, and that this was a downside of the blanket over the head. The plus side, according to Colonel Fawwaz, was if you married a real fox, you stick her under that blanket, and it keeps the other dogs away. Colonel Fawwaz really had thought hard about all of this, and it was surprising and sort of a downer the way *sex, sex, sex* was as on the front burner of his mind, so to speak, when there were like some global things happening.

As the whole disco was full of partying Saudis and Kuwaitis

tossing around American dollars, it made you wonder if Colonel Fawwaz was sort of not that unique. Anyway, I was getting kind of down about all the partying when I thought about Tommy Trang and how he was ready to die partly for these clowns, and it didn't help that Colonel Fawwaz kept running back over to me and asking *if I was having fun yet!*

I went and sat again with Princess Hayat. She put her hand on mine and we two looked at all the partying. She seemed kind of even grimmer, and it didn't make her any prettier. Colonel Fawwaz was out on the dance floor grabbing ass with the maid Leila. Without looking over, I said, "Do you know anything about Princess Lulu?"

Once again, this seemed too direct. She squeezed my hand and said, "You must kiss me." I figured it was part of the spy game, so I turned and sort of laid one on Princess Hayat. Boy, she could really kiss, and I forgot she was kind of ugly. I was just forgetting my name when she pulled her lips back and said, "You were there when this Asian man rescued Lulu from the water?"

I nodded and tried to go back to kissing her, but she pulled her head away and said, "We had the same father. No one likes Lulu but the emir, and myself. She is very strange, this half sister of mine. I would say her mind floats always on the water of her dreams."

My mission was to learn about Princess Lulu, so I stopped trying to kiss her and listened. Princess Hayat said, "Everything the emir would do to keep Lulu happy. She is bored by her traditional education as she is like a great sponge for all knowledge, so the emir has her tutored in private by many British tutors from Oxford. And she wanted to live with the Bedouin, and so he makes a safe Bedouin tribe for her to go and visit then and now. Then she wants to take care of the flamingos of Sulaibikhat, and so the emir tried to do this for her and sets up a preserve for the flamingos. And all the emir asks in return is she marry Prince Fawwaz after her first blood, and this is many a Kuwaiti girl's dream. And what does she do to repay the emir's kindness? She tried to kill herself rather than marry the colonel. Do you know this Asian man well? Is he very handsome?"

I nodded and said, "I guess Trang is good-looking."

Princess Hayat nodded and said, "I have heard he is very hand-some for an Asian man. I must tell you Lulu is mad with love for him, and when she is mad for something, she knows nothing of limits. It is too bad this Asian man is a Jew also, as this makes the love impossible. It is bad enough she has kissed him once. I myself once kissed a gardener from the Philippines, who was very attrac-tive, but at least he was not a Jew."

I didn't know Trang had kissed Lulu, but I guess she was think-ing there was some CPR. Anyway, right then there was a big com-motion from out on the black-and-white tiled dance floor. It seemed Colonel Fawwaz had noticed one of the waiters looked like Saddam Hussein. He had him clamped by the neck and was saying in English and then Arabic, "Why have you invaded an Arab brother, Saddam? Why have you done this, Saddam?"

Colonel Fawwaz saw me looking and propelled the Saddam—look-alike waiter through the laughing Arab crowd. The waiter's drinks were falling off his tray right and left, and he was looking right at me. He *did* look like Saddam, mostly because he had the same bristle mustache. The maid Leila came running over and was sort of the main cheering section for Colonel Fawwaz. Colonel Fawwaz was giving him hell in Arabic, I guess about invading Kuwait, in a real lecturing tone. It seemed to be a performance for me, as Colonel Fawwaz kept nodding at me like *is this the best fun you've ever had?*

I just stared at the colonel, so he drove the waiter to his knees with a pincher grip on his neck. Colonel Fawwaz said that the waiter Saddam Hussein was now a camel, and that the *American Cowboy* would ride him first. I shook my head and the maid Leila threw a leg over the waiter and Colonel Fawwaz kicked him and he started to crawl on all fours through the crowd. When the crowd was beginning to get bored with this, Colonel Fawwaz ran in front of the camel waiter and slapped him on the face and yelled some-thing in Arabic. Whatever he yelled caused the maid Leila to jump off and run away crying, and I turned for a translation. Princess Hayat was holding my arm, although I hadn't been aware, and she said, "Colonel Fawwaz has told Saddam if he hurts his fiancée he will kill him."

It took me a full minute to understand this last statement seemed to mean Princess Lulu was *still in Kuwait.* I couldn't ask Princess Hayat any more questions, as Colonel Fawwaz was giving the waiter Saddam a taste of his righteous anger and kicking the hell out of him with his boots, and the crowd was yelling. Then some other Saudis started kicking the waiter too, and he curled up on the floor. I walked over and grabbed Colonel Fawwaz's arm and said, "Hey, dude, cut the shit." As I walked him away he said, "But it is only play? It is all a game? Is it not fun?"

Man, was I getting tired of Colonel Fawwaz and his *fun.* Anyway, when I dragged off the colonel, the other Saudis stopped kicking the waiter, and some other waiters helped him to his feet. Colonel Fawwaz left me and walked over, pulling out his wallet. He laid hundreds of dollars on the frozen head of the Saddam waiter, and the waiter watched the money pass over his eyes to his head until I guess he felt its weight was enough, and then he smiled at Colonel Fawwaz, and all the Arabs applauded.

Colonel Fawwaz sat down on the couch between Leila and Princess Hayat. Both of them were kind of pouting, and when Colonel Fawwaz said something in Arabic to Leila she kind of turned her head away. Colonel Fawwaz looked at her turned-away head, and said something sharp, and she turned her face to him and said something sharp right back. My guess was they were arguing about his mention of his *fiancée,* Princess Lulu. Right then Princess Hayat turned and shot something at Leila that I bet was, *You really think you could marry the colonel? You are a whore and nothing more!*

The colonel looked at me with a smile as he sat between these two women, who were now sniping at each other across his bulk. It was pretty easy to follow the discussion based on the expressions, really. Colonel Fawwaz, still smiling at me, reached back as if to put his friendly arms around them and took them both by the neck. And then he did something that was kind of impressive, from a strength point of view. He stood up off the couch and kind of lifted both women into the air by the neck. They were both small women, but still, he had them both elevated, and their feet were kicking the air.

The crowd turned to Colonel Fawwaz as the two women were yelling now, and Colonel Fawwaz said something in Arabic and the crowd laughed. I got in his face and told him to put them down. He laughed and said, "You do not tell a Saudi prince what to do, Private Carmichael." He turned with his dangling women as if to march around the disco, and I moved behind him and slipped my arm around his neck and applied some pressure. He didn't respond, so I put more of a squeeze on his neck, and knocked his knees out from the rear. Now at least the girls' feet were on the ground. I was actually choking the colonel now, and he threw the girls to the floor and lifted me off the ground and stumbled toward the dance floor. As it dawned on me the girls were free, I let go of his neck, and he fell forward choking and gasping for breath. He stumbled to the bar and had a drink.

I was wondering how I was going to get out of Cairo and back to my platoon and Tommy Trang. And right then Colonel Fawwaz came over to me and smiled as if nothing had happened. He said we should go home now, and as we left the disco, he threw an arm around me and said, "Fun?"

His moods were so wild. He actually seemed to think it was all part of a *fun* evening in Cairo. And when I said nothing he stopped and took my hand, and then with his other hand placed a finger on my wrist as if to take my pulse. He tapped on it and said, "What is this?"

I said, "My pulse."

"Yes, and what makes a pulse?"

"The blood pumping."

"And what is *in* our blood?"

I looked at him in confusion and he said as he tapped my wrist, "In your blood is oil." He tapped his own wrist and said, "In my blood there is oil also. This is why America fights with us, for the oil that is in both our blood makes us brothers." He was so proud of this nonsense he almost took a bow. I guess he still thought I was this imaginary Cody Carmichael from the *Texas Oil Carmichaels,* and not a formerly stoned surfer from Huntington Beach, California.

When we got on the jet back to Saudi Arabia, Colonel Fawwaz was back in a serious mood. He was sitting across from me and kept staring at me and shaking his head. I was sick of the whole show, and just dropped my head back and stared at the ceiling, closed my eyes and tried to sleep. Then the big Arab guy was next to me, shaking my arm, and his face was in mine. Something was bugging him, so I said, "What's on your mind, Colonel?"

He shook his head and said, "That friend of yours."

"Trang."

"Yes, that friend. He has said something that has bothered me very much these last few months. Will you answer a question?"

"Go ahead."

"He is Asian."

"He is Vietnamese American."

"So his father was American."

"Yes."

"And this father. He was truly a Jew?"

I knew where this conversation was going from the first words from Colonel Fawwaz, and it amazed me how sincerely *concerned* he looked. It suddenly came to me, although it seemed impossible, that the whole trip to Cairo was set up to ask me this one crazy question: *is Tommy Trang really Jewish?*

Colonel Fawwaz shook my arm, I guess for an answer. And right then the maid Leila said from where she was lying on the couch, "Princess Lulu prefers a Jew to Colonel Fawwaz. This bothers Colonel Fawwaz so much he is losing weight and not sleeping."

I was to learn later the maid Leila was a pretty brave chick with a fast mouth. And she must have known Colonel Fawwaz wouldn't react well to this, but maybe she didn't think he'd *totally snap.* Because that's what he did next. He rose up from the couch and jumped on the maid Leila and started to slap her. I jumped on top of him and tried to yank him off, but he was a huge bastard, so I went back to choking him. This time I really cut into his windpipe, but the bastard kept slapping the maid Leila. The pilot put the jet on autopilot and came back and helped me drag the colonel off her. He was still fighting to get at her, so I slipped off my web belt and tied his hands up behind him and sat on his back for like the rest of the flight. Princess Hayat took care of the maid Leila, who was pretty bloodied around the face. And I was kind of shook up, and yelled over this weird stuff to Leila about how *a mistake had been made at birth, and she wasn't really a Palestinian maid, but like a surfer chick from California.* She didn't know what the hell I was talking about, but I think I was beginning to see right then that the freedom to wear a bikini was a deep and serious deal. Like, if there was a surfer chick scene allowed on the Red Sea, Leila would have been okay.

When the plane landed in Saudi, the pilot dropped the door and I slipped my web belt off Colonel Fawwaz's wrists and was *gone.* The prince yelled my name from the plane, but I was hoping never to see this big dude again. I turned once and flashed him the Hawaiian surfer sign of thumb and pinky as a joke. Maybe he thought I was flashing him the devil's horns, and I *was* sort of putting a hex on his whole Arab world. I walked to the edge of the tarmac, and I was suddenly lost in this crowd of good old American military personnel, and it was only then that I started to relax. I left that crowd outside the gates of the airfield, and walked along in the dark alongside the busy Tapline Road in the direction of my platoon. Americans stopped to give me a lift, but I wanted to walk. So I walked all night thinking mostly about Trang and all the random, crazy stuff that had happened to date in Arabia, and then at dawn I started thinking about the pearl, and somehow that made it better, and as it got real hot at dawn, I finally hitched a ride.

CHAPTER 6

We had a pair of chickens and a rooster at our camp north of Jubail. They were there to serve as our canaries in a coal mine. If Saddam sent some nasty biologicals at us marines, the birds were supposed to keel over first, and give us the low-tech heads-up warning about the migrating toxins. I always figured the birds would keel over, and we'd keel over at about the same second, and that would be that: *dead birds and dead marines*. Anyway, the upside of the chickens was the fresh eggs. The weird thing is that after coming back from Cairo, I suddenly became like really into gathering these eggs, and making sure the chickens were fed slops and didn't have to beg and peck all over the desert sands. I mean suddenly I was spending my free time pretending I was a chicken farmer or something. Marines notice things, and like right away people start calling me *Farmer Carmichael*. There wasn't much to actually do to help the chickens, but I spent a lot of time just *staring* at them. There was a lot on my mind, but mostly I just didn't want to be around Trang. Here's the thing: when he came up to me the morning I walked back into camp from Cairo, there was only one question on his mind: *what's the scoop on Princess Lulu?*

I like never answered him. I just grimaced and shook my head, and he said nothing and walked off with his head hanging. Of course, I had learned the crazy news Princess Lulu was probably still in occupied Kuwait, and I felt like a *real dog* not telling my main man Trang the scoop. I wanted to tell him, but I didn't. That's why I had to hang out with the chickens: I knew if I hung around Trang I'd end up telling him, and that within minutes he'd have his pack on his back and his M16 in hand and be hoofing it off toward Kuwait to rescue the princess, and probably certain death.

So I sat and thought about it all looking at the chickens. I thought about Captain Shakespear, and looked at my DIE A HERO tattoo a lot, and a couple of times jumped up to go tell him. But then I'd shake my head again and sit back down on my ass. One day while I was sitting out there wrestling with this situation, old Trang came and sat down next to me with an old typewriter. He was really totally stoked up again. He set the typewriter up on a bucket and said, *hey man, I'm writing a letter to General Schwarzkopf.* And he asked me to type it. I couldn't type, but I pecked it out as he said it aloud slowly:

Dear General,

My name is Private Thomas Trang. I will not waste your time as you are very busy with the air war. Here is the nut of it. I came to the Saudi to win a Congressional Medal of Honor. I was not born in America. But I think the world needs us to knock some heads together and spread the American Bill of Rights far and wide.

But the situation is I have been over here in Saudi Arabia and not had one single mission. I am ordered to play volleyball and be a safe driver. Sir, I am a U.S. marine and ready to fight to free Kuwait. I do not think it right that the pilots get all the glory. Saddam Hussein is evil and we should take him out ASAP as there are girls over there in Kuwait getting gang raped by these Iraqi animals while we play volleyball. I am ready to Fight for Freedom, sir! Excuse my straight talk, sir, but that's the situation.

Semper Fi,

Private Thomas Trang, USMC

After I finished typing his letter, Trang rolled it out of the type-writer and stuffed it into an envelope. He stood up and thanked me for going to Cairo to try and find out something about Princess Lulu. Trang was upbeat about his letter. I watched him jogging away across the sand, and thought *I'm saving your life, man.* My eyes looked away from Trang right then, and focused on the volleyball courts at the edge of our camp. We were hosting the Coalition Forces Mixed-Doubles Finals, and a lot of the platoon was involved in building the stands for the spectators we expected. Mostly we expected a huge crowd on account of the mixed thing—there were some good-looking female personnel volleyball players, and they wore tight Spandex. I had pitched in here and there, but Trang had refused to lend a hand to prepare for the event—he had pretty much scorned the whole thing, so he was again on the outs with the platoon.

Right then I like glance up and look down the main drag in our camp, and I see Trang stopped down the road, and he was looking toward Kuwait. And right then it happened. A bug landed on my raised hand as I waved to him. And I looked at the bug, and it looked like a cricket on steroids. And Euclid Krebes comes up to me shaking his big head and says, "These are locusts, man. This is biblical shit, man."

I wasn't sure what Euclid Krebes meant by *biblical shit,* and he started to fill me in on the Seven Plagues of Egypt. It was hard to concentrate, as the locusts were starting to get thicker, but I got the drift of his biblical reference. As an American and a U.S. marine, I did not think myself prey to any sort of late-night-radio apocalyptic vibe, but I was having sudden shivers up my spine. And then the locusts were so thick I could no longer see Trang down the road. I could see around me some of the men were doing some weird epileptic dance trying to kill the winged bastards, and mostly they were making their way indoors, as the bugs were so thick it was like nerve gas or something, and we were rendered pretty helpless.

And then I heard the crazy marine war cry of Trang coming toward me. He was yelling like to burst his lungs, *Oooraah! Oooraah! Oooraah!* I hadn't heard him this freaking jazzed in a long while, and it was like infectious, and I felt a serious pump rustling through my veins. I ran toward his voice, the mutant bugs bouncing off my face, and then Trang like grabbed me from the cloud of insects, just pulled me to him, and kind of dragged me off. Where we headed was the mess hall, and Trang like handed me one of the big pots from the mess hall and a gigantic spoon, and then I saw Euclid Krebes was there and grabbing his own pots, and he looked pretty psyched too, as if to say, *this is some fantastic times we are living through, man!*

So Trang started banging on his pots, and we three ran out the door, banging on pots too for all we were worth, and screaming our heads off in like this real primitive way. And we banged and banged and banged those pots, and the damn locusts did clear out from a small area around us, like they thought we were crazier bastards than they could handle. And Captain Pettigrew runs into our little Alamo, and his face is like covered with locusts, as was his body too, and we three just cracked up at him as we banged. He looked at himself and grinned, and then I guess Captain Pettigrew noticed the noise thing worked, so he comes out with lots of pots and pans and is like calling for his marines like he's trying to re-group at the Battle of the Bulge after getting run over by a Panzer Division of Nazis. In between passing out pans and yelling for his men to come out of the buildings he like yelled to ask Trang how he knew the pots and pans thing would drive off the locusts, and Trang yelled back, "Ancient Chinese secret, sir." That cracked them both up, given so many yo-yos in the military thought Trang was like Chinese.

So we had a crew of marines banging pots and pans up and down our main drag, and little by little the locusts started to clear. They were heading out anyway, but we clearly hastened their de-parture, like they said to themselves, *there has got to be a quieter place, a place without these crazy-ass marines.* And then the locusts were totally gone, but you couldn't stop these men, they were into drumming on those pots, man, like all the energy they had saved to go to war on Saddam in Kuwait was being channeled into some tribal drum-ming. People were just cutting loose on those pots and pans. One dude would like set the pace with some weird beat, and others would pick up on it. And then pimply Corporal Sinoma kind of jumps out there and does this kind of weird leaping dance, and Krebes said later he was like a Masai warrior, but whatever, the thing was a lot of dudes picked up on this weird leaping dance, and were cranking up and down to the local locust beat. Some people think marines are like these square killers, but man, our platoon was like into music—half the time, people had on Walkmans—and it came out now that we were some guys who could cut some serious action when a good beat was laid down.

For a while there, we marines were a band of brothers again, and there was a real fine warrior spirit. We had driven off the locusts, and now we had celebrated. But they were still just *locusts,* and not the Iraqis, and soon Trang sort of drifted away from the party. It was like Trang was the battery for the festivities, and once he was unplugged from it, the party just died. The men switched back into volleyball players. And there was a buzz going for the big volleyball tournament, but it was a different kind of buzz, as in the end it was just a *game.* I think if Trang hadn't been atop the captain's HQ the next day, people could have really forgotten the Iraqi Locusts in Kuwait and gotten into the *game,* but with him standing up there looking down like the Ghost of Heroic Marines Past, it made the whole tournament kind of stupid. At least it did for me.

I watched the volleyball tournament anyway for a while, even if I kept glancing back over my shoulder at Tommy Trang atop HQ. The Army Rangers sent a very strong team, but their guys were so beefy they couldn't jump worth a damn, and the Canadians were so team oriented they never actually went for a kill, just batted the ball back and forth on their own side of the net until everyone fell asleep. The British Desert Rats were a crazy bunch of guys who tried to spike almost every ball, and the Senegalese were tremendous players as long as they didn't have to move their feet. If the ball was out of reach of a Senegalese player, he just let it fall to the sand. Our own marines were probably the strongest team out there, but they seemed spooked by Trang—they kept making stupid errors and then glancing at him up on HQ. You may think Trang was like hanging around up on HQ to make a comment on

the volleyball, and maybe that's so, but he spent all his time looking through a scope in the direction of Kuwait and then looking at
this map he had set up on a table, and writing in a notebook. Once
I saw Captain Pettigrew up there, and Trang was consulting the
map and jabbing with his hands in the direction of Kuwait as if he
was giving the captain directions to the Kuwaiti Sheraton.

In the afternoon of that first day of the volleyball tournament,
during the British-Canadian match, I looked up, and Trang was
suddenly gone from atop HQ. I walked toward HQ and then saw
someone stumbling across the desert from the direction of Jubail,
and Trang was running to him. The *someone* was Euclid Krebes, and
he was a mess. His face was scratched and swollen purple in places
with bruises, and his left eye was just a slit. He was shaking with de-
hydration, and slipped down to the sand as Trang held a canteen to
his mouth. After Krebes drank, he kind of passed out, and Trang
hoisted him up in a fireman's carry and took him back to the barracks. When we laid him out on the rack, he cracked open one eye
and said slowly, "I was hitching back from Jubail. A limo passed me
once, and then passed me again. The third time, it slowed down
and the door opened. I looked in and there were six Arab chicks.
They asked me if I wanted to party. I got in and they gave me some
drinks. We went to a palace, through these big pink gates. We got
out of the limo and they pointed to a tree. There were eight or nine
M16s hanging from the tree."

Euclid Krebes closed his eye and slowly shook his head. He took
a deep breath and said, "They wanted me to hang my M16 in the
tree. I told them a marine never gives up his M16, even to party
with six juicy Arab ladies in a pink palace. And so right then somebody hit me in the head from behind with a baseball bat. I think it
was the limo driver. I went down to the sand. I think he was surprised I wasn't knocked out. He tried to hit me again, but I grabbed
the bat and yanked it out of his hands, but right then all those
chicks started in on me, scratching and kicking and yelling, 'USA
go home.' The limo dude got the bat again and hit me upside the
head. I was looking at the raised bat when the lights went out.
Someone else hit me from behind. I woke up in the sand in the

middle of nowhere without my M16. It must be up in that tree. I'm gonna get it back."

Euclid Krebes sat up on the rack. Trang held his arm and said, "Krebes, could you get us all back to that palace?"

The big redneck tapped his big head with his finger and said, "Man, I'm a *genius*. And there are like three roads in this sandy shit-hole of a country. Sure, I can get us back there."

So we all got in a Humvee. Krebes was placed on some bedding in the back. And we followed Krebes' directions and drove for many hours. He was popping the Tylenol-3s and was pretty happy for a guy with his head recently knocked around with a baseball bat. We came to a guardhouse and a gate, and Krebes was like, "This is it, man!" Euclid Krebes must have had his head messed up by the baseball bat, as there was like a twenty-foot sign that said, WELCOME TO ARAMCO TOWN. On the sign was a picture of a perfect American town. The guard at the gate stopped us long enough to tell us he had been a marine, and then waved us through.

And it was like, except for the heat, we had left Saudi Arabia. It was a perfect pretend Southern California suburb in the middle of the desert. There were little suburban ranch houses, each with a perfect little square lawn with sprinklers. There was a guy with a beer gut mowing a lawn. He stopped mowing long enough to salute us. Krebes yells for us to stop, and stumbles out of the Humvee in his bloody combat fatigues and lays down under some sprinklers on a green lawn. This woman comes out of the house in a yellow-striped dress and looks at him, and then goes back inside. I thought she'd call the police, but then she comes out again and strolls across the lawn like she is floating, carrying a tray with lemonade and a couple of glasses that kept flashing crystal in the brutal sunlight. I should have noted the *two* glasses right away, but I didn't. Krebes started calling her 'mom,' and this made her laugh and brush back her golden curls. She was like a mom straight from 1950s America—like she had been stuck in a time warp here in the Saudi. She didn't seem to notice how Krebes was all smashed up.

Tommy Trang was still sitting in the Humvee. He was just look-ing around at the street with this smile on his face while we talked to the lemonade lady named Ann. She said she was third-generation Aramco—which stood for Arab-American Oil Company—and had only been to the States a few times. "It's safe here," she said, which was odd, as there was a horde of Iraqis just across the border. She dragged us up to her porch to sit on like some wicker furniture, and brought us out some lemon cookies. When I looked again at the Humvee, Trang was gone.

I spotted him further down the perfect street playing baseball with five kids that seemed to come out of the shrubs. Ann's boys came out on the porch and stared at Krebes' wounds like they had never seen blood before. I asked them if they liked baseball, and pointed down the street to where Trang's gang of kids had grown to about ten. They looked at pretty Ann, and she looked down the street and said firmly that *her boys should stay on the porch.* The afternoon passed for a while without much incident, and Krebes fell asleep in his wicker chair. He was messed up bad, so it was all for the best that he crashed.

Trang was way into baseball. It looked like he and the kids were having a blast. There were a lot of other Aramco kids now on the two ultra-green lawns sitting watching the baseball game going down in the street. I saw Ann glancing down at the baseball game with tight lips, and she looked pretty *pissed.* She went into the house and I heard her talking on the phone. Then she came back out, and right then the sprinklers came on at the lawns of the houses on either side of the pickup game. All the kids who had been sitting on the lawns laughed and ran into the street. Trang stripped off his shirt, boots, and camouflage trousers and ran in his boxer shorts through the sprinklers. Soon he had all these kids charging after him. Ann beside me was shaking her head. I tried to tell her the kids were having a blast, but she just *glared* at me. And then a couple of Aramco police cars showed up with their lights going, and Ann stood up and put down her drink and drifted across her lawn down to the scene. Trang just kept running through the sprinklers. He knew the cops were there, and that all the kids had stopped following him like he was the Pied Piper, but he kept running and hollering. The cops yelled to him but finally had to go over and get in his way in the sprinklers, and they didn't look pleased.

The two cops tried to grab Trang, but he darted away. Soon they were chasing him through the sprinklers, and he was laughing. One of the cops ran to his car I guess to call for reinforcements, and then stopped to talk to Ann. He said out of breath and while pointing at Trang, "You know this guy?"

Ann said with a wave at Krebes and me, "I invited these two nice soldiers for lemonade, but their Chinese friend refused and then chased the children."

"He didn't chase them," I said. "He played baseball with them."

Right then two other Aramco police cars roar up with sirens blaring, and soon there were all sorts of cops trying to grab Trang in the sprinklers. I was wondering how it was all going to end, when one of the fatter cops stopped running and pulled out his gun and yelled at Trang. And then a big train named Euclid Krebes knocked that cop with the gun flat like he was sacking a quarterback. So then all the cops pulled their guns on Euclid Krebes, who was on his knees on the lawn. I took this as my cue, and ran back and got the Humvee. I drove it up on the lawn next to Euclid Krebes, and he sort of crawled aboard and fell over against me. Trang jumped in the rear and I put the pedal down, and we squealed out of there, with the cops still crouched with their pistols trained on us. I guess in the end they couldn't fire on three U.S. marines.

The gate to Aramco Village was down, so we blew right through it. I was feeling hostile to this fake American town in the desert, and that was when Trang yelled from the rear of the Humvee, "That was great, man!"

"Are you nuts, Trang?" I yelled.

"The baseball, man," said Trang. "I love baseball. When I was a kid just over from Nam that's all I did, man. Play baseball. But I was in Trenton. What a dive. We played on broken glass. I always wanted to live in a town like that one, with the green grass and the sprinklers and all that stuff. And Annie, man! She was apple pie, man!"

"You didn't talk to her, Trang."

"So what, man."

"So I *did* talk to her."

I didn't want to tell Trang that Annie was a shiny apple with a big worm inside. He was so high about the whole Aramco scene and started telling me how he and Princess Lulu were going to go back to America together and live in a perfect town like that one, and how the princess was going to bake cookies and make lemonade while he taught the local Little League kids how to play baseball. I tried to interrupt his flow a couple of times to remind him about the cops and blowing down the gate to escape, but Tommy Trang was in his own like vision of America and talked right over me. We are barreling down the hardball, and Trang is going on kind of crazy about all this American pie stuff, and I was only kind of half listening, when I heard Trang say, *you know, Carmichael, my father was a rapist.*

Well, *I didn't know what the hell to say to that!*

So I was just like, *ah, ah, yeah man, I guess the dude was.*

And so Trang said, *Yeah, so you can see why I'm motivated to totally do right by the princess.*

Krebes was passed out, with his ugly mouth hanging open so you could see his big pink plate of a tongue. I am like into the weirdness of this Tommy Trang idea *that because his dad was a rapist, he was going to totally be the perfect husband.* So as I am pondering this in a positive way, Trang taps me on the shoulder and asks to drive. So then Trang is driving, and he puts the pedal down, and right away passes four trucks in a supply convoy by driving in the desert around them.

Now this early in the war there were still a few Iraqi jets left in the sky—they hadn't yet boogied to Iran, as those who survived the American bombing were going to do in a few days. And I look up in the sky right then as we bounced from the desert back onto the highway, and there is an Iraqi jet, making a kamikaze run for the port of al-Jubail. And in the distance comes an American F-15, and we see this streak coming across the miles of airspace from the F-15. Trang is yelling, and Krebes glances up and says it is an AIM-9 air-to-air missile. It seemed to make the Iraqi jet into a ball of flame, but then the Iraqi jet emerged from the ball of flame. And we're all yelling in the Humvee, and right then we see a surface-to-air missile streaking up, and again it looked like the Iraqi jet exploded, but again that damn jet just *flew out of the flames,* still heading for the port of al-Jubail.

The American F-15 fired another missile, but before it could hit the Iraqi jet just did a barrel roll and fell to earth, like it had run out of gas, or luck. Trang was yelling for the Iraqi pilot to bail, but he just rode that plane down into the desert. And after we saw the fireball in the distant desert, Trang kind of lowered his head while he was driving and closed his eyes like he was praying for the pilot or something. And when he opened his eyes, he floored the Humvee, and steered it into the *middle* of the road and started yelling: *Oooraah! Oooraah!* Krebes and I started yelling and swearing too, as it looked like Trang was taking us head-on into an oil truck, but with his horn going that big tanker drove aside, and we split it down the middle. We went head-on then with all the empty oncoming vehicles heading to the port: supply trucks, flatbeds, five tons, troop transports. It got to the point where I was down on the floor, trying to pull Trang's foot off the accelerator, and he was kicking my hands away with his other foot and still yelling: *Oooraah!* So I gave up and crawled back upright and waited to die in a ball of flame. There was a third lane now in the highway, and it belonged to Thomas Trang, USMC.

And then suddenly I got on whatever plane Trang was living on, where someone is just parting the waters before you. It was like I was surfing the seventy-foot waves at Maverick's and doing all sorts of outrageously killer moves under the lip of that famous glass ax, and there was no way I could fall. Vehicles were scratching by on either side, but I was hip to the idea we were flaming in a special untouchable and primal zone. I'll tell you something: my man Tommy Trang never forgot seeing that Iraqi pilot fly out of certain death *twice* on his solo run for the port of al-Jubail.

CHAPTER 7

After Aramco we were just cruising around for hours in the Humvee with Euclid Krebes bouncing in the rear stoned on codeine, and we were taking what you might call some back roads past some massive gates, and the gates reminded me that we had set out on this day to look for the palace where the Saudi chicks lured Krebes and had smashed him up. So I shook Krebes a bit and asked him to sit up in the rear and see if any of these massive palace gates looked familiar. We went past a bunch and then Krebes' big paw hit me on the shoulder and he said, "That's the one there."

It was a gigantic pink gate of iron, and it was covered with colored lights sort of like jewels that were twinkling. I asked Krebes if he was sure, but Trang was already out of the Humvee and was ringing the bell. It was a big gold ship's bell like they might have had on the *Titanic*. Way up the driveway you could see a tree stripped of all leaves, and Krebes pointed and said that was *the tree where the chicks wanted him to leave his M16*. There was all sorts of commotion up the driveway—it looked like there were all these workmen like planning a monster party. And right then a white van slides past our Humvee, and a hand reaches out and inserts a card, and the massive gate slides open. Trang hustles in the open gate, and Krebes trots in too, but I move our Humvee up the road a bit and park it behind some Dumpsters in case we need it later, and then scale the wall. It wasn't that easy to scale the wall, as the top was covered with broken glass stuck in concrete.

When I drop down the other side into some thick foliage, a hand grabs mine and pulls me into a clearing in the bushes. Krebes and Trang are standing there grinning away, as the little dude attached to my hand *is our old camel jockey and the former-slave Ali the Bangladeshi!* He had got his shiny hair cut short, so he looked a little less like a pretty girl now. His voice had changed, and I think he had maybe even grown an inch too, so now I'd give him an even five feet. Anyway, Ali said he had been assigned to watch the palace surveillance cameras, as all the regular guards were doing work getting ready for the *Royal Wedding.* I glanced at Trang, thinking it might somehow be Princess Lulu and Colonel Fawwaz getting married, but little Ali said it was the wedding of the *half sister* of Lulu, Princess Hayat, the ghost chick I had gone to Egypt to party with and who told me Princess Lulu was still in Kuwait. Princess Hayat was being forced to marry some random cousin of Colonel Fawwaz. No wonder she looked so depressed! Anyway, right then Ali got right up in the swollen, squinting, and scabbed-up face of Euclid Krebes and said, *You have been here before!*

"Damn right I have," said Euclid Krebes. "And I came to get my M16 back, and thank whoever owns this pile for their hospitality."

So I said, "Who owns this place, Ali?"

And Ali said, like I was kind of slow on the uptake, "It is Colonel Fawwaz, of course."

"Is he behind Krebes' getting lured here and smashed up?"

"Of course," said Ali. "Who else? It is Colonel Fawwaz's palace. I told you he was a bad man when we first met. I hate him. He made me his slave after you left Kuwait."

Trang interrupted to say, "Hey Ali, is Princess Lulu here?"

My man Trang looked like he was holding his breath. Little Ali glanced at me, and then said, "She is in Kuwait."

Trang whistled. He just stared at Ali after that, so Ali said, "She has refused to leave Kuwait when the Iraqis invade."

"Refused?" said Trang. "You mean she *could* of got out?"

"Of course," said Ali. "All the Kuwaiti royals are here. But she refused and hid."

"Why did she refuse?" said Trang.

"Many reasons," said Ali.

"Such as?"

"Such as you, Private Trang."

Trang looked confused and pleased by this one, but old Euclid Krebes stepped in and explained, "If she escaped with the other Kuwaiti royals, she'd be here in Saudi with Colonel Fawwaz, and she'd be getting married today."

Trang said, "So she risked getting caught by the Iraqis rather than marry Colonel Fawwaz?"

"This is so," said little Ali. "And she has said you will come and rescue her from Kuwait."

"You spoke to her?" said Trang.

Ali looked confused and a bit pissed, and looked at Trang, Krebes, and me in turn. "Of course I have spoken to her. She told me when I left Kuwait with Colonel Fawwaz to find you and bring you to her. She says you, and you alone, Tommy Trang, will rescue her before this Gulf War is over, or she will kill herself. This is the final word of Princess Lulu of Kuwait."

Trang shot me a worried look.

All I could say was, "No wonder she's named *Lulu.*"

It was right then that Ali like pulled out a wrinkled yellow envelope and handed it to Trang. He read the letter and handed it to me. Lulu had written: *In rainstorms clams swim to the surface and open their shells for a single drop of water. Below in the dark, the single drop becomes a pearl. So it is with my love for you as I wait here in the darkness of my country.*

Trang asked Ali, "So you know where the poet princess is?"

"Of course," said Ali. "She is with my friends in the Kuwait underground. I will take you there."

Ali said we had to *meet* Colonel Fawwaz again, and that he would have to invite us to the wedding party as honored guests. That didn't make sense, but Ali said the iron rules of the Arab hospitality thing would force him to invite us. Krebes mashed his hand in his fist and said he'd like to have a private talk with old Colonel

Fawwaz, and Ali got excited by this smash talk and told Krebes not to do anything nasty until he gave the signal. So I guess little Ali wanted to knock around Colonel Fawwaz before we maybe departed for Kuwait. Trang wasn't too pleased with waiting, he wanted to rush off to Kuwait in the Humvee to rescue Princess Lulu, but I guess even to him it was clear we had to let little Ali play out his hand regarding Colonel Fawwaz, as Ali was now like our *Key to Kuwait*. I came up with that line about Ali being *The Key to Kuwait,* and thought it would make a good title of a book, but nobody else got a kick out of it.

Ali must have been on Arab time, because he clearly didn't feel the need to rush things. He showed us all the royal gardens, and then took us to like a tiled room and left us. He said with a smile that we smelled like *infidel dogs* and could not go to an Arab wedding smelling like *infidel dogs.* The room was a sauna, and there was a woodstove with perfumed wood in it tended by an old guy. The guy pointed to the wood and said the wood came from America, and then flashed us a toothless grin. There were paintings of angels on the ceiling. I had that feeling we were back in old Arabia again, which was totally cool.

We were told in gestures to strip and lie down on some wood tables, and then some beefy Arabs came in and gave us all a serious rubdown. While we were getting this rubdown, they poured cologne and powder all over us, and made some grunting sounds like they too thought we smelled like infidel dogs and that it was going to be mucho work to get us fixed up to attend the royal wedding party. Then when we were like melting into the boards, another even older guy came in and sat down in front of us and he had no eyes! Just skin over where his eyes would be! We got no explanation for the old blind guy, and he looked at each of us in turn like he could see through the skin over his eyes. And it was creepy, like he could see right into us and was judging us right then for ever after!

I guess we passed his judgment, because he settled back with a sigh that like covered all the woes of the world. Krebes was asleep, and when he started to snore, the old guy got up and tapped him on the head with one of the empty perfume bottles. Then he sat

down again and started to do this singsong thing. All of a sudden I
had to know what he was saying, and I asked Krebes, and Krebes
said he figured the geezer was reciting from the Koran. Still, for
some reason I wanted a translation, and when Ali showed up I got
one. Here is what the geezer kept saying from the Koran:

> *Let there arise from you*
> *A band of brothers*
> *Attractive to all that is good*
> *Urging what is right*
> *And forbidding what is wrong*
> *Such men shall surely triumph*

It was a good thing I asked for this translation, as my man
Trang had been in a minor slump since learning Princess Lulu was
still in Kuwait. But when he heard these words, he decided we—
me and Krebes and him—were *such a band of brothers.* I saw out of
the corner of my eye that Ali was kind of totally bummed at not
being included. Ali sent us into a steam room next, and we sat on
these stools in like a fog, so that you could barely see each other. It
opened our pores so wide you could almost look through us. And
that was when Trang asked Krebes and me if we were willing to
come with him to rescue Princess Lulu from Kuwait.

You would think this would be a big decision. Like, I was proud
of being a marine, and it meant going AWOL from the marines and
probably getting killed by the Iraqis in some nasty way as a spy. But
right off I told my man Trang *I was his brother come what may,* and
Trang jumped up and slapped me five. Then we both turned to
Krebes and he said he was *good to go* to rush old Kuwait City too, although he mentioned with a sick laugh that echoed in the tiled
steam room that he was sure we were going to be skinned alive by
the Iraqis. Later I would think pretty hard about why I like didn't
think harder about this major decision to follow Trang. I guess
sometimes you just swing for the bleachers, and wonder afterwards how you knew to swing at that particular ball.

So we stood there, the three of us dudes, in the steam room. And Trang put out his hand, and I put mine over his, and Krebes put his beefy mitt over ours. And we looked hard at each other, and Trang asked me to repeat that thing from the Koran as a kind of prayer for our good luck on our trip to Kuwait, and I did so, pushing the part about *such men shall surely triumph.* I also said, *let the spirit of Captain Shakespear watch over this band of brothers.* Krebes didn't know about Captain Shakespear, and Trang filled him in, but Krebes just looked grim when he learned about the ancient captain getting hacked to death by the swords of the Rasheed cavalry on the plains of Jarrab. Krebes brightened when Trang showed him Captain Shakespear's pearl, and explained how it had come to him via Princess Lulu, the descendant of the captain's royal Kuwaiti lover. I explained how Princess Lulu had it in her head that Trang was some sort of warrior reincarnation of Captain Shakespear, so for her this was kind of a second chance for this like ancient love affair, and Krebes thought this was totally crazy, but the craziness of it seemed to secretly please him.

And then I said we ought to make Ali an official member of our band of brothers, and there was some discussion about this as we had developed some doubts about the fidelity of your Arab in general, but I swore by him, and that was good enough for Trang and Krebes. So we yelled for him, and he caught on right away and without hesitation joined hands with us as like part of our band of brothers *fighting for good and right and saving the Princess Lulu too.*

So we were pretty damn stoked there in the tiled room. We four were ready to take on our mission. Ali ushered us out into another chamber covered in paintings of like angels having sex in all sorts of interesting ways, and he had four new servant guys holding up these spanking white Arab robes. Trang right away asked for his marine desert cammies, and Ali said they were in the wash. Trang sat down and said he'd wait, and then Ali said he had them burned outside with the rubbish. Trang jumped up and made a run for the door, but me and Krebes wrestled with him. Ali all the time was telling him that if he was going to sneak into Kuwait it would be a lot easier sneaking in looking like an *Arab.* We pointed out to Trang that a lot of special-forces dudes wore the local garb, but I think right then Trang was digesting that his decision to head to Kuwait might mean losing his beloved Marine Corps and the chance for official military greatness in general. So for a few minutes he sat on the bench with head in his hands like he was bumming, and then he shook his head and stood up with a hard-ass expression and put his hand out for the robe.

Tommy Trang looked good in the local robes, even Krebes noted it. Ali said he looked *sharif,* which was like Noble. I thought I looked pretty fine, but big old Krebes looked like he was heading back from an all-night toga party. Right then Ali got this sly look on his face, and said he wanted us to meet an important young Saudi prince. He said part of his slave duty was to hang around with this prince. It was kind of a comedown from heading off to Kuwait right away, but we were on Arab time. Also, I suspected Ali had a reason for wanting us to meet the Saudi prince, and I was right!

So Ali walks us to this like monster room, and in the middle of the monster room there was a monster purple velvet couch, and in the middle of that monster couch was a fat, fat Saudi prince about twelve years old glaring at us. Ali said something to the prince, but the important prince just *scowled.* Some crinkled old lady servant was on her knees in front of him, holding up a dripping red donut, but his mouth was too busy *scowling.* Ali bowed and said, "I present the prince Khalid Ali Abdul Aziz al Saud, great-grandson of the founder of Saudi Arabia, the great warrior Abdul Aziz." The boy took a big-ass bite of the donut right then, and the old lady caught the drippings from his chin by whipping over a silver platter with her free hand.

The fat prince pushed and rolled himself off the couch and made his way over to inspect us three. I didn't know what to do, but the kid clearly liked food, so I offered him a chocolate-covered cookie I had stowed away for my last MRE. The kid took it with a sneer, sniffed it, took a bite, and then spit the bite on the floor. Then he stepped on it and smeared it with his shoe across the floor. The old lady ran around on her knees trying to clean it up, and as she was wiping the bottom of his shoe, the prince pointed a stumpy finger at Trang and said, "You! You are not American."

Damn, I thought, *here we go again.*

But Trang said calmly, "I sure am American."

"I am Prince Khalid Ali Abdul Aziz al Saud," said the prince. "I have spoken. You are Chinese. You know kung fu?"

"No," said Trang. "I'm half Vietnamese, but I'm as American as they come. You ever heard of Vietnam?"

"Yes," said the prince. "Where America lost the war. So you are a gook?"

"Nice kid," I said to Ali.

"And now you come to my country," said the prince. "To fight for us. I hope you do not lose this war too."

The more obnoxious the kid got, the calmer Trang looked. He had this soothing voice now, and said, "To fight with your people. To be part of a great Allied Coalition to free Kuwait."

"We Saudis do not have to fight," said the prince. "My father said we do not have to fight because we have hired America to fight." And here he directed a smile at Ali. "My father said you Americans are like the Bangladeshi, our servants."

Krebes glanced at me as if to say, *can I throttle the little prince now?*

The prince waddled away, as if he had stuffed us Americans in our place. The old servant lady stuffed a bite of donut in his mouth when he opened it in front of her like a fat baby bird. I just couldn't get over how fat the kid was—I wondered if he did anything but sit around and get stuffed with donuts. The kid made a mess of the bite, and some jelly went down his robe, and the old servant lady clapped her hands and in ran some other servants, and the prince was changed as he stood there with his arms out, glaring at us again. Some of the servants were girls, and he grinned as he gave one of their tits a squeeze. He said to me, "You see, these girls are my slaves, as are you Americans."

I had pretty much enough, and motioned to Ali to get on with the tour of the royal Saudi house. He shook his head, and we followed the prince into another room. This was a toy room the size of a basketball court. It was so full of toys you couldn't even get to one end of the room. In the center of the room was a gigantic stuffed elephant about twenty feet tall. The prince huffed his way up a special set of stairs like you use to get on an airplane. When he got up there, he sat himself on the head of the elephant and yelled down to us, "This elephant is the biggest stuffed animal in the world!"

Tommy Trang shook his head, and the prince saw him and yelled down, "You shake your head! Why?"

Trang stepped forward from us and yelled up, "Because that isn't the biggest stuffed elephant in the world!"

The prince screamed down, "It *is* the biggest!"

"Nah!" said Trang. "It isn't even close to the biggest."

"Yes! Yes!" yelled the prince. *"It was made for me special by FAO Schwartz in America and it is in the* Guinness Book of World Records*!"*

Trang looked thoughtful for a minute and yelled up, "How big is your elephant?"

"It is eight meters tall. It is the biggest elephant in the world!"

Trang shook his head and said, "I hate to tell you, Prince. But a lot of kids in America have bigger ones."

"This is impossible!"

Trang walked over and started to climb up the stairs. He looked carefully at the elephant as he went up, and shook his head now and again, sadly. The prince leaned out and watched him climb. When Trang got to the top, he said something to the prince, and the prince yelled, *"Impossible!"* And then the prince just lost it. He started screaming in Arabic and pounding on the elephant. Royal retainers started running in from all over and dashing up the stairs. The kid was having a nuclear meltdown.

Trang moved aside as the servants pretty much carried the prince down the stairs. A couch was brought in, and he was placed on it. A like elder Arab jabbered with the prince and then turned to Trang and said, "You, sir, have told the prince Khalid Ali Abdul Aziz al Saud, great-grandson of Abdul Aziz al Saud, that he is wrong?"

"I told him his elephant wasn't the biggest."

"Please, sir. Tell the prince his elephant is the largest."

"Why?"

"Because he is the prince Khalid Ali Abdul Aziz, descendant of Abdul Aziz al Saud." The old retainer said this like, *why must I say what is obvious?*

"And what would old Abdul think of the kid?"

"Sir?"

"I have heard Abdul Aziz was a kick-ass desert warrior."

"This is so," said the old retainer. "A mighty warrior, the founder of Saudi Arabia."

"So would he cry over a stuffed elephant as a boy?"

The old retainer looked confused. "In those old times, there were no stuffed elephants."

"Right," said Trang. "But would old Abdul Aziz have cried, if he had one as a boy?"

"In those old times there were no stuffed elephants," said the retainer. "So he could not cry over one."

"Give it up, Trang," I said.

The prince was gobbling donuts like they were the last donuts left in Arabia. He was making a tremendous mess on his white robe, and all sorts of royal hands were trying to wipe the jellies from him and the couch as he blubbered in Arabic.

The retainer was still looking at Trang, I guess for an admission *the prince has the biggest elephant.* Maybe he thought the kid would keep stuffing donuts until either Trang said the kid had the biggest elephant or he exploded. The retainer said something to Ali, who gestured to us to follow him out of the room. I said to little Ali as we marched down another hall, "Look, that prince is spoiled as hell. He's what we call in the marines *totally unsat.* He needs a few weeks with the marines under the hot sun on a forced march."

"Maybe we should take him with us," said Ali.

We all stopped and looked at Ali, who raised his hands and said, "I make a joke!"

We slapped Ali five when he raised his hand, and the feeling generally came back of *brotherhood on the road to triumph.* The fat prince was still bugging me though, and as we moved down the halls in our robes I was like, "So why did you want us to meet the fat prince, Ali?"

Ali turned his head to me and said, "I thought you would like to meet Colonel Fawwaz's son."

All of us stopped dead in the hallway. The hall was covered with mirrors, so we three marines were all over the place. Ali continued walking and yelled back to us, "We are late for the wedding feast, come, come!"

So we ran after him and quizzed him as we walked double time to the wedding feast, and it turned out that Colonel Fawwaz was *already married* and had this fat kid, and so sixteen-year-old Princess Lulu of Kuwait was slated to be *wife number two*. Me and Trang had no idea the Arabs let you double and even triple up on wives. Krebes said he knew about this weird fact. And then I think we all were thinking about pretty little Princess Lulu giving birth to a fat and nasty little prince with Colonel Fawwaz, and it made us all want to puke. I looked at Ali, and he shook his head as if to say, *if you guys don't kick some ass in Kuwait, it will come to pass.*

Then we were sucked into this royal dining hall with like two long golden tables, and there was a scramble going on for seating, so we jarheads grabbed ourselves some. I was wondering if things were going to hit the fan whenever Colonel Fawwaz returned from wherever the hell he was, but Ali said it would all be cool, even though he admitted he didn't *exactly* know the whereabouts of Colonel Fawwaz either. The crowd of guys—no ladies allowed, of course—was mostly into grazing the food, and the servants were bringing it out on the double. I was like thinking how dumb it was for the Arabs to banish the ladies from a *wedding party*. Back home, a wedding party was like an optimum opportunity to score some loving, with the romantic mood and the dancing and all! Anyway, the Arabs had some strange table manners: first off, they ate with their fingers. Second, they would taste a dish on a platter and then return the rest if their tongue gave veto. But old Trang was right into this caveman style of eating, he shoved his hands right into platter after platter with gusto, grinning at me and nodding as he grabbed handfuls of this and that—it was a hoot to him. He couldn't keep his hands out of the food! He grabbed handfuls for me, and then started helping the old Arabs on his far side to fill up their plates, like a crazy Italian mama saying, *eat! eat!* They looked like they were weirded out by him.

The servants came down and placed a whole lamb on the table like every five feet. Trang's hands were right into the carcass, grabbing off whole chunks of meat, and distributing them to his neighbor Arabs, who now looked real *stunned* by him. And then one Arab leaned over and snagged Trang's left hand, *and it turned out the locals didn't use their left, as back in the days before toilet paper that was the hand you used to wipe your ass!* Anyway, Trang just cracked up when he understood the logic of the *no-left-hand* rule, and you would of thought I'd be cracking up too, but right then was when *I totally hit the wall.* I was a U.S. marine, a jarhead, a tough guy. But that damn lamb right in front of me was like my undoing. He has his head on and it looked like his eyes were looking straight into me, and every time happy Trang jabbed his right hand in the carcass the head jiggled and it looked like the lamb was shaking his head at me. And I just lost my appetite in some way. I'm not a vegetarian, but that lamb put me into a downer mood. It was like he found me *wanting* in some way, or suspect, and I started to look inside myself during the meal. It doesn't happen to me all that often, but when it does it can send me into a slide until I decide I'm right with the world. And everything seemed wrong suddenly: but mostly it was wrong to go AWOL from the marines with Trang. I hate to say it, but the lamb had me thinking Trang was a lunatic and I was a fool.

Well, that lamb, thanks to Trang and his fast hands, got consumed like it had been tossed into piranha-filled waters. And here is the odder thing: the less meat on those lamb bones, the more my mood started to lighten. And when the lamb was just a head attached to a gnawed-on skeleton, I got a new vibe as the lamb wiggled his head at me. It was a sadder vibe from the lamb, as if the lamb was *way gone* now and had come to grips with being consumed by the hungry hands of Tommy Trang. The lamb was at peace with being dinner, and I started to feel the same peace come on me. Like the lamb was meant to be dinner, and I was meant to go with Trang to Kuwait. Like I said, I am not always prey to these downer moods, but that lamb just threw me for a while, and then it was over. The cool thing was when it was over, I was doubly psyched I was part of this Kuwaiti rescue party. I was feeling weirdly happy, and I like reached out and patted that lamb on the skull and said: *it's cool, whatever.*

What helped me get over the downer mood was all the belching. You can't stay down when you are an American at a desert dinner party and the whole scene starts in with tremendous belches with their faces saying *they were pleased as punch with their belch!* I looked up and down the table at all the Arabs belching away like it was some sort of seismic eruption that passed from one to the next, and Krebes started in with a small symphony of belches, and then Trang let loose with a *Titanic* belch that rocked the room. Arabs all craned around to see who had burst their rib cage, and then started to *applaud us foreigners.* It was then we got on the radar of some American officers down the room at another table, and they started giving us dark looks, as we kept belching even when the rest of the Arabs had moved on. So as we belched, the Arabs started to get up and leave the table and wander away, and I thought we had offended them, but an Arab near me said with a smile that this was Arab custom: you could just ditch the table at any time as long as you mumbled something like, *alhamdulilah!* after you belched.

I didn't know why the Arabs quit the food scene, as the servants started bringing out pomegranates and custard and grapes that were cold as ice. Ali the Bangladeshi was around by the way, but he was a servant, or a slave, so he kind of hovered in the background. So we chewed on these ice grapes for a while, and I noticed we were still getting the hairy eyeball from the American military dudes down the way, and it struck me we were out of uniform and technically already AWOL. So finally it was clear it was time to move on, so we washed up at the door on the way out like the others, and then flowed with the Arabs into another room where servants were roaming with jars of incense. I gave Krebes and Trang the thumbs-up, *as here we were in old Arabia again.* We had coffee with everyone, and that got our engines stoked, and we three stood around sort of jazzed we were having this unique Arab experience.

And then it looked like we were screwed. The American officers came up and kind of surrounded us, and the look on their faces was like *you dudes are so nailed*. They wanted first to chew us out for the belching thing, and then fired a bunch of questions like *why the hell were we out of uniform* and *what the hell we were doing here* and *what the hell happened to Euclid Krebes' face?* And that's when having a genius around saved our skins for the first time. Because Trang and me were stumped, but old Euclid Krebes puts this serious look on his messed-up face and motions the general aside and says quietly, "Sir, I'm an action officer with the J-5 Planning Group. These two are my clerk and driver." I didn't know what this stuff about "J-5" meant, but the general nodded at us with this new look on his face that was *real serious*. What I gathered was that there was a top-secret group of geek war planners, called by one and all the 'Jedi Knights,' and that they used high-powered computers day and night to plan the war. Krebes started throwing some terms at the general like GBU-15s, and the floating FSCLs, and the Iraqi KARI, and the general started to glaze over as people do around computer geeks, but still with the seriously impressed look. Then he snapped back and said to Krebes, "But what are you doing *here* exactly?"

"I was told to liaison with Colonel Fawwaz, sir. Sort of keep him informed, more or less, on things."

The general smiled a sly grin and looked around. Then he said, "You mean you're here to keep him out of our hair."

Krebes tossed the sly grin right back and even winked. "Yes, sir. I feed him a lot of figures, let's say. He likes figures."

The general sly-grinned again. "I'll say he does, the dog. He likes *figures* all right. We had to send a female Air Force major back to the States because he wouldn't let her figure alone."

I was paying so much attention to Euclid Krebes and the general chuckling *over the dog Colonel Fawwaz*, that I barely noticed when Trang sort of broke off and got into a talk with an Air Force colonel. And when I beamed in, I heard Trang telling the colonel that he *hated satellites*. The colonel was apparently in intelligence, and he took the slur on satellites real personal. He got right in Trang's face and was yelling, "Where would we be without the KH-11? Where would we be without electro-optical imaging?"

"I just dislike them, sir," said Trang. "And don't forget clouds."

"Clouds?" yelled the colonel. "What the hell have clouds to do with it?"

"Can these things see through clouds?"

The colonel looked at us with his mouth open. He shook his head and said, "Lacrosse imaging, Magnum and Vortex electronic imaging—to name just *three* that can see through clouds. I suppose you have a problem with Lacrosse, Vortex, and Magnum imaging too?"

"Don't take it personally, sir."

"I do take it personally! It's like saying you don't like Jesus Christ, son. You get down on your knees like me every day and thank God for Mr. Magnum, Mr. Vortex, Mr. Lacrosse, and Mr. KH-11. This would be a different war without them, we'd be down in the trenches again going face-to-face with the enemy."

"That's just it, sir," said Trang. "They're taking all the *fun* out of it."

That bit of Trangian wisdom just about snapped the colonel in half, but that was also the moment a huge cage was wheeled into the room, like you would move a lion around in at the zoo. There was a nasty-looking character in there, and I guessed I was seeing my first Iraqi soldier. He had a buzz cut like a marine, and his face had a slash from his right ear to the corner of his mouth. The general who had been talking to Krebes said to us, "An Iraqi spy."

"Really?" I said. That was pretty cool.

"Captured him at Hafr al-Batin. He was pretending to be a refugee from Kuwait, but he had a radio transmitter strapped to him. He was sending messages to Saddam. Saudis caught him and they're real proud of it. We'd like to get our hands on him, have him send back some messages to Saddam to suit our purposes. But the Saudis won't give him up."

The Iraqi seemed to be looking right at me, and I had the sense that he was possessed by something real *evil*. He looked like a true psycho killer. As he was staring at me, that was when our host, Colonel Fawwaz, made his entrance. He was dressed in combat fatigues and carrying an M16. Right away he starts scanning the crowd, and then he locked his eyes on Trang, and slips his M16 off his shoulder, and says something sharp in Arabic.

I figured he was going to take Trang down, but instead I guess he had *ordered the door to the cage with the Iraqi be opened.* The crowd was pushing back from the cage, and in the commotion I got separated from Trang and Krebes. Then I feel someone tugging on my hand, and it is Ali, *and next to him is the bride Princess Hayat in a guy's robe!* Of course it was verboten for her to be mixing with us guys, even at her own wedding, and she pulls me to her and says in my ear, "There is little time. You must get Tommy Trang from the party now. Colonel Fawwaz has been drinking and is insane with the idea Princess Lulu prefers a Jew to him! And now this very Jew is in his own house!"

The 'Jew Thing' strikes again! Man, that one joke of Trang's was getting some mileage here in Saudi! Anyway, I had to know something else, and asked, and Princess Hayat said, "Colonel Fawwaz hates America. He plays a dirty game. He has servant women he uses to lure American soldiers here to the palace and has them badly beaten up. But quickly now, *you must go!* Ali will show you the way out of the palace, and he will lead you to Princess Lulu in Kuwait where she waits to be rescued by Thomas Trang." And then she shoved a folded-up yellow letter into my hand. I figured it was another letter from Princess Lulu for Trang, and I was right. He showed it to me later, and here is what it said: *There is a secret ocean of cool water under these desert lands from rains a thousand years old. Are you thirsty for me, Thomas Trang?*

Anyway, as soon as I felt this letter in my hand, I signaled to Trang and Krebes, and they came over as Princess Hayat kissed my ear and slipped away into the crowd after whispering with some intensity, *You must make sure Tommy Trang does not lose the pearl!* I was kind of surprised Princess Hayat cared about the pearl too, but a number of people would turn out to be secret fans of the pearl as our adventures rolled on.

Right then the door to the cage swung open. The Iraqi's hands were bound behind his back by two black servants, and then he stepped out onto the table where we had just been eating. Colonel Fawwaz steps up on the table, walks to the Iraqi, and starts beating him with the butt of his rifle. The Iraqi took the blows for a while and then made a dash down the table. Colonel Fawwaz waved his hands for everyone to get down on the floor, and then sprayed the Iraqi with bullets just as he tried to jump clear of the table. Then Colonel Fawwaz was at the end of the table and screaming in Arabic and pointing at us, and he sprayed the room a few more times with bullets. We scurried after Ali through the sea of Arabs crawling in all directions, and I guess in the local robes we all looked the same from above, as we didn't get shot.

CHAPTER 8

So we four were heading to Kuwait to rescue a princess. It was little Ali who said we should sneak in as Bedouin riding on camels. This vision of like *Lawrence of Arabia* got Tommy Trang mighty stoked up. So we wanted to get us some camels. Ali said we should proceed to the Rub' al-Khali, otherwise known as the Empty Quarter, and talk to the Bedouin tribe known as al-Murrah about the camels. Tommy Trang and me joked about 'Al Murrah' sounding like a mafia guy: *'Yo, go see Al Murrah in the Rub', he'll fix youse up with some preemo camels.'* Anyway, we hitched our way there with Arabs mostly, as we figured we were probably officially AWOL, and it wouldn't do to hitch with any U.S. forces.

It was cool to be going to see the Bedouin on their home turf. You couldn't help but think you were heading back to olden times in Arabia. And the Rub' al-Khali was the real desert thing! To date, the desert experience had been a letdown—mostly where we had our marine platoon base north of Jubail was just like crappy sand-and-gravel plains, and pretty depressing if you were expecting the shifting sands of Arabia. But this Rub' al-Khali was clearly like where all the movies of Arabia had been shot—the sand dunes were here at their best. And there was nothing *else* here for the most part—none of that ugly concrete stuff that was weeding up over the rest of the Saudi. So just being in the Rub' al-Khali put us all in a positive mood, as it was clearly the perfect backdrop for this sort of adventure. We stopped in the afternoon, and we all climbed up and sort of surfed and tumbled down the face of a dune, and it was generally a blast, although it made me miss my days of riding a king-hell swell back at Huntington Beach. But the downer mood passed like a squall, as it was clear to me I was riding a primal wave of a different sort now, and a surfer stays loose and rides the wave under his board.

So we bounced along in these Toyota trucks driven by Arabs some more, and Ali said we were heading to Jabrin, which was like one of these al-Murrah Bedouin tribes' four *oases*. When I heard that word *oasis,* I flashed the thumb at Krebes and Trang and mouthed the word: *oasis!* They mouthed it back to me, and then we pounded the side of the truck yelling, *oasis! oasis! oasis!* We were stoked! So anyway, Jabrin itself was like just patches of palm trees in an area about fifteen miles by three miles. And right away we are seeing little areas with humans and trucks and shacks, and little Ali said different lineages of the 'Jaber' strain of al-Murrah hung out in different sections around the oasis, as they had since camel time began. Most of the Jaber, Ali said, were migrating this time of year, but the emir of the whole al-Murrah tribe was hanging around here, and it was to him we would go for our camels.

Little Ali talked to some local dudes by the side of the road—who mostly stared at the scary mug of Euclid Krebes until he *growled* at them—and then a while later Ali like yelled to the driver, and we pulled over near some sick-looking trees. We all jumped out, and Ali reached up in the tree and handed us some dates. Ali acted like these were high-class dates, so we looked pleased by the taste, but it was pretty skanky stuff. Right then this dried-up old hawk of a Bedouin came walking over from like a parked truck, and he started ranting on about the old trees. Ali said this was the emir of al-Murrah, which was weird, because as I said, he was just hanging by a truck in the middle of nowhere, and there was little pomp and circumstance. But Ali said this was why the Bedouin were so cool, they believed all men were equal, so they didn't make a big show over their leadership. But Emir al-Murrah looked pretty beat down for an emir, and he seemed a little too crazy about the date trees. Ali said he was talking about the history of the famous dates of al-Jabrin, and how they were like lovingly cared for, but looking at the trees you got the definite sense al-Murrah dudes were not big into the work of agriculture, as the trees were sad cases.

This emir al-Murrah was a real talker. He branched, so to speak, right into the history of the al-Murrah tribe, not that we asked. He said—and I got all this from little Ali of course—that all those Bedouin dudes we might see hanging around this oasis were descended from one busy ancient dude named Murrah, which accounted for the name of the tribe. This original Murrah lived before the time of Islam, and thus the al-Murrah are known as the most royal of the Bedouin. This didn't follow, but whatever— it was translated. Emir Murrah said the Rub' al-Khali was full of *jinns* which were apparently like trolls, and that as a result the al-Murrahs have amazing abilities to track people and animals. This didn't follow either, but it was still cool listening to the old guy rattle on to us strangers. Then it turned out this dude *wasn't* the emir of the al-Murrah, but that the real emir was in Abquaig, so we packed up and headed there, giving Ali some funny looks.

We got to Abquaig, which was an oil-processing town, and filled with ratty metal shacks. The real name of the emir was laid on us, but it was a mile long, so we called him Emir. He was a guy about forty, and in uniform. He spoke some English, and explained the al-Murrah tribe mostly didn't do the old Bedouin camel thing anymore, but worked as the bulk of the Saudi Arabian National Guard. He actually thought it a knee slapper we were looking for a bunch of old-fashioned Bedouin on camels, and brought a lot of his comrades in the National Guard over to have a good laugh over us crazy Americans. That was when I really noticed that all the time he was talking to us, these Arabs in uniform kept coming up to the tall guy sitting next to him, who was paying out cash by the handful.

After a while, the emir got around to what we wanted, and Ali said we wanted camels for a secret mission to Kuwait. The emir seemed interested in the *secret mission,* but said sorry, he didn't have any camels. And in truth, we were surrounded by white Toyota pickup trucks, without a camel in sight. Then the emir said there were camels on the way, but they were being imported on steamer to Jeddah from Somalia. He himself was going to pick out a few of the best for the king of Saudi Arabia, and we were welcome to come as his guests, and that while there we could buy some fine camels. The emir clapped his hands right then, and I expected something to happen, but I guess he just felt like doing it.

I turned to Trang right then and mouthed: *money?* And Trang looked at me and shrugged. Ali said out loud: *you have no money?* He said it kind of loud, like he was real shocked, and all the Arabs seemed to get the gist of it, and you have never seen such surprised faces. But then the dude handing out the money like stood up. He was a real tall, real skinny dude, with an ugly black mark on his ugly wrinkled face. Picture a like Arab Abe Lincoln. And he started with this speech about money, that Ali tried to translate. This al-Murrah lieutenant wanted us to know, pretty forcefully, that wealth had four legs. By this he meant camels. He said you could only have as many camels as you could keep others from stealing, and so the number of camels you had was like an indication of your general studliness as a man. A weak man, he said, would lose his father's camels to the raids of stronger men before his father's corpse is cold.

This last bit about *the father's cold corpse* was a crowd pleaser among the al-Murrah, and they got jazzed about it and whooped a bit and puffed out their chests like *they'd never let their dead father's camels get stolen!* And the Emir al-Murrah sort of egged him on, so then the tall dude went on and said, *Can you raid on money the way you can a camel?* We all doubted this, and he nodded as if to say *just so!* He said something like, *even a coward who could not hang onto one camel when his father is a cooling corpse can have as much cash stashed as there is in the Rub' al Khali.* I wanted to move the conversation back to the incoming camels on the steamer from Somalia, *but then I noticed Trang! He was hanging on every word from this al-Murrah!*

So Tommy Trang and this al-Murrah talker became fast friends right away, even if little Ali was making all sorts of faces to indicate he didn't like this dude at all. But Trang took no notice, and the al-Murrah talker with the ugly mole and the emir al-Murrah and Tommy Trang settled into a long rap about famous camels of yore, and then they talked camel's milk from various desert regions like they were talking California wines. Tommy Trang's enthusiasm for camel talk in general clearly won over these Bedouin guys' hearts, but we were going to be here all day, so I barged in and said, "Look: we got to get back to our mission." And the al-Murrah talker with the mole turned to me and said in English, "Yes, you are going to rescue the princess Lulu of Kuwait."

We were all floored by this, as clearly no one to date had mentioned Princess Lulu. We asked him how he knew, and he got down on his knees and put his ear to the sands like an Indian scout and said *the sands talk to him.* All the other al-Murrah nodded at this, like he did have these *powers.* And this guy told the emir al-Murrah that we were a secret American mission to rescue Princess Lulu of Kuwait, *and bang! That changed everything!* The emir was totally stoked we were going to make a raid for the young princess. Best I could tell, he was just stoked by the general *heroic* nature of the escapade, which made me think how cool it was that we had decided to take on this crazy mission. And that was when old Trang said: not only were we going to rescue Princess Lulu, but we were going *to try and nail old Saddam too, if he was in the Kuwaiti theater during our infiltration.*

I glanced at Euclid Krebes when Trang said this about Saddam, and he was just shaking his head like: *we're all just so dead.* And you might of thought this big whopper about nailing Saddam Hussein would have made the al-Murrah laugh out loud, but they clearly thought *this was the excellent mother of all plans.* And the al-Murrah got to calling in all their fellow Bedouin to lay this big Trang plan on all the tribesmen within shouting range on the desert of the Rub' al-Khali, and those Bedouin got to yelling praises about it good, and at the height of all the yelling, the al-Murrah with the Mole quieted everyone to say kind of pompous-like that *he* was going to join this heroic raiding party, *to gain honor for the al-Murrah!* Man, that just went over so big with his fellow Bedouin! Suddenly, out of like nowhere, a camel appeared for us. The emir led the camel over to Trang and handing him the reins said: *this camel is the descendant of Abdul Aziz's great camel so-and-so on which the founder of Saudi Arabia took on the Rasheed!*

Trang slapped me five at the mention of the Rasheed, that tribe that old Captain Shakespear had faced down solo when they galloped at him waving swords until he was hacked up on the plains of Jarrab. My man Trang's grin said: *See? We're on the path of old Captain Shakespear!* Anyway, Trang got busy inspecting the great Abdul Aziz's camel stock like he was an old master of camel flesh. He tried to look at the huge teeth of the camel we from then on called *Abdul Aziz,* but Abdul Aziz the camel balked at this invasion, and tried to remove some of his fingers. Trang then showed all the Bedouin his hand with a couple of fingers curled inward, so it looked like he had lost a couple of digits, which all the al-Murrah found a knee slapper.

While I may not have been Cody "Cowboy" Carmichael, rich son of Texas oil, as Colonel Fawwaz thought, to my eye *Abdul Aziz the camel* looked kind of ancient and broken-down. My gut told me old Abdul Aziz the camel might of even been ridden by the actual old Abdul Aziz himself. That camel looked pretty long in the tooth is what I'm saying, and I wondered if he'd make it out of Saudi Arabia, never mind to Kuwait. But I couldn't tell my man Tommy Trang this, as he had been placed up there on the back of Abdul Aziz so all the al-Murrah boys could cheer him on to victory over Saddam. And then the emir quieted everyone down to say this camel had royal milk in its tits, and that this royal milk must only be drunk on the road to Kuwait by a man of great courage, such as our Tommy Trang. Emir al-Murrah warned that anyone else drinking the milk from Abdul Aziz the camel would get very sick, and he gave the al-Murrah guy with the Mole a sharp look, kind of like a warning.

And then the weirdest thing. It was like the al-Murrah with the Mole got into a debate with the emir al-Murrah. And the debate commenced to look like an argument, and they went into a building to have it out. Ali, Krebes, Trang, and me looked at each other, and at the building. And we all kind of shrugged like, whatever, it's all still cool. So then al-Murrah with the Mole comes running out and ties a big-ass sack onto Abdul Aziz's side, and slaps Abdul Aziz on the rump, and Tommy Trang is carried off out of the camp on the camel at a trot. Al-Murrah with the Mole raises a hand in the air and yells as best I could tell, "To Kuwait!" *And all the Bedouin go wild!* So Ali and Krebes and me start jogging after Trang and the camel Abdul Aziz along with the rest of the al-Murrah boys. So we have this huge crowd of al-Murrah sort of jogging with us out of camp, and then they all stop, and we continue jogging on into the naked desert of the Rub' al-Khali, behind Trang and the camel.

So our man the al-Murrah with the Mole is rattling on in a stoked-up way about nailing Saddam as we jogged across the desert behind Trang on the old camel Abdul Aziz, but in a way that made you think he wanted us not to think about things like *what the hell are we doing right now?* But I cut him off, and said, *for starters, dude, what is your name?*

This stopped him in his tracks. And he looked up to heaven above and then covered his face with his hands and said, "I am the Mahdi."

"Okay," I said. "You're Mahdi."

"No," he said. "I am THE Mahdi."

"Right," I said. "And I am THE Carmichael, and up ahead of us you got THE Krebes, and THE Ali, and THE Trang."

I guess I should of followed up on this THE MAHDI thing right then, but Abdul Aziz the camel picked up his trot, and I ran after my man Tommy Trang. It was late in the day, and getting cooler, which was good. I was feeling good after a while, and joked with Euclid Krebes about how we were traveling with THE Mahdi. Krebes kind of scratched his head, like he was *almost* remembering something. Ali kind of pouted, and walked with his head down, now and then throwing death glares at THE Mahdi.

There was a silence, except for sounds of our feet, and I guess Mahdi—I dropped the THE right away—felt he had to fill the silence, because he said something, *and Abdul Aziz the camel stopped.*

Tommy Trang looked down and back at us all—he hadn't said a word since we left the al-Murrah camp—it was like up on the camel he was in another world. Maybe he was dreaming he was old Captain Shakespear, who knows? But now Trang looked down, as Mahdi dropped down on his knees in the sand. Mahdi took a finger and drew what looked like a horseshoe in the sand. He sort of brushed his fingertips over it and said, "Here you see the marks of loose camel skin on the hoof. So this camel comes from the sands." He made another, sharper camel hoof mark and said, "Here you see a camel that has come from the hard plains." He diddled the sand a pit with his pinky and said, "This is a female riding-camel," and more diddling and then, "Here is the mark of a male riding-camel." He cracked open an imaginary turd and sniffed it and said, "This is from a caravan from the west that has passed a moon ago."

Krebes looked around with his ugly mug at the empty desert and said, "What the hell? There are no caravans anymore!"

Mahdi stood up and looked around with his hands shielding his eyes. He made a big show of squinting, and all sorts of expressions crossed his face, then he jabbed his arm out and said, "There! There is one! There is a caravan!" He held his arm out and said, "You see? I am a great camel tracker, as is in the tradition of the al-Murrah!"

And that was when little Ali said quietly, "This man is not Bedouin. He is not al-Murrah."

We all looked at Mahdi, and he slapped his chest and proclaimed, "I am Bedouin, I am al-Murrah. I am these things at heart."

"At *heart*?" I said. "What do you mean, *at heart*?"

"I can live on a handful of dates and a bowl of camel's milk!" said Mahdi, as if this explained things.

"But were you born a Bedouin?" I said.

"I walked barefoot, a brother to the al-Murrah. Ask any al-Murrah!"

Ali said, "The emir just kicked him out of the tribe."

"This is not so!" said Mahdi. "I have joined with you to bring honor to the al-Murrah, and the emir has wished Allah to watch over our journey, and let us rescue the princess, and have victory a hundred times over Saddam Hussein. Now I must pray!"

So Ali seemed to agree it was time to pray to Allah, and the two went off in the desert a ways to do their Allah thing. Trang was still up on the camel and looking at the damn pearl in his palm. He had a look on his face I had seen earlier, like he was lost in burning memories of Princess Lulu. Krebes was lying on the sand with his eyes closed. You would think we'd all be discussing like our *situation,* but instead we were just letting the sands fall through the hourglass without comment. Right when I was about to venture a comment on our situation *of having only one camel,* Mahdi comes running back all out of breath and thrilled, like he had met Allah, and drags us all across the desert, *and right to a little oasis!*

Mahdi said, *"Allah has led us to this oasis!"* There was an old well and an ancient trough. Mahdi was down on his hands and knees *ooh*ing and *aah*ing over the trough and saying *this was something he had not seen since his youth with the al-Murrah, a leather-lined trough!* Mahdi went to the well and looked down and mumbled thanks to Allah some, and then he took a while showing Trang a leather bucket and an old rope. It was kind of like Mahdi was an antiques dealer who had found some crap in an old attic worth millions. Mahdi couldn't get over the fact the trough was lined with leather! So to get Mahdi back on track, I dropped the bucket down the well on the old rope, pulled up a bucket of water, dumped it in the trough, and gave the camel a drink.

So then it was quickly getting dark, and the romance chilled a bit, because we had nothing to eat—or so we thought. Mahdi went to his pack and brought back handfuls of something and said, "You do not believe I am Bedou at heart, look then at these!" So we looked at all the insects in Mahdi's hands, and little Ali didn't I guess like locust—which is what they were—so he went off in the desert to pout some more. Mahdi said locusts were called *dubba,* and that true Bedouin like him thought them to signal good luck. Man, Mahdi liked to talk! He settled down to tell us about how the *dubba* hate townsfolk, and how the *dubba* once ate up all the silk of a merchant who had cheated the al-Murrah. Mahdi said the *dubba* then ate all the food, furniture, clothes, and even the flesh of the townspeople, but didn't eat the al-Murrah in the area, because like all Bedouin, the al-Murrah were beloved by God for the nobility of their hearts.

Trang was eating all this insect news up like he had been waiting his whole life to get the lowdown on *dubba,* but me and Krebes were ready to eat. I knew we were having locust for dinner, so I told Mahdi to get on with the culinary lesson. But Mahdi, as he made a tiny pit fire with some grass and scrubby twigs, wanted us to see in the light of the fire how some of the locusts were yellow, and some red. He said the yellow were called *jarad* and the red *yakhak,* and after he fried them up in a pan also from his pack, he made us taste them and tell them which were better. It was like eating burned wood chips. We all said we liked the *jarad* best, and Mahdi rejoiced, for only fools liked the *yakhak.* Trang was really into eating them, which pleased Mahdi, but I couldn't believe he liked the taste, and figured he just liked the fact he was *eating burned locusts in the Rub' al-Khali, on the way to Kuwait.*

So Trang was totally into Mahdi for bringing burned locusts into his life, and Mahdi kept talking as the desert stars came out— just the sort of talk to turn on my man Tommy Trang. It was getting chilly when Mahdi lowered his voice and told us about the old *ghazzu.* He said when he was a boy, and soon after he had been sent by his rich family to live with the Bedouin to learn about honor, he got to go with them on a few *ghazzus.* A *ghazzu* was a raid on other Bedouin, or on caravans. Mahdi said the best time for you to *ghazzu* was in January, when the desert was supposed to be popping with green grass and flowers, and the girls in the tribe were eyeballing the young guys. To hear Mahdi tell it, you'd think the Arabs used to think of nothing else but heading out to gain honor and prestige from a cool *ghazzu.* How they'd head out on camels, and then try and slither on the dunes into another camp while the other Bedouin tribe slept, and unhobble the camels and try and sneak them out, and race them back to camp. If they got away, they got prestige in the tribe. If they got caught, nobody usually got killed, but the men of the other tribe would drag you back and make you sit through a feast while you felt like a loser, and then they'd send you back loaded with food and other stuff for your tribe, but you'd have to walk and they'd leave you with only one gun. While Mahdi told us this stuff, he took something from his robe and rolled it in a ball and tossed it in the fire, and then went on about this or that *ghazzu* from the glorious past, and then reached into the fire and took out the ball, and broke it open with a knife he *also* had hidden under his robe and then tossed it to Trang, who said it was real good salty bread.

Tommy Trang said, as he ate the bread, that maybe we were on the *last true ghazzu.* Krebes and me liked the sound of that: *the last true ghazzu.* Maybe it was because we were doing something so crazy and so out on the edge, but those words just cracked us up: *the last true ghazzu.* And I think me and Krebes and Trang knew we were out on the edge on our *ghazzu,* and that was why we were cracking up so much and slapping each other five over some words like *the last true ghazzu,* laughing till we were choking and all that. Our laughter rippled all over the desert floor, and then we were all just lying back and looking at the stars over the desert, and had pretty much forgotten about Ali and Mahdi.

Ali was still sort of down about how Mahdi was taking over in the role of Best Supporting Local, and soon I heard angry talk in Arabic from over near Abdul Aziz the camel. It got nastier fast, and I was sure the two were going to come to blows. Sure enough, by the time we three got to them, the two were rolling around the desert floor and yelling Arabic and trying to get in a good punch here and there. I was surprised to see little Ali seemed to be getting the better of big Mahdi. We dragged those two apart by the ankles, and Trang asked what the beef was, and Ali said, *this man is crazy! He will kill us all in our sleep! You must make him go now!*

So that was when we all sat down for a powwow, and Mahdi brought out the hubbly-bubbly from his bottomless pack, and we all smoked—except for Trang who said it might hurt his wind— to settle into the discussion about Mahdi's sanity. And after taking a big puff and letting it out, Mahdi said, "You must stop calling me

Mahdi. It is not a name like Mike or Bill in America. I am THE
Mahdi, it is a title of honor."

THE Mahdi seemed real pleased to have gotten this news off his
chest and was looking proud and content. And then he pointed to
the ugly mole on his chin with some significance. We didn't know
what to make of this mole-pointing, but then Krebes slapped his
head and said, "You're THE Mahdi? Like Muhammad Abdullah al-
Qahatani?"

It was good to have a genius like Euclid Krebes around to keep
the conversation rolling. The mention of this Muhammad Abdullah al-Qahatani guy deflated our Mahdi like a slashed tire. He shook
his head rapidly and said, *"No. No. No. Al-Qahatani was a fake! How
could he not be? For did he not fail? So he is not the true Mahdi!"*

Euclid Krebes broke off with the Mahdi to fill us in. It turns out
the Arabs have a prophecy that the Mahdi, or messiah, will come
and clean things up when the 'Princes have corrupted the earth.'
The prophecy said he would be a guy with four things going for
him. His name would be Muhammad, he would come with a new
century during violence, he would be a descendant by blood of the
original Muhammad who started the whole Koran thing, and *he
would have an ugly mole on his face.* Through the years, Krebes said,
guys named Muhammad with Moles would pop up and claim that
they were 'the right-guided one to bring justice to the princes,' and
then usually got killed. This al-Qahatani guy who got our Mahdi
all hot and bothered was the latest. Back in 1979 he seized a big
mosque in Mecca with machine guns and started pointing to an
ugly mole on his chin and saying in Allah's name he was going to
take control of the Kingdom of Saudi Arabia, and he killed a lot of
people, and then got beheaded for his troubles.

"So we're traveling to Kuwait with a Messiah with a Mole,"
concluded Krebes. "Any you people got doubts, check out his ugly
mole."

The crazy Mahdi *pointed to his mole as if Krebes wasn't cracking on
him.* He was grinning like he was just so glad to share the news that
he was chosen to redeem those corrupt princes and get Islam back
on the straight and narrow. Ali was standing just outside of the

glow from the fire, making signs like he thought we should send the Mahdi packing ASAP. And that made a certain amount of sense, but you could see Tommy Trang was *curious* about the Mahdi, and when we were all quiet Tommy Trang said to him, "So what do you want with us *infidels* if you are The Mahdi?"

You could see right away this was a real stumper question for the Mahdi. He coughed and hemmed and hawed and talked all around the question and how the *time was not just right for him to reveal his Mahdiness to the world.* Trang stared at him, and the Mahdi rambled some more and when he was real stuck and out of breath talked about the stuff he laid on the al-Murrah about bringing *some heroism home to the Bedouin* and all that, and that was when little Ali brought handfuls of cash into the firelight and cursed out the Mahdi good, and the two went at it like cats until we pulled them apart again.

Now this made sense. The Mahdi had stolen the Saudi National Guard money he was in charge of handing out to the al-Murrah tribe. He was like their accountant or something, as he had a degree in accounting. We asked if the al-Murrah would be coming after it, and he smiled and said, they *do not know it is missing.* So I guess he had been skimming for a long time, and stockpiling, and when we showed up, Mahdi decided the time was right *to skip out of Saudi with us to Kuwait.* In his defense Mahdi said he needed the money to support himself *until such time as he could reveal his Mahdiness to the world,* which he still planned to do, when the time was right. And then he repeated that in his deepest heart—and he banged on his chest and looked like he was so moved he was going to cry—he truly believed in the nobility of our mission to Kuwait to rescue the princess and kill Saddam, and that if we would let him just follow in our very footsteps like a dog, he swore to Allah he would be of service to our mission.

I was right with Ali for kicking old Mahdi out into the cold desert night. It seemed pretty clear to me that he was a thief, and crazy as hell. Krebes wanted him gone too. But you could see Tommy Trang was kind of into him, on account of his general craziness, which was like honey to a hungry bear. But I think even Trang was willing to boot him, until Mahdi started talking about *the surprise coming in the morning.* Mahdi really laid it on Trang thick about how he had made a secret call back in the al-Murrah camp, and that when we woke up tomorrow morning all our troubles would be over, and *we would thank him a thousand times.* This sounded suspect to the rest of us, but Trang-the-Curious just had to know what was coming in the morning that was so *cool,* so after much debate we hit the sack with our K-bar knives in our hands. Ali was real pissed we hadn't run the Mahdi out of camp, and slept far off from the rest of us. One time I woke up and saw the Mahdi sitting by the dying embers of the fire, and I held my knife tighter, and then crashed again.

So then it was dawn. And I awoke feeling real alive in my whole body, and real stoked we were on a ancient *ghazzu.* Anyway, it was kind of cold, almost freezing, and the damn robe was real thin. And that was when I remembered it was winter. The camels were pissing and snorting and coughing like old men, and there was *a Bedouin boy outside a white tent!* So that was when I yelled and jumped up, and Krebes and Trang and me just rubbed our eyes like it was a dream that we had a bunch of Bedouin camped next to us. The Mahdi came over and slapped Tommy Trang on the back and said, *See, my friend! I promised you! We will travel with these many Bedouin into Kuwait! All is well! Soon you will be with Princess Lulu!"*

The Mahdi clapped his hands, and yelled in Arabic, and then to us said, *let us have some coffee!* So we go inside the white Bedouin tent, and this pretty ringed hand slips over a sort of wall, and it was clearly the hand of a woman. And it kind of waved to us, and we heard some female voices giggling. And it was so cool, and put me right into the ancient past with caravans and all, and I looked down at my own robe, and thought: *Cool! Cool! Cool!* So I settled in to watch the coffee being made by the Bedouin boy. He's got this pan on a fire that is brass but blackened with age. Mahdi passed the green beans around so we could see them, and the kid roasts them on the pan.

Soon two Bedouin men come over, and start giving the kid hell about how he is roasting the beans, and Mahdi says to us: *this is tra-ditional! To complain about the coffee making! This has been done for a thousand years!* And so then we sit outside and watch the sunrise and drink this beautiful bitter coffee with the Bedouin men, who are mostly complaining about how the kid can't make a decent cup of Joe, and then one of the Bedouin dudes who was like a grandfather starts looking at his coffee cup funny, and says something cranky to the kid, who looks scared, and it turns out the kid forgot to add *cardamom seeds*. They all jump on the kid, and so Trang says, *hey, let me make the coffee!* And Trang makes it so badly in terms of the traditional method it cheers up all the Bedouin, and we all have a good feeling as we sip a second cup as the sky lights up so pretty over the sands, and the chill is burned away by the hazy sun.

As the desert sun rose, Krebes and me looked at each other, and then back at our Bedouin. With the sun up, I guess we had both noticed the same thing about our dozen Bedouin, and Euclid Krebes put it in words, "Don't they look kind of *blond?*"

"That's what I was thinking," I said. "I was expecting black-haired dudes. But maybe they use peroxide, or lemon, like chicks on the beach back home." I was just screwing around, as I didn't think they bleached their hair. So I yelled out, "Hey Mahdi, what's up with these Bedouin? How come they're kind of blond?"

Mahdi raised his hand with one finger in the air and said, "Ah!" I waited, and he waved his hand over the Bedouin like he was a magician about to make them disappear and said in a dramatic way, "These are not just Bedouin, these are the . . . *Sulluba!*"

He laid so much emphasis on . . . *"Sulluba!"* that Krebes and me took turns doing an imitation of him, until it was clear Mahdi was getting pissed. And then Mahdi said like he was surprised, and because clearly we still needed more explanation, "Are not the *Sulluba* known to you in the West?"

Trang and me and even Ali looked at our genius Euclid Krebes, but he just shook his head. So Mahdi told us about the Sulluba. He said they were *our people*. We still didn't get it, and he said, *these are descendants of lost Crusaders! Knights who centuries ago got lost in the desert and became Bedouin!* Mahdi made all the male Sulluba come over and embrace Trang and Krebes and me like it was some sort of historical reunion, and then he had them pull open their robes, and on their chests they all had a tattoo of a cross and a sword. So Trang showed them the blue knight with the death's-head tattoo on *his* back, and a friendship was like instant. I didn't mention this tattoo before, but who could tell everything that was so cool about Trang all at once?

The Sulluba women up to this point were all kept out of sight in another tent called a *harim*. But now at a word from Mahdi, repeated by an old Sulluba, out of the white tent ran this wild young Sulluba woman with swinging hair, ululating and waving a sword. She was more or less blond, and blue-eyed, but her face was strong and fierce like the best-looking of the Bedouin, and her chin and neck were tattooed in blue. She did a kind of whirling dervish dance with the sword, and she right away seemed to focus on Euclid Krebes. She'd spin toward him waving the sword and making lover eyes at him, and then hop and spin away howling with anguish like he had broken her heart, and then dance back just to push him away with a stiff-arm, and then back again like she was going to spear his gizzard with the sword. It was pretty surprising she picked Euclid Krebes to focus on, as with all his wounds from when he was beat up by the chicks he was still looking pretty scary right then. I mean his two black eyes were turning kind of piss yellow, and his face was totally swollen and scabbed up.

Anyway, Euclid Krebes looked like he had died and gone to redneck heaven having the sword-dancing chick giving him the horned eye, and then Krebes started jumping around and kind of getting into the dance, doing the opposite of the Sulluba lady. And all the Sulluba men were into it and whooping, and four or five other fine-looking ladies and three kids came out of the tent to stare at the flame-headed Euclid Krebes doing his real lunky, herky-jerky dance moves. At one point Euclid Krebes briefly stopped his dancing and tossed his beefy arm around me and bellowed in my ear, *let he, that has steerage of my course, direct my sail — on lusty gentleman!* I never got a real grip on what that was all about, but I report it here as it sounded pretty good, and might impress those types who think marines are all moron psycho killers.

Anyway, Mahdi slipped over to me while I was pondering Krebes' good spirits and strange genius mind and said, "Tonight you will see the Sulluba dance the traditional *'Ardha'* for the king of Saudi Arabia, and this dance will amaze you men!"

At this mention of 'dancing the traditional Ardha for the king', I dragged Mahdi away to the other side of the Bedouin tent to get some answers. As best I could gather, these Sulluba Bedouin were kind of a dancing troupe who specialized in the traditional dances. Mahdi was once their *promoter*, until he left for unspecified reasons to work with the al-Murrah as their accountant. The Sulluba had been scheduled to dance for the king of Saudi Arabia the night before while we ate locusts, because he was hunting with his falcons just across the desert a ways, but the dance had been postponed for some reason, and now the Sulluba had to go do their dance for the king *tonight.* "But then after the dance tonight," said Mahdi, just about choking with excitement and goodwill, "we will all sneak into Kuwait as Sulluba to rescue the princess and kill Saddam!" And then Mahdi slapped me on the back and said, "Come, let us pack up and go see my friend the king, and he will bless our journey!" And I was like, "Mahdi, man, I thought as Mahdi you were like supposed to *slay all the corrupt princes for Islam.* How can you party down with the king if you are the Mahdi?"

And Mahdi said it wasn't yet time to reveal his Mahdiness.

CHAPTER 9

So we all head off across the desert to see the king of Saudi Arabia. And sure enough, a couple of dunes over is this huge cool scene of seriously royal tents. So I guess you can see now why Trang and Krebes and me were comrades, as we all had the same reaction! It was like: *whatever happens to us in Kuwait, this is worth the price of admission.* And we all kind of grinned at Mahdi as if to say: *hey pal, you seem crazy as hell, but for now you're cool by us for bringing us to this party.* So there was a real fine spirit in the air, and the Sulluba were whooping it up in a traditional way as we came down the dune on the camels, and all the guards and soldiers around the king scene seemed glad to see the Sulluba, especially their ladies. Most everyone took a *real long look* at Euclid Krebes, as he looked pretty nasty overall from getting beat up. But the Arabs were pretty polite, and nobody pointed at Krebes and said *what the hell happened to that messed-up dude?*

There were falcons all over the place on these sticks. I had never seen a falcon up close, so I was pretty blown away by these fierce birds. The king didn't come out right away, and we were handled by some of his like royal retainers, who kept nodding in this wise way like they expected us crazy AWOL American marines to come wandering in out of the desert with the Sulluba, and that we were doing them a great honor just by showing the hell up, which I guess was just traditional desert hospitality, but it was cool nonetheless. I did catch a glimpse of the dude I thought was the king inside this major league circus tent, and it looked like he was having coffee and listening to some ancient dude yell out stuff right into his face. Mahdi said the screamer was telling the king hero stories of yore, as he sat on cushions on all these Persian rugs, a scene just like you'd expect from the movies.

There were no Americans around as far as I could see, so I guessed the king just wanted a chance to get away from the whole official Gulf War scene and all the bossy infidel American generals hanging around pigeonholing him about this and that. So it was cool he was welcoming to us young American marines, or at least had told his retainers to like show us some red-carpet spirit. There wasn't anything to do right away, and the Sulluba had been taken away to a tent. Trang, Krebes, and me were all just staring wide-eyed at the whole ancient desert camp scene, kind of speechless. I haven't said much about little Ali recently, and that was because he was still in a bad mood about Mahdi being with us in general, and was kind of really laying low and out of the way. Then suddenly all these royal servants came charging out in robes and ran to cages filled with ugly chickens and tossed the cages in a Mercedes truck and zoomed off with wheels spinning on the sand into the desert, and Mahdi came and said that the chickens were not chickens but a bird called the *Hubara Bustard,* and that was what the Arabs liked to hunt since the earliest desert days, only there were few left in the Saudi desert, so they had to plant a few Hubara Bustards out there to make the coming hunt a good time for the old king. Krebes and me had a good laugh about the 'poor Bustards' out there about to get nailed by a hawk.

After another hour or so a lot of other royal retainers started charging around, and from these huge white tents in the rear came a stream of foreign cars, as well as a lot of armed Humvees. The Saudis must have bought the Humvees from us Americans, but they had painted them in the Saudi royal colors. The front vehicle in this idling parade of expensive automobiles was a Range Rover with the top off, and behind it were a bunch of Rolls Royces, also missing their tops. A lot of the vehicles had speakers hooked up on poles, so I guessed the king was going to have some hunting music cranking. Then the king marched out of his tent followed by a bunch of retainers in robes, and he glanced at us and gave us a cool royal nod, and then climbed up in the Range Rover in the rear, and he must have right off pushed a button, because a like royal king's throne sort of rose up a few feet in the rear, and then went back down again. I guess he was just checking the hydraulics. Then he raised his leather-covered arm, and a falcon was brought to him. He stood up and raised his arm higher, and he yanked an eye cover off the falcon with his free hand, and untied the tassels, and the falcon blinked and gave everyone a hostile yellow-eyed look, but he seemed to give us infidels a particularly long and fierce stare, like he wanted our livers. The king looked over at us too with a similar look that kind of chilled your bones, and then with a mighty cry tossed the falcon into the air.

So then the king of Saudi Arabia sat down on his royal chair in the back of the Range Rover and started singing *songs*! Mahdi ran over to say he was singing traditional songs of heroism and victory, ancient songs, *and that it was an honor to hear the king sing!* I was like getting the definite sense the Mahdi was a real fan of everything *ancient and traditional*. The vehicles spun out of the compound as the hawk was sliding away in the sky, and Mahdi grabbed my robe, and we all ran for a Humvee in the rear. Mahdi yelled as we ran that the king has sent word that he liked the look of us infidels, so we were to come along on the hunt, *again a great honor for us!*

All the Arabs in the various vehicles were singing along with the king. I think he cranked up the volume in his amplifier, because with all the engines there was no way we could have heard him otherwise. But his royal voice was just booming over the desert! Mahdi yelled the songs as we rocked around standing in the rear of a Humvee holding onto this special bar I guess put there so people could stand up. Mahdi stopped singing long enough to say that the king was in a real good mood today because he was finally away from the war and all the foreigners, which made me look at Mahdi as we were foreigners, but Mahdi yelled that we were now like in a different category, we were strangers who had arrived at the camp of a desert chief. That was cool, until I thought about it and it made me think it was saying we were no longer considered part of the general Gulf War military force, and that made me think how we were AWOL and relying on a bunch of lost Crusaders and a Messiah With a Mole to get us into Kuwait to rescue a Kuwaiti princess crazy enough to stay behind when the Iraqis invaded. So as we jammed along in the desert after the hawk in the sky I had like a sober moment, as I was no longer a marine but a stranger wandering the desert, but then I looked at Tommy Trang's grinning face, and he slapped me on the back and mouthed the word: COOL and pointed to the hawk freewheeling in the desert sky, and I looked up at that hawk for a while doing his thing in the sky and jumped back into the general good mood.

So it was a good hunt. The king's falcon made short work of those Hubara Bustards, and the king was in a good mood about it, and sang victory songs all the way back to the big white tents, and everyone in all the other cars joined in, and there was a real feeling in the air—I don't think the others were singing this hard just because they were hanging with the king. If you pressed me I'd have to say people were elevated because of that *hawk*! To see the falcon hunting, blazing down out of the sky fearlessly for the kill—it just moved something deep inside a guy, and you were like purified and noble. Krebes and Trang and me were glowing with Hawk Energy as we headed back to camp, and it was like so powerful we just wanted to bust a move for Kuwait right then and there!

So there was to be a post-hunt party with the king, but before we could hang with the king, he had to pray to Allah. But the king wanted us to be around him while he prayed, and he told Mahdi he wanted us to hear the beauty of the Koran, so he pulled out this young guy who was supposed to do Koranic simulcast while this old blind guy recited from the old book to the king. I wondered where they got all these blind guys to do the Koran reading—like we had when we were in Colonel Fawwaz's sauna. Anyway, this old blind guy recited like a swift camel, and the young translator had some trouble keeping up. So Mahdi took over, and I caught: *in the name of God, the most compassionate, the most merciful* a few times, but the rest was like words from a sawed-off shotgun. Mahdi sounded like a carnival barker trying to keep up, and we would have cracked up at this speed-reading Koran, only the king was keeping a hawk eye on us to make sure we soaked up the good word from his holy book. Sometimes the old blind reciter would stop to take a breath and the king would pick up that whip of words and just snap and crack it around the tent, and the Mahdi would race after him kind of foaming at the mouth, until all that was coming out was a kind of word spray. The old reciter was looking kind of blue, but then he pitched back into the Koran once more with the king nodding at him with approval for being *good to go,* but then the reciter just stopped and stared into outer space, and the king was deep into the words and just picked it up and carried on with his eyes closed.

I nudged Trang because it looked to me like the old blind reciter had recited for the last time. The old blind guy had his mouth open so you could see his purple tongue, and there was some brown drool coming down his chin. The king was so into whatever he was reciting from the Koran that he was sobbing with his hands over his face, which was sort of moving in a way. I waved to Mahdi, but he was too busy translating to look at the old guy. Then the old guy sort of slumped forward, and the holy book slipped off his knees to the rugs. I spoke up then pretty loud, and said, "Excuse me, King. But it looks like the old man is dead." The king opened his eyes and came out of the trance, and looked at me sort of surprised I had spoken, so I pointed to the old reciter. And then everyone was hopping around, but not because the old guy was dead, but because the holy book had hit the rugs. The king finally saw me looking at the dead guy and said, "He is in paradise with forty houris."

I said, "Houris?"

Mahdi said, "Virgins."

Well, *that* was a different take on paradise. As they carried out the body of the old reciter I was thinking, *now I understand why these Arab guys like this Islam religion so much! You die, you get forty virgins to take care of your every desire for eternity!* If they had that as the endgame at the churches back home they would've packed the rafters! If you weren't into music, where was the deep motivation to hang with a bunch of choirly angels as they offered back home? But somehow I couldn't see the ministers back home offering up forty virgins. It just wouldn't go over with the women in the audience—they'd run the minister out of town on a rail. But then it hit me that was why they kept the women over in Saudi so wrapped up in blankets and shut down generally—because if they had a voice at all in this stuff, they'd send the houris packing.

So then we were honored in that we got to eat with the king. They brought out some soup that was just okay, and then something called *kappa* that was better but not too good so Krebes called it *krappa,* and then some lamb and ribs and assorted stuff in dark brown rice, then some more lamb that looked kind of grey, with pears and carrots, and then some salad and donuts and cakes and tons of fruit and all on golden plates. And the reason I'm rattling off the menu, is that that was how Krebes and Trang and me were eating—like we couldn't stuff it in fast enough. And Krebes leaned over and said, "Better than locusts, huh?" And then I remembered we hadn't eaten much in a long time except for locusts and coffee. But Krebes was in a real fine mood and pointing to like a lamp with his knife that looked like it was once owned by Alladin and said *she teaches the torches to burn bright.* I guess he was talking in his genius way about the sword-dancing Sulluba chick.

The king seemed sort of turned on we were so hungry, and kept having the servants offer us more of this and that, and Krebes and me finally slowed down and sort of kicked back on the cushions, but old Tommy Trang kept eating like he had last been fed in the States. I knew my man Trang had a hunger, but it was like he was trying to fill up some invisible camel's hump on his back. Krebes and me looked at each other, because just when you thought he was done, Trang thrust his hand back into this-or-that plate and gobbled some more.

While Tommy Trang chowed the king talked some about falcons, with Mahdi as translator. The king said he did not breed his falcons, and said this as if we might be surprised by this, so to be polite I made some sounds like: *no way!* No indeed, the king went on, his falcons were caught by specially trained Bedouin, just as they were caught by Bedouin for King Khalid ibn Abdul Aziz. The king said it was best if the Bedouin caught them as they flew south across Arabia. I nodded, as this made some sense, but I knew as much about falcons as I did about cricket, although I was more interested in falconry, as the sight of that bird bulleting down for the kill was enough to make your heart just burst in your chest. The king also said that at the end of every hunting season the falcons were thrown up in the air and freed, which was a fine thing to do, and Krebes and I both commented on the rightness of this action to the king. Trang didn't comment, as he was still eating, and the king stopped talking to rest his eyes on Trang, and his eyes were kind of like a hawk, and that was when Trang just raised his head, eyeballed the king right back, and *let loose with the mother of all belches!*

From that belch on the king was into Tommy Trang. He patted some pillows next to him, and Trang went over and sat by him. Mahdi was just about on his knees with the honor of all this, and kept nodding at me rapidly like *things are going real well!* The king was into Tommy Trang's Vietnamese heritage, and I held my breath as I expected Trang was going to lay on him that crazy stuff about his *Jewish dad,* but Trang didn't, I think because he thought the king was a pretty cool guy, and didn't feel the need to yank his royal chain. Krebes glanced at me and shook his head like: *that was a close call!* The king went on about the war in Vietnam in a historical way that after a while sort of put me to sleep, but I could see Krebes was into it, as I guess he knew all this history and was impressed the king had such a detailed knowledge.

Then the king was silent, and so was everyone else. He was looking hard into Trang's eyes, and *Trang just eyeballed him right back.* There was a real tension in the tent, as I guess most don't eyeball the king the way Trang was doing—but they just locked their eyes and then the king smiled, and patted Trang's hand, and pronounced that *deep down Trang was a sheik!* The king said real *sheikness* was a gift from Allah. Nobody was going to argue with the king on this score, and everyone seemed amazed the king had seen this sheikness inside Trang. We smoked some fruit-flavored tobacco from the hubbly-bubbly for a while—except for Trang on account of one of his personal 'rules for military greatness' was *No Smoking*—and the king made small talk with me and Krebes, but he was just being polite, and then it was back to Trang. The king let out some smoke and asked Trang what he was up to wandering in the desert with Muhammad—that's what he called our Mahdi—and the Sulluba, and of course Tommy Trang told the king we were off to Kuwait to rescue Princess Lulu and while we were there try and knock off old Saddam Hussein if he happened to be in the area.

I wasn't surprised by now that the king took this news in stride. The Arabs were cool with craziness. He took the hubbly-bubbly again and had a big old smoke, and kicked back like he was pondering, and all the time he was holding Trang's hand in his lap. And then he switched tack and asked us how we were enjoying his country, and Krebes and me had to say the usual tourist stuff about what a beautiful desert he had here, but he wasn't really listening—you could tell he was thinking about something far away. And so then he got on this thing about the founding of Saudi Arabia. He told us for a while about his father Abdul Aziz getting on fire to kick some tribal ass from the Persian Gulf to the Red Sea and unite all the tribes in Arabia. So he told about some battles against the Rasheed, and then he turned to me and said, "It was a great adventure." And I said of course, *Yes sir, it does sound like old Abdul Aziz had some great adventures.* And then he asks me if we feel like we are on a great adventure into Kuwait, and again, I'm like, *Yes sir.*

But it was a trick question. The king put it to his retainers, sort of like, *was Abdul Aziz on a great adventure?* And *they* knew enough to hold their tongues, and it was clear the king was just itching to lay on us the truth about Abdul Aziz. So then he told us. He said, "Some foreigners forgot about Abdul Aziz's faith in Allah. Without faith in Allah, would there have been this 'adventure'?" We all chimed in with a big "No Way," as there was something about the king that made you sort of respect him and go with his line of thought. And then the king turned and looked at Trang real hard, and Trang had been looking at him the whole time like he made a certain amount of sense. The king looked at us and said, "This man looks like Abdul Aziz in the eyes!" Mahdi made it clear this was a simply amazing statement coming from the king, and Krebes and me could see that too, and nodded and smiled and so forth.

And then the king headed into some strange and unrelated territory. He went on this riff about how America was a country that was into the disease of *fact*. That we were sick with facts. He said Saudis didn't give a hoot about facts. And then the king got kind of sad and said when he was a boy everyone sat around and told stories at night. He asked us why this was so, but before we could answer he said it was because there was *hardship*! He said now no one told stories anymore because there was no hardship—and thus it was very *lucky* to have such hardship, for from it come stories! He said when you have a story to tell *then you are a man!* Without a story, *you are a ghost!* He waved his hands to the sky and said the pilots would return with no story to tell, but that we were lucky to be heading in *on the ground* to Kuwait, for we would surely look into *the very eyes of the Iraqi enemy.* The king started slapping Trang's leg and kind of yelling, "You will go to Kuwait! And, *inshallah,* if you live you will return with a story to tell! And die a happy man!"

The king then went on about how *he* would like to come on our adventures to Kuwait. After all that hedging on the word 'adventure', he just tossed it out there, but whatever. And then the king pointed to the sky and said he thought our pilots were not brave, for true bravery can only come when two men meet on camel to do battle. He said it pained him war no longer called on true men of great heart, but was now a matter of machinery and science and facts. He reached into Trang's robe and said he felt Trang had a great heart, but that he would still need *more heart* to save the princess Lulu and kill Saddam Hussein. I asked where Trang might find the extra heart, and the king said it was a gift from Allah, and mumbled some *inshallahs* under his breath, and ordered some sand brought in, which when poured in his royal hand, he like threw in the direction of Kuwait. Mahdi said this was something old Abdul Aziz used to do before battle, toss a little sand in the eyes of the enemy. Trang put out his hand, and the king ordered a bucket of sand brought in, and Trang tossed a good handful toward Kuwait, and everybody laughed and cheered, and the feelings ran real positive in the royal tent as we all tossed some sand toward the enemy in Kuwait.

The king then turned to face Tommy Trang and got serious as hell and said the success or failure of our adventure into Kuwait was basically all up to Allah, and not up to us at all. This was kind of depressing to me, as I thought even if we were AWOL, we were still highly trained reconnaissance marines, and I doubted even Allah had our kind of expertise at infiltrations of hostile environments. I was thinking on this, when the king sailed off on a riff that produced the first bad feelings. He was repeating that everything was up to Allah like we didn't get it the first time, and then for some reason he got on how in the Koran God tells Abraham to take his son Ishmael up on a hill and slay him, and Abraham was ready to do this, with the knife raised and all. I had always thought Abraham a complete *nutcase* for coming even that close to knifing his son, but whatever. The king's point was everybody had to do what God demanded them to do, and God must have demanded Tommy Trang go to Kuwait, *or why would we be going?* This was crazy to me, but I was trying to be polite and didn't say we were on our way to Kuwait *because my man Tommy Trang was so hot for Princess Lulu his balls were about to explode into blue flame.* But right then as I was holding my tongue old Euclid Krebes spoke up and told the king that the son Abraham was going to kill was *not* Ishmael, but his second son *Isaac. Whoa! You would of thought the royal tent had collapsed on our heads!* The king was choking and coughing on the hubbly-bubbly and turning red as hell, and all the retainers are grumbling when Mahdi translated the Ishmael/Isaac bone.

The king finally pulled himself together, and tried to mend some fences, and said he and us infidels had basically the same main cast of good guys like Joseph, Moses, David and Solomon and even Jesus—except, the king added with a glance at Krebes, in their religion the man Muhammad was numero uno. Well, I elbowed old Krebes, but he just had to beg to differ, and told the king he was cool they had essentially the same starting lineup, but that Jesus was the pitcher and Muhammad was maybe in the bull pen.

Well, that was the end of us hanging with the king of Saudi Arabia. We had to hustle out of the royal tent, gather the Sulluba, and hit the happy trail for Kuwait.

CHAPTER 10

So we finally headed off toward Kuwait with the Sulluba and a dozen camels. Nobody said much as we trudged out of the sandy desert and onto some ugly gravel plains. Mahdi said we were heading for the Wadi al-Batin, and Krebes said this was a dry streambed that during the Ice Age was a huge river. Krebes' info about it being a river long ago in the Ice Age upset most of the Sulluba, except for the chick who had done the sword dance with Krebes back before we saw the king. She was clearly still totally hot on Krebes, and he kept grinning at her. Anyway, the Wadi al-Batin wasn't a river anymore, which was too bad, because we had been able to carry away only so much water from the king's desert compound, as we had been in sort of a rush to depart.

That first day in the desert I saw Trang take out the pearl and look at it lying in his palm like it was a compass or something. He saw me staring at him and stashed the pearl. That night we all slept lightly. And about five in the A.M., we were awoken by the air war overhead. There were dozens of planes streaking home from Baghdad. I was jumping around in the chill of the dawn cheering them on and praying for their safe return. I was like doing a crazy war dance in the sand, and then I saw Mahdi and the Sulluba were out of their tents and staring at me like I was nuts, but I didn't care at all, and just danced a wilder dance for them. You could see the AWACS circling high in the sky as dawn came up, and I was thinking about the geniuses who could keep this sky circus aloft. I talked to Krebes about the wave of warplanes that had gone over, and he said there were F/A-18 Hornets and A-6 Intruders and British Tornadoes.

So Trang and Krebes and me were all pretty psyched to get a move on toward Kuwait that morning. We hustled the Sulluba through the coffee thing, as it was clear the Bedouins thought they had all morning to argue about proper bean-frying and cardamom. But as we were about to break camp, little Ali came up to me and asked to have a word. He took me behind the camels and asked me *if I knew why the Sulluba were taking us to Kuwait.* I said they were friends of Mahdi, but Ali just spit on the ground. Ali said the Sulluba had never had plans to come with us to Kuwait as Mahdi had promised, but that the king of Saudi Arabia had gotten wind of the situation and *ordered them to attend to us.* I said that was pretty fine of the king, given that we had left him on such shaky terms regarding the status of his Muhammad the Prophet. Ali asked me to send Mahdi packing as well as the Sulluba as they were all thieves and bad. He said that the Sulluba were generally known as the scum of the Bedouin, and had no desert experience, but lived in towns and did dances and even sold their women for money. Ali kept spitting on the ground and saying we would all have our throats cut if we stuck with Mahdi and the Sulluba.

We shoved off right then, so there was no time to do anything about this right away. Maybe I didn't say anything because I thought it was so cool to be traveling with Bedouin of any sort to Kuwait, even if they were scum. After we had trudged on the Sulluba's camels a ways, I went to report Ali's news to my man Trang, but first I came on Krebes. On the back of his camel was the wild sword-dancing Sulluba woman. She had her arms around Krebes, who gave me a big toothy smile like he was in paradise already. I glanced at the Sulluba on the other camels, and they seemed dubious as hell that Krebes and one of their ladies were hitting it off.

So then I got my camel up to Trang, and Mahdi was tight to his side on another camel, and they were having a good laugh about Krebes and the Sulluba woman. I decided not to tell Trang right then what little Ali said, because everything seemed pretty cool. I never did tell Trang what Ali said, I guess because as I said, deep down I didn't want to send the Sulluba packing, both because it was useful for our mission to travel with Bedouin and because—as I have said—it was just *so cool.* But I *almost* told him once later in the day, but at the moment I opened my mouth, my man Trang pointed to this Sulluba riding off on his camel ten yards away from us as if to say, *check out that dude.* And the thing was this Sulluba had pieces of cloth hanging from his nostrils. They were little plugs, and you might not have noticed them right away, but they were there. So Trang asked Mahdi, and he said, "It is because we smell."

"*We* smell?" I said. "What about that dude? Has he showered lately?"

Mahdi shook his head. "It is not a smell that can be washed away. We are all *hadjar* to him and so our smell is an abomination. *Hadjar* means 'people of the city.'"

"But I heard he lives in the city."

Mahdi glanced at me and said, "This is true."

"So does he wear the rags in his nose all the time?"

Mahdi shook his head and said, "It is curious."

"Why is it curious?" I said. "Why is he doing it?"

Mahdi tilted his head and then closed his eyes. I guess he was thinking. Then he opened his eyes wide and said something to the Sulluba with the plugs in his nose. I guess he couldn't figure it out, so he decided to ask the guy directly, which made sense. Mahdi listened and said nodding, "He said he has not been in the desert in many years like this as we are today. But now it is all coming back to him as we travel by camel as in the old days and he is feeling purified by the desert, and he has taken deep breaths of the desert, and as he has done so he has become revolted by the smell of *hadjar,* just as were his fathers in the old days. He thanks you for the blessings you have brought to him of his past, and understands there is nothing to be done about your smell, and says, *inshallah,* it is God's will some smell like the fresh leavings of dogs."

It was then that the Sulluba with the nose plugs sort of swatted his camel good and raced ahead of us whooping it up into the distance. I looked at Mahdi and asked if this was part of some ancient tradition, or whether the dude had just ditched us smelly *hadjar* for good. It was clear by his expression Mahdi hadn't a clue. So the Sulluba with the nose plugs was lost ahead of us over the horizon, and Mahdi nodded and said *Inshallah, like if he was gone he was gone, and why worry about it?*

Little Ali was listening to all this smell talk, and said to Trang, "Princess Lulu said your smell was the sign that you were the true one for her."

Krebes and me were like, *Trang's smell?*

Trang was like, to us, *so what's wrong with my smell, dudes?*

And Ali said the princess Lulu was not talking like his *body odor,* but about something called his *rawh.* As best we could make out Princess Lulu was of the opinion Trang's *soul smelled like that of an angel.* It sounded pretty wacky, but Mahdi said it made total sense to him, as Allah was way into smells and sniffing in the Koran. For his part, Trang looked pretty stoked Princess Lulu was talking about him in such a positive way, even if it was about his *rawh.*

And we were not done with smell stuff. Later in the morning. Nose Plugs came whooping back on his camel from the horizon, and it turned out he had found an *oasis.* He told Mahdi it had just come to him, *the smell of the oasis.* I pointed to his nose plugs, and he pointed to his heart and grinned, as if to say I guess that he *smelled the old oasis with his heart.* I think it is sort of weird to mention, but he seemed to be sitting a little taller in the saddle on his return, like he had gotten more noble or something in the last few hours.

Mahdi hopped down off his camel when we got to the oasis, and sure enough there was an old leather-lined trough just like at the last oasis, and once again Mahdi went on about how cool it was to see an old leather trough. He said seeing *two* ancient leather-lined troughs in one trip was like a sign of special fortune from Allah, like Allah was guiding our trip, and the signs of his favor were these old troughs. And that was when there was a bit of a sticking point. It turned out that the Sulluba men were beginning to feel like it *was* the old days, and that things ought to be done like in the days of their fathers. And the deal in those days was that a *woman* should be the one to ride a camel that pulled the rope that pulled up the bucket from the well. This point of view was clearly put forth by the Sulluba with the nose plugs, although it was tough keeping a straight face with his nose plugs waving around as he laid it on everyone real seriously about the need for a chick to ride the camel to yank up the bucket. But all the chicks were just sitting on the sands like as to say, *no way on the bucket, Nose Plugs.*

At first the *larger* problem—and it turned out there was one other than this bucket standoff—with the Sulluba ladies was unclear, as Mahdi was off praying, and Ali was sitting in the desert with his back to the whole scene. It was clear enough all the Sulluba women were waging a sit-down protest, and none was going to ride the camel to drag up the bucket, but it was unclear *why* they were vetoing the bucket yanking. And then Nose Plugs started pointing to the Sword Dancing Sulluba chick and Euclid Krebes more directly, and it became clear he was down on the obvious magnetic attraction between the two, and had tried to lay down some ancient Bedouin law about getting it on with infidels, and then I understood the Sulluba ladies had sided with the Sword Dancing chick that she could party down with Krebes if that was her will. I had a definite sense that Sulluba ladies were used to doing their own thing, and were real surprised and put out Nose Plugs was drawing a line in the sand. And that made me wonder if little Ali was right, that these Sulluba Bedouin ladies were otherwise the roadhouse girls of the desert. Anyway, I put the problem to Euclid Krebes, and he nodded and dragged his own camel over, tied on the bucket rope, hopped on, pulled Sword Dancer aboard, and yanked up the bucket until all the camels were watered. He made solid friends right then with the Sulluba ladies, who did some excellent *ululating* for him, but got on Nose Plugs' bad side.

By the time we stopped that evening, everything seemed mellow again, and it even seemed the Sulluba men were in good spirits and forgetting they were just a Bedouin dancing troupe that lived in the city. It was like they were all following Nose Plugs' lead and remembering the pleasures of cruising the desert under the big sky. You could just feel the joy coming from them as they put up the tents singing ancient tent-raising songs. Nose Plugs was leading them in the songs, and it was like a bunch of people remembering Christmas songs—some of them like Nose Plugs remembered all the words, and some mumbled through it, but they all kicked in on the refrain.

After the tents were raised, Nose Plugs gathered the Sulluba around and told tales of Sulluba heroism from way long ago. Mahdi tried to translate these stories, but he got so into the stories he'd forget to translate, and we'd miss so much that after a while we told him to be quiet and just listened to the Bedouin hero stories as best we could in the original Arabic under the desert sky. Trang said this was probably the way Captain Shakespear spent many a desert evening, and at that mention of the heroic Captain Shakespear, Krebes and me slapped each other five.

Before we fell asleep, Trang said to me he kept thinking about the sandy desert in the Rub' al-Khali, and how cool it would be to take Princess Lulu and just roam around those empty sands on a camel with her for the rest of their days. I guess he was basing this idea on what we had heard about Lulu growing up spending a lot of time with the Bedouin, and figuring she'd like that freewheeling desert lifestyle. But it worried me some too, as you kind of got the sense Trang was thinking: *if I rescue Lulu from Kuwait, what next?* I mean it was clear they couldn't stay in Kuwait or Saudi Arabia. I guess they could go back to America, but there was the question of us being AWOL, and maybe Trang was thinking too if Lulu was *real into the desert* maybe she wouldn't like a lot of America. So I said that maybe the two of them could like live in the Mojave Desert or Death Valley or something, if Lulu *had* to be near a desert. I guess Trang was asleep, because he didn't say anything. And after Trang had fallen asleep, Krebes said it was his considered opinion Trang was like a basket case with thinking all the time about Princess Lulu. Then the genius Euclid Krebes sort of quietly sang this stuff that follows. I made him teach it to me the next day, as I thought it real solid if old-fashioned-sounding stuff, and worthy of memory:

> *But he, his own affections counselor,*
> *Is to himself—I will not say how true—*
> *But to himself so secret and so close,*
> *So far from sounding and discovery,*
> *As is the bud bit with an envious worm*
> *Ere he can spread his sweet leaves to the air*
> *Or dedicate his beauty to the sun*

The reason I liked this so much was that it not only covered how Trang was now, but also covered how he was when we hooked up with Princess Lulu. I mean on account of Princess Lulu I'd have to say Trang later on got to totally *spread his sweet leaves and dedicate his beauty to the sun.* And I didn't totally understand it yet, but Trang's beauty was the beauty of a true warrior.

Anyway, Nose Plugs kind of slid over to us in the dawn and rattled in Arabic, and Mahdi came over and whispered that Nose Plugs was saying he was pretty sure we were being followed by some other *hadjar.* Trang and me sat up, holding our M16s, and Mahdi said, "I think it is Colonel Fawwaz's men."

We didn't even know Mahdi knew about Colonel Fawwaz, but he had known about Princess Lulu, so I guess it made sense he knew about the colonel. He made a speech about what a nasty character the colonel was, and it was clear there was bad blood between them. And then Mahdi said kind of in passing the king of Saudi Arabia had told him *a team of Saudi special-forces guys was being led by Colonel Fawwaz into Kuwait to rescue Princess Lulu!* Trang and me were like: *WHAT!* We were all over Mahdi as to why he hadn't told us this news ASAP, and he seemed confused as to why we were so interested, and I have to tell you if this wasn't an example of the mysterious Arab mind, nothing was! So we went after Mahdi to get all the details, and from the little he let on it seemed the king of

Saudi Arabia really liked Tommy Trang, had always secretly thought Colonel Fawwaz was a royal pain in his ass, and that the king's general point of view on the whole enchilada was: *Inshallah!*

In this case, *inshallah!* seemed to boil down to: *let the guy with the biggest brass nuggets between his legs win the girl!* And then Mahdi was urging us to get our asses going toward Kuwait, and I was like: *hold on there Mahdi!* And I wasn't going to move another foot until I had a question answered: why the hell *exactly* was *Mahdi* coming along? And Mahdi hemmed and hawed again and laid on us about honor and heroism and the esteem of the al-Murrah Bedouin, but I wasn't buying it, although he stormed about like he was real insulted. And then it slowly leaked out of Mahdi that the king of Saudi Arabia had promised him and the Sulluba a serious monetary reward if Tommy Trang was successful in rescuing Princess Lulu. So Tommy Trang was like: *you mean the king of Saudi Arabia is like sponsoring our team?*

And that *was* the deal: *the king of Saudi Arabia was sponsoring Team Trang.* Actually, it turned out all Mahdi had to do to collect his reward was to return with the *story* of what went down in Kuwait. And the Sulluba just had to dump us at the gates of Kuwait, and then skedaddle back to Riyadh to get paid by the king. Little Ali came over to me after we moved out of camp that morning, and he seemed relieved to know Mahdi and the Sulluba's motivations were monetary, as he felt this was about the only damn thing that would make them safe to keep around.

You might be wondering about the dudes maybe following us, and if they were Colonel Fawwaz and his Saudi special-forces men. Trang and Krebes and me were planning on doing a area recon to our rear to check them out that morning, but Nose Plugs pulled out his nose rags and like walked back and made a big show of sniffing the desert air and reported back to us that the smell of *hadjar* in the rear was now gone. He said that maybe they had just been a passing Iraqi patrol. *Ah, excuse me dude?* we said to Nose Plugs. *A passing Iraqi patrol,* he repeated. And of course that was when Mahdi passed on the news that we had spent the night in Kuwaiti territory, and had passed over the Saudi-Kuwaiti border, such as it was, sometime in the previous afternoon. He hadn't bothered to tell us about the border, and we couldn't get a straight answer as to *why* he hadn't, and he got in a big huff and riffed some *inshallahs* at us and waved his arms at the expanse of the desert, and when I kept pressing he took my M16 and dragged a line in the sand and sort of motioned for me to step over it, as if to say, *there is your border, happy now?*

So Mahdi was for the first time getting kind of cranky, and when I thought on it, I decided it was because we *were* in Kuwait and it was kind of stressing him out to think there were *real* Iraqis around. Mahdi wasn't the only one who was changed by being on the Kuwaiti side of the border. Euclid Krebes told me a couple of times as we packed up and got the Sulluba going again *that we were all going to die.* He said this with a grin, and slapped his M16 and said, *locked and loaded!* And Krebes liked to point to Tommy Trang, who was out scouting ahead of us on that old camel Abdul Aziz, and who would circle back to us and tell us to *move it out, move it people,* and you could see Trang was feeling *unbelievably* stoked he was finally in enemy Iraqi territory and on a real mission and closer to rescuing Princess Lulu. You know, the more nutty and dangerous things got as we went deeper into this infiltration, the more Trang looked like a surefooted surfer up on the mighty wave he was riding.

Anyway, just after prayers for the Islamics in our raiding party a few hours later, we came upon the enemy. We had saddled up again on the camels, and Trang was out front a hundred meters, when he turned around and signaled with a closed fist for us to stop. And like a hundred meters ahead of Trang these two Iraqi soldiers were standing there. They had just emerged from a trench in the sand. And Trang made no move to get off his camel Abdul Aziz, and we were all frozen in place, and then those two Iraqis *made their move!* They flopped on their backs and kicked their legs in the air and waggled their hands. None of us moved, as I think we were all thinking the same thing: *they've released some biological toxins by accident on their own position!* But then they stood up and waved to us, and jumped up and down, and then flopped on their backs again. And that was when Krebes said, "They look like dying cockroaches!" And that was exactly what they looked like, and we all had a good laugh, and our whole party followed Trang's lead in advancing on these two dying cockroaches, who were now waving shreds of white cloth at us.

As we came closer to them they reached into their bunker, and they pulled out their rifles. This stopped us, but they just had those rifles long enough to fling them in our direction, and then they ran toward the rifles and started kicking them around the desert angrily and glancing at us, and then kicking them around some more. Then more dying cockroach, and more white flag waving. Trang got there ahead of us, and they scrambled across the desert floor on their knees and grabbing his ankles started gibbering in Arabic and I guess begging for mercy. Krebes got off his camel and did the right thing by checking them for concealed weapons, and then he made to bind their hands behind their backs with some rope he got off one of the camels, but Trang told him not to bother, as they were clearly miserable, starving creatures. The look on Trang's face as he looked at these two begging for mercy to him was one of like total surprise mixed with some serious sadness, and I guess he had imagined a fiercer and more noble enemy.

We didn't actually know what to *do* with our two Iraqi prisoners of war, and were kind of on this topic when I saw one of the Iraqis pointing back toward Kuwait City and gibbering on, and right then this thing sort of flies over our heads. That was the first time the Iraqis started grinning, when I walked over and picked up an *arrow*. The shaft was white fiberglass, like a surveyor would use to mark land, and the arrowhead was some metal cut from a food can. I scratched my head and handed the arrow to Euclid Krebes, who handed it to Trang. And we all looked to where it came from, and the Iraqis made it clear there was one soldier over there, and this dude was *afraid to surrender*. Little Ali talked to our two Iraqis, and the Iraqis said until recently they had been kept in their trench by these roving bands of Iraqi enforcers called the Mukharabat, who executed anyone they found away from their trench, and also by a fear of us Americans, who they had been told would like torture them to death by slow roasting over an open fire.

Right then another arrow came toward us, but this one had been shot kind of high, and was sort of drifting and wobbling in the air. Trang leaned out and plucked the arrow from the sky just before it hit the ground, and this impressed the Sulluba Bedouin mightily, and they *ululated* for him. Mahdi turned to me right after Trang snagged the arrow and said, *the arrows of fate, they do not miss.* I gave Mahdi a confused look and Mahdi snapped at me, *these are words from the Koran. Allahu Akbar!* Anyway, Trang then walked toward the solo Iraqi's trench waving the arrow, and when he got about halfway there he made a big show of snapping it over his leg and holding the broken ends aloft. Little Ali ran up next to Trang and started yelling at the Iraqi dude in the trench that he would come to no harm, and then the two Iraqi prisoners ran up and did the same, and then they ran ahead to the trench, but when they got there they sat down and sobbed.

There was a dude in there, and he had sliced his own throat with the top off a metal can, and was still pumping blood down his chest and it was just one unholy mess. I guess he was brother to one of our Iraqi prisoners, who got down there in the trench and held him like a baby and sobbed. The other prisoner told Ali how the Iraqi brothers had been taken from their house at night to be made into soldiers, and told if they failed their family would be strangled to death. After a while my man Trang got down in the trench with Ali and the other Iraqi, and they sort of talked and tried to pull the sobbing guy away from his brother. The Iraqi guy didn't want to let go, so they sort of wrestled, and Trang and little Ali came up pretty bloody.

Well, we gave one Iraqi prisoner a canteen of water, even though it was like almost our last one, and some proper white cloth for waving. And we told the Iraqi that when his pal was done with his heavy grieving for his brother, to walk him to Saudi Arabia. Trang had a note made up by Ali in Arabic and English explaining that these two had surrendered to him, Thomas Trang, USMC, and they were to be treated in accord with the Geneva Convention and the Red Cross and fair and square. Krebes wondered if it was wise to alert everyone in our military we were in country illegally, and that was when it became clear Trang expected our infiltration to be such a roaring success that when it was over we would all be embraced back into the military fold with all sorts of honors, and that notes like this one sent back with the prisoners would become like part of the historical record and kept behind glass in the First Marine Expeditionary Force Museum. Euclid Krebes went off again on HUBRIS, and how Trang's head was so big it was a wonder he could carry it on his shoulders.

My man Tommy Trang's HUBRIS impressed the hell out of one little person, and that was Ali. When we pulled out and left the prisoner Iraqis, he was up on the camel Abdul Aziz sitting behind Trang. We rode for a long time without stopping then, because Tommy Trang was on fire to get to Kuwait. After a couple of hours under the insane desert sun, some of the Sulluba were kind of slumping in their saddles, I guess as a dancing troupe in the city they had lost some of their historical desert fortitude. Trang started belting out some traditional Marine Corps marching jodies from up on his camel to like get the Sulluba in the martial mood, and it worked for a while, but then the Sulluba slumped in their saddles again. And then there was some weird curse or something, because everyone started scratching their crotches, men and women alike. Mahdi said there were no bugs in the desert, but we all disagreed. He yelled the bugs were in our imagination, but he was scratching as fiercely as any of us.

And then the itch went away as quickly as it had come, and we went back to being a band of Sulluba Bedouin out in the desert west of Kuwait City. See, that was the thing. We were making like Bedouin just doing their desert thing regardless of the war, so we were traveling in this big loop, like we had no interest in Kuwait City at all, but were strictly desert wanderers. It was crazy to me that anyone would buy that Bedouin would be out here with the bombs and all, but later that afternoon Nose Plugs pointed to a small band of camels way north on the horizon.

Toward sunset, I kicked my camel and got up near Trang and Ali on old Abdul Aziz in the lead, and I near fell off my camel as I listened to Tommy Trang the Vietnamese American marine. He was going on and on about—no joking—*the Bill of Rights.* He was running over those rights backward and forward and getting Ali to recite them. I rode back and told Krebes about Trang rattling on about the Bill of Rights in such a stoked way, and he didn't think it as strange as me, and kicked his camel up to join in the conference and throw in his genius ten cents. I guess I was kind of embarrassed, as my Californian family was American as far back as anyone could remember, and I couldn't have told you squat about the Bill of Rights. Anyway, that was the beginning of Trang's education of little Ali as to *why* America was totally worth laying down your life for as a marine.

Ali, Krebes, and Trang passed the time up there wrestling with the Bill of Rights, and I guess they weren't looking ahead as much, because it was Nose Plugs who spotted something in the desert sands ahead. It looked like a small black plane had crashed in the desert, and as we got closer it looked more like a little missile that got crunched up. The writing on it was in English. We all got off our camels and circled around the thing and speculated some as to whether it was a missile or a little plane. If it was a plane, about the only thing that could of piloted it was a *monkey.* I thought to glance at Krebes, and of course I saw he knew what it was but was waiting for someone to ask him, so I asked and he said, *it's a drone, man.*

I was like, " 'Drone'?"

Krebes looked at me like I was an idiot. "Little fake airplane we sent in before the *real* planes with live *pilots* got sent in."

"What did we send them for?"

"So Saddam would like *think* they were planes with live pilots and turn on his radar systems and light up his missile sites so we could see where they were and then the planes with pilots could come in and blast them."

For a while we just broke out what water we could, and the Sulluba and all of us but Trang got off our camels and sat around the drone not saying much at all. Trang stayed up on his camel with Ali like he was waiting for us to get up and get a move on again for Kuwait. I had the feeling—although it wasn't said by

Trang—that he wanted *to get away from the drone*. And I guess I was right, given the short discussion that was to follow. Anyway, then it was clear the sun was setting, and so Krebes and me and Mahdi and the Sulluba lay back on the sand to let that happen, and Trang got down from his camel finally. He walked all around the drone studying it good, and then sat on the tail end of it looking down at us all chilling on the hot sand. Ali stayed up on Trang's camel Abdul Aziz like he was keeping the camel engine running in case Trang wanted to make a quick escape.

After a while I was almost asleep when I heard Trang say to the desert air kind of quietly, "If they don't need pilots for this drone thing, how long till they don't need pilots at all?" No one answered Trang, and I sort of drifted into sleep again, and then Trang said a little louder and woke me up, "And if they don't need pilots, man, how long till they don't need us dudes on the *ground*? How long till they have drone soldiers, robots to do all the *fighting*?"

I opened my eyes enough to see my man Tommy Trang was standing up now. There was a look on his face like he had never been more serious in his life, and he was glaring off toward Kuwait City like a hawk. I guess that explains the difference between Trang and Krebes and me. Because Krebes and me couldn't get any steam up over the issue of drones at all. Krebes and me were damn good marines I guess, and were clearly fired up or nuts or stupid enough to join Tommy Trang on this crazy incursion into Kuwait, but in terms of worrying about the 'big-picture' meaning of drones, Trang was like standing all alone.

And a few minutes later, Trang had us mounting up again, and heading off toward Kuwait in a big hurry. For a while we were galloping the camels, and it was like Trang was afraid if we didn't hurry, the Gulf War would be like over and settled by the drones and the jets and he'd never get a chance to win a congressional Medal of Honor.

CHAPTER 11

When we finally made camp that night, Euclid Krebes went to gather a little brush to burn for coffee. It turned out Krebes was a coffee hound, which was good as it was mostly what the Sulluba had to offer in terms of supplies. There wasn't much to burn in this scrabbly, gravelly desert, but when Krebes wandered back with what little he had found to burn, *the Sulluba lost their minds!* The Sulluba were both furious and looking scared at the brush in Krebes' hands. It turned out Krebes had yanked out the *ausaj* bush, and that this *ausaj* bush was protected by jinns, and that these little jinn-trolls got mighty pissed when their *ausaj* was abused. The Sulluba looked at Krebes like: *what will you do now to make the jinns chill?* And Euclid Krebes settled in to make coffee after shaking the bush in Nose Plugs' face and saying: *inshallah!* Trang and me thought that *inshallah* was pretty funny, as it was as if Krebes was saying, *Allah Wills the Coffee From this Ausaj Bush, So Deal!*

The Arabs were constantly tossing *inshallah* in our faces whenever things got screwed up, so it was nice to toss an *inshallah* back in their camp. But man, they had no sense of humor when it came to Allah. And since we were on the topic of screwing up, when Krebes had his coffee made, he got into the topic with Mahdi of: *where the heck was Kuwait City?* The problem was we marines had no map and no compass, which was a screwup, but we hadn't expected to head out when we had for Kuwait. Plus, at the time we headed out we thought we were with experienced desert Bedouin, and not a dance troupe from the city, such as were the Sulluba.

So Krebes took a sip of java and opined to Mahdi that he and the Sulluba were afraid of Iraqis, and so leading us further north into the empty desert. Mahdi laughed, and then got angry when he saw Krebes was serious, and said *by Allah he would never do such a thing,* but that they were cleverly circling in a wide loop so as we would look like traditional Bedouin. Nose Plugs jammed his finger over Krebes' head and said in the morning we would see Kuwait City, by the will of Allah. And Krebes nodded and said *he hoped Allah knew where the hell Kuwait City was because nobody else seemed to,* and that was when Nose Plugs let loose with a whole lot of anger directed toward Krebes, and Mahdi let on that Nose Plugs was still not happy with the friendship of Euclid Krebes and the Sword Dancing Sulluba lady, and that the relationship should go no further toward any international boogie-woogie in the sands, or Nose Plugs was going *to show some ancient Bedouin wrath.*

Sword Dancing Sulluba lady had spent that whole day riding on the back of Krebes' camel with her arms about his waist, and although they didn't say much to each other without Ali's help, it was clear Euclid Krebes felt he had found the *real deal* and it seemed Sword Dancer felt the same way about her big redheaded redneck genius marine. At one point Krebes insisted little Ali try to tell Sword Dancer that he, Krebes, *was soaring on Cupid's Wings,* and Sword Dancer looked pretty baffled but pleased. Ali told me he used the word *Locust* for Cupid, but as I said, Sword Dancer got the basic idea. It wasn't that strange, marines throughout history were always falling for the locals, and dragging them back to the states. Krebes had already rode up to Trang a dozen times this morning to thank him for like inventing this expedition, as it led to his meeting Sword Dancer.

That night we were all hanging by the little coffee fire deep in a pit in the sand, and man, could you ever see the stars out here in the desert when the wind blue the haze from Saddam's oil fires away! Mahdi checked out my interest in the night sky and whispered in my ear, *Are you harder to create, or the heaven He built?* I was like, *hitting me with the Koran again, Mahdi?* And Mahdi was real pleased with my guess and tossed me a stoked, *Allahu akbar!* But right then Sword Dancer jammed a knife with some violence into the sand and announced—with Ali as translator—that she just *had to lay on us the dream she had the night before she met us.* The Sulluba guys looked real serious, like Sword Dancer's dreams were a real big deal. So we infidel marines were cool with a little campfire story, and were like *lay on us your mighty dream, O Sword Dancer!*

So Sword Dancer told us her dream, as follows: She was doing the Bedouin thing in the desert, and she saw a dude pulling water from a secret watering hole in like Jarrab. This dude was wearing golden armor. He had the beautiful face of a noble warrior except for a sword wound on his cheek, and the fact he was an infidel foreigner. He was beautiful she repeated, but sweating, as you don't wear golden armor in the desert with half a brain. So he was *sweating,* Sword Dancer repeated a third time—as if we marines were idiots—and in great need of water, to slake his *mighty thirst,* and yanking away at a rope made of real silver that reached down into the secret watering hole. That was cool, a rope made of real silver, and I told Sword Dancer I liked that and the golden armor best about her story. I might have made a crack about *her secret watering hole,* but she was Euclid Krebes' chick now.

Anyway, in her dream Sword Dancer told Sir Golden Knight he would be cooler if he would take off his golden armor in the desert, but he ignored her and kept yanking away at the silver rope which was already piled mightily at his feet. Sword Dancer said she figured the knight had been dragging up that silver rope for days, and yelling to the desert about how mightily thirsty he was to drink from the *special well.*

At this point Sword Dancer paused and walked over to Tommy Trang where he was sitting by the fire. She inspected him good, reaching in his robe and giving his nipples a squeeze, and messing with his grin like she was checking a horse's teeth. She said she was looking for *certain marks.* She pulled his robe off his shoulders and kind of let out a war whoop, and I guess that was one of the marks she was looking for: *the blue knight tattoo on his back.* She gave the knight tattoo a slap, and then looked real sad and plopped down on the sands. She pulled at her blond hair and *ululated* for us, and then she chilled and went back to her dream.

Sword Dancer went on about Sir Golden Knight and the Sacred Well. But now as she told the story she was on her knees like ten inches from Trang's nose, and weeping. Trang grinned at me like *is this Arab lady great, or what?* Anyway, Sword Dancer told Trang she was sure glad he wasn't wearing verses from the Koran in a leather bag around his neck the way some Bedouin do, as these same verses can stop her powers from working, and Trang needed her powers. Trang said he would never wear Koran verses in a leather pouch around his neck to stop her powers, and this relieved Sword Dancer. She said in the dream she pleaded with Sir Golden Knight not to drink from the sacred well, as it would kill him. She said she told him she would bring him something cool to drink from the bottles on her camel, and that he should take off his armor. But the Golden Knight dude ignored her, and kept yanking on that silver rope, and Sword Dancer stood by watching, and around sunset the old bucket came bouncing up the side of the well. The knight pulled harder when he heard the bucket, but when it came up the knight fell to his knees vomiting, and the head of a beautiful young woman rolled across the sand. Sir Golden Knight soon expired, as Sword Dancer couldn't get him out of his armor, and plus he was full of grief and his heart broken, as he loved the beautiful young woman on seeing her face in the bucket.

Well, then Sword Dancer finishes off this like Golden Knight dream stuff by saying, *Tommy Trang should stay away from the princess Lulu and leave Kuwait right now.* Well, that was a great story! I mean, it took us right back to old Arabia to have this wild story told around the campfire like we were on an ancient *ghazzu!*

So nobody had a *better* story than that one from Sword Dancer, so for a while nobody talked much to anyone, and after a while we all decided to crash. I admit I was kind of wondering if Trang had like been weirded out by Sword Dancer's dream, so I asked him. Trang shook his head, but something was on his mind. So we both lay there on the sands, and then he said into the desert night, *I'm sick from her beauty, man, you know? And I'm getting sicker every day. I'm going to die, man, if I don't get to Kuwait City and see Lulu soon.* So this was a really *totally* surprising statement coming from an ass-kicking jarhead marine like Trang, and I was like, *yeah, man. Ah, we'll do what we can to get you to Kuwait City. You hang tough there, bro.* I was kind of wondering if the weird poetry stuff Euclid Krebes had been recently spouting was like totally messing with his head. I mean: *sick from her beauty?* That didn't sound at all like my man Tommy Trang. But maybe Krebes was right and Trang had been feeling this lovesick all along, and the love acid in him was like just leaking out now.

So then we all crashed, but we were soon awoken by this yelling and I think just about everyone sat bolt upright and grabbed their weapons. And then I started to laugh, because it was Euclid Krebes out there under the desert sky slam-dancing with Sword Dancer. And man, *they were full of the juice of life!*

Sometimes it sounded like they were scampering around the desert and nipping at each other like desert dogs, and then like the desert floor was rumbling, and then a whole lot of ululating and groaning from Sword Dancer, and lots of calling on Jesus Christ by Krebes and who the hell knows what Sword Dancer was saying next, but whatever it was it was said at *high decibel,* and she was alerting every Iraqi in the desert for thirty klicks that she was a Sulluba getting the love sword from an American marine here in the desert!

So this howling of Krebes and Sword Dancer went on and on, and it became clear none of the rest of us were sleeping, so one by one we got up and sat by the embers of the coffee fire. Everyone was there finally except for Nose Plugs, and it was good to see all present grinning at the sounds of love, especially when they really shot the moon. After a while Trang and me started to clap, like to show our appreciation for a good *ululation* from Sword Dancer, or some sort of gonzo marine *oooraah* yell from Euclid Krebes. It was good to see Trang wasn't so *sick from her beauty* that he like lost his sense of humor.

And Mahdi the Messiah piped up during a lull and said he had been taught by an old al-Murrah Bedouin dude how to tell from a woman's footsteps in the desert whether she was a virgin or not, and he went on at some length trying to explain how sex changed the way a woman walked, and the other Sulluba dudes were way into this, and wanted to know all about this lost art of virgin detection. And that led the Sulluba guys to get on a riff about the virtue of their ladies—except for Sword Dancer mind you—and how if anyone tried to touch one of their ladies—except for Sword Dancer for her virtue was, *inshallah*, clearly a thing of the past and was never that intact anyway—*there would be hell to pay!*

And then I saw some of the Sulluba guys glancing at each other, and I wondered if this line of thought about revenge had them wondering where *Nose Plugs was at right now.* I said something to Mahdi, who said Nose Plugs was being tended by the other Sulluba ladies in their tent, and he wasn't feeling too well. And the next morning it was clear Nose Plugs was feeling a lot worse, and Trang and me were getting a lot of dark looks from the Sulluba.

So I went and talked to Mahdi, who said for some reason Krebes had followed Sword Dancer into her tent late at night when their passion was like finally spent, and that Krebes *had tripped over the sick Nose Plugs.* Mahdi gave me a significant look.

"So what does this all mean?" I said.

"It has made him much sicker, this touch of the foot of Krebes."

"Why so?"

"It is a Sulluba belief that those who have sex are unclean until they have washed. So Krebes was unclean, and his touch has made the sickness grow."

It came out that the Sulluba were now united that the only way for Nose Plugs to survive his sickness was to keep Krebes and Sword Dancer from doing the wild thing for a while, and Trang was the one who decided to tell Krebes. It didn't go all that well with Krebes, and you could hear his point of view was that it was time to dump the damn Sulluba—except for Sword Dancer who was apparently with us for the duration now—and make our way into Kuwait City. But if the message to cease and desist didn't go well with Krebes, it went even worse with Sword Dancer, and you could hear her really screaming at Mahdi off in the desert in the other direction.

So things got complicated for a while. Euclid Krebes wouldn't push on to Kuwait unless Sword Dancer came with us. That was fair enough, and was cool by Trang and me and even Ali. So we were ready to head out—on some camels Mahdi bought for us from the Sulluba—when Krebes motioned to Sword Dancer to climb aboard *his* camel, but she kept staring at the ladies' tent. From inside the tent, Sword Dancer was catching hell from the Sulluba ladies. I looked to Ali, and he said the Sulluba ladies were blaming Sword Dancer for Nose Plugs' illness, and were telling her that *Nose Plugs said he would die if she left with us.* Ali added that Nose Plugs was confessing through the ladies *long held feelings* for *Sword Dancer,* and that the ladies were demanding Sword Dancer remain with them and marry Nose Plugs and continue as part of the dancing troupe.

One look at Sword Dancer and you saw she was pretty pissed and disgusted by all of this stuff coming from the ladies in the tent. She rolled her eyes to the heavens, and flared her nostrils, and violently shook her head. But the pleas kept coming from the tent, and it was getting hotter, *and Kuwait City was waiting!* I looked at Tommy Trang, who gave the word to Krebes that although we needed him, he was free to stay with Sword Dancer. *Whoa!* I guess someone in the tent spoke English, because after some chatter in the tent we got an earful from Nose Plugs himself, although he did sound pretty sick, which as translated by Ali was to say *that Nose Plugs would kill him if that unclean infidel dog Krebes stayed with the Sulluba.*

So there you have it again! Dig a little under the skin of the Arabs, and right away you find out they really think we are *infidel dogs.* Trang and me kind of grinned at each other and shook our heads like, *don't you just hate being called an infidel dog?* Anyway, we were still stuck as to what to do, and Trang and me kind of looked to Euclid Krebes, *who looked at Sword Dancer real sadly.* I mean I've never seen the Redneck Genius Marine so clearly suffering. He got off his camel and strode over and took her in his arms and said stuff like *not to marry Nose Plugs, but to wait for him,* and *he'd come get her when the mission was over and he had helped his friend rescue the princess Lulu as he had promised to do.* Little Ali was like under his eighteen-inch biceps as he held Sword Dancer and translating his love promises.

So I have to say Sword Dancer really let loose with some regret. She wailed and tore her robes some and pulled her hair and dropped to her knees in the sand. And then she stopped all this and just stared hard at the tent where Nose Plugs was, and she let loose with a volley of Arabic, and out marched all the Sulluba ladies to stand in the sun. And then Sword Dancer was inside the tent, and I heard Nose Plugs say something to her that from the sound of it was like words of *love and thanks,* and if I had to translate, I'd say Sword Dancer said sharp in return: *stuff it, Nose Plugs!* There was a lot of kind of whining talk from Nose Plugs and everyone was trying to pretend not to listen and it sounded a little like he was laying on her some *singsong poetry,* and then there was silence.

For like ten minutes we three marines sat there on the camels, looking at the tent and the Sulluba women standing there in a line and up at the hazy sun, and anywhere but at each other. Because I don't think any of us wanted to show in our faces what we each thought had happened in that tent. One of the Sulluba women finally said something to the tent like: *hello, anybody in there?* And still nothing. So finally Krebes got down off his camel and walked toward the tent, and just as he did so, as if on cue, came all this wailing from the Sulluba ladies! Next the Sulluba ladies all rush into the tent, and then started screeching like ten cats in a bag, and Sword Dancer came stumbling out with like the robe just about ripped off her back, and she kind of ran over and hopped up on Krebes' camel and gave an order to all of us that was like, *move it out, marines!*

Tommy Trang and me looked at Krebes, *and he just looked so bummed!* I mean he really looked regretful, like if Sword Dancer had just *chilled* and waited for him back in Saudi Arabia until our mission was accomplished, all would have been so cool, and he could have taken his Arab lady back home to the folks in Georgia. But Krebes just fixed her with this royal sadness, and she started to get it and kicked the camel like as to make it move out, but even the camel turned his head like to look at her sadly. And then all the Sulluba were gathered around Sword Dancer and yelling, and some of them dragged out the body of Nose Plugs from the tent to show us as if we didn't already know, and Krebes reached up and plucked Sword Dancer off his camel and set her on her feet on the sands, and then climbed back up and spurred his ankles into the side of his camel and rode out of camp.

Euclid Krebes never looked back, and after he went a ways, Trang and me followed after him, and we never looked back either. Out of the corner of my eye I could see Mahdi and little Ali were riding on a camel together off to the side. Trang and me kept a distance back from Krebes to like give him some space to breath and consider all the sadness that had just gone down, and then from behind us back in the camp we heard some sounds that made your spine tighten into steel. You just wanted to plug your ears, but the damn sounds carried over the desert a long ways, and the Sulluba seemed to be taking their time about their justice. I never got a chance to ask Krebes if he thought he did the right thing given those terrible sounds from back in the camp we left, all he would say to me when I rode near him on my camel later that afternoon was this: *she made blessed my rude hand.* I will never forget the genius Krebes saying that weird stuff while holding his huge redneck marine hand out to me, as he totally looked like nothing mattered more to him in this world than the status of his *rude hand.*

CHAPTER 12

It struck me that we no longer looked totally Bedouin without the whole Sulluba caravan, but we at least were on camels and in the local robes, and *maybe* we could pass from afar for some wandering Bedouin dudes. Tommy Trang was content for the moment to just follow big Krebes—who was slumped on his camel—across the desert. I guess we were *all* actually pretty glum on account of what just happened with Sword Dancer, and from an American point of view the thing with the *water* kind of finally broke the tragic mood, and got us back in the saddle, so to speak.

I haven't said much about it, but your Arab need to stop *everything* to pray five times a day can really get to be a pain. I mean many of us Americans pray too, but when we have a job to do like slipping into an occupied country to rescue a princess, maybe we do it on the fly. But for your Arab, it has to be this major production. Little Ali seemed to take the Western view on things and praised Allah on his own time as far as I could tell, but Mahdi was big into the *hold everything, I got to hit my knees toward Mecca*. So while we are trying to follow Krebes at a respectful distance Mahdi hits the sands to pray. And I don't know why we didn't just leave him to catch up to *us*, but we waited as Krebes marched on.

And because we were watching Mahdi, hoping he'd finish chatting up Allah ASAP, that was when it became clear he used an awful lot of water in the prayer thing. The dude damn near took a shower. He took water from our last canteen and washed his face, hands, arms up to his elbows, and even his *feet*. This *ablutions* part of the prayer process took most of the time, so we had to gallop the camels after Krebes before settling back to follow him at a distance. And then later in the day Mahdi stopped to do his Allah thing again, and that was when Trang commented that we ought to conserve water or we'd be out of the stuff. And Mahdi said sharply, "Better out of water than out of Allah." And Trang jumped off his camel, and waited until Mahdi finished splashing the water around, and then Trang reached out and touched his arm! Mahdi was furious and spluttering and saying he'd have to do all his ablutions again as he was touched by an infidel, but Trang grabbed the canteen and climbed back up on his camel. And then we headed out pulling Mahdi's camel with us.

I had to glance back to see what Mahdi would do about his ablutions without water, *and he was down on his knees giving himself a sand rubdown!* And then he seemed to whiz through his prayers, and then was running after us. He caught up to us and after catching his breath called Trang an infidel pig and all sorts of probably worse things in Arabic because Ali kept raising his eyebrows and glancing at Trang as if to say: *good thing you don't speak Arabic!*

All the screaming from Mahdi turned Euclid Krebes around, and he trotted back to us. And Krebes kind of looked at Mahdi with wonder, because the Mahdi was so absolutely ballistic about *the interruption of his ablutions and prayers!* And then Mahdi was venting *all sorts* of outrages at us infidels, stuff that was totally unrelated to Tommy Trang's giving him some hell about water usage. As far as I could tell, everything that had ever happened to wrong Mahdi or Saudis or Arabs through the ages *was our fault.* But then the like huge *blame it on the Americans* thing ceased, and Mahdi climbed on the camel, and spurred in his heels and headed out, and then glanced back at us with a look of concern like: *are we going to get the princess in Kuwait, or not?* I looked at Trang, and he was grinning like, *what a goddamn madman was Mahdi!*

That was the cool thing about Tommy Trang. He like didn't get pissed at Mahdi's crazy rant, or take it personally, but just seemed to be attracted to it in a way, like *he was a lucky man to have collected such a crackerjack example of Arab looniness.* Trang appreciated the whole essential Mahdi package in a way that was way beyond Krebes and me: *the Messiah with a Mole thing, the al-Murrah Bedouin rip-off, the vague connection to the dancing Sulluba, the mission to bring a good bedtime story back to the king of Saudi Arabia.* I think Krebes and me would have sent Mahdi packing right about now if this had been just *our* mission.

It was later that afternoon, as we trudged along together, that Mahdi rode up next to me alone. We had finally turned toward the east, so we were making our move toward Kuwait City. Mahdi said nothing, just kept glancing at me. None of us had said much, as I think Sword Dancer's fate, not to mention that Iraqi soldier who slit his throat, was still kind of ruining the vibe. And then after a while Mahdi rode a little closer to me and patted my camel on the neck. And his leg was brushing mine as he rode by my side, and he said, "It is curious."

So I said after a while, "What is, Mahdi?"

And Mahdi nodded and seemed to be glad I had bothered to respond to him. So he continued, "It is interesting about camels."

I waited a minute and then said, "What is interesting about camels, Mahdi?"

He patted me on the back, like my responding had made him sure we were friends. And so he cleared his throat and said, "It is interesting. In the old days a lost camel would find his way to his summer well without fail. But now most camels come from Somalia and so know of no summer well. So if you left one of these camels we are riding here in the desert, what would they do?"

"Look for the nearest oasis?"

Mahdi raised his finger excitedly, "Exactly not! I promise you he would stand right here until he died!"

And with this like lesson on camels, and after a significant look at me—the Arabs can really toss a significant look your way— Mahdi turned his camel and headed to the rear of our little patrol.

And what with Trang teaching little Ali a civics class on America, and Krebes bent out of shape about what went down with Sword Dancer, I was left to wonder about why Mahdi laid this little camel lesson on me. And best I could come up with was Mahdi was maybe like a modern camel, and that he didn't have a summer well anymore so to speak, so he was just wandering around the desert in his life real confused, which would account for all the weird things he had done to pass his days. Then again, maybe he was just crazy.

And then an American plane went over our little camel raiding party. A small transport plane, with the side cargo door open. And I wondered if they had the binoculars out and could tell we were not Bedouin, but I guess they were too busy scattering their load to look close. They were tossing out a few of these tiny boxes on parachutes every once in a while, and one floated right down in our path. I wondered if it was some sort of bomb, but it didn't explode when it hit the ground, but just sat there with its little parachute covering it up. We marched up to it carefully, and then Krebes hopped down off his camel and with the tip of his M16, lifted up the parachute. And there on the sand was a little green boombox radio. So Krebes picked it up, and turned it on carefully, as you still couldn't help wondering if it was a trick. And he turned it on kind of loud, and it was real surprising to hear The Clash's song "Rock the Casbah."

Trang started yelling to *turn it off! turn it off!* But I guess Krebes liked this song, as he just turned it up more, and started doing his redneck's idea of dancing right there in the desert sands. And then we all were grinning, because he was two hundred fifty pounds of real lousy dancer. Plus, it was good to see him dancing and taking a break from being hit so hard by the whole Sword Dancer love thing. While Krebes shook his heavy marine bootie, Trang came over to me on his camel and said, *this radio must be some psyops thing.* For some reason Trang was real down on the radio, and my best guess was because it kind of was like the jets overhead—they ruined the mood of being on an old-fashioned *ghazzu.*

When "Rock the Casbah" was over, an Arabic voice came on and little Ali said the guy was telling the Iraqi soldiers how wrong Saddam was to invade an Arab brother, and giving detailed instructions on how to surrender. Next they played the "Star-spangled Banner," and we all sang it with our hands over our hearts and sitting up straight in the saddle, and pretty much yelling it out over the desert sands. That was a stoking moment, and I still can see Krebes with tears rolling down his cheeks, singing at the top of his leathery lungs. As I might of said, I think Krebes at this point would get the MCP—Most Changed Player—Award for our incursion into Kuwait. I mean the dude was really sort of a redneck bastard when we first met him back at boot camp, and now he was dancing and getting weepy. And the wild thing is I think Krebes was really awake to his speedy changes, and he kept telling me he *blamed Trang* and that it was *all Trang's fault.* You got to understand Krebes said this with a slow smile, and he didn't really *blame* Trang, but was *totally appreciative* of him. Krebes traced his own personal changes way back in time to when Trang first invented the pearl-diving expedition from the USS *Inchon.* I was dubious and said *Trang was just like into grabbing free pearls, man.* And Krebes shook his mighty head like I was a fool and said *Trang was the genius who opened the golden door, Carmichael, and we assholes all walked through.* That was pretty cryptic and way beyond me at the time. Anyway, when the Arabic guy came on with some more about how the Iraqis should surrender, Krebes turned down the radio, and we sang the "Star-spangled Banner" again, and this time Ali got in there with his voice and he seemed to have already memorized the words, so like I said he was a real quick study.

So then we had that amazing *can-do* American mood back totally. And little Ali was clearly on our team, and we busted across the desert deeper into Kuwait in one camel row yelling the marine *oooraah!* Mahdi was kind enough to hang back and not ruin this American moment for the four of us. And we said the usual stuff right then: *like hey, man, I just want to say, whatever happens, I'm proud to have served with you.* And right then Euclid Krebes jumps off his camel and cranks up the radio again and starts into this air-guitar thing there in the desert sands. And the song he is doing the excellent air guitar to is "American Band" by Grand Funk Railroad. He was just jamming on his imaginary guitar to the words:

We're coming to your town!
We'll help you to party down!

Anyway, that song kind of cracked me up, because we *were* sort of an American band, heading to the town of Kuwait, and maybe we would even get a chance to teach the locals to party American-style! And so after his air-guitar performance was over Krebes got back on his camel and we slapped each other five every way you could, which took some camel shuffling. After that even the camels seemed to march a little stronger, like the positive American energy had gone right to their funny-looking heads. And right then I was really thinking hard about Trang, and wondered how this dude had gotten so outrageously fired up about America given his personal history with American marines raping his mother in Vietnam. And so I rode up next to Euclid Krebes, and put the question to him, and he said like it was simple, *roses grow best in shit, man.*

I like wanted Krebes to elaborate, so he told me how half-breed Vietnamese American kids left behind after we pulled out of Saigon got their faces kicked on a daily basis, and had like no *rights* at all—which Krebes figured related to why Trang was so into the Bill of Rights. So then Krebes went drifting off into some heavy Vietnamese history lesson and was losing me, *when we saw the limousine in the sand.* Even from far off you could tell it was a limousine, and Trang headed right for it, I guess he figured maybe Princess Lulu was inside. And as we got closer we could see there were black-clad figures moving around the vehicle. And when we rode up, they came running to us, and they were four Kuwaiti chicks who had been trying to escape from occupied Kuwait. They knew nothing about Princess Lulu. Trang right away started digging like a happy dog at one of the wheels. The rest of us men joined in the digging, except Mahdi who opted out I guess on account of being a potential messiah, and who instead talked to the gals and found out they had been stuck for four days, and without water for two.

One of the gals then opened her hands and started to pray, and Trang asked Ali what she was saying, and he said she was thanking Allah for rescuing them from the forces of evil.

"Tell her," said Trang, taking a breather from his digging, "that *Allah* didn't rescue her. Tell her she's being rescued by Private Thomas Trang, United States Marine Corps, and his fellow marines."

Little Ali looked at Trang and grinned like *okay, I'll tell her,* and when he did we saw the Arab gal shaking her head and she rattled angrily back at Ali, who reported, "She said it was Allah who sent you to rescue them from the forces of evil. All is in the hands of Allah."

You could see this *thanking Allah* sort of bothered Trang, and he stopped digging and kind of climbed out of the hole he was in near the tire. He then turned to the same praying gal and asked her to open the trunk. She refused, and Trang got the keys from the ignition, and when he opened the trunk, we were like, *Whoa! No wonder you Arab gals got bogged down in the sand!* The whole trunk was chock full of coins and jewels and gold bars and Kuwaiti and American bills. Trang turned to the praying gal and said *why didn't you take out this money?* And the gal through Ali said the limousine was not stuck on account of weight of the loot in the trunk, but due to *those darn forces of evil.*

Tommy Trang seemed to lose a little of his steam for the rescue of the maidens in distress. And the thing was they didn't once *thank us* marines and Ali as we slaved to take all the loot out of the trunk, but looked at us kind of like we were going to steal some jewels the whole time, and even got kind of pissy about how we were repacking the loot after we got the limo out of the sand by some miracle. We kept having some of the loot left on the sand when the trunk was full—some servant must have been real good at packing to get it all inside. And they wouldn't let us put the last of the loot in the limousine itself, for some damn reason. So then the praying Kuwaiti chick starts giving Trang some hell, just laying real bitchily into him and Ali said she was saying she once had *bad Asian servants like him,* and Trang burned her with a hardcore look, and then starts reaching into the trunk and flinging the jewels and gold all over the sand.

And the four Kuwaiti girls just jump on Tommy Trang and are clawing at him and shrieking. Euclid Krebes just started cracking up with a real loud guffaw, and then so did me and Ali. But then it was clear these girls were like serious, and were going for Trang's eyes with their extra long fingernails, so we peeled them off him one by one. First I got one, and then Krebes, and Ali was able to yank away a shorter one, until just the worst of them, the *really* bitchy one, was still going after Trang like a wildcat. Trang finally got her arms pinned to her side—he had her in a kind of bear hug—and she was still kicking her legs into his shins. And he carried her over and shoved her in the limousine and slammed the door. So we did the same with the other girls, and then Trang made us pick up all the jewels and loot from the sand and toss it in the backseat. And when we had picked up every last jewel and coin and bill, Trang tossed in the keys. One of them hopped in the front seat, and the limousine zoomed away.

It was a relief to see them gone. Trang, Krebes, Ali, and me just stood there watching the limousine race away south toward Saudi Arabia, and I guess we were thinking, *so much for our first try at maidens in distress!* And that was when little Ali said the girls had told him for a couple of hours each day they had run the air conditioner, and that he had noticed they were almost out of gas. I don't know why Ali hadn't told us this sooner. Ali was bummed, as he thought we would laugh about the out-of-gas thing, and Trang had to explain that American marines didn't want *any* chick cooking to death in the desert in a limousine period. This surprised little Ali, you could see that.

Trang really had to digest the way things hadn't gone as he had planned with these Kuwaiti maidens in distress, but we all reminded him that *four bitch chicks does not a country make,* and we still had a mission to focus on. And right then Euclid Krebes started to air guitar that song "Bad to the Bone." And I saw Trang's eyes light up when Krebes got to that cool line, *When I walk the streets, kings and queens step aside* . . . So Trang kind of slowly snapped back into shape, and even drove us on our camels past sundown into a dark and starless night until we couldn't see each other, so we stopped and made camp. And we had no fire that night, as we were real near Kuwait City, plus we were out of water and had nothing to cook anyway. Mahdi offered up a couple of locusts each, and eating the locusts got us back in the ancient *ghazzu* mood. Mahdi laid on us some stories of the al-Murrah in battle, but he went on a bit too long about the lineages of this-or-that mighty camel between each little bit of action, and so we fell asleep with his ancient storytelling voice in our ears. I should mention before I fell asleep I saw Trang letting Krebes hold the pearl, which kind of bummed me out some as he had never let *me* hold it—but whatever, not a big deal.

Anyway, what a surprise in the morning for us marines! Trang woke me up at just before light by whispering in my ear not to move. I sort of rolled my eyes to the side to look at him. He said he had been scouting and five hundred yards away was a mobile SCUD launcher complete with a SCUD missile that must have moved in during the night. Maybe you've heard about these missiles, but they were like the only thing Saddam really had as far as armaments that was a real pain in the neck for our side. Krebes whispered they were really homemade pieces of crap as far as missiles go, but our side was having a hell of a time locating these mobile SCUD launchers. *And here was one right near us!* Krebes had sort of slid over to us like a desert snake, and then Ali did the same, so our four heads were like together as we thought what to do. Although it was pretty clear in ten more minutes it would be light enough that the SCUD crew *had* to see our camels and us, and we were surprised they hadn't already as we could now see their big SCUD! *But maybe they were asleep too, who the hell knew!*

It was obvious to Trang we had to attack ASAP to get the jump on them. That seemed a little less obvious to Krebes and Ali and me, but we were still good to go! I don't mention Mahdi, as he made it clear he needed to sleep a little longer and had no personal interest in SCUDs. So we decided to sort of move out away from the camels and Mahdi, and loop around in two parties: Trang and Ali would come in as one pincer, and Krebes and me the other. At this moment Krebes like raises his hand like he was in school and says he has something important to say to us. And we expect some operational input, but the genius Euclid Krebes closes his eyes and lays on us to *never forget that a greater power than we can contradict hath driven our intents.* That kind of was confusing to say the least, and it took a full minute to recover the stoked warrior mood, until we were all just grinning away again at the *prospect of this first mighty action!* The best thing about this action was that we knew how hard America and the allies were trying to nail these SCUDs from the air, and if we took one out it might save some lives back across the border. And just before we headed out, Tommy Trang slapped his shoulder and said our old refrain: *DIE A HERO!* So we all slapped our shoulders and said *DIE A HERO!*—even little Ali! And then we gave each other the thumbs-up, *and we were finally off to our first real battle!*

We kind of crouched over across the desert sands. And there was sweat pouring into my pits, and I was repeating to myself for motivational reasons: *remember Captain Shakespear!* And then as we ran toward the SCUD I looked over at Krebes and he glanced at me, and his serious-as-hell warrior expression broke into a grin, and he *winked at me!* I mean, that took real style, to wink at someone as you head toward *unknown numbers of the Iraqi enemy!* So then we sort of spread apart, me and Krebes, and we are close enough to start ripping some rounds but are waiting for Trang to open up on the other side of the pincer as per our mission plan. But instead of firing from Trang, I hear him giving the marine *oooraah!* loud enough to wake up old dead Captain Shakespear himself, and I'm thinking: *what the hell?* But then Krebes and me were close enough to the SCUD that it dawned on me we ought to have seen some sign of the enemy by now.

Well, it was kind of a letdown to discover that there was no *enemy,* and that there was really no *SCUD.* It was a decoy SCUD, made of like wood and fabric. I guess with the sun rising from Trang's side in the east he realized this before us, so started yelling *oooraah!* It was a pretty good decoy from afar, but when you got up close you saw what lousy Iraqi work had gone into this thing. It was like slapped together, with paint drips all over the place and holes where I guess they just ran out of fabric. It was on a real metal trailer, only it was a boat trailer. So we still had some serious battle juice in us, and I guess we decided to do a dumb thing, but what the hell. We all backed off from this decoy and fired a couple of rounds into it, just to calm our itchy trigger fingers. Trang looked real bummed, like he had really had his heart set on some action!

And then, as little Ali even got to fire a couple of M16 rounds, was when we heard what sounded like marine Cobra helicopters. And damned if they weren't playing the *William Tell* Overture just like in the movies! For a second I just wanted to cheer, until it was clear we were kind of *in the way* of this American attack, and looked for all the world like the Iraqi crew for this SCUD dressed as Bedouin. The helicopters came sizzling across the desert so fast, and opened fire so fast, that there wasn't much to do but hit the sands. And then I saw Trang had thrown off his robe and was jumping around trying to wave off the U.S. attack! I guess Trang thought we'd all be killed if he didn't wave them off! And right then Euclid Krebes jumped from the ground and ran the ten yards over and just totally flattened Trang, like a tackle sacking a quarterback. Rounds were spraying all the hell around, and I at least was slithering across the sands as fast as I could away from the SCUD.

Then the Cobra helicopters were gone, and the SCUD was burning, and I glanced back over my shoulder to see Krebes was still lying there on top of Trang. And I yelled out, and little Ali came out from *inside the SCUD!* The SCUD was just obliterated, but Ali had for some crazy reason decided to hide *inside it,* and he had survived by some miracle. I stood up and yelled again to Tommy Trang, and then I saw him moving under Krebes, and the way big Krebes sort of fell off Trang's back like a big sack—well, my heart just cracked right then.

Euclid Krebes was a mess. He had taken a round right through his back, and when he rolled over, you could see all the blood on his gut. The round must have passed at a sharp angle through his back and right into the desert sands. Trang went right to work on

Krebes without a word, making his robe he grabbed from the ground into a compress on his gut. The sands all around were already soaked. Euclid Krebes' big redneck head was in Trang's lap, and you could look into Trang's eyes and see this ferocity screaming out from inside them saying *no way you are gonna die, my big friend!* And that was when Trang started yelling to Krebes over and over, *I'm going to get you help, man, gonna get you help.* And he yelled to little Ali to like *go get his camel.* Ali ran off, and was back with old Abdul Aziz the camel in a flash, and along with him came Mahdi. Anyway, that was when Mahdi bent down over Euclid Krebes and took his hand and said, "You are going to meet Allah, my lucky friend."

Trang like lashed out with a fist to the jaw and knocked Mahdi flat on his ass. He deadlifted Krebes' two hundred fifty pounds and sort of flopped him on his busted gut over the camel Abdul Aziz, and hopped into the saddle. Krebes didn't make a sound. It goes without saying my man Trang was kind of out of his head. He hopped on the camel and started galloping *south-east toward Kuwait City!* So I like ran alongside the camel yelling, *"Trang, Trang, what the hell?"* And as that camel charged off, Tommy Trang was like yelling over his shoulder at me, *"Got to get Krebes help. Fastest into Kuwait City. Wait here twenty-four hours. I'll probably be taken prisoner. If I'm not back in twenty-four hours, you and Ali rescue Princess Lulu!"* And that was when I raised my eyes to the south and saw the famous water towers of Kuwait City in the distance.

CHAPTER 13

When I walked back to our original camp from that morning, I saw that our other camels were history. The helicopter pilots had riddled them. Ali came up and I asked him how old Abdul Aziz the camel had survived, and Ali said the crafty old camel had broken his hobble and taken off in the desert away from the other two camels at some point in the action, and that Ali had found him lying on his side like he was playing possum. So maybe he *was* of Abdul Aziz's camel stock, because if that was true, he was a crafty old beast.

Right then I guess I just wanted to keep talking camels with Ali, as you just want to talk about something ordinary like baseball back home when some really bad thing has gone down. Because it was clear to me from the wobbly feeling in my knees and buzz in my head that if I thought about old Euclid Krebes and Tommy Trang straight on I was going to just sit down and sob into my knees. *Some tough marine!* But I knew my man Krebes was a goner, and was probably dead already from blood loss as crazy Trang rode him into Kuwait City, and that Trang was by now maybe a POW, but probably dead too.

And then it was like my whole head cleared and I was just so pissed at Tommy Trang, and at myself. This whole thing about going AWOL to rescue the princess *was just insane from start to finish!* The whole thing was like this drugged state of mind, and now I was like sober again, and just wanted to kick myself in the ass. I decided if Tommy Trang made it back I was going to drag him back to Saudi Arabia, even if me and Ali and even Mahdi had to tie him to a camel.

Then I got it into my head that I should follow Trang's tracks, so I could come on the Iraqis when he got in trouble and help him out. *I was pretty sure that was what Trang would do for me!* But I wasn't Trang, so I sat there not knowing what to do next, so I decided to wait the twenty-four hours and then decide. After all, there was an outside chance Trang would make it back. *That was sure what Ali thought!* He sat looking toward Kuwait City for the camel Abdul Aziz to come ambling back with Trang. And little Ali's faith sort of cheered me, and I sort of moved around the big badass mood and got back on my feet. And I sat next to little Ali for a while, hoping some of his faith would like rub off on me, I guess. And I talked some to Ali about his faith, and it turned out Ali was sure Trang was coming back because Trang carried the damn *pearl.* And for me that was kind of depressing to learn, as I had figured Ali's faith was like in Trang the United States marine. And that was when I looked over my shoulder and found Mahdi with his hand deep inside the guts of one of the dead camels. And he already had this little fire going, and that was kind of crazy, but I heard myself muttering *inshallah!* If the Iraqis see the fire, they see the fire. And I damn near laughed out loud to hear myself using the all-purpose Arab *inshallah!*

Anyway, Mahdi said when he saw me looking at his hands in the camel's gut *that he wanted me to eat something special.* He had a serious knife in his hand, and was opening up the guts of the camel even more, just happily sawing away. And he said when someone goes to Allah it is the Bedouin tradition to make a celebration of it, and so he wanted me to try some camel liver, which was a very great delicacy. Crazy Mahdi looked sincere about the celebration thing, and Trang would have clocked him for it for sure. But then I thought about the Islamic belief in the forty virgins waiting for a guy, and that made me chuckle a bit, and I asked Mahdi if this virgin thing was true. And he stood up and as he did so he yanked out the camel liver from the guts of the camel—this huge bloody football of meat—and he walked to me and said quietly that he was sure Krebes was already in the arms of Sword Dancer, as *inshallah,* they were meant to be together in eternity, and praises to Allah, *now it was so!* And Mahdi held the camel liver speared by his knife over the fire, and it sizzled, and Mahdi looked at me with this tragic and knowing look that gave me the chills, like he *did* have a direct phone line to Allah, so was up to speed on Krebes and Sword Dancer riding the camel together in paradise.

When your good friend just took a round that tore open his guts, your stomach will *just say no* to camel liver. And my stomach at first was disgusted by the bloody mess Mahdi was cooking, and I had to look away into the desert to keep from vomiting. Mahdi kept smiling as he cooked and muttering *inshallah* to himself, until that was like all I heard: *inshallah, inshallah, inshallah.* And then when I looked over again I saw little Ali had been handed a juicy hunk and was just gnawing into it, and he stopped to look at me, but then he buried his teeth back into the camel liver. And I guess we hadn't eaten in a long time, so it made sense for Ali to be hungry. But it sure looked like Ali was really *digging* the taste of the camel liver, kind of like he was at a feast, and what with Krebes dead or dying and Trang captured or dead, that didn't seem right—but he was just a twelve-year-old kid, our Ali.

And Mahdi started going on about like the ancient practices of the Bedouin. It was like he was talking to himself. And suddenly Mahdi started insisting there was *nothing like camel's urine to keep a man from being backed up in the crap department.* And that information kind of woke me up, and I looked at him. He jumped up when I glanced at him like he was real happy and started filling me in on how when he was with the al-Murrah Bedouin he drank a glass of camel's urine every day, and sometimes two glasses, *because the taste was that good!* I like shook my head, as this was over the top. Two of our raiding party were gone, and this Arab *was selling me on camel's piss!* He was holding out his hand like he was holding a glass of camel piss, and then pretended he was tossing it down the hatch and rubbing his stomach like *what could be better in the morning?* And then he marched over to me with another imaginary glass of camel piss and held it out to me. I just stared at his empty hand, and then *I laughed one of those small laughs that just erupt like a belch.* I didn't want to laugh, but like after all that had happened that morning, handing me a glass of imaginary camel piss—well, it was like the straw that broke the camel's back. And so I laughed, and after that I even ate some camel liver. And man, *it was the best thing I had ever tasted in my life.* I just chomped on that camel liver until there was camel blood all over my chin and chest.

So after that we three all pretty much just sat baking in the sand. And we like pulled robes over our heads, as it was getting roasting hot. Mahdi went and drained the camels of some blood, so we had that blood to drink at least. And it was too hot to even *think* about how I was really going native with the camel-blood drinking. It was too hot for anything but waiting for the sun to set. I just looked at my marine boots a lot and watched the flies suck on the salt stains. And nobody said anything, but then late in the afternoon I hear Mahdi say: *inshallah.* He said it real quiet, and kind of like someone would say: *oh damn!* And when I came out from under my robe I saw he was pointing to a little black cloud in the north. And I blinked in the sun and shrugged, and he went back under his robe. But I kept my eyes on that black cloud, and it kind of expanded into these black billows in the sky. And then there were flashes of lightning inside the black billows, and then it seemed to race right at us across the desert. The winds were slow at first and kind of felt good given the heat, but then they started to fling sand at us.

Mahdi and Ali kind of crawled over to me, and the three of us dug like three mad dogs in the sand until there was a little pit. The sandstorm just blasted right over us right then, and we three just dove into the pit and curled around each other while still kind of digging. And we all just kept digging down as the sandstorm roared like a jet taking off on a carrier and it felt like we were getting hit by a sonic sandblaster. I was like: *hey man, this is real bad, this could like kill you!* And I heard Mahdi just *inshallahing* for all he was worth and rattling some Koran too. If you squinted out through your fingers and from under your robe it looked like the horizon was on fire. Then there was a cool breeze, and some monstrous black clouds came wailing towards us in a solid wall, and I was like: *good god almighty, we are so screwed!* We were in a black-as-hell situation, and there were red flames in it, no kidding! The whole scene turned scarlet then, and the sky was just cracking like glass breaking, and then the storm sort of slid off us, and I heard Mahdi say something like *al-hamdu-lilah* over and over, which he said was *thanks be to God,* and I was like you got that right, Mahdi my man!

Mahdi said we were lucky because sandstorms coming down from the Euphrates Valley region can last for five days, or even a couple of weeks. And Ali said such a situation would have made it very hard for Trang to find us again. And man, we had sand like in every orifice. My M16 was just so screwed with sand there was like nothing I could do with it. Mahdi and Ali just sat and chilled while I rubbed myself, so after a while I sat and chilled too. And there was nothing but us three kind of sitting there—and I don't know if I was even waiting for Trang right then, for man, I was truly just glad to be on the other side of that sandstorm.

But Ali was still waiting for Trang. He was like the lookout on an old ship at sea sent up the mast to look for land. He just kept scouring the desert with his swollen eyes. He did that for four hours, and in the late afternoon he jumped up and started running toward Kuwait City. And I jumped up and ran after him, and of course all Mahdi could say was *inshallah!* And our Ali was waving his arms and that was when I saw a shape wavering in the heat of the horizon. It was like the black shape was melting around there, but it was a man, and finally we got close enough to see it was Trang. If it hadn't been Trang, but an Iraqi, I guess we would have been screwed. And I was punching the air with my fist when I knew it was Trang, and kind of leaping around—I was that glad to see him.

But I stopped jumping when I saw he was naked. And he was kind of stumbling along with his head down, and then he raised it and he must have seen us, but he just lowered his head and kept stumbling to us. And then we got to him, and Trang kind of fell into my arms, and I lifted him over onto my shoulder, and carried him back to where we had hunkered down from the sandstorm. I lay Trang down so he could sit in our pit like he was sitting up. His skin was rubbed red raw, like he had the worst sunburn you could imagine. There was something like a hunk of camel's liver in his hand, and I remember thinking, *he's eaten camel's liver too.* But right then Mahdi came with a hunk of bloody camel and put it in his mouth, and Trang just slurped away at it and gnawed as Mahdi held it to his face.

And after a while the camel liver—even kind of seriously sandy—like revived him and Tommy Trang told us what had happened. He had made it to the outskirts of Kuwait City, and Krebes was still barely alive, although out of his head. Trang said Krebes knew he was near Kuwait City, and kept talking like a good marine about the *mission.* And right then Trang saw an Iraqi patrol on motorcycles zooming at him across the sands. Four guys, and they circled him when they came up on him. And Trang had ripped off part of his robe, so he was like up on the camel trying to make his point by waving this scrap as a white flag. But these Iraqis just ran up and yanked Trang off the camel, and kicked him around the sands four on one, and then they yanked Krebes down too. Trang said when they did that he tried to get up but someone butted him in the head with a rifle. And then the Iraqis were standing over him yelling at him about George Bush and the Bombs, and they kicked him some more, and then one of them sprayed old Abdul Aziz the camel with bullets.

And then one of the Iraqis started laughing and said in English, "I am doctor! I take care of the sick American!" And all the Iraqis laughed. And the first Iraqi bent over Krebes with his knife and cut away his bloody robe. And then he raised the knife with two hands and plunged it into Krebes. Trang was held down by the other three Iraqis as the first Iraqi sawed open Krebes' gut. Then he reached inside with his knife until he was like up to his wrists, and he pulled out Krebes' heart. He stood up with the heart in hand, kicked Krebes, and walked over to Trang. He made the other three Iraqis strip Trang and hold him up, and then he held the heart under Trang's nose and said, "You take back. You show President Bush." And he grabbed Trang's hand and shoved the heart into his palm and closed his fingers around it. Then they tied Krebes' neck with a rope they secured to the back of one of their motorcycles, and then all the Iraqis roared back toward Kuwait City.

So Tommy Trang lay there in the sand without saying a word after that, just staring up at the sky filthy with oil smoke. And little Ali took off his robe and put it over Trang like a sheet. And when I looked over again Trang had passed out. And little naked Ali sat cross-legged by Trang's head while he slept. And Mahdi sat next to me and took my hand and said something, sort of a poem. So I asked, and he said this is what he said:

> Cling one and all to the rope of God's faith
> And do not separate
> Remember God's blessings
> For you were enemies
> And he joined your hearts together
> And now you are brothers

I nodded at Mahdi like to say *thanks man,* because best I could make out Mahdi was saying he was once our enemy, since we were infidel dogs, but now he was on our team. It was a nice thing to say, but what struck me was that he figured *we brothers were still going to punch on into Kuwait City.* I wasn't sure about that, and just sat looking at Trang, and at how his fingers were wrapped around Euclid Krebes' heart like the claws of a hawk.

After a couple of hours, Trang started to talk again, but he didn't open his eyes. He said when the sandstorm hit, he just lay facedown in the sand. And in the roar of the wind he thought he could hear voices. And he said he saw little Ali beckoning to him out in the sand and he walked toward him, and Ali showed him how the winds had scooped away the sands to reveal a like ancient stone slab. And on the slab was a ancient stone coffin covered in weird carved Arabic letters. And he said Ali told him not to go near it, but he walked down in the pit and over to the coffin. And then he said I was there, and that we two pushed the heavy top off the coffin to look inside. And there was an ancient woman in there dressed in yellow robes, and she was covered in gold jewelry. Her hands were tied together by a golden chain, and then Trang said: *her head was cut off from her body.*

I kind of wished Trang hadn't told me about this like vision he had in the fury of the sandstorm. Because with the present situation and circumstances, we really had enough to deal with without weird visions. It was weird enough by far that my friend was holding my other friend Euclid Krebes' heart in his fingers. *That was all the weird I needed right now!* But as I said before, as we went on with this trip into Kuwait, my man Trang was having these weird visions, and I thought this one was worth reporting. But still, I didn't have anything to say to Trang about this vision, as I was kind of ready to deal with the *facts* of our situation, strange as they were!

And then I really started to notice the heat. Sometimes you think about things that suck, and sometimes you don't—*but the heat was really getting to me for some reason right then.* It was like it was this evil heat snake and it was heading its fanged head down my throat every time I opened my mouth to take a breath, and it was just parching me out from the inside. It was like suddenly I was aware *I was a sack of water in a skin bag as a human,* and now that water was just drying right up as I sat there until there was going to be nothing left but the bones in the bag. And while I am bumming on this sensation, Mahdi—I guess to fill the local airways with some chatter—starts going on about how the desert has always been a great place to get religion, and how all the great religions—but especially the greatest Islam—arose from the desert. Mahdi just didn't shut up, and I was suddenly just too fried to open my mouth to tell him to clam up. And Trang was lying there like a dead man, with little Ali by his side and I guess waiting for him to jump up like some soldier Lazarus and say, *I'm back people, let's kick some ass!*

But nothing happened until sunset. Mahdi ceased on the world religion class, and we were just four dudes wheezing in the heat, and not even really waiting for what was next. It was a state of mind beyond *whatever.* We might have sat there and never gotten up again, just been covered over by the like eternal sands. *But no!* At sunset I hear little Ali make these sounds, and I open my crusted eyes and look at him. And he is sort of pointing back toward Saudi Arabia. And so I turn my creaking head to look, and there are these camels coming towards us with the sunset behind them. The first thing I thought was *I'm dead* and this is like *the grim reaper coming in Bedouin style.* I was that totally fried. But Mahdi starts *inshallahing* happily, and nodding like to say *it is so right what is happening.* And it real slowly comes to me that *I know these camel dudes in the distance,* and then *bang!* I understand it is the *Sulluba!*

And they stopped their camels and just like were there on the horizon and nothing happened, but then they dismounted and walked over to the side, and started *dancing!* I smiled at Mahdi, and he reached out and patted me on the shoulder and said, *they dance the famous and ancient gaysa! A dance for the hero!* And you could just hear drums and tambourines, and they were done up like parrots and really whirling some dervish over there in the sands at sunset! And I kind of crawled over to Tommy Trang and shook him awake, and he finally cracked open his eyes. I held him up so he could see them dancing, and his eyes blinked, and then I saw his eyes open wide, and I swear they exploded with the most intense light, but I guess they just caught the sunset at the right angle.

CHAPTER 14

So Tommy Trang was lying there on the sand like a dead man after the desert sun had set and the Sulluba departed and then *wham!* out of the blue he like thrust Krebes' heart up into the sky and said, *Krebes wants us to kick some Iraqi ass.* It was a real startling thing to have happen. One minute all is silent, and then you see this bloody hand with a heart punch upwards, and Trang indicates Krebes' heart is indicating to him we should *get on with the mission to Kuwait City.* So we all stumbled to our feet and just started walking toward Kuwait City. A weird little squad were we, by the way. Our fearless leader Tommy Trang was marching ahead of us naked as the day he was born, and clutching Krebes' heart in his fingers. The Iraqis had taken his M16, so he was without a weapon.

No one was going to argue with Krebes' heart. Ali and Mahdi both seemed to really believe Trang was in consultation with Krebes on the other side, and it seemed to move them both greatly. And although Tommy Trang didn't act like he was *joking,* I operated on the idea Trang meant Krebes would have *liked us* to kick some Iraqi ass. But Trang was sure acting like Krebes was *leading* our party. Trang walked ahead of us in the dusk toward the distant oil fires and every once in a while he like thrust Krebes' heart up violently into the sky, and the other three of us would jump a bit like we were hit by an electrical shock, as it was always kind of surprising.

There were these little lights across the desert here and there, and I took them to be Iraqi patrols. Sometimes it looked like one was heading towards us, but then I remembered the Iraqis were real low-tech, and probably had no night-vision capabilities to pick out us four crazies. One time this Iraqi patrol clearly on motorcycles was heading straight for us, so that their headlights were like kind of in our eyes, and then *wham!* up shot Krebes' heart, and the motorcycles broke off. That was kind of spooky, but I chalked it up to coincidence. But not Mahdi, he was doing a lot of *Allahu akbar*— God is great—under his breath. Little Ali was so excited he was *hyperventilating.* I had to hand it to Trang, because whatever it was he was up to with the heart of Euclid Krebes, it was totally motivational, in an insane sort of way.

And then we came to this huge sand berm built by the Iraqis. They must have done it with dozens of bulldozers, as we had to climb up one side that was pretty significant in size. And Trang was ahead of us climbing, and when he got to the top of the sand berm he like thrust the heart into the sky, and once again, it was a weird but powerful moment. And when Mahdi and Ali and me got to the top nobody said anything, because there was this huge trench down there in front of us, and there was just enough last light to see it was like full of dead Iraqis. And as we walked down into the trench, I saw that all the seriously toasted Iraqi soldiers had their mouths open in like a scream, most with their heads thrown back like they were *screaming at the sky!* There were hundreds of these corpses, all screaming in the same fashion, and sometimes the skin was just burned right off their faces, so it was like skulls screaming with their white teeth and all, and Mahdi was so upset he did some praying right there toward Mecca, and we stood around him as he did this, and a little moonlight came and cast itself on our little party as Mahdi did his Islamic prayer thing.

Tommy Trang was just jabbing Krebes' heart over and over into the night sky as Mahdi prayed, as if to say *we warriors are here to kill Saddam and bring an end to this sort of horror scene.* Anyway, it was like later on some army dude would tell me those Iraqis were killed with fuel-air explosives, and that they had all died gasping for breath if they weren't roasted to death right away, as these explosives like sucked all the oxygen right out of the air. But I'll never forget seeing all those burned dead guys like addressing the heavens as if to say: *why me?*

So then we moved on to the top of the other side of the trench, where there was another sand berm. And when we humped to the top of the sand berm we came on this group of Iraqi soldiers, we damn near smacked into them. Tommy Trang had the heart held high, and he kind of lowered it slowly, and these Iraqi dudes were so close we could hear them breathing—they were all out of breath from climbing the sand berm. And damned if the moon didn't come out again and put the glow on us. They all had like the thousand-mile stare, and for a second you might have thought these were ghosts. But then I registered they were all carrying shovels, and that they were heading in to bury some dead, and then I saw some looking over their shoulder like they thought they might be being followed, and I understood they were doing this at the risk of being AWOL and shot.

And from behind me came like a whisper of *inshallah* from Mahdi, and with that word the Iraqis just filed past us and slipped their way in a line down into the pit of death. And right there was when I registered all the fried Iraqis I had just witnessed, and I just dropped to my knees and started booting all over the sand. I was lifted up by Mahdi and Ali with hands under my pits, and saw Trang looking at me with real sympathy, and I had to say something to like restore my marine dignity, and I said, "Hey Trang, put some goddamn clothes on, would you?" And damned if my man Tommy Trang didn't look down at himself with surprise, as if this was the first time he had noticed he was naked. But then he grinned at me and I saw he was pulling my leg, that he *knew* he was naked, and *knew* he was carrying the heart of our dead friend, and I guess, well, that grin from Tommy Trang that said he was *semi-sane* made it all *slightly* acceptable, and I grinned back, and he nodded and turned again toward Kuwait City.

Trang didn't get too far, because Ali yelled from back down in the trench with the dead Iraqis for us to *wait the hell up!* I guess he had slipped back down in the trench with the Iraqi burial detail for some unknown reason. We stood looking at each other like *what's Ali up to?* And then he came running back up the wall of the trench and in his arms were a bunch of Iraqi uniforms! Ali like had stripped some of the less-burned corpses down there. Ali dropped the uniforms to the sand, and pulled out an Iraqi officer's uniform and held it out to Trang. And I was like wondering if he would put it on, but Trang was psyched to get dressed up like a Iraqi colonel, and kind of laughing, like this was an excellent break for our team, to score these uniforms. Ali then dropped his robe and slipped into a Iraqi private's uniform. I stood there holding a dead Iraqi's uniform in my hand, and then thought: *surf the weirdness, Carmichael!* So I dropped the robe to the sand and got dressed up like a Iraqi sergeant.

So we marched on dressed as Iraqis—except for Mahdi who opted to stay in his robe—and came on these bunkers that were all blown in, and right then as I am wondering how many Iraqis are buried down there under the sand, there came the sounds of a couple of big bombers. So we all hunkered down in the sand, as it was clear the sound of the bombers overhead in the night was like getting louder, and then we felt the first bombs hit and with the earth shaking ran toward one of the blown-in bunkers. But we didn't quite make it there when the *big bad bomb* exploded. It was like a small nuclear bomb went off in the distance, and Trang and me agreed a few minutes later when we had recovered a bit that it was a fifteen-thousand-pound Daisy Cutter. It hit about a half mile north of our position, but the shock still sent the four of us flying sideways. The whole sky was neon yellow and red when it hit, and even with my eyes shut the inside of my head was lit up. I guess the Coalition forces dropped some napalm on some oil-filled Iraqi trenches also, because when we stood up there was this huge wall of fire in the distance.

The concussion from the Daisy Cutter left me kind of shaking as I stood there. It was like all the bones in my body were jiggling, and I think an eardrum popped, because I had a pretty intense pain. And that was when it *really* started to come home to me that

Trang was made of different human materials. Because I had always thought I was pretty tough, but that Daisy Cutter just left me quaking and shaking in my joints. But you looked at Trang and you felt better—he still gave off a vibe that was like a *shrug*. Anyway, soon we were marching after Trang again, and we came on more Iraqis. These guys were like splattering their tank on top with black paint, I guess to try and make it look like the tank had already been hit. They were yelling at each other as they worked, and we sort of skirted them in the dark and kept on for Kuwait City. At dawn we slipped into some abandoned Iraqi bunkers, and spent the day zonked in there, with one of us fake Iraqis keeping watch on two-hour shifts for stray *real* Iraqis. I had that old Manfred Mann song "Blinded by the Light" stuck on replay in my head for some kinky reason—maybe because of that big bomb that lit up my head like a halogen. Anyway, we slipped out after dark again, and continued our forced march for Kuwait City.

And then as we marched I was wondering what we were going to do when we got into Kuwait City *exactly*. I mean *how* were we going to link up with the Kuwaiti Resistance? Ali had said Princess Lulu was with the Kuwaiti Resistance, but as we crossed the first ring road way at the farthest edge of the city, I wasn't sure how we would find them. But it turned out it wasn't that hard. We broke into an abandoned office building, and Ali took the phone, called a number, and started rattling in Arabic. And then Ali was arguing some, and he was shaking his head like he couldn't believe something, and then he clicked off. And so then without a word little Ali like took the lead of our little squad. As he walked Ali announced he had wanted us picked up, but that this dude Khaled, the leader of the Kuwaiti Resistance, had said the vehicles were all out on a mission, *and that we would do well to walk*. Ali didn't seem to believe the vehicles were all out on a mission, and he was in a lather about it.

Ali seemed to know Kuwait real well. So he led us along all these like random concrete suburban streets in a section of town called Bnaid al-Gar. There were broken concrete holes along the roadside every twenty yards, and Ali said the Iraqis had stolen the streetlights and shipped them back to Iraq. Turned out the Iraqis had at first stolen like everything in Kuwait that wasn't nailed down, and now they were working on shipping back things that *were* nailed down—or stuck in concrete, like the street lamps. Anyway, it seemed like most of the mega-houses we were slipping past were surrounded by some sort of concrete wall, and then without a word Ali like suddenly slithered up and over this one wall. Mahdi and Trang and me waited hunched in the shadows, and then a metal gate opened and there was this tall young Arab guy motioning for us to enter. As he walked us inside he said his name was Khaled, and that he was the leader of this cell of the Kuwaiti Resistance. He didn't seem fazed at all that three of us were dressed like Iraqis in uniforms that I noticed in the light of the room were scorched pretty bad in places.

Khaled was one of those dudes who wore his hair over his eyes like a sheepdog, so he could always be flipping it out of the way. He was also one of those guys who liked to glance in the closest mirror. When he was introduced to me, as he was flipping his hair, he shot a hard look into the closest mirror like *the fierce Kuwaiti Resistance leader Khaled greets the American warrior!* He wore his Levi's extra tight, some dark wraparound shades, a leather jacket—as the room was like frigid with air-conditioning, and a whole bucket of aftershave—the guy was like a nerve toxin weapon with his aftershave. What hurt his overall badass look was that everything about him was kind of caved in: his chin, his nose, but mostly his chest. And the reason I note all this stuff about Khaled right off is: I had time to stare at him as we were introduced, because the usual Arab chitchat about the desert weather took like ten minutes with him, as he couldn't answer a simple question without studying his various warrior poses in the mirror.

Anyway, we were in a sort of serious bachelor-pad room. There was a pool table, and a mega stereo system with speakers the size of coffins, and some posters of blond American semi-babes sitting on motorcycles with their legs spread. Ali was quickly at the fridge helping himself to a soda. At first the twenty or so Arab guys milling around the pool table looked at us nervously as they smoked and mumbled, and then Khaled flipped his sheepdog hair and said some stuff in Arabic, and they all brightened and one by one came over and like wanted to slap us five. Ali came back and said Khaled had told them we were a crack CIA team here to liaison with the Kuwaiti Resistance, and that our coming signaled that their particular Kuwaiti Resistance cell had been recognized by the American military as the very best and most heroic cell and one to get behind and support with Stinger missiles and other cool high-tech American toys. I asked little Ali where Khaled got this idea, and Ali said *this is what I told him* as if to say to me: *you thought we could just come in empty-handed?*

It was clear the local Arabs were thrilled by the honor, but you could see they were also weirded out by the fact Trang was carrying a hunk of something bloody in his hand. Khaled said something softly to Ali. I saw Ali shake his head, and then pull Khaled off in a corner to whisper something to him. Khaled was clearly impressed by whatever Ali was saying, as his eyes were huge and glued to Trang. And right then I saw Khaled like whispering to another Kuwaiti Resistance fighter, and you could see some gossip was going around the room. I went over to Ali and asked what he had told Khaled about Trang. Ali said he had told them Trang was holding the heart of an Iraqi soldier he was going to grill and eat later in the evening.

The resistance fighters were so nerved out by Tommy Trang after that they kept moving away from him wherever he went in the room. It was then I started to wonder what had happened to *Princess Lulu's pearl*. It would have sucked to have lost it, but I was pretty sure the Iraqis had it now. Still, I asked Trang, and I guess I should have known nothing bad would have happened to that special pearl. Trang like smiled at me and said it was in a really safe place. And so I said: *no way man!* I slapped Trang five on account of the weirdness of his still cruising around with a pearl up his ass, and he appreciated my enthusiasm.

Anyway, it turned out little Ali had gotten the word from the Kuwaiti Resistance leader Khaled that he totally knew where Princess Lulu was, but that tonight it was impossible to get there as there were extra Iraqi patrols out, and so would put the princess at great risk as we might reveal her hiding place. Little Ali also informed Trang and me that Khaled had told him the *Iraqis* knew Princess Lulu was still somewhere in Kuwait, and were doing all they could to locate her to use as like a bargaining chip, or just to kill for sick fun. And then little Ali said he had learned not only were the Iraqis looking for Princess Lulu, but old Colonel Fawwaz was in Kuwait with a squad of Saudi Special Forces, and he was looking for the princess too!

This news about the Iraqis and Colonel Fawwaz of course made Tommy Trang want to get to Princess Lulu ASAP, and Trang dragged Ali over and tried to convince Khaled that we had to rescue Princess Lulu tonight, and that got us in our first of many arguments with Khaled, as he took it that Tommy Trang was suggesting he was like not heroic enough. And little Ali took over and stopped translating for Trang, and I guess laid it on thick again about how we were sent because word had reached *the emir of Kuwait in exile, the king of Saudi Arabia, the Coalition high command, and even President Bush* that Khaled's cell was the bravest and the one to back in Kuwait. So Khaled chilled, but you could see he was a real touchy guy.

There wasn't much to do except sit down on the couches and hammer some whiskey and Pepsi with these guys. And my ear was still hurting from the Daisy Cutter bomb, so the drink took away some of the pain. And there were a lot of big pillows in the room, and when I sat down no one took much notice, but when Trang sat down it was like all the guys jumped to grab a pillow. And someone asked Trang if he wanted a whiskey and Pepsi, and Trang was screwing around and said he wanted a whiskey and *Coke,* and there was total silence in the room. The Kuwaiti Resistance guys were clearly upset by this request, but also not going to crap on a guy who ate the hearts of dead Iraqis. And Ali told Trang that no one drank Coke here because *Coke did business with the Jews in Israel,* and I thought: *here we go!* But maybe Trang was too beat from the last few days to screw with them and say he was a Jew too, because he just glanced at me with a look like: *that crazy Arab Jew thing again,* and then asked for a straight whiskey.

So most everyone had a drink, and I guess heroism was like in the air, because the conversation got onto *war cries*. It turned out a couple of these Kuwaiti Resistance fighters were in college in the U.S., and spoke okay English. They took over the translation, as like little Ali finished his drink and fell asleep on the pillows. Anyway, the guys wanted to talk war cries, and by that they meant *Bedouin war cries*. It turns out among the Bedouin there are like family groups called *fakheds,* and that each *fakhed* had a war cry, and that each war cry was the name of a great camel of yore, or the name of an honored sister. So your basic Bedouin would go into battle screaming the name of a favorite sister or a famous dead camel.

The guys were really into naming some famous old camel names like they were famous horses from the Kentucky Derby, but as I looked around the room, I wondered if any of them had any Bedouin blood at all. So I asked, and you would have thought I'd asked if they were *Jews*. I guess it was an insult, to say the least. And then I asked if any of them had any Bedouin friends, and this question *too* was an insult. So I asked if any had ridden a camel, and they all said they had done this. Anyway, my questions were too factual and like ruining the mood, and Ali had woken up and was giving me a warning look. So the conversation went back to *fakhed* war cries, and these guys decided after a few more whiskey-and-Pepsis that they wanted me and Trang to have a war cry based on a famous camel or an honored sister. So that led them into stories of famous camels, which took some hours. And someone brought out a hubbly-bubbly, and we all smoked some—except for Trang on account of his *wind*—and the guys talked in Arabic among themselves for a while. And then one of the guys asked Trang if he was going to pick a *fakhed* war cry, and Trang looked at the guy and said: *Princess Lulu.*

The general consensus was that this wasn't right, it had to be a famous camel or an honored sister. Still, given that Trang was a foreigner and *ate Iraqi heart for dinner,* maybe he should be allowed to yell out what he wanted when he went into battle. And then there was some fast Arabic jabber back and forth that I took to be about Princess Lulu, and I asked one of the guys what they were saying.

And he glanced at Trang and said he would say nothing bad about this Princess Lulu, but then he started to crack up over his own seriousness. So then Trang got real interested, but still, none of the guys wanted to say anything, because clearly *the Iraqi heart eater* was hot on Princess Lulu, and I guess no one wanted to risk pissing him off. But the conversation was at a dead halt, and Trang looked at Ali. So Ali did some fishing in Arabic, and the guys sort of hedged, but then Ali reported. He said everyone knew Princess Lulu was considered the biggest looney tune in the Kuwaiti royal family, and that the royal family was embarrassed by her as she had tried to kill herself and then stayed in Kuwait rather than marry Colonel Fawwaz. Rather than being here to rescue Princess Lulu, the word was Colonel Fawwaz was here *to find and kill Princess Lulu so she wouldn't dishonor the families more*. The Kuwaiti Resistance said that they were modern guys and not into honor killings and that as long as they had her in custody, the nutty Princess Lulu was safe from Colonel Fawwaz. That was when I first wondered—when this crazy 'honor killing' thing popped into my American ears— if maybe Princess Lulu was nutty to the point of suicide *because* she grew up in Arabia. In the end I learned Lulu *was* pretty nutty, but she also turned out to be as stoked about freedom as my man Trang.

Anyway, there was some quiet for a while, and then the leader Khaled came and stood before Trang and swore that Princess Lulu was still a virgin, and that was to say none of *his men* had been allowed near her. Trang nodded, but Khaled went on to say that all *his men* saw she was beautiful as the greatest Kuwaiti pearl of yore, but that none of *his men* would dishonor her, as might be possible to do in a war situation with all the chaos of war. Khaled swore by Allah that she was with *only his best and most honorable fighters,* who respected the virtue of a woman, and that if one of *his men* put a hand on her plump and milk-full young breast, he personally would cut that hand off. Khaled pulled out a nasty-looking knife and waved it with a *swish* in the air, and repeated that *anyone who tried to dishonor fair Lulu would have to answer to him*. All the Kuwaiti fighters jumped up and pulled out knives and *swished* them around and yelled their *fakhed* war cries, and swore by Allah that they too would make quick work of anyone dishonoring the famous beauty Princess Lulu of Kuwait. The Kuwaiti fighters really put on quite a show with their knife waving, and it became clear they must not have a lot of whiskey-drinking experience, because they were all pretty trashed.

So while the Kuwaiti fighters were losing themselves in mock knife fights to protect the honor of Princess Lulu, little Ali kind of slid over to me and Trang and like said Mahdi the Messiah was in the backyard of this building. We hadn't seen Mahdi in a long time, and Ali said he was sick, but kind of wiggled his eyebrows a bit. And it came to me what the eyebrow thing meant, and I said, *he's been drinking?* And Ali said 'the Messiah' had a bottle of whiskey by his side, yes. This was not a big surprise somehow for a guy as messed up in his thinking as Mahdi, but what Ali said next *was* a surprise: *it was his opinion that these Kuwaiti Resistance guys didn't have any idea where Princess Lulu was, and that was why Khaled had gone on so long about protecting her virtue.* Ali said these Kuwaiti Resistance guys *had* been taking care of her, but if she had skipped out maybe it was because *Khaled or one of his guys had tried to put the move on her, or worse.* Ali said a couple of the former Kuwaiti Resistance guys were missing, and that these two guys were friends of his and *really* good guys. Ali had been told by Khaled these two good guys had been killed by the Iraqis during a big heroic raid, but that he thought this was all a lie, and that these good guys might have taken off with Princess Lulu to keep her safe after Khaled tried to jump on her.

Trang suddenly jumped up in a way that stopped all the knife waving, and a number of the more drunken fighters fell over with surprise. All the fighters were frozen and staring at Trang, who said he needed a barbecue grill, and was *real hungry.* He took out Krebes' heart and put it on the pool table and motioned like to eat it, *and this needed no translation.* He pulled over Khaled and put his arm around him like they were old friends, and motioned for Ali to translate. He said he thought Khaled was the greatest of Kuwaiti fighters, as were the brave Kuwaiti men in this room, and that was why President Bush had sent *us* to link up with *them* for the *very greatest mission of the war.* Trang was silent for a moment, and looked into the drunken face of each of the Kuwaiti Resistance dudes. And then he picked up Krebes' heart and said that this was not an *Iraqi* heart, but the heart of one of the American members of our CIA team *who had failed to follow his orders on the way over the border.* Trang said that *he would cut out the heart of anyone who failed him or Khaled in any way or fashion.* Then Trang paused and said that if anyone had anything to tell him about anything—say, the status of Princess Lulu—they should do it *right now,* or risk having their heart cut out and eaten later. I had to hand it to Trang, once again the dude proved he could really think on his feet.

None of the Kuwaiti fighters said a word, but all stared at Trang like they really believed that he would cut out their heart. Trang looked kind of bummed by the lack of response. Anyway, after a while one of the Kuwaiti guys asked if he might ask what *exactly was the greatest mission of the war that they were all going on?* And Trang kind of glared at him and said *we are here to kill Saddam.* And that stopped the party like everybody had been shot in the head, until Khaled raised his knife in the air and let out a *fakhed* war cry, and one by one the others all raised their knives in the air and whooped it up too. But the mood was one of: *man, we better whoop it up good or this crazy CIA mother will cut out our heart right here and now.* They were like looking at each other like: *yea! kill Saddam! Whatever this crazy Chinese guy says!* And the thing was they didn't seem to know how to stop whooping, but went and filled their cups with whiskey and kept whooping and glancing at Tommy Trang until he waved his hand in a fierce way and they all shut up.

CHAPTER 15

The next morning we awoke to Khaled on his knees before Trang with a coffee, and going on for some reason about how they would be *brothers now and in paradise.* Khaled was all excited about what a *big day* he had planned for us, and how he had been up all night making *arrangements* like he was some sort of Kuwaiti tour guide. Trang sipped the coffee, and then handed it to me—and that gesture pissed off Khaled, and he charged from the room. That was so Trang—he was aware Khaled was ignoring us and he was saying: *hey man, don't ignore my people.* So I took a sip of the coffee, and handed the cup to little Ali, and to my surprise he handed it on after a sip to Mahdi, who was looking like one real hungover Arab messiah.

Trang ordered three more coffees from Khaled when he came back in, and Khaled frowned and left us alone again. While he was gone Trang said he didn't have a good feeling about these Kuwaiti Resistance guys, and wanted us to bust out and find Princess Lulu on our own. Ali shook his head at this, and said it was of course a big city crawling with crazed Iraqis, and the only connection we had to Lulu was Khaled and his cell. Trang was clearly bummed about this, and walked back and forth in the room with his coffee, and every once in a while snuck a look out from behind these heavy-duty velvet curtains into the street. I got up and looked out too, and it was like looking out into a suburban street in like San Diego or something. All concrete low-slung houses, very ugly. But to be honest, it looked quiet enough—you wouldn't know by looking out there was any sort of war on at all.

Next thing we know Khaled is back in the room with his party face back on, and he's all revved up about *how the vehicles are here and all is ready and we must hurry and oh what excitement today!* Anyway, Khaled couldn't get us out the back door and into the trunk of this white Toyota fast enough. And Trang seemed really *good to go* this morning, almost as revved up as Khaled. So we two hop into the trunk, and Khaled says *inshallah* and slams it shut on our heads a little too fast, and I got konked good, but whatever. Little Ali and Mahdi get in the backseat of the car along with a couple of Kuwaiti dudes, and some others pack in the front. I hear a couple of other vehicles roar up, and the voices of the rest of the Kuwaiti guys as they pack into those vehicles. And my head is like in Trang's ass, as the trunk isn't that comfortable, and I hear something, and it is Trang chuckling, like as to say, *this is just so crazy as to be excellent!*

It was cool to see Trang back in top form, kind of a *bring-it-on-baby* attitude. He reached around and like patted me on the shoulder. And then we both rocked back and got whacked, as the Toyota squealed away. And it did cross *my* mind that these Arabs might even sell us out to the Iraqis, *but Trang seemed sure we were heading toward the best operation yet!* His excitement was massive, and he was jiggling his legs like a maniac. I whispered like: *chill, man, chill!* But instead Tommy Trang started banging his fists on the trunk door and yelling if they had any Arab *ghazzu* music and if so to *crank it up!*

And so someone popped in a tape, and I guess Trang's powerfully stoked vibe had passed to everyone in the car, because all the Kuwaiti guys were singing at the top of their lungs. But it wasn't Arab music, but an American band called *Devo*. And the song had lines like: *whip it! whip it good!* sung in this weird sort of mechanical way. And that song snapped Trang out of his pumped mood, I guess because it ruined the feeling we were on an ancient *ghazzu*. You would have thought being in the trunk of a Toyota would have ruined the *ghazzu* mood for Trang, but whatever. But the Kuwaiti dudes were having a fine old time singing and I guess swaying together, as the whole vehicle was rocking back and forth. It struck me that these Kuwaiti warriors needed a couple of lessons in like how to be *swift and silent and deadly* like a U.S. marine.

When the Devo tape ended, I guess Tommy Trang too was thinking about the marines, and what we had left behind to go on this mission to rescue Princess Lulu. It was getting kind of hot in the trunk by the way. Anyway, Trang said to me quietly, "Do you think if we do some good work over here in Kuwait the marines won't court-martial us for being AWOL?"

I said, "I don't know, Tommy. I think we're kind of screwed there."

And Trang said, "I guess we'd have to do something *big* to get off the hook."

"If we like killed Saddam, yeah, they might cut us some slack."

"That big, huh?"

"I think so, yeah. That big."

"Well then, we'll have to kill him. But I hope he comes to Kuwait, I'll tell you what. I'm not all that psyched to bust on to Baghdad."

Trang didn't say anything else. The vehicle hit some potholes and we both bounced off the inside of the trunk roof. It was strange hearing Trang like talk about getting back in the marines after all this, but even stranger that he *really thought he had a shot at killing Saddam.* But as I lay there stuffed in the hot trunk I started to think: *maybe!* I mean Saddam *might* come to see his troops in Kuwait, and if he did he'd probably march around in the *open,* not worried there was a expert shot like Tommy Trang getting a bead on him. So if you think about it, the reason it was *possible* he might get a shot at Saddam was because my man Trang was so *crazy* that he was here in Kuwait *where Saddam would never expect him to be!* And right then I am back on *Team Trang.* And as I light up from the inside with visions of knocking off evil Saddam Hussein, right then as I am just glowing to be in a Toyota trunk with my man Thomas Trang, USMC, he says to me, "Hey man, I've got a vibe."

So I say, "What kind of vibe, Trang?"

"You won't buy it," says Trang, which is weird to say, as I had just bought the *kill Saddam* thing to some degree, and that would be hard to top.

"Go ahead," I say. "What's up?"

"I'm getting a vibe from Princess Lulu."

"A 'vibe'?" I say.

"Like a message," says Trang. "Coming in real strong from the pearl."

"What's she saying?"

"That we're about to link up."

"Excellent," I say.

Trang was silent for a while, and then started whispering these problem sounds like: *ohh ohh ohhh.* So I say to him, "You got a problem?" And then it hit me like a brick to the head: Trang was getting the news from the *pearl, and the pearl was hidden where the sun never shines.* And I guess I was right because Trang said, "Yeah Cody man, this is kind of a lot to ask, but I got to get something out if I'm about to hook up with the princess Lulu."

"No way, man," I said. "I'll do some crazy shit like try and kill Saddam with you, but I *ain't* plucking no pearl from your ass."

"I *ain't* asking you to pluck it out," said Trang. "Just don't be bummed while I fish around in there. I got to get it shined up before I see Princess Lulu. She's gonna want to see it right away, for sure."

"Tommy Trang," I said. "My face is like six inches from your crazy ass. You put your fingers anywhere near your ass and I'm hitching back to Saudi."

Trang was silent after that, but I knew he was itching, so to speak, to get that pearl out. But suddenly Trang says quietly, "Shot over," which is a term used for like enemy explosives heading your way, and then he starts to crack up. I asked Trang what was cracking him up, and he said he had to like *pass some serious gas.* He said the pearl up there had him constantly gassed up, and that when the gas popped around the pearl plug it was usually pretty nasty. And right then it happened, my man blasted a nuclear one. Trang had gotten me into this whole thing, but this was *unforgivable.* It was so bad my eyes were watering, and I was gagging, hollering, and pounding on the roof of the trunk, and the Kuwaiti guys must have thought I was getting killed, because a minute later they pulled over. The top flipped up and I rocketed out of there, and the Kuwaiti guys and little Ali and Mahdi ran around to see what the hell was going on, and I made a joking show of marching down the street saying *that was it, I was heading home to California.* Trang seemed to think I *wasn't* joking, and he ran after me down the street saying he was *sorry, man, sorry, and it was all the pearl's fault, and it did something to his plumbing.*

With a grin I let Trang know I was joking, and he slapped me on the shoulder and said: *DIE A HERO!* and *Remember Captain Shake-spear!* And I slapped him back in the same fashion and said the same stuff, and then we slapped Ali with the same words when he came running up—although he had really come running up to wisely *hustle us Americans out of the Kuwaiti street.* And that was when I looked around, and saw we were on a street that was on a sandy beach, and there were all these fancy concrete-and-glass beach houses lined all along like you might see in Malibu, but nobody at all around. And Trang runs around the corner of one wall, I guess to crouch down and fish out the pearl and give it a shine. He comes back out and of-fers to let me hold it, and I was like *thanks man, maybe later.*

Little Ali was like tugging on Trang's hand to get him in what he called a *villa.* All the other Kuwaiti dudes were already in there, and they had stowed the Toyotas out of sight, and there was not a sound in the street. And right then Trang sees some flowers on the porch of a huge peach villa next to the villa Ali is tugging him to-ward, and Trang jumps the wall and makes a run for the flowers. And I guess the house wasn't empty, because as Trang ran back to us with the flowers in his hand this dog is gnashing his teeth at his heels, and Trang almost made it over the wall, but the dog got a chomp on his calf, but I was like over the wall in a flash and beat that dog over the head with the butt end of my M16, which was still by my side, although I haven't mentioned it much.

The owner of the villa came whistling out right then and call-ing off the dog, and when she found out we were Americans, man, she was all apologies, and this classy Arab lady really made us *feel fine about being here to liberate her country.* She took us inside her villa and cleaned out the puncture wounds in Trang's calf with some real care, and when she got the picture Trang's trespassing purpose was to gather flowers for like a *long-lost lady love,* man, this really *turned her on some,* and she like got out her clippers and went to town and chopped down all the flowers in her villa so that Trang was carrying this tower of flowers in a fancy crystal vase. This Arab lady was then suddenly seriously weeping over Trang going AWOL and sneaking into occupied Kuwait to rescue the princess, and it was like cool because *it clearly translated across borders and into her Arab mind what Tommy Trang was up to!* And Trang is appreciative of her water-works, and whips out the pearl and places it in her palm, and tells her the ancient story of Captain Shakespear and his Kuwaiti princess lover, and she gets all weepy again over this ancient love story.

The Arab lady now *had* to come with us back to the other villa to see Trang link up with Princess Lulu. I kind of caught Trang's eye as if to say *we don't even know Lulu is over there in the other villa dude,* but Tommy Trang *was sure Lulu was there somehow,* and had also decided this Arab lady was A-OK, and I agree she did make us feel *real fine* about what we were up to in going AWOL and busting a move into Kuwait, and we hadn't had a lot of cheerleaders to date, Arab or American.

So the Arab lady like loaded me up with flowers too, and then made a pile for herself to carry in a basket. And then we had to wait while she put on a fancy dress she said she wore mostly in London when she went shopping. And then we headed back out into the oil haze and went through this secret gate and over to the other villa. I still wasn't even sure why everyone was acting like Princess Lulu was in this villa. I mean no one had announced *officially* that she was here. *But man, ride the big wave,* I told myself. And as we came into the yard of the villa next door, little Ali pointed us around to the rear, so we did so and he ran ahead and like opened this tinted glass door, and the other glass door was opened from the inside by like a smiling Khaled.

You got this blast of cold as you stepped inside the villa, and the lights were off and the windows covered with curtains so you couldn't see anything much, and then *flash!* a spotlight from the ceiling came down on like the kitchen table, and it was covered in silver cloth that shimmered. And standing on the table was none other than *Princess Lulu!* And all around her in a half circle like from some *musical* were the Kuwaiti Resistance guys, and they all had their hands out and raised to her, which was a nice dramatic touch, and I wondered who had organized it. It turned out it was Lulu who organized this spectacle, with help from Khaled.

The first time we saw Princess Lulu she was vomiting seawater and not at her best, and the second time was with the emir of Kuwait, and she was pretty much drugged and under wraps, but then you could tell at least her Arab face was *awesome,* mostly because her blue eyes were so huge. But now as she wasn't vomiting or under wraps I could take in her whole Arab babe look, and right away I also noticed some things about Princess Lulu worth mentioning because they were kind of *curious.* Like she had decorated her young babe face and hands with blue swirling Bedouin henna markings! She also had on some strange clothes, which she soon enough told me she had sort of *adapted* from the Bedouin. She wore a kind of fancy pancho of black and blue and scarlet with braids of gold. She later told me it was called a *farwa* and mostly Bedouin guys wore it, and showed me how the inside was all lamb's wool, which seemed like hot for the desert. She was wearing a gold *aqual* on her head, which was the rope the Arab men wore to keep the towel on the head, but she was just kind of wearing it like a gold crown of sorts over her shiny black hair, which was a clever thing to do. Her long hair went down to her waist in like six plaits. And on her wrists and around her neck were all this silver jewelry with lots of precious stones that were gleaming in the kitchen light, and this she told me later she had *designed herself* based on Bedouin designs. She also wore silver finger and several nose rings, let us not forget those.

So Princess Lulu has all our attention, and flips her head so her plaits kind of whip around her neck and says to Trang with some seriousness, *So are you the hero sent by Allah to fly me from the golden bird-cage?* I wasn't sure, but figured she meant the whole rich little *country* of Kuwait was like her golden birdcage. Trang was kind of stumped as he stood there with the flowers—rare for him—and then said just, *yeah Princess, let's blow this birdcage!* Princess Lulu looked kind of bummed by this response—I think she was looking for some like high poetry from the tongue of my man Trang—but then she gave him a real buttered love look and all was cool.

Anyway, Princess Lulu was a *real piece of work,* as they say. Which was very cool as we really didn't know much about her, and what if she had turned out to be a dud in the end? That would have sucked, if she had turned out to be like one of those rich bitch Kuwaiti chicks stuck in the sand. Now to your average citizen she might seem like a little flaky with the face painting and the stuff about the golden birdcage, and my own taste ran more toward Leila the maid and your basic athletic beach surfer babe, but I came to see Princess Lulu's flaky style was like a sign of something cool deep in her trying to flower in her locked-down Arab world, and not *just* flakiness. Anyway, did I mention Tommy Trang was so blown away by the whole spectacle of Princess Lulu he tripped on the Persian rug when she like held out her ringed hand to him from the table? And how the vase with the tower of flowers went flying and exploded on the marble floor and Trang like landed in a bed of flowers at her feet? I mean: to each his own, and if blue swirling henna markings on a chick's face burn Trang's torch, what the hell?

Ali and I kind of helped Tommy Trang up off his knees and carried him forward to like take Princess Lulu's hand, and she pulled him up on the table as we pushed his sorry ass from below. That was when I noticed his calf wound from the dog was dripping blood, but when I looked up he and Princess Lulu were just standing close and eyeballing each other, and right then the classy lady from next door started to ululate, and the Kuwaiti guys grabbed Princess Lulu and Tommy Trang and carried them around the room in circles doing some sort of Bedouin war dance or something.

And every time Tommy Trang spun around on the shoulders of the Kuwaiti Resistance guys I like caught his eye, and you never saw a guy happier—it was like *just being here* with her he was in paradise already, and once again I had a real strong feeling that I had done the right thing to like help bring these two crazy kids together. And I started to think about Euclid Krebes, and wondered whether he was looking down and thinking it was worth it, just accomplishing this dance for these two here in the villa on the Persian Gulf. It was kind of a weird idea to think that one *ululating* dance for a couple of near strangers was worth a life like Krebes', but as I looked beyond Princess Lulu and Tommy Trang and out onto the oil-slicked waters of the Persian Gulf I like kind of tumbled into this mellow zone and then got hit in the chest with this momentary brick-in-the-chest thud of *absolutely it was worth it!* And right then I thought about Euclid Krebes holding his hand out to me from his camel and saying about Sword Dancer *she made blessed my rude hand,* and saying it with a look like he was sure nothing in his life mattered more.

And there wasn't a lot of time to think these deep thoughts about whether it was worth it to lose Krebes to bring together these international lovers, because the dancers carried Lulu and Trang through a big set of dark glass doors, and into a room where there was a huge feast. I was like *hey! This is an occupied country! Where did this feast come from?* But that was the thing about the Iraqi invasion—in a lot of ways, things went on for *some* rich local people kind of semi-normally—it was a very weird war.

And then Khaled is by my side, and he is saying how he helped to orchestrate this feast, and seeming *real pleased* I was so surprised. So after Lulu and Trang are seated up at the head of this huge circular marble table, Khaled like sits next to me. And it turned out Khaled was a real rich guy who had a servant from Pakistan who had shown a talent for cooking, and he had sent the guy to a special cooking school in Paris, and when the Pakistani guy came back Khaled had like ordered him to update classic Bedouin dishes. And Khaled was really hopeful I'd love the meal, because he was going to make a cookbook of Bedouin dishes after the Gulf War was over and sell it in America, and if there was interest maybe even open some restaurants in New York and San Francisco, as he had rich Kuwaiti relatives in both cities.

I guess Khaled felt the need to say something to all at the table before the chow, so he stopped wringing his napkin in his hands and stood up and clinked his glass just like we do in the marines when we want to make a toast. Only Khaled used a ring on his pinky to clink the glass, as the locals had no knives or forks. Anyway, Khaled said this: "Once it is said there were hailstones in the desert, so too before us we see Thomas Trang and Princess Lulu together. *Allahu akbar.*" I slapped Khaled on the back when he sat down, as it was a pretty classy little toast, in my opinion, and totally nailed the miracle quality of the whole saga. And Khaled, I got to say, did not seem like a resistance fighter right then—I mean he was all weepy about Trang and Lulu, but mostly I think about his toast and how it moved *him*. Trang was eyeballing me because Khaled was crying into his napkin and shaking his head. And in a way that was pretty cool, because it just showed you once again this sort of romantic thing has some international currency. And I just started thinking hard about the damn old pearl in a crazy but positive way, like the pearl was the local representative for this international romance thing.

And then I shook my head to clear it, and found all eyes were back on Princess Lulu and Tommy Trang, as I guess Lulu had asked to see the *pearl,* which was weird, as I had just been thinking about the pearl. And I was nervous for a second, but Trang had it in his pocket, and like fished it out and it looked all shined up. Trang like turned and winked at me, and Lulu took the pearl in her hands and closed her eyes and looked like she was saying a prayer or something. And then she stood up and sort of sang some in Arabic for like five minutes, and all I grabbed onto was Lulu was apparently thanking Allah for bringing Tommy Trang to her by reciting some Koranic stuff about noble warriors, and I was kind of bummed she left out Krebes and Ali and Mahdi and me and laid on us stuff from Allah. But that Lulu was a cool chick, and she left her seat and came and gave me a kiss on the cheek, and did the same for Ali. She skipped Mahdi, and at the time I thought it was just a mistake.

Princess Lulu then popped a candle out of a serious silver candlestick holder and placed a bit of paper in the hole and then placed the pearl there, so it was like the pearl was there for all to see! And she placed the candlestick holder in the center of the table, and then Khaled jumped up and fiddled with the lighting so there was like a spotlight on the pearl, and man, it really did glow in that light. And you couldn't help but think about how this pearl had been held by Captain Shakespear when he was out in the desert on the warpath with Abdul Aziz and wanted to think about his royal Kuwaiti princess lover, and how it was with him when he stood his ground at the plains of Jarrab and was hacked by Rasheed swords, and how his Kuwaiti lover had probably pulled out her hair when she got the pearl returned with bloodstains, and how each Kuwaiti daughter of that lover had gotten it down to Princess Lulu, and how now we were here sort of celebrating in a serious romantic way how the pearl had brought together Princess Lulu and Tommy Trang for like a second try at an international romance.

So one second I am totally into the glowing romantic mood of the pearl, and then I am seeing Captain Shakespear get hacked to death. I mean I really am *seeing* the guy and it was really weird, and it wasn't *pretty* to see him bleeding to death in the sands. And I am thinking: *to hell with the pearl!* And I like want to *blow the party and grab Trang and head back to Saudi.* So I like blinked and right then we start to eat, and someone fills my glass with wine, and I like chug it down. And so then Khaled grabs the bottle from a servant and fills it up again and says it is time to eat the *saleeg*. And the *saleeg* is like put right in front of me, and it is a *lamb's head boiled in milk!* Khaled jams in his hand and yanks the lamb's head aloft with milk dripping from it, and this lamb's boiled eyes were checking me out *in a seriously questioning way!* And for a while Khaled is going on about how the lamb's head was cooked to his specifications, as would be described in his new Bedouin cookbook, but I didn't hear much as the lamb and me were in a sort of staring contest, and the lamb won—*I had to look away.*

Luckily this was a real feast, so Khaled moved on to other foods he wanted me to sample. Like he was in a real rage about something called *sayadiah,* and he started to apologize because technically it wasn't a Bedouin dish but a fisherman's meal from Jeddah on the Red Sea. It made Khaled real happy that I agreed that nobody in America was going to complain if he slipped a meal from Jeddah into an otherwise Bedouin cookbook. This agreement got Khaled so jazzed he dragged me from my chair out of the room to show me where the *sayadiah* was cooked behind the villa on what looked like lava rocks from a sauna. So Khaled was waving his hands in front of me explaining how you burn onions in oil, add water until the water is black, and add rice and lemon and salt. I was trying to concentrate on the culinary details to take the vision of the lamb's staring eyes out of my head, and it kind of worked. Then I was raced back to my seat and Khaled poked at my fish to show me how nice the white fish looked against the brown rice, and then he watched carefully as I ate the *sayadiah.*

Up at the head of the table, Princess Lulu and Trang were like digging into what looked like a whole roasted lamb. Again, you would have thought those in Kuwait were suffering for food, and when I mentioned this to Khaled he said, "But we are the resistance fighters! We must eat, or how will we fight?" Anyway, the roast lamb at the head of the table was steaming hot, but Lulu and Trang were just cranking their right hands—as was the traditional Arab way—into the carcass and ripping off hunks and feeding each other stuffed mouthfuls and laughing away as the grease or sauce or whatever got all over their chins and clothes. And looking at Lulu I was thinking: *she gets as stoked as Trang about something as simple as chowing down!* Then I felt Khaled patting my arm to tell me there was another course for me, and it was something called *mootabug,* a thin dough filled with banana and white cheese. Now that *mootabug* was good stuff, and cleaned out the vision of the lamb's eyes totally.

When I looked up again, Princess Lulu was waving her hands, and I guess telling Trang some story. I like beamed in on the conversation and heard Lulu say that when her mother was about to give birth, she went off to visit her Bedouin midwife in the desert. But she could not find the midwife, so ended up giving birth to Lulu in a cave, but died from the effort. But several days later the midwife had a dream, and it led her to the cave, and there she found Lulu's dead mother with a suckling baby at her breast. And I guess the deal was the dead mother's breasts had remained operational after death. And Lulu said from that point on she was raised by the Bedouin midwife because the midwife felt so bad about missing the birth, and also because she saw the dead mother nursing as like a sign from Allah that Lulu was special.

Little Ali had like beamed in on this story too, and waggled his eyebrows at me to say *did you hear that whopper from Princess Lulu?* And I like looked at Trang, and he was looking at *Lulu with like a look that she was just the coolest girl he had ever met by far.* It was a frozen sort of look, like if he blinked she'd be gone. And soon enough I figured out that part of the mighty attraction of Princess Lulu for Trang was that she could really tell some whoppers with a straight face. Anyway, to be honest I was probably wearing a dubious look on my face right then after her stuff about nursing the dead mother, as unlike Trang I was worried right then she was a little *crazy.* But Trang right then was one happy dude to be hooked up with this maybe crazy Kuwaiti princess, and biting with gusto into a dessert called *turroomba,* which looked kind of like a donut, and he got so jazzed about the *turroomba* that he waved it and yelled out, *"Hey Cody, try a turroomba!"* And Ali like grinned and mimicked Trang yelling out *try a turroomba!* in Arabic, and all the Arabs cracked up, because I guess *turroomba* also somehow meant *enema.* And for the rest of our time in Kuwait, whenever Princess Lulu proclaimed some totally crazy stuff as factual—which was pretty often as I guess like Trang she found facts kind of boring—and I would look dubious, Trang would like jump in with, *Hey Cody, try a turroomba!*

So then the party was pretty pleasant again, and a large silver bowl of water was carried in, and it was like it was from the Crusades. And everyone took a drink from it as it was passed around, and that felt very cool and ancient. And then the table was cleaned up by the servants—who were actually some of the resistance guys—and when they took away the tablecloths Khaled got excited and waving his hand around the table said most of those at this very table were *artists!* It turned out they were not artists, actually, but *actors*! And when I heard that I just hung my head down and shook it and kind of snorted like as to say: *would somebody please send us some professional soldiers in this war!* And Khaled wanted to know why I was snorting, but I didn't explain about how the Sulluba were a *dancing* troupe, and it seemed crazy that our Kuwaiti Resistance fighters were *actors*! So Khaled didn't know why I was snorting and shaking my head, but he sort of patted me on the back and said the old *inshallah* a few times like that covered this weirdness.

Khaled started rattling to the table of fighters or actors or whatever they were, and Princess Lulu started clapping her hands with glee. It turned out that was how Princess Lulu knew these Kuwaiti guys in the first place, as she had done a little secret acting with them when she wasn't running around the desert with the Bedouin drawing henna tattoos on her face and hands. I say *secret* as she wasn't supposed to be allowed to be in their plays as a chick and a princess. And as I learned later from Khaled, it turned out all her life she had been really on fire to be an actress and someday head to Hollywood to star in some infidel movies, and it was a cause of personal heartbreak she was totally shut down by the emir in this regard. The word was she was constantly in hot water with the emir for trying to slip out dressed like a guy and hang with the actors like Khaled, and so in the final months before the emir got her engaged he pretty much kept her locked up in the palace. And then when Lulu heard she was engaged to old Colonel Fawwaz, the emir not only had to keep her locked up, but *doped up* too.

Anyway, in a flash they all decide to put on one of their plays, one that was supposed to be a real local crowd-pleaser. So Khaled gets up on the table and starts pulling up the lines of what I took to be imaginary sails, and it is explained by Lulu that he was a sea captain in old Kuwait heading out to get pearls. And a number of other Kuwaiti guys jump on the table and aboard the old *dhow*, which is what Lulu called the ship, and made like to do sailing stuff. You couldn't tell really what they were doing—some were clearly manning the lines, but others were waving their hands in the air, and others were leaping around like the deck was on fire. I glanced at my man Trang, and he nodded back at me like *this is very cool,*

whatever the hell it is they are supposed to be doing on this dhow! Well, according to Princess Lulu—who served as like a voice-over narra-
tor—all they were doing was heading out to the pearl beds on the
old dhow, and they took their time doing it as there must not have
been much wind, and then the actors all sat down on the dhow I
guess to wait in the burning sun to get to the pearl beds.

It took a while to get to the pearl beds, and the Kuwaiti guys did
their best acting to make us understand they were baking in the
sun and running out of water and really suffering. And then from
the like kitchen of the villa there was a tremendous smashing
sound, and that woke me right up until I understood it was the
kitchen servants making the sounds of a terrible storm at sea. And
all the actors put their arms around each other and leaned from
side to side together, like they were swaying on high seas. And it
must have been a terrible storm, as then the guys were rolling
around the table! But then they all crawled to their knees, and
made like they were all working together to bail out the boat, and
Khaled the Captain was standing over them sort of cheering them
on. Captain Khaled really tried to rally the troops after that to save
the dhow, but I guess the dhow sank, because in twos and threes all
the Kuwaiti guys slipped off the table until there was just Captain
Khaled, and then he sank slowly to the table and into a bow and
the thing was over.

I thought it was an okay play about a dhow sinking and everyone dying, but *man,* the Kuwaiti guys who were *not* in the play were
really *moved!* There were only like four of them left over, but they
were all pretty broken up about the dhow sinking. And when I
looked around, a lot of the actors were broken up too, and some
were wiping away tears! And Princess Lulu was clapping away, as
were Trang and me and Ali—and even Mahdi—but I think we
three guys were just being polite. I mean none of us were crying
like Princess Lulu about the play, and I looked at Trang and he
shrugged back at me with a grin like as to say *something about sinking
dhows really gets to these people, make a note of it.*

So when I got a chance, as the Kuwaiti dudes were all congratu-
lating each other like *no my friend, it was truly you who were wonderful in*

this play, I asked Khaled why the sinking *dhow* was such a tearjerker for the locals. Right away I could see it was the *wrong* question, as he was offended and said *"was it not for you too?"* And then Khaled pursed his lips and looked to the ceiling and said, "Do you not see, my friend, the truth? Now there are in Kuwait no more sinking *dhows*! No one in Kuwait dies anymore out of a hunger for *pearls*!" I guess it wouldn't have been the same play if it was set on an oil tanker.

Lulu was gone from the wartime dinner party for a while after this for some unknown reason, and I got caught up in some random Arab chitchat with one or two of the actors about how fine they were in the play. And then Lulu comes back into the room, and it kind of looks like she's now in a golden bathrobe with wings, but she sees everyone looking and raises her arms and flaps them like a bird and says it is a Japanese wedding kimono. No explanation as to where she scored this golden kimono, or why she opted for the costume change. Lulu was never big on explaining, but then again, neither was Trang. So anyway, Princess Lulu sits down next to Tommy Trang in the wedding kimono at the round table. No one is saying anything, but all are staring at Princess Lulu. I was kind of hoping no one else would speak so I could just keep looking at her blue eyes, which were what we call back in the States 'bedroom eyes.' Trang like reached out to take her hand, but as he did she turned it over and said *look at what I found upstairs.*

When last we saw Princess Lulu with a bug it was a centipede, and now she had some sort of bug in her hand again. She was looking down at it, and her eyes were like misty with tears, and she said, *I do not know its name.* I took this to mean she knew the names of most desert bugs from hanging with the Bedouin. Lulu said, *when I do not know the name of a bug and it is beautiful I call it a 'wonderful bug.'* This made her laugh in a sweet and childish way and glance around at all of us. Ali like held a candle over the bug, and we all crowded closer and oohed and aahed over the bug. I oohed and aahed because Trang was grinning from the wonderful bug to Princess Lulu and to all assembled like he was the proud *father* of this bug. It was almost too much for me. Trang hadn't shown a bit of interest in a bug—other than locusts—as long as I had known him, and now my friend the warrior was pointing out to Khaled the pretty gold lace on the edge of the wing tips.

Khaled for his part was just using this as a chance to ogle the Princess Lulu's superior tits up close, because it looked like she wasn't wearing much under the kimono, and the kimono was kind of hanging open. So I must have looked pretty dubious about this bug love-fest, because I suddenly saw Princess Lulu eyeballing me through the crowd of admirers. And she said, "Cody Carmichael." She used my full name a lot from there on, Princess Lulu. "Cody Carmichael, do you know this wonderful bug that has come from foreign lands has spoken to me?"

Uh-oh. That's what I'm thinking. *Uh-oh.* Because she seemed *serious as hell.* And I thought right then she *was serious as hell.* Later on I'd understand she liked to yank people's chain with a straight face as much as Trang, and she didn't *really* talk to bugs. Anyway, at the same time, there was some *truth* in her chatting up bugs, because she was crazily into the wonders of nature. As the pilot told me on the way to Egypt, this was a chick who cared more for nature than any other human being—until Trang, but then he was sort of a force of nature! But the thing was, it took me a while to figure out Lulu's virtues, and in these days I still had her marked as a young fiery babe of old Arabia, and a bit of a nutcase.

But the thing was right then my man Trang was digging this bug-talk stuff from the princess, and he's eyeballing me like, *aren't you going to ask what the wonderful bug said to the princess?* And I'm not! No, I'm not going to ask. I don't know why, but at that moment I was homesick for some American-style *common sense.* But anyway, Lulu the Magnificent wasn't done with holding center stage. She like leaves the room again and returns with this jewel-covered silver case, and the wonderful bug is placed in this case she says is like from Yemen, and it is closed with a snap and sits quietly on the table in front of Princess Lulu. And that was when the princess Lulu said something kind of interesting. She raised up the closed silver box with the wonderful bug in her two hands and said, *this was how I was in Kuwait before the coming of Thomas Trang.* And then she opened the silver box and took out the wonderful bug and as she tossed the bug toward me said *and this is how I am now.* And the damn bug like flew twitching around all our heads, and then landed on me and sat glued there for the rest of the evening, twitching its antennae toward me like two scolding fingers.

So then Princess Lulu asks if anyone wants to hear a poem she has written while she was endlessly waiting for us marines to show up in Kuwait. And all the Kuwaiti Resistance dudes are like, *right on, lay us on a poem, Princess Lulu!* And suddenly I am like chilled out, because something breaks in me and I'm like, *she's just a poetry-writing sixteen-year-old girl, we have these types in the US of A!* Nothing *too* weird here. So Princess Lulu stands up and places the silver box carefully in the lap of my man Tommy Trang, and then she like takes his hand. I guess the poem was like for *Trang.* Princess Lulu throws a like fierce look around the room and raising one arm of her kimono says real slow:

> *Desert flaming*
> *for a hummingbird*
> *sipping from the well*
> *of your lost oasis*

Now I didn't see any birds in the desert other than the king's hawks and the hunted Hubara Bustard, never mind *hummingbirds,* and would the little bird have to fly to the bottom of the well to sip the water? Anyway, the poet Princess Lulu was like torching a blue-eyed gaze into Trang that would make your hair crinkle. Last time I had seen a look like that was when the king of Saudi Arabia's hawk was eyeballing me like he wanted to eat my infidel liver. And Trang looked kind of pinned to his chair by that hawk look, but mighty pleased by it too. I guess one of the cool things about loving a certifiable chick is her *love* has a flaming-arrow quality you don't usually find in the totally sane. Anyway, the words to the little poem started to pinball around in my jarhead, and I had nothing to do so I started to think about the *words.* And I figured that 'hummingbird' was Lulu and the 'lost oasis' was Trang. And then I decided the 'desert flaming' bit was pretty cool: *like what if the world was on fire to see if like your love works out?* I mean most of us from the USA don't think the universe cares all that much about our love life. But I have to admit suddenly I was like kind of infected again with this idea that *maybe the universe had a major plan to bring together Lulu and Trang.* But then that seemed totally crazy, so I let the idea drop.

So anyway, nobody is moving, and Princess Lulu is just holding Tommy Trang's two hands—and Trang's hands are in turn wrapped around the old pearl he has plucked off the candlestick. And this is getting to be a bit much, but what the hell—*these kids were into the old pearl!* Anyway, nothing else is really happening, and so we are all just quiet and waiting for these two to break off the *special pearl moment.* And then Khaled and his resistance dudes start to do real quietly their *Aiyah! Aiyah!* thing, and they get the *Aiyahs!* going like in a chant, and then louder and louder, and then right when they are like pounding on the table or clapping along with their chant like camels heading into battle, they break off into a lot of *Allahu akbars,* their *Allah is Great* thing, and for me at least that mention of old Allah kind of poisoned the pure love vibe of the general *Aiyah!* mood. Anyway, I was thinking about everything and kind of spacing out, when I looked around the room, and Princess Lulu and Tommy Trang were gone.

CHAPTER 16

So Princess Lulu and Tommy Trang were gone from the party. I was worried about them, but Khaled said he knew where they were and they were safe. He seemed to indicate they were at a villa down the beach, and that they were being guarded by his fighters. I wasn't sure about how safe they were guarded by these Kuwaiti *actors,* but I understood Trang wanting to get away and be alone for the first time with Princess Lulu. It dawned on me that although Tommy Trang was *crazy* about Princess Lulu, he had never really *spoken* to Princess Lulu in private. This had never seemed to bother Trang, like it was all so clear to him she was the one from the get-go there was nothing to say about it. I was now curious how the dude *knew* she was the one, because from what I could see it was turning out he was *right.* I just never *totally* know things—even following Trang was something I had some doubts about like every day. Anyway, I crashed later on the couch, and in the morning woke to the quiet sounds of the oil-slicked waters of the Persian Gulf sloshing up on the beach at dawn.

I went out through the glass doors and sat on the beach, and once again you would not have known there was a war on at all. So as I am sitting there on the sand, watching the sun struggling to break through the oil haze, Khaled comes out with a tray with breakfast. And he wanted me to try his soft bread with black honey from some place called *Hadramaut,* and some white goat cheese, and these tiny green olives from Lebanon. What made it excellent was Khaled had made so potent a coffee—even if it kind of looked like sewage in the cup—to wash this stuff all down. And Khaled went on and on about breakfast recipes, and it was fine sitting there thinking about how happy Trang and Lulu must have been down the beach in one of these villas and talking about international breakfasts with Khaled like we had not a care in the world.

And then we started to talk about Princess Lulu, and I got to questioning Khaled about how she wanted to be an actress and go to Hollywood and all. Khaled suddenly got all pissed and yelled out, *Lulu is crazy!* Khaled chilled after that outburst, and asked me if I liked the play about the sinking dhow. I was like, *sure Khaled, a great play about a sinking dhow.* Khaled was pleased as hell I liked the dhow play, but then got on a loud rant about how *crazy Lulu was always pushing their acting crew for Shakespeare and other infidel plays!* He got totally fired up about this, and kept asking me, *Why must we do Shakespeare when there are many famous Kuwaiti writers?* I didn't know what to say, and Khaled ranted on that Lulu's whole problem was that she *read too much infidel shit* generally, and that all this reading has made her unhappy with the orderly Islamic life found in Arabia.

Anyway, as the sun rose it became clear Khaled had a real head of steam up this morning. Maybe he drank too much of his fine coffee. But suddenly Khaled was up in front of me kind of acting out what he would do to Saddam if he met the dude in hand-to-hand combat. And that mock fighting got his juices going, and he stormed into the villa to wake up his resistance fighters. So I got up off the beach with my coffee to follow him inside, and they were all sacked out here and there and kind of blankly looking at the leader Khaled, who was making a speech about how they were going to *kick some Iraqi ass today!* I mean that was the *gist* of it, and the rest might of been like the mighty story of Islam, who knows? Every once in a while he'd stop sort of yelling at the sleepy dudes on the floor, and glance at me, and I took it my job was to pump my fist and say something fired up, so I'd lay on them a Marine Corps *oooraah!* yell, and this seemed to please Khaled a great deal.

Next thing I know the coffee is on in some big pots, so I had some more, as did the Kuwaiti resistance guys—they were really slugging the bitter stuff back. And Khaled was still railing at them, and I guess his stoked-up energy, plus the coffee, kind of seeped into the room, because soon the Kuwaiti guys are clearly catching the martial mood. I was like wondering where all this was leading to, but soon enough I know, because Khaled gets right in my face with his coffee and olive and goat cheese breath, and is saying, "It is time to strike a blow against Saddam!"

So I am like, *excellent, let's sit down and make a mission plan.* But the *plan* thing got a big negative from Khaled, who seemed to think only cowards make plans, not heroes of the resistance. So I gave up and got back to cheering them on and slugging coffee, and soon I was kind of fired up myself. I mean maybe I was in a confused state, what with Tommy Trang linking up with Princess Lulu. It was like, *what exactly was I supposed to do now?* So maybe that was why I was free to get fired up with the Kuwaiti guys, because I didn't have anything else on my agenda, and kicking some Iraqi ass did seem like a cool way to spend the day. The way Khaled was making it sound, *we were going to clear the Iraqis out of Kuwait today! We would have a great victory!* These Kuwaiti guys really knew how to have a pre-battle pep rally, but part of me, the whole time we were all yelling, never really thought they were going to leave the villa—but I was wrong!

Soon from out of the closets and the storerooms the guys were bringing weapons—fresh M16s and ammo and grenades and the like. I am shown all this stuff, and a lot of it was just out of the box, so to speak. And Khaled is in my face fingering a grenade and saying, "Today we will show *this* to Saddam!" And next thing I know all the guys are like slipping out of the villa and heading toward the Toyotas, and Khaled is waving for me to come, and I was thinking I shouldn't go, but then I was like, *I guess that's why I'm here, man, to link up with these fighters!* So I think about leaving a note for Trang, *Goat cheese in the fridge, see you after the great victory,* but then I just head out the door after the warriors. Little Ali and Mahdi had *no* interest in going with the crazy guys, and Ali looked at me like I had a death wish or something.

They had me down on the floor of the Toyota, but I wanted to see the passing scene, so kept popping my head up. And there wasn't much to see except the nearly empty streets heading toward downtown Kuwait City in the distance. And that was the direction we were rattling towards, and Khaled and the guys discussed as we went along how to avoid the Iraqi sentries on some roads, and so we took some weird detours through some lots here and there. I tried to ask what exactly *was* our heroic strike against Saddam going to be, but Khaled kept saying, "You will see! A great one!" And Khaled taught the guys to yell in English, *Kill the Bastards!* So that was yelled a lot, and I wondered if we were on a suicide run right into the center of the Iraqi command in Kuwait City.

But I guess I shouldn't have worried about that! What happened was we came to a roundabout, where there was a big mosaic of Saddam Hussein sitting there in the island. The Iraqis must have went to some serious effort to get this mosaic of Saddam down here to Kuwait. But there was the face of the evil guy who caused the whole mess, kind of beaming down at us with a sort of airhead smile as we squealed around the roundabout in the Toyota. We went around and around while the guys yelled out the window shaking their fists at the portrait of Saddam, and then when they were all done making their statements about Saddam's mother and goats, they like pointed their rifles out the window and start spraying the painted tiles with rounds. The guys were crawling over each other to empty their clips, and then popping back in to smash in another clip. Khaled was damn near out the window as he pulled a grenade with his teeth and tossed *that* up at Saddam. It like bounced off Saddam's bushy mustache and back to the concrete. We were on the other side of the roundabout when it went off, but still caught a couple of pieces of stray shrapnel through the window, and one of the Kuwaiti guys got nicked under the eye.

The bloodied Kuwaiti was holding his face with both hands and yowling. I like peeled his hands away from his face and it wasn't much of a wound, but it did bleed. I looked up and had to yell right then, as Khaled was still squealing in circles around the monument, and I told him to *get the hell back to base,* or at least away from the roundabout. He didn't respond, but kept grinning over his shoulder at the wounded fighter like he was really *pleased.* So I like slapped him on the shoulder and let out with the local cry: *aiyah! aiyah!* and added: *a great victory! a mighty victory!* This seemed to register with Khaled, and he grinned and yelled: *aiyah! aiyah!* and we went squealing away from the monument with all the boys rocking the car with their various *fakhed* war cries and the like, and the guy with the scratch wailing through his hands like he was heading to Allah pronto.

So I was in this vehicle with all these crazy screaming Arabs, and I suddenly just sat back in my corner of the seat and looked out the car window at the passing ugly concrete scene of the streets of Kuwait, and I was suddenly just chilling. Sometimes things get so crazy you just kick back and enjoy the ride, as if you are now safe in the hands of the gods of craziness. But the guys wouldn't let me chill, as each wanted to slap me five, I guess as a sort of international way of saying: *Hey, man, don't chill, join in the victory party! Aiyah! Aiyah!*

So then, to show soldierly brotherhood, for a few minutes as we hightailed it back to the beachfront villa, I taught them all to do the Marine Corps yell of: *Oooraah!* So they all, one after the other, let loose with their various Arabic *oooraahs!* I guess because they were actors mostly, and wanted to get it right, they had me do it over and over so each could examine his brother Arab warrior's like *oooraahbility,* so to speak. And they all examined my face after each *oooraah!,* to sort of gauge my opinion. So now their mood was like serious, like it really mattered whether they can *oooraah!* and that was when I kind of crashed in mood and was like: *get me out of this goddamn vehicle!*

Mostly I think I wanted to report to Trang the situation with Khaled and the Kuwaiti Resistance, and that we were in bed with the original gang that couldn't shoot straight. And as I am thinking we are closer to the villa, suddenly the Toyota is yanked to the side and we squeal to a halt and there is a lot of Arabic and the guys are out of the car and making a wild charge after some old guy in a filthy robe who is like skulking near the side of a concrete house. And it is clear he's an old dude, as he kind of tries to hobble away on stiff legs, and the Kuwaiti Resistance guys like catch up and knock him down with their rifles and start whacking the hell out of him. Then he is dragged to his feet, and dragged by his armpits to the car and shoved into the backseat on like top of me. And then *Aiyah!*, we are off again!

So the old dude in my lap stinks, and he is getting pummeled by rifle butts, and I am getting whacked here and there, so I yell out to Khaled, and he yells out for the guys to cut it out. And so I have a moment with this shivering old dude on my lap to ask Khaled *what the deal was,* and he yells over his shoulder: *Aiyah! He is working with the Iraqis! He is a sympathizer! He is a Palestinian! We know this of him! We will find out all he knows!* Well, that was all the break they would give in the pummeling action, and went back to pummeling him with their fists, and I got so sick of it I like started to swing back at the guys from behind the old Palestinian, who had like pissed in my lap, and then we like came to the villa.

I am out of the vehicle in a flash, and kind of carried the old dude with me, as he was in my lap. And he tried to like hobble down the street, but the boys were on him. I had a grip on him however, so there was like a tug-of-war between me and the guys for the Palestinian. Khaled came over and tried to break my grip on the old guy's wrist and I am like saying to him, "What did he do, man? What exactly did he do?"

But I guess I was coming up against that Arab dislike of facts, because my questions really pissed off Khaled. He damn near spit at me to say, *"He is a sympathizer! We all know this! He is a very bad man! He will see justice!"*

So I was like, "Who? Who? Who told you he was a bad man? What proof do you have?"

And Khaled kept saying, "Muhammad knows! Muhammad knows!"

I thought this was their *main man Muhammad,* but a ugly resistance guy got in my face and nodded vigorously and Khaled said slapping him on the shoulder, "This is Muhammad! He swears the truth!" So right then all the Kuwaiti dudes do a smart thing, they all drop the Palestinian and gang up on me. And so they break my grip on the old guy, and Khaled drags him in the house. And when he is in the villa, all the guys forget about me and run after Khaled and the old Palestinian.

So I stand there for a second or two looking at the door of the villa, and then take a breath and march inside. They are taping the guy in a chair. I guess they were prepared for this sort of thing, as I saw three different guys holding rolls of tape. They had his mouth taped shut too, and his pants were down at his knees. Khaled cut the head off an orange power cord with a knife and stripped the wires some, and plugged it into a socket. The old guy must have decided I was his only chance, as he was giving me a real wide-eyed plea to like *save his ass.* But I had to admit, I was new to the local scene, and wondered if maybe as crazy as these Kuwaiti dudes were, they did know something I didn't about this Palestinian guy's guilt? It seemed like they had just grabbed him because he was a Palestinian, but could I be sure?

But when I saw Khaled was planning to put the hot end of the power cord to the old guy's balls, that was when I tried to pull the cord from his hands. And man, Khaled was one unhappy Arab! He like started yanking back on the cord, so we are both yanking and trying not to touch the hot end—it was kind of like two guys dancing with a orange rattlesnake. So then I give a yank that pulls it from the wall so at least it isn't *hot,* and right then there is a big commotion from the front of the villa, as a car has pulled up. And some guys are carrying the dead body of somebody up the walk, and all I can think is: *Where the hell are the Iraqis? How could they miss all this commotion? They must be idiots!* And the dead *headless* young Arab guy is carried into the room, followed by someone with a shopping bag *with the guy's head in it,* and there is a lot of wailing, because the dead guy was in the resistance. He looks pretty bad, this guy—aside from missing his head he's like clearly riddled with bullet holes. All the Arab guys are suddenly quiet and looking at Khaled, as I understand this is like his *cousin,* and there is a note pinned to the dead guy's chest, and Khaled leans down and reads it and yanking it off waves it at me and says, "This is a message from the Iraqis! It says, 'Give up the princess, or we will kill you all, one by one!'"

I guess the Iraqis had like picked this dude up, tortured him, and dumped him in front of Khaled's family home. As I was to learn, that was the Iraqis' thing, to pick someone up, torture or kill them, and then dump them back in front of their family home. It turned out the death of this young cousin of Khaled was the first actual fatality in this cell of the Kuwaiti Resistance, because other than today's firing on Saddam's portrait, they had been mostly into the business of late-night money and jewel burial, which was not a high-risk activity. So anyway, Khaled is down on his knees, looking into the bag with his cousin's head and grieving, and when he looks up he yells at me, *"You have brought bad luck to us!"* How he figured *that* I have no idea, but your Arab seemed to like to blame somebody else for his troubles. So then Khaled climbs off his knees, and you can see he's in a fury, and it isn't going to go well for the Palestinian. Khaled goes and plugs back in the power cord from the lamp, and he's just about to juice the old guy's nuts when there is a yell like, *"Yo!"* and in comes Tommy Trang in just his Iraqi camo pants. I guess he's like strolled in from the beach side of the villa, and his back is covered with sand like he's been sunbathing, and he's got a dive knife he must have found at the other villa strapped to his lower leg—not the leg that got bit by the dog, the other one.

So Trang like takes in the whole scene at a glance, and nobody is moving. The Kuwaiti boys still clearly had a feeling Trang was a crazy heart-eater, and it was like they were frozen, waiting to see what this crazy ninja would do next. Tommy Trang did look pretty tough and serious. And I guess my man Trang was no fool, as he seemed to have a grip on what was going down. So Trang like reaches down and pulls out the dive knife, and he goes to the old Palestinian and grabs the dude by what hair he has left and shoves back his head so his neck is exposed, and he lays the knife on his neck and runs it across real soft, so it reveals a little trace line of blood. And then he turns to me, and in a pissed way says, "Why didn't you kill this traitor? What is wrong with you? Are you a coward? Are you afraid of blood? Are you a woman?" Khaled translates all this in an amazed way, *and all seem pleased when Trang walks over and like punches me in the gut!* It was a hard and surprising hit, and I like dropped to my knees and then *Trang like kicked me over!*

I have an idea what Trang is up to, *but he was playing the role of the badass pretty strong!* Anyway, he goes back to the Palestinian and tells the Kuwaiti guys he's going to slit the old dude's throat right now, and *some Arab should get a glass so all can drink his blood.* Then when one Arab goes off to get a glass, Trang like starts saying he's going to torture the old guy himself and eat his nuts, to get him to *name names!* And then he looks at all the Kuwaitis and says, "You boys don't want to see what I'm going to do!" *But the Arabs do want to see!* But Trang is already dragging the Palestinian out the door by his arms, and the chair the old guy is sitting in is bouncing down the steps. Trang like picked up the chair and the guy and carried them both to a Toyota. He opened the door and tosses the chair and old man sideways into the backseat. Then Trang holds out his hand, and someone tosses him the keys. So Tommy Trang yells to me, "Have these warriors get a barbecue going on the beach, when I get back we'll all eat Palestinian heart for dinner." So when that parting line was translated as the Toyota squealed away, *it went over big with the Kuwaitis!*

There wasn't anything to do but wander back in the villa. The Kuwaitis were glancing at me like I was a coward, but the glow of crazy Trang's doings had them all stoked up, and they went back into *aiyah!* pep-rally mode. I don't want to hang around with these nutty Kuwaitis and the headless cousin, so I go out the rear doors thinking I'll head down the beach and circle back to the road and catch up with Tommy Trang, and right then Ali like pops his head over the wall of the villa of the lady with the flowers. So I climb over the wall. And Princess Lulu comes to me with her arms out and asks if I am okay and feels my gut, so I guess little Ali was watching the whole thing and reported back to her. She gets all serious, and I am looking in her mysterious blue eyes as she tells me *Allah has sent me to Kuwait for a reason*—I guess other than helping link her up with Tommy Trang—*and that soon Allah will lay this reason on me.*

Ali like grabbed my hand and dragged me out the front door, and soon me and him are running down the empty beachfront street. So as we are running down the street, little Ali is like laying all this *gossip* on me about Princess Lulu and Tommy Trang. I guess little Ali was sleeping outside their door like a dog or something, and he told me the two like didn't do the wild thing, *but just lay together talking all night about the future of Kuwait.* That was what linking up with Lulu did to Trang! She like lit his hero fuse, and soon enough he was this human firework exploding all over Kuwait! I mean he was always crazy, but with Lulu around he just got crazier about not just becoming a hero, *but doing some good!* And this is weird, but one of those screamer songs from the 1970s jumped into my skull right then, the one with the words: *FIGHT! FIGHT! FIGHT! I'M TNT! I'M DYNA-MITE! I'M THE POWER OF LOVE! WATCH ME EXPLOOOOODE!* It was because of that song I came up with the idea of calling him TNT, for like at least two of his initials. Trang wasn't into my calling him TNT, so I only said it in my head when he had us doing some totally crazy shit in the coming weeks, like joining an Iraqi attack on the Coalition forces in Saudi Arabia, or sitting under a podium with Saddam Hussein about to lecture over our heads.

Anyway, right then we saw Tommy Trang pulling into this deserted driveway in the Toyota, and we hopped in the back. Trang said to me, *sorry man, about whacking you in the gut,* and I said, *that's cool.* And so then we have to deal with the old Palestinian. He's untied, but sitting in the backseat looking like he was about to wet his pants again. And the old dude can't speak English, so little Ali like digs into his life story for me and Trang. So we get this whole long story from the Palestinian. The guy had been in prison for five months before the Iraqi invasion *because he lost the dog of some rich Kuwaiti family!* Turns out the locals can't even officially *have* dogs according to the Koran, but as witnessed by the bite on Trang's leg, *people still owned them!* Anyway, the old guy lost a favorite Chihuahua of some rich Kuwaiti lady and *wham!* into the clinker. There had been no trial, and no charges. The old dude said there were dozens—Indians and Pakistanis and Bangladeshis mostly—in the prison without charges because their families were too poor to put up money for their release.

So Tommy Trang asked how the old guy had got out of the prison. And the Palestinian said his getting out during the Iraqi occupation *was what caused all the trouble!* Because the Kuwaitis believed he must have collaborated with the Iraqis to be let go—*that the only good Palestinian was one who was still in jail!* He said he had gotten out by answering to the name of someone who had died during the night. He did not know why he did this. And the Iraqis blindfolded him and dragged him to a courtyard and left him baking in the sun, and then just tossed him out the prison door. That didn't make a hell of a lot of sense, but that was how the old dude said he got freed by the Iraqis.

The Palestinian dude was starting to shake again, and started begging us to like not push him into the street, because he had nowhere to go, and would either be picked up by Iraqis or Kuwaitis. I am like looking at Trang to see what he's thinking, but I guess he was still stuck on the old dude's story about all the Bangladeshis and Pakistanis and the like stuck in the prison *with like no charges and no trial.* And Trang like wants the old Palestinian to take us to the prison tonight so he can get a look at the joint. But the old sorry dude just looks terrified at the idea, and little Ali tells Tommy Trang it is crazy to ask the old guy to lead us there, and besides: Ali knows where the prison is!

When the old Palestinian gets the vibe he doesn't have to lead us back there tonight, and Trang assures him we won't like toss him out of the Toyota, he chills a little. And so then he taps his old skull and says he memorized the names and addresses of as many prisoners as he could while he was in the prison. So Trang slaps the steering wheel and says: *yes!* And so Ali like finds a pen and starts writing the names of these prisoners onto a paper bag he found on the floor. And Tommy Trang kept glancing at the growing list of names with a real pleased look, *like we have really done some good work here!* We are like in the Toyota in a random villa driveway, and every once in a while a car goes by and we all duck down. Weird, but we still hadn't seen any Iraqis.

So Trang is stoked we have this list of screwed prisoners, and says he can't wait to tell Lulu how we'll make our first heroic operation with the Kuwaiti Resistance to bust these guys out, as the old Palestinian had said the prison was lightly guarded. But right as

Tommy Trang said this he like stares at me like as to say *am I crazy?*, as I guess it came to him the Kuwaiti Resistance guys might not be good to go to bust these servant prisoners out, given how they treated the old Palestinian. And I take this opportunity to lay on Tommy Trang my heroic morning mission to like shoot up Saddam's portrait in the roundabout, and me and Trang can't help but crack up laughing over our affiliation with these wacky Kuwaiti warriors.

And then Trang is like real serious again, because he's been made really bummed to hear all these foreign servant dudes are in prison without charges and trial for stuff like *losing a dog*. Remember how hot Tommy Trang was on the *American Bill of Rights,* and you can imagine how upset Trang was about this being done by the country we were like trying to *liberate*. So we are on a downer about the Kuwaitis in general as we all decide to head back to the lady's villa to see Lulu.

CHAPTER 17

So when we enter the lady's villa, I see this chick standing there in the hallway who isn't Lulu, and I knew her right away, although it seemed like a hundred years since I last saw her: *it was Leila, the maid of Princess Lulu, the girl behind the curtain, the girl with the centipede in her private parts, the great love of Colonel Fawwaz, the girl who really belonged on a beach in California.* The last time I had seen her was when me and Colonel Fawwaz returned from our fun trip to Cairo, and she had mouthed off and said how bent Colonel Fawwaz was about Princess Lulu being in love with a supposed Jew like Tommy Trang, and she had got the crap knocked out of her for her troubles by the big colonel.

And I guess she had been mouthing off to Colonel Fawwaz again, as she had a purple shiner and a pretty bruised face overall. She had a load of orange makeup on, and I figure she had done some triage on her face to try and make herself presentable. But with the purple eye and the swelling, all the heavy orange makeup did was make her look like she was heading out for Halloween. That sucked, as in her former state she was a real beach babe. It made me feel less than friendly toward big Colonel Fawwaz.

Anyway, Leila the maid seemed really pleased to see me again, and held both my hands and looked me in the eye and said how great I looked, and I said likewise back to her, as it seemed the right thing to say. But she took that as an opportunity to lay into how

Colonel Fawwaz had messed up her face, and Lulu came down-stairs right then and we all kind of took our chairs out on the back porch because Leila went into the story of how she had just snuck into Kuwait, and started back like when she was born in Jerusa-lem—no kidding!

It became clear we were going to get a *lengthy story* told to us right here in a villa on the Persian Gulf at twilight. And so after wrapping up her childhood in Jerusalem, Leila told how she had loved Colonel Fawwaz even though she knew he was a very bad man, and how after a lot of arm-twisting, *he recently agreed to blow off Princess Lulu and marry her.* But right after their secret engagement, she saw him getting ready to make a trip in the desert, and there were all these Saudi soldiers with him night and day, and one of the sol-diers told her Colonel Fawwaz was going into Kuwait to *find and kill Princess Lulu before she could dishonor both the Saudi and Kuwaiti royal families by getting it on with Tommy Trang,* and the brave Leila confronted Colonel Fawwaz and got the crap knocked out of her. Leila the maid didn't mention the detail about Tommy Trang being a supposed Jew, and I wondered why she hadn't, *and decided in her world this was too awful to even mention in polite company.* But the crowd—Khaled and the fight-ers were now there listening to her saga too—was taking her story at face value: *Colonel Fawwaz was busting a move into Kuwait to kill Princess Lulu before she could pop her cherry with an American marine: after all, Trang was an infidel dog, and that alone was pretty bad in these desert parts.*

So then Leila the maid was telling us how she had decided to *follow* Colonel Fawwaz and his posse of soldiers into Kuwait so she could try and warn Lulu. She only carried a backpack of water and a handbag full of dried fruit for herself. The Saudi team traveled only at night, and during the day slept in holes they dug in the sand. Leila the maid every day scraped a shallow trench in the sand with a piece of wood she found, and lay down in it and waited for evening. By night she snuck close enough to the Saudi team to hear them—and they talked all the way to Kuwait about girls they had boned, and by the time they got to Kuwait City, the maid Leila was so disgusted she said if she had a machine gun, she would have shot all these disgusting Saudi men down! The maid Leila turned to me and said: *you Americans are not the true infidel dogs, it is these Saudi men who are the dogs!*

I wanted to know how the maid Leila had found us here at the villa, and she said it wasn't too hard, that when she got in the city she had called Khaled's *mother*. We all turned to look at Khaled the resistance dude in the dark, but he seemed pretty calm about it, like *of course he kept his mother up to speed on all his doings*. Soon I would learn about Arab mothers and what they know, and the mothers would be put to some good use—but for now I was wondering what would happen to all of us if the Iraqis got ahold of Khaled's mother.

Anyway, I don't know how it came up exactly, but suddenly we were all talking about like *doing something*. So next thing I know, Trang is going on about *how he wants to bust out the Palestinian and other foreign prisoners he has learned about*. And Khaled and his Kuwaiti resistance dudes are way down on this idea like: *who the hell cares about some random servants?* But little Ali right then kind of hinted loudly in Arabic I guess that Khaled and his resistance dudes were probably just a bunch of women, and the situation kind of rolled along, picking up crazy steam, *and suddenly it looked like we were going tonight to free the prisoners.* And next thing I know, there are Princess Lulu and the maid Leila strapping on M16s and some web belts with hand grenades brought by the resistance dudes to the party, and Tommy Trang and me were like: *whoa ladies!*

Princess Lulu argued Kuwait was *her* country, especially as she was a royal *princess,* and she had been on many a *ghazzu* with the Bedouin. She got right in Trang's face and eyeballing him said: *I will fight for my country!* I wasn't all that into the wonderful bug or the poem thing myself, but this martial Princess Lulu was really kind of attractive. And then the maid Leila said *she* was certainly coming, as many of the men in the prison were Palestinian, and she was Palestinian. Khaled got kind of bummed at the mention of the Palestinians in the prison. Tommy Trang said *if Princess Lulu and the maid Leila went, he wasn't going at all,* and he sat back down.

So then the maid Leila made a flowery speech to Princess Lulu saying that she agreed it was too dangerous for Lulu, what with the

Iraqis and Colonel Fawwaz out there wanting to kill her, and that she would ask *to fight in the name of Princess Lulu,* to sort of make up for being the temporary fiancée of a guy like Colonel Fawwaz, who now wanted to kill her beloved friend Lulu. Khaled and his resistance fighters seemed to like the sound of this and think it just and right and a good way to say *sorry,* but Princess Lulu said she was going into this battle, *and that was a royal final word.* Khaled looked at Trang, and Trang shrugged and said he was *maybe okay* on maid Leila coming if she *did what he said to the letter,* but no way on Princess Lulu.

Man, Princess Lulu was pissed at Tommy Trang. She was one fiery sixteen-year-old Kuwaiti gal, and let loose with a long volley of Arabic, and Ali gave up the simulcast and summarized for Trang: *Lulu hates you, now and forever.* But Tommy Trang seemed to get a serious kick out of seeing the burning fire in Princess Lulu. I mean he did until she tried to follow us out the door on the mission, and me and him and some of the Arabs had to like carry her back into the villa kicking and yelling *and like tie her to a couch with the help of the lady of the villa,* who promised to like read to her while we were gone from the stories in *A Thousand and One Nights.* That was the first time we had to tie down Princess Lulu for her own good, and it wouldn't be the last. Man, what a crazy fireball was that princess!

So Ali is like in the lead Toyota with Trang and Khaled and the maid Leila and me, and the rest of the Kuwaiti warriors were following in two other vehicles. And the thing I noticed was that little Ali kept looking at Trang with this look of wonder and respect, and it turned out little Ali knew some of the servant class from Bangladesh that were in this Kuwaiti prison, in some cases for like years. I guess he never thought someone would think to bust these guys out as a first order of business, *and if Ali could have kissed Trang's feet as we busted down the hardball, I think he would have!* I mean if Ali didn't already worship Trang, this was a capper.

Anyway, Ali knows the whole layout of this like ancient mud building where the prisoners were housed. And Ali said there were some fighters guarding the prisoners, but like only four or five— and to Ali they had looked like the half-wits of the Iraqi army. Ali also said it was lucky for us that the prison was on the north side of downtown Kuwait City, and that we would not have to go far. And Trang then spoke up and said with a kind of laugh that if Khaled didn't mind, he'd like to have *some sort* of plan for the mission other than just driving up like Bonnie and Clyde, lowering our guns at the Iraqis, and demanding the prisoners. Khaled kind of tilted his head to the side grudgingly, like, *Okay man, if you insist.* I think Khaled's plan actually was just what Trang had said, and afterwards I wondered if maybe *things would have gone better for at least one of our raiding party on this ghazzu if we had just driven up and jumped out firing.*

But as marines we liked a mission plan. So as we drove through the backstreets of Kuwait in the dark we talked about the layout of the old building, how much room there was on the like plaza in front, how many prisoners there were inside, and what the hell we were to do with them once they were free! For Trang and me this was a sticking point, but Ali and Khaled thought the important thing was that *we bust out the prisoners, and the rest was up to Allah.* So we concentrated on the bust-'em-out part of the operation because the Arabs didn't want to talk about anything else and were really interested as far as I could tell in just firing their weapons. And as we tried to make a mission plan the maid Leila kept telling us that she wanted to be a central part of the plan. I got the feeling she had like a real Arabic *Joan of Arc* vision, and that she wanted to do some-thing real memorable. Trang and I vetoed her time and again, and told her to just stay with the vehicles and chill until we made our escape after the action. But Leila gave us an earful of Arabic that made Khaled laugh at us, and even Ali grinned and refused to translate.

All of a sudden Leila switches gears and sort of spun into a riff on how old Allah had sent Trang to rescue Lulu from her rotten life, and Trang set her straight and said kind of angrily that *Allah had not a thing to do with us busting into Kuwait,* but Leila just smiled at him like he was a nice fool. Trang turned to me and said with a laugh, *man, how do we get these people to knock it off about thanking Allah all the time?* So anyway, when Trang settled down and once again told Leila she was on the sidelines for this operation, we parked like around the corner from the prison in a dark spot. Trang had all the cars turned around so they would be headed back toward the villa. Khaled congratulated Trang on this piece of the 'mission planning,' until Trang told him to clam up. So then we all snuck up—Khaled, Ali, Trang, and me—and peeked around the corner at the prison. And that was when we saw that it was a plain solid concrete box with only two small barred windows and a big solid wooden door across the front—*it was going to be like attacking the Alamo.*

It was clear to Trang and me that we had to get the Iraqis outside into the open, but how this was to be done I had no idea. And then as we huddled I saw the maid Leila was like listening in on our mission planning, and I didn't think much about it right then. But it flashed to me what a brave chick she was in mouthing off to Colonel Fawwaz way back when on the plane back from Cairo. Anyway, she saw me glancing at her and dropped her hand off her M16's trigger to flash me this like *salute.* Then I got my attention back in the huddle, and Trang was talking about circling around to the rear of the prison to see if we had a better chance busting in from the rear.

So Khaled is giving Trang some hell about why we just don't start *hurling grenades* and such, when one of the Toyotas like squealed backwards, and peeled some rubber to turn around. And Trang like jumps in the way of the vehicle as it makes for the plaza, and bounces off the hood. And it is of course the maid Leila making like Joan of Arc, Arab version. Khaled right away lets out an *aiyah!* and wants to raid the prison after her, but mostly he got some stares in the dark from the crouching Arab fighters.

We look around the corner, and the maid Leila is parked in front of the prison and has the hood up on her Toyota, and is leaning in like she wants to change a spark plug. And she has like tied her T-shirt in a knot around her waist in a classic sexy way, and her ass is waggling back and forth from under the hood, and the Iraqis are just racing out of the prison.

She was a brave crazy chick, the maid Leila. Only the classic sexy T-shirt was maybe too strong an *I'm-a-slut* statement here in Arabia, because after making some fake efforts at interest in her engine, the five or six Iraqi soldiers are like grabbing at her tits and her ass and like pushing her back and forth between them and laughing. And then one grabs her by the hair and starts to push her toward the entrance to the prison, and I hear Trang next to me flip his weapon off safe and say something fast to Khaled, and as he jumps up I hear Khaled let out with an *Aiyah!*, and we are fanning out from behind the corner into the courtyard with our whole crew of fighters.

None of the Iraqis are prepared for this and we have them by the balls, but our Arab fighters showed no sense of fire control. They are just unloading their clips toward the prison screaming *Aiyah!* and I guess *fakhed* war cries, and it is over in the ten seconds it took us to charge the prison. The Arabs and Ali stormed into the prison, and me and Trang stopped and bent over the body of the maid Leila long enough to verify she had died. And then Trang and me follow the rest of the fighters into the prison, where we find a whole mess of yelling going on between the twenty or so foreign prisoners in a single big caged room. Ali runs outside to the plaza and then runs back in with a set of keys I guess he got off one of the dead Iraqis. And Ali flings open the gates, *and damned if only two of the prisoners moved out!*

We were all dead silent for a second, and then everyone is yelling their heads off angrily in Arabic, and it becomes clear *the majority of the foreign prisoners are afraid to leave the prison!* And little Ali looks to Trang and yells, *they are afraid of being picked up by the Kuwaitis as collaborators! They say they are being treated well by the Iraqis!* Trang looks at me real bummed and I don't know what the hell to say! Right then a Kuwaiti Resistance guy runs in and says we have to vamoose pronto as they killed a couple of Iraqi soldiers outside and they can hear more on the way. So last thing I saw inside the prison was these sorry foreign prisoners looking at the open gate like: *should I stay or should I go now? If I stay there will be trouble, if I go it will be double.*

When I got outside the prison, I scooped up poor dead Leila in my arms. I thought Trang was right behind me, but when I turned around, *no one was there!* With Leila in my arms, I ran back inside the prison and found Trang *talking to the prisoners with Ali as translator as if he had all day!* He was still trying to convince them to make a run for it! There was a lot of yelling from outside the prison as the Kuwaiti

Resistance dudes now had the vehicles idling right in front. And then one of our vehicles squealed away. So I kind of shoveled Trang out the door with Leila's body in my arms.

So as we drive back to the villa we are all pretty glum. The body of the maid Leila was now in the trunk of the Toyota. And I was suddenly daydreaming about surfing, and the chick in my daydream who was surfing the waves near me was Leila, and she looked pretty happy, and waved to me with a look like: *isn't it cool to have nothing better to do than ride the waves?* And I thought how fine Leila looked in this red, white, and blue bikini, and how freedom is all about a chick in a red, white, and blue bikini free to ride the waves, and the right to party on the beach by a fire after sunset with said chick, and even the right to lick the salt off her soft cheek if you are so lucky. And as Leila was stone dead from bullet holes, I snapped out of this daydream, and was suddenly pretty wrecked about Leila in the trunk, but at the same time stoked I was a follower of Tommy Trang, who was—in his own crazed way—'fighting for our right to party,' so to speak.

Anyway, there were no *Aiyahs!* on the way back, and no way to spin this as a *great Victory over Saddam!* And to make it worse, Khaled the resistance fighter was loudly blaming the whole screwup on Trang. He was hinting that if Trang hadn't been so into *mission plans* we could have all stormed the prison right from the get-go, *and the maid Leila would never have had a chance to do her crazy thing and be killed!* Khaled wanted Trang to agree that in the next mighty attack we would just run right up the center, *guns blazing!*

It was pretty clear my man Trang was blaming himself totally for the death of the maid Leila. He was just staring out the window looking really crushed. It was weird to see him so flat and down— it made me see how I was generally used to Trang always buzzing with some new rush. I was also kind of wondering what we were going to say to Princess Lulu, as she was probably not in the best of moods anyway having been tied up when we left—and now we were returning with the body of her friend Leila, who had risked her life sneaking back into Kuwait to warn her Colonel Fawwaz was coming to kill her, and had been killed by friendly fire in a total snafu of an operation. And I have to admit I was also thinking that if and when Colonel Fawwaz got the news the chick he was really hot for—the maid Leila—had been killed in an operation run by Tommy Trang, well, he was going to be that much more down on Trang.

Man, that princess Lulu was one wild chick! I say that because there was always a *surprise* when she was around. Like, when we walked in the villa there was someone asleep on the couch with a blanket over her, *but it was the old lady!* When we woke her up, man, *was she pissed at Princess Lulu!* I guess after the lady had read a couple of dozen nights of *A Thousand and One Nights,* Princess Lulu had done some heavy-duty *acting* about how she was so grateful to the lady, and how wrong she was to want to go on our *ghazzu,* and so on, until the lady like agreed to untie the princess so she could go to the bathroom with some royal dignity. And the minute she was fully untied: Princess Lulu *vamoosed!*

It turned out all this had happened only twenty minutes earlier, so with little Ali, Trang and me bolted back to the Toyota and went on a mission to track her down. And we drive the streets near the villa for a while, until down at like the other end of one we see two Iraqi soldiers in a huddle around someone. So we ditch the vehicle and slide down the street with M16s in front of us, and sure enough we can see Princess Lulu is in the center of these two guys, but the weird thing is this big *bird* like in the arms of Princess Lulu. And the Iraqi guys are yanking at the bird's legs, and Princess Lulu is *clearly giving them some low-level royal hell to like leave her and the bird alone!*

The Iraqis and Princess Lulu were so into their bird argument that Tommy Trang and me walked right up behind them and put the muzzles of our M16s to their heads pretty much before they were aware we were there. And what was really weird was after looking real scared and surprised, the two young Iraqi dudes like start scanning the skies and Ali said they were saying: *it has started! It has started!* So it was clear they thought the American invasion had started already, and we had like just parachuted in or something, so Trang decided to go with that idea, and made some military signals down the street and so forth, and yelled up the street, and tried to make it seem like there were lots of fellow American GIs in the vicinity. But Trang didn't need to act, as those two young Iraqi dudes were unarmed—it turned out they had sold their rifles for food a few days earlier as they were starving, and they couldn't wait for the war to be over, and had wondered what the hell had kept America from just busting into Kuwait weeks earlier.

So it was nice that Princess Lulu was stoked to see Trang and Ali and me. And she said she was coming to link up with us when she came on this *flamingo* in the road, *and that is in fact what the bird was!* It was so covered with soot from the burning oil wells it looked damn near black, *but if you looked close, you saw it was a flamingo!* And I didn't *know* Kuwait had flamingos and said so, and that was when I got a real earful from Princess Lulu. It turns out not only was there like before the Gulf War a bunch of flamingos at some local place with mudflats called Sulaibikhat, but that Princess Lulu had like spearheaded a drive to make their home a sanctuary. Princess Lulu was like known in some quarters as *Princess Flamingo,* she was so crazy about these big pink birds. And she feared the flamingos had all already been killed by oil spills, or Iraqi mines, or by hungry Iraqi soldiers—but that here was one in her arms! And to hear Princess Lulu go on about the flamingo, you would have thought *Allah reached down from heaven himself and placed it in her arms!* I just kept staring at Lulu: poet, actress, bug lover, flamingo protector, willing warrior—man, the girl was a blazing pinwheel. No wonder the emir had a hard time keeping her on the Islamic straight and narrow, so to speak. I'm no matchmaker, but it now struck me hard that this was the only girl who could *maybe* keep up with Tommy Trang.

Anyway, the deal with these two teenage Iraqi soldiers was this: they were starving, *and wanted to eat the big, dirty bird for dinner.* They had no idea Lulu was a princess, nor did they care much—*they just wanted to eat!* But now that us Yanks were here, I guess they figured they were *prisoners* and that as soon as we got them back to some prison camp, *they would be eating like kings.* They started showing us this like leaflet with a cartoon drawing of Iraqis sitting around with Americans having a pig-out on what looked like pizza. Trang said to me, "Hey man, the psyop people have been selling surrender to these guys with pizza!" And I guess the two Iraqis knew about the word *pizza*, as they brightened up and said, "Pizza!" So Trang called them Pizza One and Pizza Two, and we tried to figure out what to *do* with them.

So the Iraqi Pizza Brothers are in a good mood now, and laughing about the idea that a few minutes earlier they were ready to eat *flamingo*. Princess Lulu wasn't laughing, and wanted to get the bird back to the villa to like clean off the soot and oil or whatever, as she didn't think it was in the best of shape. But I guess Trang wanted to yuck it up with Pizza One and Pizza Two a bit, maybe because when they were gone we'd have to tell Princess Lulu about the status of the maid Leila. So Trang like asks if they want a Coke with their pizza when we get to the prison camp, and this translates, *but makes those Iraqis pissed!* As Coke is sold in Israel, and *so is real bad!* The Jew thing again, this time from *Iraqis!*

Anyway, we told Pizza One and Pizza Two to head for the Sheraton in downtown Kuwait, and there they would find their pizzas waiting, along with all the Pepsi they could drink. And they want to hang with us, as they are rightly dubious as there hasn't been any sign of an invasion by the Yanks since we started talking, so we have to chase them off with our M16s. And then there we were on a Kuwaiti street corner with Princess Lulu and her flamingo. So we start to be like *So how ya been, Princess?* And she's more or less like, *How you guys been?* And we're all like *fine fine good good* in the way people are when they don't want to get down to serious business. So we all just walk back to the Toyota, with the flamingo kind of like craning his neck around to look at me kind of questioningly. And this is weird, but it made me remember other birds and animals—mostly dead ones—that had given me the creeps on this adventure. Like the lamb back at Princess Hayat's wedding party that kept jiggling its eyes at me—that lamb looked like it had a damn question for me too.

So we get in the Toyota, and Princess Lulu sets the flamingo down on the seat next to her and tries to clean it by putting saliva on her fingers and rubbing the bird's feathers. And then she is crying, the princess Lulu. And we ask her what is wrong, and she points at Tommy Trang and says *she can tell by his face something very bad has happened.* So Trang grips the steering wheel hard and tells her right out about the status of her friend the maid Leila in the trunk, and she weeps some serious tears with some heavy *ululating* and tries to clean off the flamingo even harder with her saliva.

And then we stop down the street from the two villas, and I know Trang is thinking, *where do we go?* Can't go back to the old lady's villa, as she's pissed at Lulu. And don't really want to go back to Khaled's villa, as those local resistance boys are wacky. So right then everyone is quiet in the car, and we like just sit there for a few minutes. And then Princess Lulu makes her strange speech. It turns out Princess Lulu is pretty sure *Allah* is up to something in trading her the maid Leila for a flamingo. She pointed out how weird it was that she was known as 'Princess Flamingo,' and right when her best friend is killed fighting for Kuwait, *a flamingo comes to her on a street corner in the middle of a war.* You could hear Princess Lulu's sixteen-year-old brain working this out for herself as she talked, as she kept tossing in a lot of the old *inshallah, inshallah, inshallah* stuff the way an American might say *um, um, um* when they are thinking. But she got fired up as she *inshallahed* her way toward her mighty conclusion, which was that Trang and her *were about to do some great things for Kuwait in the coming days,* and that it was like *all already planned out by Allah,* and all Trang and her had to do was *be hip to signs from Allah like the flamingo.*

So by the time Princess Lulu was done with her speech, she was in a mighty fine mood! *All was going according to Allah's plan!* It was too bad the maid Leila had to die, but in the big picture *known only to Allah,* why, *it was a great thing!* Princess Lulu looked at us with this tearful but beaming look like: *don't you guys get it? Hooray! Thank Allah the prison operation was a total train wreck! Thanks to Allah the maid Leila stormed the prison and got riddled by a bunch of trigger-happy Kuwaiti kids with M16s!* On the other hand, to be honest, I think Trang and me were a little *relieved* Princess Lulu had like come around to this *crazy Allah-colored glasses view of things,* as I think we were both wondering—she was a girl who had tried to commit suicide rather than marry Colonel Fawwaz after all—if she might be a little *hysterical* about the maid Leila's death. And because we were relieved, we didn't try to talk her out of her *flamingo-is-a-sign-from-Allah* point of view right then. And I'd like to mention that all the time she was laying this *Allah-has-a-plan stuff on me,* the damn flamingo was still craning his neck around at me and laying a big beady eyeball on me. And bird eyes are like snake eyes, they don't have like the least bit of warmth in them, so at one point toward the end of her rattling on, I reached out and tried to push the flamingo's head so like he wasn't eyeballing me, and the damn bird bit me on the finger!

There was a certain amount of blood, and right then Lulu finally put a clamp on the grand-Allah-plan talk, and like took my finger and popped it in her mouth and started sucking like a vacuum cleaner. And she's smiling at me and saying around the finger, *I know you don't believe me, Cody Carmichael, about the flamingo. But you will see! You will see! All of nature speaks to us as signs from Allah! You must read the signs from Allah! Everything is a sign from Allah! This flamingo is a sign from Allah!* I mean I *think* that is what Princess Lulu was saying, it was hard to tell, as she had an Arab accent, and was talking while sucking my finger, which I might add was so sexy it almost convinced me to *salemt,* which means to go Muslim. And as she talked and we sat in that Toyota, my man Trang is like beaming at her again like, *isn't she a pearl?* That's what he called her when he was really thinking she was an amazing *find* from here on in, and he seemed to get a kick out of saying it, on account of Lulu turning out to mean *pearl* in Arabic. I mean generally my man Trang was starting to glow like a phosphorescent flare right about now on account of crazy Lulu.

CHAPTER 18

A few days later Khaled the resistance dude ran into the villa and yelled out *yo!* I guess he picked that up from us, and right then it cracked Trang up and he said *yo!* back, and so forth for a while. And then Khaled says as he flipped the hair from his eyes, *the Kuwaiti Resistance Has News!* He said it like he was blowing a damn trumpet, but what the hell do you want from an *actor.* Anyway, the *news* was that Iraqi tanks in Kuwait were moving secretly to the border with Saudi Arabia as we were chilling wondering what to do next, and there was a big crazy invasion of Saudi Arabia planned by the Iraqis!

It was obvious to Trang what we needed to do! We needed to bust back to Saudi Arabia to warn the American forces of the attack! I like pointed out if it was this major an attack the U.S. would like pick it up on satellite, but Trang pointed to the dark sky outside and said: *what if they don't see it through the clouds and smoke from the oil fires?* Trang seemed kind of pissed at me for even mentioning the Americans might already know about the coming Iraqi invasion, like I ruined the *beauty* of the thing. I mean, we had a serious heroic mission here! We might save hundreds if not thousands of U.S. and Coalition lives if we could just bust back to the border before the Iraqis were done getting it together and attack!

As I *could* see the beauty of this mission, I soon was as totally stoked as Trang. And it was also a chance to like make up for the snafu at the prison. So we are all inside the villa with Khaled and his

Kuwaiti Resistance warriors, and all are raising their M16s to us and screaming *Aiyah! Aiyah!* And luckily Khaled and his resistance boys had *no* interest in sneaking past the Iraqi tanks to warn the Americans of the attack, as you could tell by their fake *aiyahs!* they thought *we* were going to certain death, and *they* were going to go back to burying money and keeping an eye on the babe Princess Lulu. And Princess Lulu had no interest in sneaking into Saudi Arabia at all what with her crazy royal family all hanging there and wanting to kill her to preserve their honor. She wanted to stay in the villa and nurse the flamingo back to health and like wait for our return. She seemed to feel by the time we got back from this mission Allah would have revealed to her about the *Big, Big Plans* he had in store for us.

Little Ali was a different story. Tommy Trang wanted him to stay and keep an eye on Princess Lulu. He didn't trust Khaled and the Resistance Boys to do squat for her in a pinch. But little Ali was primed to be part of our heroic mission to save the Americans from the Iraqi attack. I mean he just loved America and Americans, and like begged us to let him come—he pointed out he actually knew the way to the Saudi border, and all the cool places to hide along the way. So that was the clincher: we needed him to get us to the border fast, and the lives of hundreds of Americans were worth more than a larger risk for one Kuwaiti princess, but it was still a monster decision for Tommy Trang to leave Princess Lulu alone again, you could see that. But as I have said, in some weird way I got the vibe he was now on fire to get into battle *for* Lulu, like some knight of yore fought in his lady's name.

So it was a cool thing we are wearing Iraqi uniforms, as we figured they'd make it easier to get to the Saudi border. Anyway, Khaled thought our Iraqi uniforms looked too *clean,* and we had of course washed them in the villa's washer a few times, as they were stripped off dead guys. But Khaled wants our uniforms to look like we have been in the desert for weeks, and we strip down and he and his boys go in the rear yard of the villa and kick the hell out of those uniforms in the dirt, like there were real Iraqis in them—and they had a real fine time doing it! So they would have torn them to shreds, but we rescued them and put them on. So when we are duded up 'filthy Iraqi' style like the local soldiers, Khaled and the boys like want to rub our faces with ashes from the grill, I guess to make us look more like your basic swarthy Iraqi. I thought Trang looked like a Vietnamese American marine in an Iraqi colonel's uniform with ashes on his face, but whatever, we were off.

Princess Lulu gave Tommy Trang a big kiss right on the lips in front of all of us which got a round of *aiyahs,* and like tried to make him walk under a Koran, and told him to more or less kick some Iraqi ass so he could maybe get his heroism written up in the *Il-liyyun.* As best I could make out—Lulu was kind of too fired up to explain—the Islamics believed there is some place called *Seventh Heaven,* where there is a book the *Illiyyun* where all the good deeds are recorded by your personal angel reporter. Trang listened to this Muslim stuff from Lulu and grinned at me like, *my own personal angel reporter, can't beat that!* It kind of bummed me out right then Trang found it all so funny and curious, as at that moment I found it pretty creepy that a smart chick in the Modern Age was buying into such high-octane wigginess.

Anyway, the main thing here is Lulu was still way into Trang doing the heroic-warrior thing. I guess she figured it was all part of Allah's big-ass plan as signified by the flamingo, and right then she was still totally tied into that whole *inshallah* stuff. Anyway, Trang and me like skipped out on the Koran walk, but I got a kiss from Lulu too, as did little Ali. Khaled and all the fighters gave us hugs like we were heading to paradise and should say *yo!* to Allah. All of this from the time we found out about the coming Iraqi attack was done like in a huge hurry, by the way.

So then we busted out the door and like hopped in the Toyota with Ali at the wheel. We didn't know he could drive, but he was pretty good—and he was supposed to be our private and so the driver. I guess every Iraqi available had like headed to the Saudi border as the streets were pretty empty, and roadside guard stations were empty. So we buzzed along and Trang's legs were twitching away, as he was real worried we'd not get a chance to warn the Americans. And then little Ali saw an empty Kuwaiti garbage truck, and he said these things were used to move the Iraqi supplies to the front, and if we were in one, nobody would bother us. It seemed like a pretty noticeable way to travel, like heading to the Saudi-Kuwaiti border on an elephant, but Ali's mind worked in curious ways. Those curious ways were like Trang's, who saw the beauty of the garbage truck like: *what Iraqi would think three crazy Americans would be heading to the Iraqi lines in a garbage truck?*

Ali was real pleased to be included as one of the *three crazy Americans*. And he like hopped up in the garbage rig, but it wouldn't turn over. It was starting to get dark as Trang headed under the hood, and he somehow got the spark plugs out and cleaned them, and after he hot-wired the rig, we were on our way. Little Ali said the Iraqis had no ability to repair their equipment, they just used it until it died on the desert, and grabbed something else. I was suddenly proud of all our marine support units who worked so hard back behind the lines of glory to keep our vehicles and equipment in top shape. Even in the overlooked stuff like repair and maintenance I had a strong feeling right then as we headed toward the battle that the American way of doing things was the *right way*— right down to the level of how we clean spark plugs and change the oil on our tanks and vehicles.

I tried to turn Trang and Ali on to my heavy thoughts concerning *spark plugs and oil changes and the American way,* but they were not too interested. I don't know why, but I get in these moods sometimes where I just sort of ride the wave and chill. I knew we were heading toward a battle from the wrong side of the lines, but I was just buzzing in a crazy way, and sure it was going to be cool somehow—at least right at that moment I was, which accounts for my mellow thoughts on spark plugs and the American way. So that was my mood as we came at dusk on a ragtag squad of Iraqi soldiers heading toward the Saudi border. And Trang said: *blow around 'em.* And Ali looked at him and said: *mines.* So I guess we couldn't get off the road right now, and as we came on those dudes they like just stepped aside, but not far off the road. I guess some saw Trang was like an Iraqi officer through the window and sort of saluted in a half-assed way, and then we started to hear some clumps on the back of our garbage truck.

It was clear the Iraqis were jumping up on the garbage truck. Ali looked behind and verified like: *they are jumping in the garbage truck!* So I guess these Iraqi dudes just saw the empty open rear and decided to catch a ride to the front. Every once in a while we heard them *clumping* around back there, and then we heard someone giving a tired speech—so I guess there was an Iraqi officer of some sort, and he was like halfass trying to get them stoked for battle. We started to come on more and more of these sad-sack Iraqi squads in the road, and there was a lot of yelling now from the rear of the garbage truck, so I guess lots of the Iraqis were like cramming in there and hitching a ride, and Ali said others were hanging on to the sides like garbagemen do back home.

The best thing about having all these Iraqis hanging on the rear was that they made us look that much more *official.* We'd like come on Iraqis now and beep the horn to get them out of the road faster, and the dudes hanging on the side of the garbage truck were like screaming at the dudes in the road to give way, and Ali said as best he could tell from the Arabic these dudes were like screaming we were a special unit or something, I guess to keep any more Iraqis from like piling in the rear. And I have to say *you never saw a sadder-looking specimen of soldier* than those dudes we passed on the side of the road to Saudi. They were the most *unsat* bunch of dudes! Starving, crapped-up, exhausted—kind of just shuffling their feet. And they all kind of looked so much the same—most featured the bushy Saddam mustache—that after a while I was wondering if we were like seeing the same sorry Joe Iraqi dude over and over. It didn't help that for a long time the road to Saudi was like looking exactly the same too.

It was getting darker all the time, and then we heard a lot of clumping again in the rear, and little Ali said the Iraqis were like bailing out and like heading in a line in the direction of like these trees. I was like *trees, dude?* And Ali said the Kuwaitis had planted these trees in the desert, called the Wafra Forest, and that he could see there were like tanks kind of right over there with their engines running. I looked out and you could like barely see the tanks, but they were there all right—and their engines were running. So the like clumping is still going on in the rear, and man, we like brought a *lot* of lazy Iraqis to the front! And right then this one Iraqi like was running along the side of our truck, and he was like motioning ahead like a crazy man and Ali said he was saying: *mines*. And then he was walking off toward his squad and the tanks in the Wafra Forest, and Trang kind of slowed down the garbage truck, and then we stopped.

But right away we heard something clump back there, so we knew we still had at least one Iraqi. Which sucked, as one was too many in terms of the alert he might give! So Ali had this bright idea, and Trang said, *yeah, cool!* And he like flipped the lever, and we heard this mighty grinding sound as the hydraulics started to work back there, and I guess that big garbage truck mouth closing just scared the hell out of this Iraqi kid, because he was like screaming and cursing and soon enough we saw him running toward the Wafra Woods too. So Ali and Trang gave each other high fives for thinking about this clever way to clear out the Dumpster, until Trang decided he was bummed that we had helped the enemy at all, what with them about to attack the Coalition lines and all.

Unless you are like way into the Gulf War you might not remember that the Iraqis made this one large-scale sort of suicidal tank and infantry into Saudi Arabia. And there we were on the Kuwaiti side that evening just standing there in front of the garbage truck with the Iraqi tank battalion off to the West of us in the Wafra Forest revving their engines, with serious clouds in the sky, and no sign on the Coalition Saudi side that they were pulling any forces into position to counter this Iraqi tank attack. So Trang was stoked in a weird way, because there was no doubt this situation called for some Captain Shakespear heroics. So we all slapped each other on the shoulder and yelled: *remember Captain Shakespear!* Trang also yelled out: *Lulu! Lulu! Lulu!* I guess that was now his personal *fakhed* war cry, like the Bedouin of yore. Anyway, the only problem was there was a barrier minefield ahead of us.

And it was right then that little Ali took out a pack of cigarettes and a lighter and started to light one up. Tommy Trang and me like flicked a look at each other like: *what the hell?* And then Trang slapped the cigarette from little Ali's lips as he was about to light up. And Trang was furious. I thought it was about the stupidity of flashing a lighter in the near dark of the border just before battle, but Trang was real pissed that like Ali was thinking of *smoking!* Trang was like: *man, do you know what this stuff does to your wind? How you gonna be a marine if you got shit for lungs?* So I knew my man Trang was real pissed to hear him *swear*, but right then Trang switched moods and like raises his hand and says to little Ali: *slap me five, little Bangloman!* Trang made that up on the spot, *Bangloman*, for Bangladeshi man. Ali raised his hand and slapped Trang five, but he was looking real confused.

So Tommy Trang took the lighter from Ali. And he like admired it in his palm, and flicked the flame a few times. So then he ran back and got behind the garbage truck, I guess in case there was a sniper over there on the Coalition side, and he raised the lighter over the top of the garbage truck and started to flash it on and off. And it is *Morse code* and Trang is like flashing, I guess because it was a short message: YO.

Ali and me and Trang kept a sharp eye on the Saudi side of the border, but we got no return message. There was a string of Saudi border patrol posts over there now manned by Saudis and U.S. marines. They were *supposed* to keep an eye on the barrier minefield twenty-four hours a day, but I guess they were not on the lookout for a tiny flashing *YO* from us AWOL knuckleheads.

And so then Trang started to flash: IRAQI ATTACK! IRAQI AT-TACK! That really took a lot of thumb action to flash. I guess because Trang's thumb was now pretty tired, he next just flashed again: YO! YO! YO! And then finally Ali like started to slap my shoulder, and we saw there was a tiny light flashing back, and Trang and me spelled it out as it came in, and it said: FUK U, IRAQI.

So we were pretty stoked, and flashed back: IRAQI TANK AT-TACK. That took a long while to flash out with the lighter, but we were so jazzed to be talking to the good old boys of the good old USA!

But right then we got: U FUKS WISH!

So we flash back: WE USMC.

So we get: KISS MY MARINE ASS, IRAQI.

Man! These guys were *Marines!* Trang, Ali, and me were dancing around behind the garbage truck in the desert and doing a sort of low-decibel version of the marine seal call of *oooraah!* Maybe we shouldn't have taken time out for that however, as right then we hear the engines of the tanks in the Wafra Forest revving up, and we look over and you can see the lead T-62 tanks are moving out of the woods.

So Trang flashes: WAFRA FOREST!

And the last flash we got from the other side was: *SEMPER FI!* Which were the sacred words of the Marine Corps, so we were real happy, as we knew they had gotten our message and were busting to get on the horn to HQ to alert our side. And Trang gets all serious and shakes my hand then little Ali's hand and says to him, *Semper Fi, Marine!* And Trang looks long and hard at Ali and then says to me, *Can we make this little Bangloman a U.S. marine?* And little Ali from Bangladesh looked so proud and like puffed up his chest, and I'm like, *Hell yes!* I didn't know the legalities, and although as we were AWOL and he was not a U.S. citizen it seemed real doubtful, as Ali might have just helped save the lives of hundreds of U.S. marines and other Coalition forces, I figured there was a good chance whatever we decided to do here on the battlefield might get approved from on high later on!

So Trang had like Ali hold up his right hand and repeat, *Do you swear to uphold the Constitution of the United States of America . . .* And then we all sang the Marine Corps hymn there as the Iraqi tanks rumbled toward the border. And I was thinking the whole time: *we did it man, we saved American lives!*

So I was kind of thinking too that Trang and Ali and me would now like turn around the old garbage truck and like head back into Kuwait to link back up with Princess Lulu and like think about getting her out of the theater of operations before the coming Coalition ground invasion of Kuwait. That made common sense to me. But then my man Trang had *other ideas.* I guess he was still feeling like he came all this way to be in a real battle, and here was one right in front of him about to go down! And he turned to me and said quickly: *let's do it for Lulu.* Something about that *for Lulu* stuff kind of stuck in my throat, as it seemed less stoking for our team as a *whole* than the pure warrior cry of *remember Captain Shakespear!* Anyway, *I* at least yelled our *remember Captain Shakespear!* as we three started running down along the side of the barrier minefield toward where the Iraqi tanks were making their way across toward Saudi. Trang yelled to me and Ali as we jogged behind him that the Iraqi tank guys must know the way to get through the mines. It was getting even darker as we ran toward the tanks, and you could now just make out that behind each tank was a squad or so of Iraqi soldiers.

About the only thing that was cool, and kind of surprising, was that none of these Iraqis had spotted us and shot at us yet. But we were in Iraqi uniforms, and I guess any of those that might have seen us running toward them would think: *here are some more Iraqis coming to join the mother of all battles!* Trang like slowed down as we got close to the line of T-62 tanks, and we walked some, and then there was a break in the column of tanks heading single file through the mines. When Trang saw that break he used it as a chance to like run into the gap in the line so we didn't have to like interact directly with any Iraqi troops. So then we were in the long snake of tanks and forces heading across the barrier minefield, and it was so weird and wild and crazy I just got in that mood again like I used to get when I was surfing: *nobody can touch us, man. We are in the ZONE.*

We were in a sort of empty zone in the snake of Iraqi tanks and soldiers, which helped the feeling that like nobody could touch us, but then the lead Iraqi tanks slowed up and the tanks behind us caught up. So then as the tank behind starts like clipping us in the ass, we have to step aside a bit to let it pass, and fall in behind that tank with four Iraqi soldiers. We kept our faces looking toward Saudi and outward toward the minefield, and it was dark enough, and we were lucky enough, that no Iraqi yelled out right away. And then we noticed these Iraqis weren't looking nowhere but toward where they figured death was coming from: *up in the sky!* They were like head-bobbing birds—they'd walk glancing at the tank ahead, and then scan the night skies. So to get along, go along—Trang and Ali and me all thought that at once, so we fall in behind these four and as far back as we can without getting run over by the next tank and make like bobbing birds. And looking up at the cloudy, dark night like that, a dozen feet from four Iraqis—well, then my good feeling evaporated, and I *too* started waiting for the Coalition to let loose the sky dogs of war, and pummel us into hamburger.

That Trang was a funny guy though—all of a sudden I think I am tripping, *because I hear some humming real low.* And little by little I make out what it was, and it was that old song *Yankee-Doodle went to town!* Over and over Trang whistled that little tune I hadn't heard since I was a kid. And then Trang started singing the song, and I sang it quietly with him, and sort of chuckled, because I remembered as a kid wondering why Yankee-Doodle called the feather in his cap 'macaroni.' Anyway, the song was like the sort of thing you remember with a real warmth, because you haven't heard it in a decade, and it was like it was a totally lost thing of real value, and you wonder why you ever let it go. I mean that was how I was feeling about it as we marched along in the Iraqi attack toward probable death. Some soldiers have always said there are no atheists in foxholes, and you kind of burn right back to praying your ass off—but we weren't doing that God thing—we were whistling "Yankee-Doodle," and it was like better than a prayer, and carried us on like wings right across the minefield—most of the way!

I say 'most of the way' because all of a sudden Trang stops whistling, and says to me, "I got a bad feeling if we don't bust a move we are going to be too late." So then he put wings to his feet, and we are charging past the four Iraqis, and running alongside the T-62 tank, and running past more Iraqis, and more tanks. Some Iraqis yelled out to us as we ran, *but we were just flying past tank, soldiers, tank, soldiers, tank, soldiers . . .* until we were near the head of the line of Iraqi tanks. I guess Trang thought we should get on the Saudi side so we could like shoot back at this column of tanks and soldiers. And Trang slowed down behind this one tank toward the front of the line where there are only two Iraqis, and right then a like hand reached out in the dark and grabbed my arm and like said something kind of friendly in Arabic. I bet he was saying, *No need to hurry to death.* And I like said nothing, but this made him grip harder and say it again. And then he like *shined a flashlight in my face! The dumbest thing you could do on an infiltration!*

And the dude was so surprised by my face he like dropped his rifle. And it got crunched by the tank behind. I'm like whispering, *Trang, Ali, ah dudes, we have a situation here.* And the Iraqi is muttering to the other Iraqi, and he comes over as we jog along and says in this heavy Iraqi accent, "American?"

And Trang is right there and whispers, "Yeah, dude, we be of the US of A."

And the Iraqi like starts laughing in the dark, and he is slapping Tommy Trang on the back as we run. So I relax a bit, as the Iraqi seems *cool.* And right away the Iraqi wants to know what side we are on, and Trang says we are trying to get to the Saudi side.

"So you can kill us?" says the Iraqi.

"Yeah," says Trang. "But I think we'll be too late."

And the Iraqi looks up at the sky like for the jets and the bombs, and says, "Yes, you will die with us."

I like break in with, "Hey man, don't you want to kill us?"

And the Iraqi laughed again. It was cool he was in such good spirits. And he says to me, "I do not want to kill you Americans. Americans are very good. George Bush is very good. Why would I kill you? I want to be you." And it turned out this Iraqi dude had been to college for a couple of years at the University of Southern California, and had been visiting his family back in Iraq when he got grabbed and stuck in Saddam's army. And get this: *the dude said he was way into surfing while he was at USC!* So me and him start seriously talking up the waves, and Tommy Trang I guess got bored with this mellow talk of liquid mountains, as he grabbed my arm and said, *Come on, man!*

So we were across the border now in Saudi, and right behind the lead Iraqi tank. The tank was firing shells on one of those Saudi border patrol outposts. And I'm wondering: *where are the Yanks?* And Trang moves away from the Iraqi tank, and Ali and Trang and me

go running sideways down the Saudi front lines just inside the
mines in the dark. And a few minutes after that the skies open up,
and the Iraqi tanks in the rear of the snaking line come under fire
from our jets in the sky. But a lot of Iraqi tanks make it across the
border, and are firing wildly. I was like ready to stop to watch the
slaughter of the Iraqi tanks from the sky, but Trang was busting to
get into the town of Khafji. So we humped our way there double
time, and got there just after a half dozen Iraqi tanks rolled into
the narrow streets of the Saudi beach town.

So all around us in the streets of Khafji there are the booming
sounds of Iraqi tanks firing randomly, but all the action was in the
sky in terms of Coalition response. The town itself seemed kind of
empty of Coalition forces. So Trang and Ali and me were like *who the
hell are the Iraqi tankers firing on in the streets?* Because as far as we could
tell they were just blazing away at the concrete buildings in Khafji
for the hell of it. So we sort of stop running through the streets,
and chill for a minute in front of like a drugstore. Tommy Trang
was clearly kind of bummed, as we had busted our balls to get into
a heroic ground battle here on the allied side in Khafji.

I guess the Coalition response was to like *give* Khafji to the
Iraqis for the time being, and let the flyboys hammer the tanks in
the rear of the minefield, and when those Iraqis in Khafji were isolated, take them out at leisure. Right then we hear an Iraqi tank
coming down our road, and we three like scuttle back into the
shadows of the storefront. And right in front of us the tank fires
off a round down the street, and blows up a building that looked
like a little hotel. I like am holding Trang's arm in the dark, as I
want to hold him back if he decides to like John Wayne this tank,
but he isn't that crazy I guess. His legs were just twitching away—
the hundred-proof battle juice was pumping hard in his veins.
And then a Cobra attack helicopter like takes out *that* Iraqi tank at
the end of our street, and molten metal flies back in our direction.

And then down there where the Iraqi tank was hit and burning
we see some Iraqi soldiers, and Trang yells the marine call of *oooraah!*
And jumps in the road and starts firing crazily at them, and they

dive behind the burning wreckage. So now we have something to do as marines, and run down the road to the burning tank, but the Iraqis have crawled off.

And so the warrior Trang is totally fired up as he *finally* got to pull his trigger in a battle, and we start charging down the streets, and we keep seeing Iraqis at the other end of the streets, but as soon as we open up they like scatter! It was getting really frustrating trying to find some Iraqis to engage in a decent firefight, and we tried to hold our fire and move closer before firing, but the Iraqis were nervous as rabbits, and ran away from any motion! And right about then as we have just fired on some fleeing Iraqis, we hear this American voice from like the top of a building yelling down, *"Yo! Up here, marine!"* And there is a *head* up there with night-vision goggles on staring down at us, and we hear footsteps running inside, and this big wooden door opens, and there stands a U.S. marine. He is like in face paint, and the night-vision goggles are up on the top of his head, and he like flashes a light in our faces and says, "Yo! Motherfuckers!"

And the dude is like slapping us on the back and ushering us in, *and I know this voice!* And he's like using our names: *Fucking Trang! Fucking Carmichael!* And it is *Lance Corporal Sinoma from our old recon platoon!* He's like, *was that you crazy motherfuckers flashing us about the tank attack?* And we are marched up on the roof of this two-story building, where there are like five other guys from our recon platoon. And all are so cheered to see us, and we all take time out for a lot of backslapping, and it would have been so cool a like reunion, except Sinoma kept saying, *you guys are so fucked, man!*

Anyway, the deal was these dudes got caught up at a Saudi border station without our Captain Pettigrew when the Iraqi attack came, and like pulled back to Khafji and were like laying low and just radioing the situation to the Coalition side. So for the next like six hours or so we chilled on the roof with them watching the Coalition jets hammer the Iraqi tanks in the desert into flaming fireballs one by one, and in between explosions we told them of our adventures. They were totally turned on to the infiltration of

Kuwait with the blond Sulluba, and Sinoma showed this T-shirt he wore that said: MY DADDY WENT TO THE GULF WAR AND ALL HE BROUGHT HOME WAS THIS STUPID T-SHIRT. Of course they wanted to know if Tommy Trang and Princess Lulu had done the wild thing in the sack, and were kind of bummed when Trang said he wanted to get married first and do right by the princess. There were a lot of comments that Trang was a fricking idiot, and Corporal Sinoma said Trang should have dug in between her brown royal Arab thighs ASAP. And Trang kind of cracked and grabbed Sinoma and growled real pissed an inch from his pimply face, *hey man, do I look like some asshole rapist marine?* Nobody but me knew what the hell Trang was talking about there, so all let the topic drop fast. Later I would remember this thing with Sinoma when I was thinking back about what made Trang so endlessly crazy about being a righteous marine hero.

So anyway, word comes on the PRC-104 radio in a few hours that the Iraqi tanks in the barrier minefield are pretty much nailed, and then there is a lot of static, and then it comes that the decision has been made to let the Royal Saudi forces have the honor of kicking the remaining isolated Iraqis out of Khafji. There was a lot of jeering about this decision from us marines, and I understand that later in the morning, the Saudis made no plan, but just yelled *Aiyah!* and tried an up-the-middle run into Khafji, and had their asses kicked. But by then we were long gone. Because at about 0400, Tommy Trang came over to me and little Ali and said, *we better bust out before light man.* And Trang saw me glance at our marines kind of chilling on the rooftop, and he said, *hey man if you want to stay with these dudes, no problem.*

And the brain part of me *did* want to stay, but I shook my head and my lips said *no way, man.* I mean the first time I followed Trang was when we were in Colonel Fawwaz's steam room, and it was like when you just point your surfboard down some massive wave and do it with just a powerful rush, but now it was like a *decision.* Anyway, the marines from our platoon all stood and like shook our hands before we left and wished us luck and called little Ali *Private Ali, USMC* which turned him on. They told us they'd testify about how we flashed the warning about the Iraqi attack across the barrier minefield and generally assisted there on the rooftop if it would help at our court-martial. And Private Sinoma said to Trang, with a laugh, *go back in there and kill Saddam, would ya buddy?* And Trang said, *that's what I aim to do,* and the guys laughed because they didn't know Trang was pretty serious. Anyway, I followed my man Trang down the stairs and back into the dark streets of Khafji.

So we see like *nobody* as we make our way out of Khafji. We see a number of burning tanks in the town, but we stayed away from them as the light from the flames would have made us a visible target. And we leave Khafji and are crunching across the gravel double time back along the track the Iraqi tanks took into Khafji, and soon we come upon the like charred remains of dozens of Iraqi tanks. And as the whole area was mined, we *had* to pass pretty close to these burning monsters, and we saw a lot of like burned Iraqis and burned Iraqi body parts littered about on the tanks. It was real hot when you passed the tanks, and it was like we were cooking along with the dead Iraqis, but then you were past them and back into the darkness. The smell of burning flesh made you want to vomit, so I think we three all held our breath as we hurried by the tanks.

I guess not all the Iraqis were killed. Some of the Iraqi soldiers and tankers were smart or crazy enough to like run into the minefield *and like lay low!* I saw some exploded mines out there and passed a few Iraqi body parts that had been blasted by mines back into the road. What with us being lit up as we passed the burning tanks, I suppose sooner or later we were going to be spotted. And I figured we'd be shot, but then I hear these feet behind me, and a voice says, "Hey USA." Trang like starts running, like he doesn't want to hear this, and Ali and I like follow his lead. But then I hear another set of running feet in the dark behind us, and jabbering in Arabic, and I'm like saying ahead to Trang and Ali like, *I think we have a situation here, dudes.*

And we just keep on running, and pick up the pace. But I glance over my shoulder and there are like a half dozen of the sorry Iraqi dudes running without weapons and waving their hands and yelling: *George Bush! George Bush!* And I guess their voices sucked in every living Iraqi hiding out there in the barrier minefield, because when I looked back again we were like being followed by a near platoon of sorry scraggly ass Iraqis. Trang like puts the pedal down, *and we try to outrun them.* And we do so, even with little Ali holding us back a bit, *until bang!* We run into a couple of dozen more Iraqis just camping in the tank road. I guess these were Iraqi dudes who never ran into the barrier minefield. And they barely looked up as we ran up, but we had to stop. And the pack of surrendering dudes in the rear like caught up, and suddenly we were caught in this crowd of Iraqi soldiers gibbering in Arabic and pidgin English and throwing up their hands in surrender.

Tommy Trang looks at me through all these waving hands of the crazed Iraqis, and you can see he is like *totally glum.* And so we both look at little Ali, and the *Bangloman* like tells all the Iraqis to shut up, and explains that we three are going back into Kuwait. *Man, they were some pissed Iraqis when they heard that!* I guess they figured we were sent out to round 'em up and bring them to a POW camp! One who spoke English started giving us some *Geneva Convention about how we had to accept their surrender!* And we were like *look dudes, we accept your surrender, okay? You guys have officially surrendered, okay? But we're kind of busy, and can't take you back to a POW camp.*

So then Tommy Trang like tears off his own T-shirt under his Iraqi colonel's uniform and finds this metal bar blown off a blasted tank. It was still hot metal, so he wrapped another piece of cloth around the base. And he like makes a surrender flag. And he gives that to the Iraqi dude who was into the Geneva Convention and tells him to like gather all the dudes and walk them across the Saudi lines and when they got to U.S. Forces to yell out a secret password: 'Yankee-Doodle'. The only thing that made these Iraqis happy was when we told them the secret surrender password was *Yankee-Doodle.*

And for good measure Ali and I make two more surrender flags with our T-shirts. And these surrendering Iraqi dudes are all pretty glum that we are not personally leading them in to surrender, and in that bummed state watch us pull out and continue our trek back into Kuwait, and when I looked back the dudes were all standing there with the white flags in the tank road as if they were *unsure what the hell to do*. And I am sorry to report that as Trang and Ali and me broke out of the barrier minefield there was a massive explosion right where we had left those Iraqis standing with their surrender flags. I guess the U.S. Cobra helicopters had sniffed out those dudes, and thought they were a still active Iraqi company, and not a bunch of sad sacks caught between a rock and a hard place.

CHAPTER 19

We made it back into Kuwait City just before dawn on a motorcycle we found ditched in a bombed-out Iraqi bunker. All Tommy Trang did was unjam the stuck clutch and the 500 cc Suzuki ran like a charm. It was a serious squeeze with three of us on the seat, and little Ali's ass was hanging and bouncing off the rear fender much of the way. We blew right past all sorts of sorry Iraqis trudging their way back in the dark, but none said a word. The craziness was so stoking of this situation of us busting back to Kuwait across the desert on a motorcycle after our first battle that my mind was just kicking over with energy. And my stoked-up mind had this old tune bubble up from below, and it was that screamer song by the British band Queen with the words:

—
I want to ride my bicycle!
I want to ride it where I like!

So at first I just had those words in my own head, but then it started to crack me up as it was like the right song in some spooky way, so I started to yell over the engine. And then little Ali started to yell them out, and even Trang joined in, which was cool, as he had that thing about modern music ruining the *ghazzu* mood.

At dawn we ditched the motorcycle when it ran out of gas just inside Kuwait City, and it was clear we had to go to ground for the day. I spot the Sheraton Hotel in the distance, where we got like put up by the emir for rescuing Princess Lulu ages ago. Trang and Ali and me sort of head on foot for the Sheraton as it is getting easier to see us three lunatics. And when we arrive at the Sheraton after much skulking along the streets the hotel is buzzing with action. We like hide in this alley under a trashed vehicle to survey the scene. The hotel has got some generators and satellite dishes, and it is clear this is like the place where the international reporters are hanging.

So we three slip across the street, and down another alley behind the Sheraton, and there is an old Iraqi dude back there smoking a butt. And we have to wait a while but sure enough he drifts off to take a piss, and Trang jumps the fence and we follow and all drop down inside the grounds. So we are standing there at dawn in the rear of the hotel near a pool filled with black water. And there were a couple of old overweight American guys hanging by the pool at a table filled to overflowing with empty beers. And they looked like old-fashioned reporters, and were cool old guys too, and told us three to pull up a chair.

We hadn't taken off our Iraqi uniforms. But no mention of this was made by these reporters, I think because these old dudes were pretty baked from drinking all night—or maybe they were just waiting for us to spill our story when we were moved to do so. So we chilled with a beer each—even little Ali as he generally seemed to be quickly mellowing on his own Muslim thing—and they were smoking cigars and talking about their adventures reporting in the good old days in Nam, and it was clear they missed those days something bad of like hopping by helo around the exciting front. It sounded like there was always a ground battle going on in those days in Vietnam, so you didn't have to knock your nuts together looking for one like here in the Gulf War.

So then Trang sucks back the rest of his beer and says, "My parents met in Nam." And these guys were stopped by that and I could see they were doing the arithmetic, and Trang like went on about how his mother was raped by a squad of U.S. Marines in a village near some place called Hue.

Now, as I said, these two reporters were really pretty squint-eyed baked, and they are *way* into Tommy Trang's story. So Trang is pleased they are pleased as he's a friendly guy, and starts in with our whole story about going AWOL to rescue the Kuwaiti princess, and our adventures with the Sulluba sneaking in as Bedouin, and how we are just back from the battle at Khafji—which it turns out they haven't even *heard* about yet as there has been no official military briefing back in Saudi—then backtracks to our rescuing little Ali from being a slave after the camel races, and all of a sudden the two reporters start to *crack up*. And it is clear these fried reporter dudes have decided Tommy Trang is like totally yanking their chain in a wild way about their having nothing interesting to report in this war except a bunch of planes dropping bombs from the sky, and they start to like lean forward and slap him on the shoulder and say, like *you got us, man* and *have another beer, my man.*

So Tommy Trang doesn't take it well that they think he is full of it. So the reporters decide to play along some more and one takes out a reporter's pad and pretends to scribble and says, and *what did you say was the name of this Kuwaiti princess?* And the other reporter grabs the pad and yells, *no, no, this is my exclusive! I told him to sit down! I offered him the first beer!* And one of them says to Ali *so you were a little slave camel-jockey in Saudi, right?*

So another reporter is chilling out by the black pool now, and he starts to drift over to see why these old reporter warhorses are cracking up. And in the break in the laughter my man Tommy Trang stands up and says kind of proudly, "Her name is Princess Lulu and she is going to be my wife." And with that Trang turns and walks away, and as Ali and me follow him this new reporter who has wandered over to eavesdrop says to the others, "Hey, I heard about a young Kuwaiti princess trapped in the country, from some sources in Riyadh!" And then there is like a scramble as the three of them come after us, and we three like bolt back over the fence.

So even to us crazy AWOL marines, it is clear we can't march back to the villa in the middle of the day. And the reporters are trying to open the fence around the hotel, and that shaking brought the Iraqi guard running, and we three just had time to jump into this stinking Dumpster. I mean it didn't smell as bad as burning Iraqis, but still, you had to breathe through your mouth. Trang and Ali and me all knew we were going to be there until dark. And we had been up all night at the battle for Khafji, so we all decided it was a good time to like catch forty winks. So we got to moving the garbage around, trying to make ourselves a garbage bed with some minimum of comfort. And if you have just been sneaking into battle from the wrong side of the lines, you aren't too picky about your bedding. I mean we were all like asleep in a few minutes.

And when we woke up it was real late in the afternoon. I looked at Trang from around the edge of a bag of garbage and saw he was wide awake. Trang looked serious as hell and kind of fierce too, so I was like, "What you thinking so hard, man?"

And Trang said, "I'm thinking about those Iraqis who wanted to surrender this morning. They were afraid to go forward, and afraid to go back."

And I was like, "It sucked, man."

And Trang was like, "It's their own damn fault."

So I was like, "How you figure that?"

And Trang was like, "Americans would never have put up with a nasty dude like Saddam running their lives."

"And?"

And Trang said, "So because the Iraqis couldn't keep their own house in order, we have to come over and like clean up the mess, and a lot of sorry-ass Iraqis had to die this morning."

So I said, "Where are you going with this, Tommy?"

And Trang was like, "So it's clear Saddam has to go. I've been saying that all along. Which is why *we three* have to try to nail him while we are over here."

Here we were back on sure ground, as Trang *had* been saying this all along, even if it still sounded crazy that *we* were going to nail him.

So I said, "We got to nail Saddam. Agreed."

But Trang sort of groaned and said, "But at the same time, we got to do something about the *Kuwaitis,* and the *Saudis* too."

I kind of knew where he was going, but Trang clearly wanted to talk so I said, "Why man?"

And Trang like nudged Ali, who had been sleeping all this time and said, "Ask Ali, man. I mean he was their *slave.* That ain't right. And what about that thing with whacking women around in the streets of Saudi? These Arab folks need a Bill of Rights bad, if not a democracy."

To summarize what you might call the *Kuwaiti International Garbage Talks,* we three agreed Saddam had to go with a silver bullet in the brain, but we *also* agreed Saudi Arabia and Kuwait needed a Bill of Rights, and to lose the royal thing, and become *democracies.* And you might think it totally crazy that like two teenage AWOL marines and a Bangladeshi ex-slave were like doing so much heavy international thinking in a garbage bin, and I mentioned this to Trang. And he was quiet for a minute, and then Trang turned his head and informed Ali, *In America you can think things out for yourself!* So we were fired up there in the garbage because Trang's *thoughts* had like cleaned up a dark cloud that had been hanging over the whole Gulf War operation from the get-go about U.S. marines fighting and dying for a bunch of rich royals who didn't have a good word to say about freedom and democracy.

So having cleared the air, we were all feeling stoked! And Tommy Trang started to whistle "Yankee-Doodle" again, and we whistled with him. And then we sang "America the Beautiful," and "The Star-spangled Banner," and all three verses of the Marine Corps hymn. And when we got to "The Star-spangled Banner," we all three lay there in the dumpster with our hands over our hearts. Soon it was dusk, and we were not singing loud at all, in case you were thinking we'd attract enemy attention with all our fine singing. And Trang slapped Ali five and told him he was going to make an excellent American marine! And then the last thing we had to do before leaving the dumpster was discuss with Trang how cool and beautiful was Lulu, and this went on so long Ali was like shaking his head at me behind Trang's back like to say: *the man is sick with love!*

We crawled out of the mountain of garbage bags after dark. And we hoof our way through alleys and backstreets toward Princess Lulu, and we find her at Khaled's villa. And I was wondering how *Princess* Lulu was going to take Trang's brand-spanking-new plan—as he explained it to me—to like dump the Kuwaiti and Saudi royal families ASAP in favor of democracy. So we march into the villa, and the first thing we see on the marble floor is this fine-looking flamingo, looking in the pink of health, so to speak. And Princess Lulu comes out and pretty much wings herself through the air into the arms of Tommy Trang, and he swings her around, and it was fine to see *this much like international love in front of your eyes.* And when Lulu and Trang are done spinning and generally surfing the stoke of gripping each other tight, Princess Lulu gives me and little Ali hugs and kisses too, and then she like falls to her knees and starts quietly crying, because I guess even with her huge faith in Allah's big plan, a minor part of Lulu wasn't totally sure she'd ever see us three again. And I didn't think about it at the time, but this crying was the first little crack in Lulu's like loss of faith in Allah's big plan when it came to maybe losing Tommy Trang in heroic battle. But since we were back safe and sound, Princess Lulu was pretty soon up off her knees and back into talking about *Allah's plans* for all of us. And her and Trang were so excited to talk to each other they did that *no you talk first thing,* and then Tommy Trang like looked Princess Lulu in the eye and said straight out, *I think we should dump the king thing here and in Saudi.*

Now as Princess Lulu was a *princess,* you might have thought she would have a big problem with this idea. But right away she starts nodding and looking at me saying, "That is exactly Allah's plan!" Apparently she had gotten the word from *above* while we were gone to Khafji that Allah's big plan for us all, as signified by Allah sending the flamingo to replace maid Leila, is that we should bring some democratic reforms to Kuwait. I mean in those days

Lulu still pretty much figured *everything* was like Allah's plan, and it took her a while to figure out *Allah* probably didn't want democracy in Kuwait, *she* wanted democracy in Kuwait, and the reason *she* wanted democracy was because she knew at some level that only in a democracy would she be free to get it on in peace with the infidel Tommy Trang. So to recap, at this point in Lulu's sixteen-year-old life she still *had* to think it was old Allah talking to her about democracy, and not her own American-style common sense.

Anyway, as a result of the COMING SOON: DEMOCRACY TO KUWAIT announcement, we were all feeling fine. And there were a lot more hugs and kisses for all! And as I was in the midst of this lovefest for democracy, I see Khaled and all the Kuwaiti fighters are like filtering into the room. It turned out they had been like all watching pro wrestling on satellite elsewhere in the villa, but it was a lousy match, so they were checking out what all our noise was about. And Khaled right away caught on to our good feeling over bringing democracy to Kuwait, and as our little party congratulates each other, the word goes around among the Kuwaiti Resistance fighters, and they start to argue! And man, a party of Arabs can really argue! There were like serious in-your-face debates going on with a lot of finger waving among all the fighters!

Little Ali and Princess Lulu took turns telling us how the whole thing was shaking down with the Kuwaiti Resistance dudes. It was all about democracy, all this arguing, and at first it was cool to see they were getting all hot about it, *as I figured it takes two to tango!* I mean *some* of these resistance dudes were into democracy, and getting in the faces of those who were cool with a emir. So Princess Lulu, Trang, Ali, and me take seats on a couch, as it was clear this was going to be a long night, but what the hell: *they were maybe deciding the future of their rich little country.* It turned out there had been a democratic movement with some reforms in the past in Kuwait, but nothing much had happened recently, but what with all the royals out of the country, *some* of these local boys agreed, it was the time to make some changes!

But Khaled, the leader of the Kuwaiti Resistance, was not one of those totally hot for a democracy. And he had a real weak understanding of democracy, and after he asked me some questions, he was pretty angry. All the resistance fighters listened in on our conversation, as Ali translated for them. It went like this:

Khaled said, "But of course only the rich men pick the president?"

And I said, "Every citizen votes for the president."

Khaled said, "But only the *rich* are citizens, yes?"

I said, "No man, *everybody* eighteen and over is a voting citizen."

Khaled said, "Of course, but not the servants. *They* do not vote."

And I said, "Yeah man, the *servants* vote for the president."

Khaled was stunned by this news about the servants voting, and you could see more than half of the resistance dudes were with him. But then Princess Lulu spoke up in Arabic, I guess to nail a point me and Khaled had skimmed. What she said was: *in America all the women get to vote, even the female servants.*

This just damn near made Khaled and about half of the fighters fire their rifles. It made me wonder what they taught the local Kuwaiti kids about America. Not much, I guess. Anyway, Khaled and the resistance went back into a more heated argument, and then Khaled like started *pointing to the door.* He was demanding *anybody who wanted female servants to vote hit the road.* And he was serious, and about half of the resistance left the villa with their rifles! And then Khaled turned to Princess Lulu, Trang, Ali, and me, *and told us we had to go too if we had such crazy-ass ideas!*

So Trang and me stood in front of the villa cracking up, as it struck us as pretty funny we had gotten the boot from Khaled's resistance team for just *saying* chick servants should get the vote. And then Ali like marched us with Princess Lulu and the other exiled resistance dudes back to the villa of the lady with the flowers next door. And there was a long powwow at the door, as the lady was still bummed about being ditched by Princess Lulu way long ago when we busted back to Khafji. So Princess Lulu came forward and told her she was like real sorry, and then the lady listened to Ali explain why Khaled had kicked us all out. And Ali told her that Khaled had kicked us out because *we were fighting so that rich women in Kuwait could vote!* Ali told me he had limited it to *rich* women, as he didn't think the *servant thing* would fly. And this lady was way into that and ushered us back into the villa. And so we all sit down with the remaining resistance dudes to talk things over, and it turned out that what we had was a room full of *poor* resistance dudes who were not even voting citizens of Kuwait.

So we had split into two resistance cells: the rich Kuwaitis led by Khaled who were for the emir and the other royals, and the poor in Kuwait who were for democracy. But who was *our* leader? Little Ali said we should vote on it, and as none of these poor Kuwaiti dudes had ever voted, they were pretty jazzed. So we all wrote down the name of our leader on a piece of paper, and the lady read off the results. And Tommy Trang was elected our leader *by a slim margin.* I say 'slim' as most of the Kuwaiti dudes had voted for themselves, as I guess they had a strong sense of their leadership ability. And when it was announced Trang was the leader, most of them were pretty pissed, so we had to explain that you didn't *always* get your first choice in a democratic election.

Anyway, Trang as the leader of his own cell of the Kuwaiti Resistance was on fire! I mean he was really charged up that our cell was going to like try and bring democracy to Kuwait. And he rattled on about democracy as little Ali translated, but it was clear the local boys had little idea what the hell he was saying. So I told Trang he had to like simplify it for the locals, and Trang decided to like give Kuwait an American-style *Bill of Rights.* So Princess Lulu gets pen and paper and like translates the rights into Arabic as Trang recited them, and wrote them up with a very pretty and flowery hand, and then she pulled some watercolors out of a bag she carried from Khaled's villa and made the whole document real fine along the edges. Looking at Lulu painting on the edges of the *Kuwaiti Bill of Rights* it was clear she was not only an actress and poet, but an artist too! The only artistic types I had known were the dudes who spray-painted surfboards back at Huntington Beach, and I always had a solid respect for their talents. Anyway, Lulu saw me like admiring her handiwork on the Bill of Rights, and like opening her pretty flower blue eyes wide said to me, *you know how I feel in my heart, Cody?*

And I was like, *I sure don't, Princess.*

And she said this: *I wish but for the thing I have.*

That was kind of a cryptic riddle, and made me right away think of old Euclid Krebes and the poetical things he used to spout. Anyway, Lulu like went right back to watercoloring, because I didn't say anything right away—I didn't know what to say! And then like it hit me: she means *Trang!*

So anyway, the Kuwaiti dudes went over that Bill of Rights with a lot of Arabic jabber and a lot of coffee from the lady until the early hours of the morning. And you could feel a real fresh wind blowing in the room, but maybe it was just the air-conditioning. What I mean is I was way into what we were up to, but didn't expect it would amount to much more than like a civics lesson for these poor Kuwaiti dudes. Maybe I was just tired, even with the endless coffee. But Tommy Trang and Princess Lulu never got tired that night! I guess love can really fire you up to save the world! I mean they had a *seriously* excited time discussing all the excellent new rights coming to town right after we killed Saddam and dumped the emir.

I remember at one point that night Lulu talking about some royal Kuwaiti aunt of hers by the name of Souad. I guess this Souad was a poet—although her books were outlawed in Kuwait—and sort of an inspiration to Lulu through the years. So Lulu like laid on us some poetry by this Souad, and one line of the poem went like this: *democracy is when a woman can talk of her lover, without anyone killing her.* Maybe it had more rhymes in the original Arabic, but whatever, you could see why Lulu was into it. I crashed after the poem, and at some point I like woke up to see Tommy Trang was making all the fighters sign the bottom of the new Kuwaiti Bill of Rights in their own blood, and the Arab dudes were into that!

I watched as they signed in blood, and then Trang had me do it too, so I poked my thumb with the tip of the knife. And the lady was voted in as part of our resistance group, and she signed the document, although with a pen. It turned out her husband had a fully equipped office, so we all trooped to this office and ran off like a hundred copies. Then our democratic Kuwaiti Resistance dudes announced they wanted to sneak around Kuwait and post these xeroxes right then on like walls, and to me that shows you how stoked they were about the *Bill of Rights,* as they hadn't shown a lot of enthusiasm for risking their lives to date. But we had run off a hundred copies with everyone's *names,* and *that* didn't seem too bright to post around Kuwait, so we ran off copies without our names for like public display.

And Trang was so stoking proud as he sent those young Kuwaiti dudes off into the dark with the message that not only was there a cell of brave resistance fighters helping to rid Kuwait of Iraqis, but that the same cell was now planning on bringing *democracy* to Kuwait after the war. Actually, Trang wanted to go with the resistance dudes, but they wouldn't hear of it—they wanted him to stay at the villa and like work on the new *constitution* he had mentioned. So Trang promised to do that, although you could see he was bummed to have to stay home and think about a constitution when there was a real mission under way. And as soon as the Kuwaiti dudes were gone Trang said he wished Euclid Krebes was still around, as the truth was he wasn't as up to speed on the U.S. Constitution as he was on the *Bill of Rights,* which was kind of a direct and simple top-ten cool political idea list.

So Tommy Trang kicked back on the couch and shut his eyes like he was trying hard to remember the American Constitution, when Princess Lulu pops in the room. And right away I'm thinking: *should I still call her Princess Lulu if we are now a democratic movement?* Well, what happened next relates. It turns out that the lady's husband—who was probably partying and getting laid in London— was one of those geeky dudes who was into talking to people when he was home on like a *ham radio.* And so Princess Lulu dragged us to another room to like stare at this ham radio, and the lady starts like fiddling with switches and stuff to get the thing going. And she hands the mike to Princess Lulu, and right then our Princess Lulu clicks the switch and starts chattering in Arabic.

As little Ali has gone off with the Kuwaiti fighters to like post the *Bill of Rights* for post-war Kuwait around town, it is up to like the lady to tell us what Princess Lulu was up to. And Princess Lulu was telling everyone who was out there in ham-radio land that she was no longer the *princess* Lulu of Kuwait, but was now just an average *Lulu*! And then she got into explaining that she was with a new resistance group that was aiming to get rid of the Kuwaiti monarchy—of which she was a *former* member—and replace it with a bunch of men and women elected into a Kuwaiti congress by all the people in Kuwait in a popular election. You could see Princess Lulu—I mean citizen Lulu—was being *carried away* by all this, as she was laying on a lot of flowery stuff and talking rapid-fire in Arabic about what a great revolution this was, not unlike the American Revolution, and how after the liberation of Kuwait there would be a Golden Age in Kuwait, like had never been seen since the ancient days of Athens, and how if the people of Kuwait could only endure a little longer, all their pain would be worthwhile, on account of the democracy they would all enjoy, and so on, and so on. Man, that Arab girl could really talk!

I admit I kind of wondered if she was telling all this good news to like one ham radio geek in like Cairo. And to be honest, the more Lulu talked into that mike, the more bummed I slowly got. It seemed like Tommy Trang just kept adding on more and more *impossible stuff* we had to do before skipping out of Kuwait. Like first we were just going to rescue Princess Lulu, and then there was the crazy stuff about killing Saddam, and now we were supposed to help turn Kuwait into a democracy. So I guess my face showed how dubious I was, as Trang like said, "What's up, man?"

So out of my mouth came the words, "We got to bail out of Kuwait, man. This is all crazy, man."

And Lulu heard me as she chattered, and kind of turned to me and smiled and taking her finger off the TALK button said, "You are very right." And she turned to Tommy Trang and like as she took his hand said, "Let us leave Kuwait." And then she said to me, "How do we get out?"

She looked half serious, so I was like, "I don't know Lulu, and I don't care if we go on one of those old *dhows* or something. Let's just go *somewhere,* and you two can grow old together and watch your kids grow up and go to their senior prom, all that corny American stuff."

And Trang like slapped me on the shoulder and said, "You *are* so right man, let's get the hell out of here in a *dhow!*"

And Lulu yelled, "We will leave right now!"

And then Trang and Lulu *cracked up laughing* at the very idea they would *bolt in a dhow* right when they were in the middle of fighting to bring democracy to Kuwait. And I'll tell you right now, Trang *never* really wanted to bolt, but little by little Lulu started to have a different take on this question. I mean Lulu was crazy for freedom, but *nobody* in the end was crazier about it than Tommy Trang.

CHAPTER 20

Anyway, we finally crashed that night after founding the Democratic Resistance of Kuwait. And when we woke up, who do we see chilling on the villa's couch *but old Mahdi the Messiah!* I had like dropped Mahdi right out of my mind, as he had been missing in action since we arrived in Kuwait City. Anyway, there he is sitting on the couch wearing this nasty thin sword. It is like tied to his side by some sort of red sash. Mahdi saw me looking at his sword and stood up and whipped it out of the scabbard and swished it around the room. Then Mahdi like walked over to me and told me to feel the blade with the back of my nail and I'm like: *that's sharp dude!* Mahdi told me *this very sword* had been used for countless beheadings on order of some long-ago ruler of Kuwait named Mubarak, and that the sorry dude about to lose his head had to hold a bowl to catch the head and all the impure blood that spouted from the neck.

What are you going to do when you have a crazy Arab dude with notions of being a Islamic messiah hanging around swishing a nasty sword and rattling about beheading? All I did was like sort of hint around as to that maybe we were busy, but Trang—he like comes right out and says with a laugh: *what the hell do you want, Mahdi?* And Mahdi like makes Trang laugh harder because he puts away the swishing sword and it is soon clear all the messiah wants is *like someone to make him some breakfast.* What a lazy dude was Mahdi! He wanted to like knock off the Saudi and Kuwaiti royalty but he was too lazy to make his own breakfast! So Ali like went in the back and whipped something up so we could lose the Mahdi.

We all chilled in the living room with Mahdi as the messiah dude chowed down. And what quickly becomes clear was he already knew all about our brand-new movement to dump the Kuwaiti and Saudi monarchies. But something got lost in translation, because Mahdi did not seem to register at all that we were like hoping to produce a *democratic* Kuwait—and I guess Saudi Arabia—when like the royals were gone. No, as Mahdi shoved food in his mouth, it became clear the democratic goals of our movement had escaped him. All his ears heard was the rumor that we were trying to bump off the Kuwaiti royals, *and this had got his blood boiling!* I guess as *Mahdi* he thought Allah had like tapped him for the job of bumping off royals to like replace them with more pure and strict Islamic dudes. And he like kept pointing to the damn mole on his chin as if to say, *I'm the Mahdi, man! I'm the one in charge of bumping off royals! You infidel dudes have to back off my like Allah-appointed historical role!*

So a couple of times Trang tried to inform the messiah with the mole that we were aiming to bring democracy to the Arab locals, and that the heavy Islamic thing was like definitely not part of our agenda, and would be seen as a serious step backwards by our people. But the messiah dude wouldn't hear what Trang was saying about democracy, just jumped up and swished his sword and said that this very sword of Mubarak will make the royal heads roll, *and that soon he would reveal he was the Mahdi to the world!* And then after this huffing and puffing Mahdi would sit back down and go back to his chow. As he was spilling food all over his white robe and it was all stuck in his beard, after a while I kicked back and chilled a bit and felt a bit like Tommy Trang did about Mahdi: *What a pure crackerjack example of Arab looniness!*

Anyway, Trang and me had to stop laughing about Mahdi, as Lulu came in the room and didn't think Mahdi was funny at all, and neither did our little Ali. Maybe we should have listened to these two more, but Mahdi seemed like such a clown at the time! I mean he couldn't even feed himself, never mind start a Islamic revolution. It was also Lulu's opinion that Mahdi might someday

try and slay *her,* as she was a royal, even if a former one. I guess Lulu
didn't like the looks Mahdi was giving her as he waved Mubarak's
sword. So Lulu whispered we should find a new villa ASAP. Tommy
Trang wasn't too worried about crazy Mahdi, but he said if our
Lulu wanted us to find a new home, we would find a new home! So
we ditched Mahdi right there as he was stuffing his face with breakfast and ranting about Allah, took our stuff and the flamingo on a
sort of leash, and walked down the beach.

So we break into this real plush villa down the shoreline some.
And like it wasn't very far from the old villa, but it seemed to make
Lulu happy to be the hell away from the sword-swishing Mahdi the
messiah. And whoever owned this new villa had like a real crazy
antique royal taste in furnishings. I mean the whole place was filled
with this wooden gold furniture that was like built for giants.
Overall, as we had been in a palace and a number of villas, I got to
say your basic Arab taste was pretty cheeseball. So anyway, we sat
around on the couch at this new villa and talked about the democratic movement we had just founded and Lulu opined how
maybe the whole Arab world would like get inspired by us and start
to dig hard into the democratic way! That night we all just talked
endlessly about democracy, and tried *not* to think about crazy
Mahdi waving the psycho sword of Islam, or how big Colonel
Fawwaz was sniffing around in Kuwait somewhere grinding his
teeth about 'Trang the Jew infidel' hanging with his fiancée Lulu, or
how we had been pretty lucky in not getting killed yet by any Iraqis
in general.

Finally I couldn't talk about the *joys of democracy* anymore and
went outside the new villa to sit on the beach and listen to the slap
of the oil-soaked waters for a while. While I was sitting there I had a
strong feeling we were getting closer to the ground war, as the
Coalition bombing was wicked heavy. And then finally Tommy
Trang comes out of the villa and sits down next to me, and neither
of us said anything for a while. Of course, I think we both *wanted* to
say something about all the Arab psychos after us, and it was all bottled up inside, and then Trang started to laugh, and then I couldn't
help it—*I started to crack up too.* And Trang was like grinning away

and saying: *what dude? what? what's so funny?* But then the two of us were just rolling on our backs, laughing like maniacs as we thought about how *this had become one hell of a crazy-ass ghazzu we were on!*

We finally chilled and just sat there looking into the dark waters of the Persian Gulf and listening to the *kabooms* of the Coalition bombs from across the desert, and that was when Ali came outside and sat down with us, but clearly something heavy was on his mind, as our little Ali seemed pretty glum. So Trang and me were like *out with it, Bangloman.*

And Ali said to Trang, "Will you *salemt*?"

And Trang didn't even know what this was, to *salemt*. So Ali was like very serious as he said, "To *salemt* is to become a Muslim."

Trang laughed and said, "Come on, little man. Me? A Muslim? I'm an American, end of story."

And Ali said, "But how then can you marry Lulu? *She* is a Muslim. *She* believes in Allah as the one god, and Muhammad as his messenger."

And Trang said, "She's free under the Bill of Rights to believe in Allah or Ronald McDonald or whatever. But she's not going to let old Allah stand in the way. Lulu's cool, Ali."

And little Ali got like huffy, and stood up and said, "You are a great man, Tommy Trang. But in this you are a fool. Lulu is not *'cool'*—she is a Muslim."

I like looked at Trang in the dark and said, "You worried this old man Allah's going to mess with Lulu and you?"

And Tommy Trang like slapped me on the back and said, *"Inshallah, dude, inshallah."* Which Trang thought was pretty funny, using the local lingo as if to say, *Whatever, man, whatever.* And I had the weird feeling Trang was kind of curiously *into* the whole problem of Allah, and was kind of *looking forward* to seeing how it all played out between Lulu, him, and Allah. But Allah was in no way a *major* concern, Trang was clearly still gunning for Saddam Hussein, and into helping turn Kuwait into a democracy, before we all sailed off into the sunset on a *dhow.*

So you might have thought we were done with the Allah topic, but little Ali was just sitting there with a totally glum look, so

Trang finally turned to him and said, "Hey, Ali, chill. Me and old Allah are like this, man." And Trang held his two fingers together, to show how *close* were Trang and Allah. And then Tommy Trang started totally cracking up as he looked at his own fingers held aloft. And then there was a sound from behind us, and we all turned around to see Lulu standing like a few feet behind us, looking at Trang's raised fingers. And I guess by her face it was the first time she really totally digested that Allah was like *a big joke to an American like Trang.* And so Lulu like said something in Arabic that sounded pretty pissed and ran back in the villa.

Trang grinned at us and shaking his head went back into the villa. Even when she was a total hothead he was still nuttily into Lulu. And so then we had like an hour or so where Ali and me sat there on the beach while Trang and Lulu chatted about Allah in the villa. And it turned out Ali had found some American-style playing cards in this villa, so I like taught the little *Bangloman* how to play poker, while we waited for Lulu and Trang.

So then finally Lulu and Trang were in the doorway of the villa, and man, *they both looked exhausted!* I guess they had really gone to the mat over old Allah. And Trang said to me and Ali, *it's cool.* And although he looked tired, Trang looked reasonably happy—like it had been an interesting experience to wrestle this hard over something as curious to him as this local phenomenon Allah. I think Trang never had any doubts that Allah could be skirted as a problem between him and Lulu. But a look at Lulu told a different story. She just looked exhausted, and kind of more depressed than I had ever seen her—like someone had tried to tear her heart out. Looking at her face, I was pretty sure Lulu and Trang had pretty much *only agreed to chill on Allah for now,* and like hold continued talks on the topic *after* they had like brought democracy to Kuwait.

Anyway, the next day Ali got on the horn to talk to some of his old Kuwaiti friends in hiding and discovered—to our total and serious surprise—the Bill of Rights posted on walls around Kuwait had like been noticed by the Kuwaiti locals and there was a real underground buzz going on about who we new democratic resistance dudes were and what we were up to! It turned out this *Bill of*

Rights was like a powerful recruiting poster or something, and it sure opened my eyes as to like the *inspirational power of tossing a cool idea like democracy on the table*. I guess some of the Kuwaiti kids who were like in hiding decided that they'd be willing to risk their young lives for something as excellent as a democratic future for Kuwait.

In a flash of inspiration Trang decides we should become a larger-scale underground movement if there were all these young Kuwaiti dudes hungering for democracy. It was that simple: Trang just said, with a serious stoke in his voice, *let's open it up to more of the locals!* So over the next few days we enter a crazy new phase of like laying the groundwork for this larger underground democratic resistance organization. It was weird because we had just founded this democratic resistance movement and now here it was already expanding! But as you might have seen by now, with Trang around you had to buckle your seatbelt, as the dude just always had his golden arms open to the newest possibilities in any situation.

So suddenly Trang, Lulu, Ali, and me find we have all this sort of heavy *bureaucratic* work to do in terms of vetting a lot of possible members of our underground democratic resistance movement. It sure was a good thing we had little Ali, as he knew some of these mostly poor Kuwaitis—and we had both male and female—and he also seemed to have a nose for the solid-gold Arabs versus the sort of dubious players. I should say we didn't exactly invite those like interested in our movement right to our beachfront villa, but Ali and Trang kind of scouted around and set up a sort of organizational HQ in an empty and bland house Ali found several streets inland and away. Nobody was to know where we were keeping the princess Lulu, and we went to great lengths to like do all our operational stuff at this random concrete house.

Little Ali was like over there at our new HQ doing interviews all the time, as every time we tapped one new fighter, he or she had a number of friends who wanted to join, and Ali had to vet *those* friends. We did the usual thing with a resistance movement, we like made a bunch of separate cells, and none of them were to know about the other ones, and we made one solid Kuwaiti the leader of each cell. And we spent a lot of time sneaking from the HQ back to the villa while looking out for Iraqi patrols, and it seemed like we were constantly on the go, *but were we doing anything in terms of fighting Iraqis?* I mean soon we had like five cells set up with five or more members in each, but it seemed we were like *marine staff officers!* And you could see this was getting Tommy Trang down even more than me—he wasn't cut out *to be behind a desk.*

It was Lulu who like told Tommy Trang one night when we came home from like doing more interview work at HQ that he needed a *ghazzu.* I guess she sensed her man was like getting down in the dumps, and the minute she said that word *ghazzu* you could see Trang's face light up! *Ghazzu* was a word that went with *Captain Shakespear* and DIE A HERO! and all that stuff that like made my man Trang's heart tick. So we all chilled out on the sofas in the villa and like tried to come up with a cool *ghazzu.* But all that bureaucratic work like *knocked something right out of us*—I mean at least us *guys* were like totally out of *cool ghazzu ideas!*

But not Lulu! Her mind was just *fizzling* as she sat on the couch holding her man Trang's hand. I mean it was like her imagination had been bottled up in Kuwait for like the last sixteen years, and starting now it was just going to *explode* for our democratic resistance. That was one of the cool things Trang did for Lulu: he gave her outlawed imagination a little American spot in the desert on which to land and flower. Anyway, we guys are like so burned out with the office work at HQ we just stare at her as she gets on this excited riff about how our democratic resistance movement needs a *name!* I didn't see how this related to a *ghazzu* for Trang, but we are too burned out to argue. And as Lulu is like throwing out heavy names like *Popular Front for Democracy in Kuwait!,* and even worse ones like *Jihad for Kuwaiti Democracy!,* and we are looking dubious at her, just then the flamingo walks in front of the couch. That pink flamingo like had a kid's wading pool that she chilled in all day, and she had like the free run of the villa. And Lulu like jumps up and points her finger to the sky and says: *Flamingo!* So we all like catch on right away, and so we are *Operation Flamingo!*

Lulu was really jazzed about the name *Flamingo* as it like tied together for her the memory of the maid Leila and the role of Allah in all that was going down, and it *was* a cool name, but still, we needed a *ghazzu*! But we had to learn to trust Lulu, and right after she like got the name Flamingo she like orders Ali to like find some cardboard. There was still a bit of the princess in Lulu—she like was always ordering little Ali around—but he worshipped her like she was his queen, after all she was hooked up with Trang, who was to Ali like a king!

So anyway, Lulu like took this piece of cardboard Ali had found in the old garbage and like starts sawing away with a knife. And we have no idea what she is up to, but finally you could see it was *the cutout of a flamingo!* So like Lulu wants us to get some pink spray paint and like wander around Kuwait at night and spray up these flamingos all over the place, *as like a sign that our democratic resistance movement is present and accounted for!*

Tommy Trang tried to have some enthusiasm for this idea, but it was Ali who carried the ball. He like jumped on the phone, and starts jabbering, and hangs up a dozen times, and makes new calls. And that was one of the odder things too about the Iraqi invasion—the local phone service wasn't compromised until late in the game! And it was Ali who like showed us how powerful a *tool* was the phone, as soon he had located a like warehouse that had all sorts of spray paint, and it was like one of the few warehouses the Iraqis hadn't yet pillaged. So Ali is like on the phone again, and has one of the cells heading there to break in and get a bunch of paint, and he makes plans to meet them near our HQ later that night. And Trang was psyched to go, but Lulu told him he and me had to stay home and work on the new *democratic Kuwaiti Constitution.* Man, was Trang bummed! I kind of glanced at Lulu right then, because on the one hand she was the one who suggested Trang needed a good *ghazzu,* but then she clearly wanted him to stay home. What I am saying is right then I was guessing Lulu might have some growing doubts about losing Trang to some heroic action—even if it was old Allah's plan!

Like that night little Ali and one of the cells roamed around Kuwait spray-painting flamingos here and there. And Ali didn't show up until just before morning, and it turned out he had a hell of a good *ghazzu*! He had gone so far as to sneak up and paint flamingos on like a couple of Iraqi tanks, and some Iraqi antiaircraft guns. Trang and I were pretty jealous as he told us of his adventures on his *ghazzu*, and *bummed we hadn't seen how cool it was right away!* Because when we went to HQ later that day, the phone there was soon ringing off the hook. And it turned out a lot of the young Kuwaitis that were in hiding really were stoked to see this flamingo painted all over the city, and to know as the phone word spread that there was a new group out there *ready to give the finger to Saddam!*

So we are all pretty happy with the flamingos to say the least, as the word came from some of the resistance dudes that the Iraqis were like pissed as a whacked hive of bees. You wouldn't have thought the Iraqis would have wasted much time with the spray-painted flamingos, what with the air war smashing them from the sky, but the word was they were like *busting to nail us!* And the next night we like made more flamingo cutouts, and sent out resistance dudes with more spray paint, and more of the cells got involved in this cool *ghazzu* of throwing flamingos in the face of the Iraqis. And more and more young Kuwaitis were wanting to join our movement, but we didn't want the fun to get out of control, so we like decided to chill for a while in terms of signing up new members until we like knew what we were doing next in terms of an operation.

And then one day little Ali brought someone to our secret villa. We were kind of surprised Ali did this, as no one was supposed to know where we were keeping the princess, out of natural fear of the news getting to Colonel Fawwaz, the Iraqis—or now even Mahdi. Anyway, Ali walked into the room a tall, skinny old Arab lady and tells us she is like *Khaled's mother!* The first thing out of her mouth is: *she has seen Colonel Fawwaz and his men in Kuwait.* That made us sit up and take notice of this old lady! It turned out her family was close to the Saudi royal family, and had known Colonel Fawwaz since he was a fat little boy. And she told us—as if we didn't know—that Colonel Fawwaz was just out of his mind with wanting to find and kill Princess Lulu for hanging with the infidel Tommy Trang. And so that was why she had tracked us down through Ali at HQ, to warn us about Colonel Fawwaz.

So after we thanked her again, she like took a sip of tea—Ali had brought in some tea—and said she wanted us to know *how she was real down on her son Khaled*. He had like told her all about our splintering from his group over like democracy, and I guess Khaled had added in disgust that we were like into *everyone* voting, even *servants and women!* And I guess he was surprised when his mother came down on him like a ton of bricks and told him to like go apologize to us, *and told him she was for women voting!* I noticed she didn't say *servants voting,* but whatever. The deal was she like wanted to be a part of our Operation Flamingo which she somehow knew a lot about, and little Ali let on to us this was a big deal, as I guess Khaled's mother carried a lot of weight with like a lot of local Kuwaiti ladies.

I glanced at Trang as we like all sipped *tea* with Khaled's mother. And to be honest Trang was looking kind of bummed and bored again. I guess he was thinking *if we've got a bunch of Kuwaiti mothers on our side, what are we going to do, have a cookie sale for the democratic resistance?* And Trang was just wrong, because these mothers were like a huge secret local force, and as Khaled's mother talked we began to see she already had the *mothers sort of already organized!* She had like a phone web going of mothers, and they like organized the movement of food and stuff to those who were in serious hiding. And this sort of made Trang sit up and take notice of Khaled's mother! And you could see Trang's mind was starting to work: *what she was saying was she had dozens of eyes all over Kuwait watching the Iraqis' every move!* And that was like when Trang got clearly stoked and asked her *if the eyes of all these Kuwaiti mothers could like start to keep track of all the Iraqi staff, troop, and armament movements around the city.* And Khaled's mother said she could *absolutely* do this with her mothers, *only how would the mothers know what to look for exactly?*

So right then Trang and Ali and Lulu and me got to work like sketching out a sort of *manual* for the mothers of Kuwait. We included drawings of what the insignia were for the various Iraqi enlisted men and officers, so if the mothers had binoculars they could see if there were any high-ranking Iraqis hanging around. And Trang like drew sketches of the various Iraqi tanks and armaments, because although most of these were on the Saudi-Kuwaiti border side of Kuwait, they were always being moved around. And that was when I came up with the term *Motherweb*, for like the web of Kuwaiti mothers, and all were into this name. We gave the contact number as the phone at our HQ, and what that meant was someone had to be over there all the time, and that someone turned out to be little Ali.

We printed up this manual for the mothers on the Xerox machine in the villa. And as we had to print a lot of copies, we were like suddenly turned into office workers. That was a bummer overall, except it gave Trang and Lulu and me a lot of time to jabber together as we printed and stapled the manuals. Of course we went over for the hundredth time with Lulu all the stories of our slipping into Kuwait to link up with her, and how wild it was that Lulu and Trang had linked up again after their initial kind of random meeting in the waters of the Persian Gulf. And Lulu like said with a serious look: *Inshallah! The truth is I was there to die, and you to steal pearls from our waters!* And Lulu then thanked Allah that she wanted to drown that night rather than marry Colonel Fawwaz and that we wanted to rustle pearls from her waters. I wasn't all that into thanking Allah, so I tried to move the conversation back to the more practical questions like: *and where the hell will you two go when we get out and when exactly are we leaving and how about soon?* But Lulu always teased me back and said like *find us a dhow and we will go right now!* It was like a joking refrain from Lulu: *find us a dhow.* She was joking then about leaving, but as I said, toward the very end of the operation she had a different point of view.

Anyway, as we xeroxed and stapled, we also let Tommy Trang rattle on once again about democracy and what a cool thing it is that America has this powerfully excellent vision to share with the world. And generally I was way into hearing Trang tell it straight, but after a while that night, I wanted him to talk about something else except *democracy.* So I was like Trang, man, you should *write these thoughts down on democracy and share them with the local people!* And Lulu was like, *Cody Carmichael has a great idea!* And Trang and me looked at her like *he does?* As I was generally not known for ideas, I guess. And what came out of it was more Lulu's idea, as she ran with the ball in an excited way and decided we in Operation Flamingo needed like a *newspaper.*

Trang and me thought that was a cool idea, but we were not reporters, we were marines, even if AWOL. But Lulu was jamming on the idea, and said we could have like articles on democracy, and run the Bill of Rights, and have like lighter stuff like cartoons about the Iraqi occupation. And Trang said it would kind of get in the Iraqis' face if we like ran *an account of the coming and goings of the various Iraqi troops as was reported by the Motherweb,* and when he came up with that idea *he got real stoked about the newspaper!* So we put the word to Ali, and he put the word to the cells, and soon we had a bunch of Kuwaiti guys and gals who like had an interest in reporting, and also others who had access to a small printing press at the local Kuwaiti university.

So we met a lot with the new reporters for the *Kuwaiti Flamingo Democrat*—the like name of the new paper—at HQ, and there were some skilled and serious former Kuwaiti newspaper dudes in the bunch, and they were primed to do an excellent job. So they like put out this four-page underground newspaper in about four days, and it was distributed all over Kuwait by the cells, and even delivered right to the Iraqi HQ. And once again, the word came back that the Iraqis were just blowing gaskets, and that just made all of us crack up, and feel fine, and it was a real golden time for Lulu, Trang, Ali, and me, after that first issue of the *Kuwaiti Flamingo Democrat* came out. We opened the doors again to new recruits, and added another like five cells.

So we were feeling excellent, as I said, except Trang was clearly running a fever in his need for a *ghazzu.* And Trang and me talked a lot about his *need for a ghazzu* at HQ between like meeting with reporters, or cell heads, or new recruits, or checking in on the new Motherweb about Iraqi troop movements. And one day Trang was like so upset he like swept his fist across a table of maps and knocked a bottle to the floor. That wasn't like him, but he was *real* frustrated. And damned if his *sweeping the bottle to the floor didn't produce like another idea for some of our new cells.* It was Lulu who looked at the bottle and laughed and said: *Operation Broken Glass!* And the deal was our guys went out at night and littered the road with broken glass around the Iraqi installations, so cars and vehicles were like popping tires right and left, and every morning the Iraqis had to send out sweeping crews near the installations and gun positions.

Lulu in this period was like on a raging boil with enthusiasm and imaginative energy. She came up with another cool idea after Operation Broken Glass. She got some of the cell members who were also artists, and they like made up these mock *Kuwaiti road signs.* The signs looked exactly like the real thing. And now we knew from the Motherweb where all the Iraqi positions and operations were, and these fake road signs said stuff like: SLOW IRAQI ATROCITY ZONE, or NEXT RIGHT, IRAQI RAPIST HOTEL, or JUST AHEAD, DEATH TO SADDAM! So that idea went over big with the cells, and they all wanted to put up fake road signs. And of course the Iraqis tore down the fake signs as fast as we could put them up, but our cells just kept throwing up new ones. And we reported on the signs in the *Kuwaiti Flamingo Democrat,* and then Lulu did something even *more* clever that kind of followed from the road signs. That girl was just *foaming* with cool ideas during this period. It made me wonder how many other girls in Arabia were just like shut down totally in terms of their creative talents and in need of like liberation by a posse of crazy American marines.

Anyway, we had been slipped a lot of photos that brave Kuwaitis had taken throughout the Iraqi occupation, and Lulu like wrote up this fake pamphlet from the 'Iraqi Ministry of Information.' And in the pamphlet she ran the photos along with fake captions. Like she had a photo of all these buildings destroyed by the Iraqis, and she captioned it, GLORIOUS NEW CONSTRUCTION BY ORDER OF SADDAM, or photos of dead Kuwaitis in rows after the Iraqi invasion and the caption, THE HAPPY KUWAITIS GREET THEIR LIBERATORS, or photos of the Kuwaiti prisoners being beaten in Basra with the caption, EDUCATION UNDER SADDAM, or photos of the empty hospitals and the caption, ONLY THE BEST MEDICAL CARE UNDER IRAQ. And this pamphlet was printed and distributed around Kuwait, and was of course a great underground success among the Kuwaitis, and once again pissed off the Iraqis as far as we could tell. And Lulu was just basking in the glow of what she had done with this pamphlet for a few days, as I guess using your native talents after hiding them under a blanket for sixteen years or so can give you a superior buzz. And we didn't know it at the time, but those were Lulu's golden days. If Lulu had more time living under some sort of American-style personal freedom, she really would have flowered, I bet.

CHAPTER 21

I guess our luck couldn't hold out forever. We had a lot of totally brave young Kuwaitis running around at night on various *ghazzus,* and sooner or later one of them was bound to get caught by the Iraqis. And Ali took the call that this one Kuwaiti guy named Yussuf had been picked up, tortured, and dumped headless on the steps of his parents' house, as was Iraqi tradition. So we scrambled to vacate our HQ, and gave the word that all the cells were to chill until we figured out how badly we were compromised. Little Ali and Trang and me took shifts keeping an eye on the HQ, and the Iraqis never showed up there, so I guess this young Kuwaiti didn't break, so we were pretty amazed at his courage, and the word went out on the Motherweb and to the cells, and we all honored Yussuf's heroic memory. Trang spoke of him as a real Captain Shakespear–type dude, and for a couple of days would talk of little else but this guy Yussuf, and his bravery.

So we chilled on our resistance activities after our dude Yussuf was killed, and that was when the dead Saluki showed up. A Saluki is a royal Arab hunting dog. Some like cell member got in touch with us and told us about the dead dog. And Lulu like asked some questions about what the dog looked like, and when she got off the phone she looked pretty bummed. And the Saluki was brought to her, and when she saw it, even with its head pretty much blown off, she said: *Colonel Fawwaz is sending me a message that he is in Kuwait and will kill me.* The deal was the dead Saluki was a descendant of one of the famous dogs of Colonel Fawwaz's grandfather Abdul Aziz al-Saud the founder of Saudi Arabia, and one of countless engagement gifts Colonel Fawwaz had *tried* to give to Princess Lulu.

So what with Colonel Fawwaz and the Iraqis both gunning for Lulu—not to mention crazy Mahdi and his sword of Islam—I was once again for departing from Kuwait. I was into our democratic resistance activities, but thought real strongly right then Lulu, Trang, Ali, and me needed to find a *dhow* and vacate. So I introduced the idea kind of jokingly once again and said: *hey friends, can we like find that old dhow now and let someone else kill Saddam and bring democracy to Kuwait?* And Lulu didn't answer the question straight, but stared at me and then said kind of seriously, *the first thing you should know is here in Kuwait a dhow is really called a bhum or a barghala.* And Lulu then ran around and got a piece of paper and like drew a *bhum,* and it had a sharp, long bow like a knife, and a flat stern and two masts. It looked real cool and ancient. Lulu said the stern had to be painted black with a white ring, and she drew it like that! And then Lulu got into the drawing the way real artists do, and she got out her watercolors and made it real pretty. And then she gave the drawing to me and said: *a bhum for you, Cody Carmichael, as you are always asking for one.* But then Lulu was suddenly hot on drawing and watercoloring, and she was one of those imaginative types who like forgot the world when she was doing it, which is always kind of beautiful to see! I mean I *never* forgot the world! Like I was totally aware as Lulu started happily watercoloring a *barghala* that Colonel Fawwaz *and* the Iraqis were like hound dogs trying to sniff out her trail!

Lulu kept working on her *barghala,* and raised her head suddenly to me and said if she *had* to escape from Kuwait on one of the boats she'd prefer the *barghala* over the *bhum* because it was more fancy and beautiful and had these huge rear windows in the stern where she and Trang could like lie together and look out at the Persian Gulf. And then Tommy Trang said with a laugh that maybe we could find someone to make us a *barghala,* and then we could sail away when we had accomplished our various missions in Kuwait, and head off to like the pearl beds. And that was when Lulu laughed, and it turned out she was laughing because when we had first met her it was in the waters right off downtown Kuwait City, and we had told everyone we were there looking for *pearls*. It turns out the pearl beds—and there were some left—were actually like way south of Kuwait and toward Bahrain. And Tommy Trang took Lulu's hand right then and said, *I knew what pearl I was looking for,* and Lulu like was into the romantic moment, and I like winked at Trang and said *nice recovery, dude.*

Anyway, when the romantic thing was over for the moment the talk of pearls and *barghala* continued between us three. And we didn't have much else to do but talk as we were laying low resistance-wise, and Lulu got on to the old art of Kuwaiti boat building, and Lulu knew of this one old guy who was still barely alive, and he was like once this major builder of the finest *bhums* and *barghalas* in the days of yore. And so as always with Tommy Trang it wasn't enough to just sit around and *talk* about this boat-building dude, we needed to like go *seek him out,* and I guess see if he was up for a like wartime commission for a boat. As we snuck to his place in the dark that night—and he wasn't far away here on the Persian Gulf shoreline—I got the impression Tommy Trang really expected this dude could like build us all a *barghala*, and that Lulu and Trang—and Ali and me if we wanted—would like spend our days cruising for pearls in the peacetime Persian Gulf and like anchoring in the friendlier country of Bahrain when we needed a shower or some supplies.

So we got to the shoreline house of the old boat builder, and he was like not in his house but in this huge shed, and in the shed was like this half-built boat: *and damned if it didn't look like the barghala Lulu had drawn!* And I guess nobody came to visit the old master builder much, and he was a real antique Arab. There was dust all over the *barghala* like he hadn't put a tool to it in years. So the old boat builder was pretty deaf, so Lulu had to yell Arabic into his hairy old ears, and then he reached out and gripped her hands real fast in this vice grip and started rattling on in Arabic like he had just seen *Allah.*

And it turned out that once long ago this dude had like had a commission from *Princess Lulu's father, the brother of the emir, to like build the most beautiful barghala of his career in honor of the coming birth of Lulu.* And so the old dude had worked and worked, as I guess there was something about *Allah watching him* on this commission. And then the old dude started to weep some, as Lulu's dad *had never come to pick up the barghala, as Lulu's mom had like died in childbirth.* And the old dude said Lulu's royal dad had paid him never to build another *barghala,* and like he was still getting money to *not* make any *barghalas* even though Lulu's dad was dead. And he tossed a lot of *inshallahs* around, so I guess his view was his not building *barghalas* anymore was like the will of Allah. So then he stood up and stumbled his old legs over to the *barghala* with a hammer and chisel and did a little chipping, and then said to Lulu that he felt he was now free to finish this *barghala* for *her, as it was the very one that he had started like sixteen or so years earlier for her father.* And then he raised hammer and chisel to the sky and kind of shook them and cried out *Allahu akbar!*

I was like looking at Trang like to say: *no fucking way!* I didn't say it out loud, as Trang wasn't into swearing, but I was thinking: *no fucking way!* But you could see by Trang's face *he was thinking it too!* And then I started to get this like weird chill up my spine. And I think we two young Americans didn't really know *what* to say! But Lulu knew what to say, and of course it was *Allahu akbar!* She was totally sure Allah was behind this! And I mean it seemed to take a little of the thrill out of it for her, as I guess she was totally used to Allah having lots of tricks up his sleeve, and was like calmly: *there you go, Allah does it again!* So Lulu was totally like nodding and thanking Allah, where I was left just blown away and thinking: *no fucking way!* And to tell you the truth, I think this *barghala* thing was like a serious turning point for me. I mean, looking back on all that went down in Arabia, I think the idea there was some sort of big-ass plan at work in pushing Trang and Lulu together sort of finished breaking through the surface waters of my mind right then.

Anyway, the ancient boat builder was just in a rage to get back to work, and said in the morning he would call up his two sons who were like computer programmers, but who were really boat builders at heart, to come help him knock out the old *barghala.* And Lulu asked if she could go aboard, and the old dude said it was her boat, she could do whatever the hell she wanted. He kept calling her Princess, by the way, even though she tried to tell him about her giving that all up and our democratic movement.

So Lulu zipped up the ladder, and Trang followed. And they stood up there on the *barghala* together, and you could just see them out there on the Persian Gulf cruising around and doing some ancient pearling. And I guess Lulu said to the old guy that her man Trang was hot on doing some pearling when the *barghala* was finished, and the old dude said he himself was once a pearl diver. So Trang like whipped out the big pearl from his pocket, and the old dude took it and his old eyes kind of misted over, as I guess way back when Captain Shakespear was around they had such glorious pearls, but now, no more.

The old dude like put his tools down right then, and started to slip back into his personal history of yore as a pearler. And he let us know even when they could have them, diving suits were verboten, as unfair. And Trang like said: *unfair? unfair to the pearls?* And the old dude nodded like: *yeah, unfair to the pearls.* And Trang looked at me like: *that is excellent!* And the old dude said the pearling had to be done in the hottest months of the year, so you really suffered. And again Trang was like nodding as if to say: *so be it! The hottest months!* And somehow the old dude caught on Trang was like into the suffering aspects of proper pearling, so he like addressed Tommy Trang and warned him that he would have to put up with *sores and skin troubles and maybe even scurvy,* and that he would be allowed to eat nothing but *rice and dates and damn near starve,* and that you worked from dawn to dusk until your lungs collapsed, among jellyfish and sharks, and that generally it was the worst experience under Allah.

And so my man Trang was like standing in the *barghala* looking down at the old man like: *yeah, old man, bring it on, you can't break me, I'm a United States marine!* And the old man was real jazzed by the look on the face of Trang, and he rustled around in the back of the shed and like brought out this ancient bit of filthy cloth that you might have rejected to clean the oil off your car's dipstick back home and handed it to Trang. And the deal was this was the very loincloth the old dude had worn when he was a pearler, and he wanted Trang to like have it! *A great honor!* So Trang being Trang he like stripped down and put on the ratty loincloth, and the old dude started to weep. I tell you what, I would not have put *my* balls in that crusty old rag, but such was Tommy Trang!

Trang and Lulu were so hot on the *barghala* that there was no way we were going to leave the old boat-building dude that night. I like settled in against a wall, and the old dude went back to work on the boat and Trang kind of hovered around him to get his first lessons in *barghala* building. I guess Trang figured he ought to know something, in case the thing broke down out there off Bahrain. The ancient dude had a lot of stored-up boat-building energy after a sixteen-year work stoppage, so he was good to go—and the two pretty much worked through the night. I like fell asleep on the floor, and at one point I woke up to see Lulu and Trang lying together in what would be like the rear bedroom of the *barghala*. They were like touching heads together and whispering, but when the old dude came back from like the shitter, Trang got up to help him hammer a board on their boat, while Lulu just lay there in the rear of the *barghala* with her eyes squeezed shut like she was in pain. I remember thinking: *I wish this thing was done enough so we could splash it right into the gulf tonight!* Later on, when our operation against Saddam was over, Lulu would admit she was secretly thinking the same thing once or twice as she lay there alone in the back of the *barghala* that night.

A few hours before dawn as we like slipped back to our villa we almost got picked up by a random Iraqi patrol. We only got away because Lulu turned out to be a real speedy runner for a little girl with such a plush figure. The Iraqis actually fired at us when they saw we were getting away. So we ended up in the basement of a random villa, and as we sat there in the dark Lulu suddenly plunged into this manic rap about how Tommy Trang was just like some dude named *Antar.* And Lulu is like *Antar did this* and *Antar did that,* like we are up to speed on who the hell this *Antar* dude is in the first place. Trang had to like grab Lulu's arm and kind of shaking it say: *whoa Lulu babe! Back it up! Who is this Antar?* Lulu looked a little pissed and said, *I have read the stories of your lands, why have you not read mine?* Anyway, it turns out *Antar* is like some Bedouin warrior dude who lived back in the sixth century, and was just like our own Lancelot. So we were cool with that, and told Lulu *to lay on us the news of the mighty Antar!* And so Lulu heads into this wild saga of how Antar saved his lady by slaying a lion while his own feet were bound together, and then ran off to take on forty thousand Bedouin in solo battle, among other excellent warrior doings. And Trang like stood up when she was finally done and opening his arms wide like he was talking to a huge crowd yelled: *I am Antar!* And Lulu and me had a pretty good laugh, as Trang was playing it like he was *serious.*

When we got back to our villa that morning, I right away wished we had gotten on the *barghala*—even unfinished—and taken off and away from the Gulf War. Because little Ali was standing there looking real, real bummed. And he signaled like he wanted to tell Tommy Trang something in private, but Lulu like caught the hand sign and said: *what is up, Ali?* And still Ali didn't want to tell, but when he did it was like clear why he didn't want Lulu to hear the news. The deal was the Iraqis had announced they were going to kill three random Kuwaitis a day until Princess Lulu was given up. The Iraqis were like blaming Princess Lulu for all this Flamingo stuff! And while we were learning how to build a *barghala,* the Iraqis had killed two men and a five-year-old girl they had just randomly snatched off the street to prove they were dead serious. And the Iraqis had done some real nasty stuff to the little girl, and my man Trang looked at me with the fiercest look like, *we absolutely got to do something!*

So our Lulu was real upset, too. And upset ran to hysterical pretty fast, and I am sorry to report my first reaction was: *let's hit the barghala! The thing will float!* I thought we could skip out and spread the word Lulu had vacated Kuwait. But Lulu got ahold of her weeping, and then she asked to hold the pearl, and when it was placed in her hands Lulu said to Tommy Trang, *I will give myself up to the Iraqis. I cannot let my people die for me.* And Lulu didn't mean like: *I'll do it later today after a final cup of tea!* She like handed the pearl back to Trang and headed pronto for the door of the villa. And that was when I really saw she was a pretty heroic chick under all the craziness of drawing swirling blue henna lines on her face and chatting up Allah. I mean she was not just ready to commit suicide *for herself* like to avoid marriage to Colonel Fawwaz, she was ready to off herself *for others*—and that's two totally different cups of tea. And that was when I started to think about the *pearl,* as it seemed like everyone who touched the damn thing ended up dying while trying to save others. Krebes, Leila—they both died trying to help others, if you think about it. But then I shook my head to clear it, as blaming the pearl for random deaths in wartime seemed totally crazy.

Anyway, Trang is like trying to convince Lulu giving herself up to the Iraqis was *not* the best course of action, but she opened the door to the villa and headed toward the road. And Trang just picked her up kicking and yelling and carried this heroic chick back inside. And as I have said: she was a wildcat! Tommy Trang like was standing there holding this kicking, scratching, yelling, weeping princess, and he looked at me like: *what the hell do I do with her?* And I was like shaking my head like: *you signed up for this buddy!* So Trang said kind of bummed, *Get some rope!* So once again we had to tie down Lulu. And even when she was like tied down she kept up kicking and squirming, and was clearly hurting her own wrists and ankles. I don't think I have ever seen anyone lose it like that! So finally Trang like got on top of her to kind of hug her and hold her steady and he held her wrists and whispered to her like you would a child that it was all going to be okay, and Khaled's mother was called and took a look in the room and said, "I will call a doctor friend."

So this Dr. Abdullah came and gave her a tranquilizer. He looked real pale and scared, and he left us with a couple more syringes and some pills, and then he vamoosed. All Dr. Abdullah said the whole time he was there was, "So this is indeed Princess Lulu?" And Lulu stopped struggling long enough to say, "I am just Lulu. Lulu of the new democratic Kuwait."

So eventually Lulu was chilled by the drugs in her veins, but she still was glaring at Tommy Trang and me with like the eyes of a hawk. And round and round the merry-go-round conversation went, and it went like this:

Lulu said, "You can't keep me tied up until the end of the war."

Trang said, "I'll keep you tied up until we solve this little problem."

Lulu said, "It cannot be solved but with my death."

Trang said, "We got to be smarter than the Iraqis."

Lulu said, "I am ready to die for my people."

Trang said, "You won't die."

Lulu said, "I will die."

It always boiled down to these two teenagers saying: *you won't die! I will die!* Anyway, Trang like took time out from arguing with Lulu about death long enough to tell Ali to call a meeting at HQ of the best of the resistance cell heads. And Trang wouldn't leave Lulu to go the meeting, I guess he remembered how she got free when we went to bust the prisoners out of prison. So he told me to go, and to find some solution to the problem of the Iraqis killing civilians in order to get Lulu.

So I go with Ali to HQ later, and one by one the Kuwaiti cell heads showed up. And these dudes were looking at me with such real human concern, and I could see they all knew the situation with Lulu tied to the bed and wanting to give herself up to the Iraqis. It was like, and I hate to say it, but it was like Lulu was *really* some sort of royalty to them now. Anyway, the coffee flowed all night, but nobody had a genius idea, until word came on the Motherweb while we were putting our heads together that the Iraqis had like blown to bits several houses with RPG rockets in the belief Lulu was in them. And Ali asked questions, and it turned out for some reason the crazy, lazy Iraqis hadn't like checked the rubble for dead bodies. And Ali hung up the phone and was just grinning from ear to ear, and we were all in the dark. So little Ali said: *don't you see? They have tried to kill Lulu! We will let them think they have killed her!*

Ali wasted no time, but got back on the horn. And he found a Kuwaiti girl's body at the morgue who had been in another Iraqi attack and was pretty blown up. And so then Ali like got on the horn to Khaled's mother and scheduled some citywide heavy-duty crying and ululating for the next morning over the 'dead princess.' And Ali told Khaled's mother to tell all the mothers the princess was *really* dead, I guess so the wailing would look realistic. And then Ali told Khaled's mother that *there would be a funeral march starting at the souk in downtown Kuwait at noon for all the mothers!*

Man, it wasn't enough for Ali just to have a good idea, he was like becoming more like Trang—he had to go whole hog! I mean I would have just let the local mothers do their wailing from the windows and rooftops, and put the word out the princess was dead, and hope the Iraqis took the bait. And maybe we'd lay off the resistance activities for a while longer. So when Ali got off the phone I was like *what the hell was that about a funeral march, Bangloman?* I mean this was still occupied Kuwait, and because of that we sort of made it a commonsense rule to like *sneak around*. But Ali's idea, as he explained it, was to *put the whole Motherweb on the streets of Kuwait the next day walking behind the casket of the 'dead princess.'* Ali thought chances were pretty good the Iraqis would not fire on a bunch of mothers, and that this show of 'Mother Power' would really get everyone inspired in Kuwait.

I went back to report the decision to have like a parade in downtown Kuwait the next day. And of course Lulu was real bummed hearing about the dead Kuwaiti girl, but also pretty turned on by the idea of a funeral march. She thought it was pretty funny that she would get to attend her own funeral. And Trang was generally impressed with Ali's idea of a march, but jumped up when Lulu said she'd like to attend her own funeral. He was like *no way are you going!* And Lulu was like *last time you didn't let me come on a ghazzu my maid Leila was killed!* I didn't think this made a lot of sense, but whatever. Then Lulu started to yell at Tommy Trang that it was *her* funeral, and besides, she could be there in disguise *as all the Kuwaiti mothers would of course be under their blankets!* It looked like we would have to tie her up again to keep her away, so Trang gave in and Lulu got to go to her own funeral. But the only way Trang would agree to let her go was if *he* got to go so he could be by her side with an M16 under *his* blanket. Lulu thought this was pretty funny, and that night they tested a rig of some big old lady pillow tits for Trang so he'd look properly female under his blanket.

Tommy Trang made it clear that I was *not* to walk in the funeral march, but to be there on the sidelines with Ali and the rest of our democratic resistance boys heavily armed and undercover, so that if there was a snafu of monster proportions, we could like lay down some covering fire so Trang could grab Lulu and make tracks to safety. So Trang and Ali and me and the Kuwaiti dudes with us stayed up late drawing the funeral march route from the souk, and sketching in our positions. And the more we made plans, the more it was clear we would be pretty obvious as there was no real *cover*. So the decision was made that Ali and me and the Kuwaiti dudes would *all* have to be heavily armed and blanketed Kuwaiti women too, only we would not walk in the parade, but hang around the fringes, like we were women too nervous to get right in it. So there was a logistical problem or two that night, like where would we find enough blankets to like go over our heads?

That night we broke into a series of villas all along the waterfront, and gathered enough local female garb. While we were doing this detail stuff, our Ali was out with a resistance cell getting the poor dead Kuwaiti girl's body out of the morgue, and rustling up a casket, and generally chatting up Khaled's mother a whole lot on the phone all night about the logistics of the funeral march. Man, Trang and me agreed that our Ali was going to make a hell of a Marine Corps officer someday!

So our march was scheduled for noon the next day, but we were all hidden away in nearby buildings in downtown Kuwait before dawn, so we could filter in with the other real mothers when they arrived. So around ten in the morning, we are on the sixth floor of this building looking down, and we see all these Iraqis showing up in force. And this doesn't look good! So we are all holding our breath, and then the Iraqi troops start to like line the road, like they are lining up for our parade. And the strange thing was they looked real casual, not like they were there to bust heads. And then they all let out a half-assed cheer, and it turns out *they* are having a parade too!

Down the road comes a bunch of Iraqi dudes dressed in loincloths, and they are pulling what looked like a Roman chariot.

There are like two dozen of these loinclothed, bristle-mustached Saddam-like Iraqis, and they are just dragging this chariot, and in the chariot is a huge Saddam Hussein figure. It was a pretty lousy float, like it was done by a bunch of bored vocational school kids ordered to do a 'Spirit of Saddam' float for the Fourth of July. And there were all these loudspeakers around Saddam's head, and some like message was being broadcast at high volume from the chariot. The Iraqi dudes lining the street were just standing there as it passed, and Ali stuck his head out the window to try and pick up the Arabic. And Ali said the float was to like proclaim that Saddam was a new king of Babylon, and would do just like some ancient dude named Nebu-something who *was* the king of Babylon, who like drove the Jews out of Jerusalem way before the year zero.

So once that wacky historical stuff about the Jews was over—and it really made us wonder again about Saddam's sanity—all the Iraqis pretty much vacated the street. So by about 11:00 A.M. the street was almost empty. And that was when the mothers started to filter into the street in black, blanketed clumps of two and three, and then those clumps banded together. And if you stuck your head out the window you heard ululation going on not only in the street, but like all over the city! I mean people were sticking their heads out and letting go from the rooftops with some real grief for their princess Lulu! I looked at Lulu and she was in tears next to me. And so then we saw like a bunch of our fighters dressed as mothers carrying out the coffin, and the Kuwaiti mothers rushed over, I guess to help carry the dead girl. And as there really was a dead girl killed by an Iraqi RPG rocket in there, it really was pretty sad. And so then Trang and Lulu ran down the stairs to get out there and mix in with the mothers. And I ran down with the Kuwaiti fighters and Ali and we took our positions on the roadside with our rifles knocking on our knees under our robes.

Man, it was hot under the robe! And the funeral procession just started marching along, and all the mothers are wailing. And a couple of Iraqis showed up, but they just watched us for a while, and then they were gone—I guess to report. And so the mothers marched and the mothers wailed, and it was like: *where are we going with this?* I mean what do we do if the Iraqis just let them march and go home and don't believe it is Lulu in the casket? But then a bus showed up, and a bunch of scruffy Iraqis led by an officer got in the road like fifty feet ahead of the marchers, and they lowered their rifles and barked an order I guess was *stop you mothers!*

But those mothers of Kuwait kept marching carrying the casket right toward the rifles, and the wailing of the mothers picked up. I guess that made sense, *as they really thought Lulu was in the coffin and was a hero who died for their freedom!* But the wailing was so strong from the mothers I had to believe there was a lot more behind the grief! I mean these mothers were really totally *angry and upset,* and they kept marching toward the Iraqi rifles. And I remember thinking *how brave were these mothers of Kuwait!* And that was when one of the mothers ran ahead of all the others and started to yell at the Iraqis about *how they killed Princess Lulu,* and Ali in his robe next to me suddenly said like under his breath: *oh, oh!* And that was when the Iraqi officer just shot that brave mother down, and all the other mothers dropped the casket and scattered. I said to Ali: *here we go, bro!* And I flipped up my robe and opened fire, as did Ali and the democratic Kuwaiti boys, and the Iraqis scattered like rabbits for cover. And in the midst of all the firing, one of the mothers ran forward and like scooped up the brave mother who had been shot down by the Iraqis and ran carrying her right toward our guys, so we had to cease fire.

And then we were all bolting back to our rally point behind some buildings, and when we all got there we saw it was of course Tommy Trang who had scooped up the shot mother. And I am sorry to report that the mother who was shot while making sure the Iraqis knew it was Princess Lulu in the coffin was none other than Khaled's mother, the one who had like founded the Mother-web. And Trang like said in this breaking voice, as he stood there holding her dying body in his arms, that Khaled's brave mother reminded him of *his* Vietnamese mother, as both were so totally crazy about freedom and democracy at any price. Looking at my friend right then, I was pretty sure we were not going to leave Kuwait until Trang had done something *big* with his soldier talents to try and save this crazy Arab world.

CHAPTER 22

And a few days later little Ali came home from our *new* HQ—
we had moved it twice because of Iraqis seen snooping around—
and said the Motherweb was back in action and had reported there
was a great rush of important-looking Iraqi vehicles coming down
from Baghdad. And Ali like explained the Motherweb was real sure
there were something real heavy-duty going down, as they had
never seen this kind of beehive reaction among the local Iraqi officers and men. And Tommy Trang like slapped me and little Ali
five, and looked significantly at Lulu, who nodded and said *Inshallah*
kind of quietly. I guess even then Lulu was sure it was Saddam
Hussein coming to town just so her man Trang could get his shot
at him—but of course Lulu figured it was *Allah* throwing out this
opportunity. Man, Trang and me glanced at her with some humor
like to say: *enough about Allah already!*

Anyway, Trang jumped into a kick-ass overdrive, and told little
Ali to stay on the Motherweb and get up-to-the-minute reports
from the mothers. And the reports we got were real excited, and it
became clear there was going to be like a secret gathering of the Iraqi
General Staff in the Kuwaiti Theater of Operations—what the Iraqis
called their 19th Province. And so Tommy Trang got more and more
stoked, and started going on about how this *was our big chance to like
prove we were right in going AWOL into Kuwait by knocking off a bunch of the
Iraqi general staff officers.* I guess Trang was already thinking explo-

sives—that we would like somehow blow the building where they were meeting sky high! And then Trang like looked at me and smiled this secret grin and I knew he was thinking, *And who knows, man, if our luck holds maybe Saddam will be there too!* But this was too big a like hope to state openly, so we remained just stoked with the possibility we might like knock off the majority of the Iraqi General Staff.

The reports from the Motherweb continued over the next few hours, as we hustled back to Khaled's villa to like look in his cellar to see what armaments and munitions the rich guy had hidden down there. Ali was real jumpy while we were over at Khaled's, as he said the word on the street was the resistance dude was totally blaming Trang for the death of his mother in the funeral march. Trang didn't seem too concerned about Khaled, as he said to Ali, *hey, tell the dude to take a number!* Anyway, Khaled had a real fine collection of weapons, but the best thing we found was like some serious C-4 plastic explosives. We didn't know what we were going to do with them, but we were pretty sure they would come in handy if we had to blow some building up! So we were all stoked to get a move on toward the action, and I had pocketed all my previous late nights thoughts on like all of us bolting from Kuwait. I mean bumping off the Iraqi Officer General Staff—and maybe even Saddam Hussein himself—that was like a historical action worthy of Captain Shakespear!

So Tommy Trang stood there grinning with the plastic explosives in his hand like they were the Holy Grail, or something. And he looked at Ali, Lulu, and me like *real significantly,* as if to say with this powerful stuff *we really might pull this off!* And we all reached out and put our hands over the plastic explosives, kind of like we were throwing our vibes into the stuff to like *do us right!* And there were electric and non-electric blasting caps, time-fuse, detonator cord, clackers—the works! We really had to laugh at Khaled: *he had all this expensive war stuff stashed, but he was more into cooking.* And so Trang explained what was kind of obvious: all we had to do was figure out where the Iraqi officers were having the big powwow about how they were getting creamed from the sky in this war, and get in there before them, and like put the explosives where they would do the most damage. And then we hide somewhere down the street, and at the right moment, *kaboom!* There were some details to figure out, but that was the mission plan right then. But the minor problem that came up right away was: *Lulu was throwing her two cents into our plans as if she expected to come on this most major ghazzu of all!* And I glanced at Trang with some significance as she was still giving *Allah* credit for like this mission existing at all, and he said to her straight out and pretty firmly, *you can't come, Lulu.*

Well, she didn't lose it to the degree we had to tie her down or anything, but she really carried on. She like was saying to Trang, *if I don't go, we will not be married!* She was kind of crazy, our Lulu, and she reached the point of saying, as she picked up the phone, *that if she couldn't come she'd call the Iraqis and warn them of our plans.* Trang just stared at her, and she cracked up laughing as she held the phone up, as of course she was bluffing. But you know, she was serious about coming, and *serious about calling it off between her and Trang* if she couldn't come along. So Trang had to like come up with something, and in the end Trang said, *you can come to watch the explosion from down the street, but you can't sneak in to place the explosives.* Lulu was cool with that, to my surprise.

And Lulu like went to the door of the villa to like look out into a sudden rain. I followed her and she started to tell me how much the Bedouin loved the rain. And right in the doorway of the villa Lulu found a small fat red *spider.* And she cried out like it was a real *score* to find this spider. So she scooped it up and showed it to me in her palm and said it was called *bint al-mater,* or daughter of the rain, and said to the Bedouin the spider was *a symbol of eternal love,* the kind of love that feels like you are standing in torrents of rain after weeks of hot sun in the desert. And Lulu like placed the *bint al-mater* in my hand and said, "You know, now Thomas Trang and I are alone in this world. I have given up my kingdom and Allah with my love for him."

Lulu stood in the door of the villa after the rain stopped, and she sniffed. I mean she really *sniffed.* And then she turned to me and said, "My parents died when I was very young. My grandmother was my friend, and she would take me to Mutlaa Ridge to 'sniff the wind.' We would go there with a picnic in the evening when it was cool, and watch the birds, and smell all that is beautiful that is carried on the wind in the desert." So like right then Lulu touched me on the shoulder, and we stepped out on the patio of the villa and I tried to sniff the wind. But the wind was full of the smell of oil fires burning, not to mention the sounds of the heavy Coalition bombing, so we went back inside.

Anyway, little Ali on the Motherweb began to piece together the situation with regard to this planned Iraqi General Staff meeting. And this might surprise you: a couple of the mothers on the Motherweb had like stopped just looking out their windows, and were like actively chatting up Iraqi soldiers. As you might have guessed, many of the Iraqi soldiers were not all that into Saddam! And more than that, some of them were ready to be bribed for information. I mean a lot of these Iraqi soldiers were at this point getting *really, really hungry.* So a couple of our mothers had started quietly like giving them food and jewels and what have you in exchange for information. It was a dangerous game these mothers were playing, but as has been seen in the funeral march, a lot of the local Arab ladies were real *ballsy.* So this is a long way of saying little Ali had the time and place of the meeting all wrapped up a few hours later!

And the deal was the meeting was scheduled for like early the next morning. So we decided to head out ASAP, so we could maybe sneak into the building, plant the explosives, and find a nice hiding place down the road to watch the fun. So we packed up and headed out that evening without further comment. Trang took a brand new M16 rifle from Khaled's cache, and I carried all the plastic explosives and my old M16, and Ali carried the blast kit and extra ammunition. And then Trang had like an inspiration, and ran back to like the lady's villa, where we had done all the xeroxing. He wanted the original copy of the Bill of Rights for Kuwait that Lulu had written up in Arabic and watercolored a lot of fancy stuff on. I was kicking myself for not keeping an eye on this cool historical document myself. And I saw Trang fold it neatly and put it into his side cargo pocket, and I noticed he put it on the left side. So Trang saw me looking and reached into his right cargo pocket and pulled out the sort of rotten hamburger remains of Euclid Krebes in a plastic Ziplock bag and said: *the dude wouldn't want to miss nailing Saddam!*

By the way, we were all wearing the local robes, but Trang had decided to still wear the Iraqi camouflage trousers *under* his robe, as he said it made him feel more like a *marine,* as well as gave him a means to carry the hearts of old brothers-in-arms and historical documents like the first Bill of Rights for Kuwait. I figured he was also carrying the pearl as usual, but didn't feel like asking where it was! So given the heroic size of what we were heading out to do, I kept thinking there should be like some huge parade for us, with bugles blowing and stuff! I mean this was a major-league action! And I also kept thinking: if it was this easy to maybe nail Saddam, why were there not dozens of recon marine teams in here trying to do the same? But there were no bugles, we just all slipped into the Toyota as soon as it was dark and with Ali at the wheel, as he knew the way to the like warehouse where the meeting was to go down, we were off to like kill Saddam, or at least his General officer Staff.

So on the way to the warehouse Lulu, Ali, and me were in a serious mood. I mean it was a serious business what we were going to try and do. But Trang wanted to talk about it! Trang kept telling us *we were like on a mission of historical proportions!* Trang wanted us to like talk about how surprised all the senior American military officers would be when the news came we had like taken down Saddam. Tommy Trang like pretended I was George Bush, and he was like a senior aide coming in to whisper the news during a press conference. And then *he* pretended to be President George Bush and said as if to a camera: *I have just gotten word that Saddam Hussein and all his senior officers have been killed in an explosion in occupied Kuwait.* And Trang imagined all the reporters would go wild with questions, and President Bush would smile and say: *I know as much as you do at this time. We believe it was part of an organized resistance movement within Kuwait.* And then Trang said President Bush would like hurry down to the Situation Room saying over his shoulder to like all his clueless generals: *find out who the hell did this!* And Trang imagined word would go out to General Schwarzkopf to like figure out what the hell happened ASAP, and little by little word would filter back from the marines who saw us at Khafji, and knew we were heading back into Kuwait and gunning for Saddam, that these two crazy-ass heroic marines, Privates Cody Carmichael and Thomas Trang, were known to be working on plans to take down Saddam. And how President Bush would like put the word out that we were no longer AWOL, but had been ordered to go on this risky mission by like the top brass. And the way Tommy Trang saw it, we would like be given the congressional Medal of Honor in the Rose Garden—even little Ali when we explained he was a U.S. marine as of Khafji when he gave him a battlefield enlistment—and then he and Lulu would like head off to their golden future as national heroes.

So what I am saying here is I have never seen Trang so stoked. I mean all the way to our appointment with history in the Toyota he like wouldn't shut up. As you have seen, he was not the most talkative guy normally—but on this ride he was like a heroic chatterbox. Not that we minded—I mean I think the rest of us were a little concerned something might go wrong during the actual *appointment with history.* I didn't take a poll of Ali or Lulu, but even Lulu looked serious. But old Tommy Trang, he was just on a roll, he was just sailing into history with his mouth running on overdrive! He could see it all in detail, down to the like individual roses in the Rose Garden!

And then Trang looking at me real seriously said, "You know, I got to thank you for busting into Kuwait with me, Carmichael." That was real cool of Tommy Trang to say, and I like slugged his shoulder and said, "Remember Captain Shakespear!" and he punched my shoulder back. And right then as we traded punched shoulders, I guess a modern song finally bubbled up into old Trang's head. And he started suddenly roaring out this pounding anthem that everyone knows, and I joined right in, as it was just a stoking song to sing with your comrade-in-arms while on the way to maybe knocking off Saddam:

> *No time for losers,*
> *Cause we are the champions of the WORLD!!*

Trang finally got quiet when Ali pulled into an alley and said he saw a Iraqi guardhouse ahead, and from here on in we had to like hoof it. So Trang like wanted to do one last thing before we got out of the car, and that was to hear the Bill of Rights for Kuwait read by Lulu in Arabic. So Lulu did a fine job of this, and made her voice like real pretty and singsong. And then we tossed our various packs on our backs and slid down the alley. All the way to the empty factory where the Iraqi staff meeting was to take place I kept thinking: *it can't be this easy!* But it was this easy! I mean we saw some distant Iraqis, but none like near us as we skirted along sticking to the shadows. And then when we were like near the factory, it was a snap to like pick out the empty building from which we would squeeze the clacker and watch the explosion at a distance the next morning.

So we went to this building, and Trang set Lulu down in a corner and told her to sit tight until we came back from setting the plastic explosives in the factory. And that was when Lulu made it clear that she was not going to be left out of such a mission of historical proportions. I guess the problem was Tommy Trang had like painted the glory of the thing so hugely that she had decided that as the only *actual* Kuwaiti, her country would look at her funny if she wasn't there for the whole operation. Lulu, in short, felt that some actual Kuwaiti should set the explosives under the feet of Saddam, or at least touch them when they were in place, so it could be said in the history books they were set under Saddam by the brave citizen Lulu.

Tommy Trang was on such fire to get on with the operation, and it looked like such a cakewalk, that he agreed. I think he also figured Lulu was not going to like let us get on with our appointment with destiny without a lot more chatter, and in doing so the damn factory might like get guarded. So Trang was like, *come on Lulu!* And we were off again. It was only about a couple hundred yards away, the factory. There were no numbers on the building, and there was no way we would have found it if not for our little Ali. I guess in normal times the factory had been like a milk-processing plant, and all the milk equipment had long ago been sent packing to Baghdad. So then we were like in an alley right next to the building, and we all hunkered down there to listen for any sign of Iraqi troops. I remember thinking: *this is crazy!* If we Americans were like having a meeting of all our top brass including General Schwarzkopf, we would have had the place armed to the teeth days before!

So as there was no sign of any Iraqi guards, Trang flashed the thumbs-up, and we slid inside. And when we were in this big empty hall we could see in the moonlight the marks on the floor where all the heavy like milk pasteurizing equipment had been removed, and we could see some preparations had been made for the meeting, as there were rows and rows of American-style folding chairs. And then Trang like nudged me, and we all turned, because there on the wall of the factory like forty feet high was a huge portrait of Saddam Hussein! And on this sort of stage in front were all these random velvet and gold royalty chairs they must have stolen from the various Kuwaiti palaces. So we all grinned at each other, as it sure looked like the big Iraqi cheese Saddam Hussein himself would be here bright and early.

We all slid up to the stage, and then Trang like crawled right under it. It was a real crappy wooden stage, but it had been surrounded by all this like fancy drapery, and covered with a bunch of Persian rugs. And Trang stuck his head out from under the like three-foot-high stage, and gave us the thumbs-up again, as this was clearly the place to set the explosives! And without further ado, Tommy Trang like motioned for the plastics and the detonators. And so I like crawled under the stage to see what it was like and lend a hand setting up the plastics. And I could hear Lulu and Ali having some fun sitting in what would be Saddam's chair over our heads, and little Ali was making these sounds like *boooom!* And so those two were having fun, and Tommy Trang and me were pretty happy setting the explosives down below.

Then the plastic explosives were set, and we were just so close to doing the dirty work to achieve our objective. And Trang and me slid out from under the stage, and we had to laugh, as Lulu like was sitting up there in this real massive golden chair. Lulu said this was her only chance to even *pretend* Trang and her were like the emir and emiress of Kuwait. I was surprised she wanted to pretend this, but I guess you can take the girl out of the princess, but you can't take the princess out of the girl, or something like that! I mean, no matter how much you are into democracy, there is still a part of you that is into playing emir and emiress. So I guess that was where Lulu was coming from, that like ancient human interest in royalty. Anyway, Lulu wasn't happy with just having Trang like as emir by her side! No, she wanted Ali to kneel down, so she could like *knight him.* I asked where she had heard about knights, and she said: *Cody Carmichael, do you think they have taken each and every book from me?* Anyway, you could tell little Ali *loved* Lulu, and wanted to play along about the knights, but he kept glancing at Trang like, *Would you tell her we gots to go?* But Trang, he was just looking at Lulu with that soggy look like, *Isn't she the coolest?*

So like when Lulu asked me to kneel down so she could knight me *Sir Cody of the Royal Order of the Democratic Flamingo,* or some damn thing, I just had to bring these two back to reality. And Lulu was pretty cool about it, as I guess she knew it made sense to like get ourselves into hiding for the night so we could end the Gulf War in the morning. So just as Tommy Trang is offering his arm to Lulu to help her off her throne, that was when the Iraqi vehicles started screaming from all directions. And we all like glanced at each other, and bolted for the door, but by the time we got to it the headlights from the Iraqi vehicles barreling down the road had it lit up. So we ran to the back of the factory, but the doors there were locked. And the windows were all stuck—although we didn't have much time to try more than a couple as we could hear all these Iraqis yelling in front of the building. We were caught like mice, and there was nowhere to go but back under the stage.

And we got under the stage just as the twenty-or-so Iraqis barged into the big factory room. Man, these were some crazy Iraqi clowns. I mean they were all arguing with each other right away, and you got the sense that none of them wanted to be here, and they were all blaming each other for random stuff. They were just really *unsat,* to use a marine term. And I could see out a crack between two sections of the cloth around the stage, and I watched all these Iraqi dudes sort of mill around and smoke butts and give each other dirty looks. I guess they had been ordered out here to like guard the factory for the night, and the reason they came screaming up in their cars was they were late, and probably got yelled at by some officer back in Kuwait City to like get the hell out here—but of course the *officer* didn't come out!

In the Marines we were taught that on every mission you give 110 percent. If the U.S. Marines had been assigned to guard this factory for a big meeting of the top brass, we would have been out here days earlier to secure the site. And we would have brought in trained dogs to like sniff out the plastic explosives—such as we were carrying—and we would have searched every inch of the place five times, and then done it again. We would have set up sectors of fire, and put marines and heavy guns on the roof and the roofs surrounding the building, and we would have searched and secured all the surrounding buildings too. So as I watched these Iraqis settle into the seats sort of slouching, and watched many of them nod and take a snooze, and others like just hung around looking bored and cranky—well, all I could think was how proud I was to be—even if AWOL—a United States marine!

And when I was feeling that enormous pride, that was when I turned my head around to look at the faces of Trang and Lulu and Ali. And that was when it really hit me. I mean I knew we were trapped here, that these unsat Iraqi dudes were going to slouch through the night and that we would still be here when the Iraqi brass arrived in the morning. And my mind followed this track as I looked at the deadly serious faces of my friends, and as I thought of Saddam Hussein coming to sit in the like golden chair over our heads, that was when I looked back at my man Trang's eyes. And the fact it took me so long to figure out what Ali, Trang, and Lulu understood right away was *because it was something I would never in a million years think to do to myself!*

The way Trang and Lulu and Ali were staring at me, I knew they had made *their* decision already, and were waiting to see what *I* wanted to do. I suppose that was polite of them, as clearly it should be unanimous. And my reaction was: *no way!* I'll say it again: *no way!* No way was I going to blow myself up to knock off Saddam Hussein and a bunch of his top brass. I thought it was an excellent plan to blow up these Iraqi dudes from like a remote location down the street from this former milk factory, *as they were evil no doubt and had to go!* But blowing *myself up* to get rid of this evil dude *seemed out of the question!* And so there was Trang staring at me with the simple question in his eyes, and I like shook my head as to say: *we part company here, man.*

And so Trang like nodded at Lulu and Ali and set down the clacker. And he gave me a grin like: *just as well man, I didn't really want to die!* And I thought: *whew!* And then after a while Trang and Lulu like lay down together, as there was plenty of room under the stage. And damned if Trang didn't like take out the *Bill of Rights* for Kuwait, and the two of the like democratic lovebirds looked at it for a while. And then my friend and his girl Lulu—it is hard to believe but—*they fell asleep in each other's arms!* It almost impressed me more that they were able to fall asleep in this situation then that they were willing to blow themselves up to rid the world of Saddam Hussein. And little Ali like curled up at their feet like he was their dog or something. He might have dozed here and there, but every once in a while I'd look over and little Ali would be staring at me with these sad eyes, like I had really let him down.

I didn't fall asleep. I mean I was more awake then ever. I was like *glowing* I was so awake. I could have run to Khafji and back. I could have raced a camel to Riyadh. I could of swum back to California. I tried to sleep, and I even tried to count sheep. And then damned if the mind doesn't wander, and I kept thinking about all those dead Iraqis like fried in the trenches with their mouth open looking at the heavens and going: *why me?* And in my mind I kept counting these french-fried Iraqi dudes. It was like a weird obsession I had that night: *One Iraqi, two Iraqis, three Iraqis . . .* I could like see the scene so clearly, as if it was all lit up. And then I started to count all those Iraqis who had like run after us trying to surrender yelling: *George Bush! George Bush!* And so I counted those now-dead Iraqi dudes. And then I suddenly was seeing the coming ground war happen, and I was seeing all these Iraqi dudes, hundreds of them, blown to bits and going up in flames. And that led me to think about the Americans who might die in the coming ground war, and I saw their like widows getting handed the folded flag, and their kids crying. And it was the American kids that finally got to me, to be honest.

So I took a real deep breath, but quietly. And then I looked at Trang and Lulu and Ali, and it like came to me *that these were my best friends in the world.* And when I thought back on my life, *the best days by far were these days I had spent on this ghazzu with my man Tommy Trang.* It was like the king of Saudi said to us: *when you face death you have a story to tell, and you are a man alive!* And it was like I couldn't remember much about my life back in California when I was a stoner surfer, but every *second* of my time with Trang was like hotwired into my brain. And it was weird to think, but it was Trang who had given me this story to tell, *he had in some way made me really alive!* If you don't know what it means to be really *glad* you are alive, I can't help you—but if you are lucky enough to have had this feeling, *then you know how high I was!* And you know, it was because I was so alive thanks to my man Trang, that like the prospect of cashing in my chips in a few hours made me like really want *to ululate in some heavy grief!*

And then it was dawn, and that bloody Arabian light was breaking into the factory. I was like the only one awake in the whole room. And I hadn't slept a wink. And I was like: *this is my last morning alive, that sucks!* Because some switch had like flipped in my brain, and I was like: *damn, got to do it! Don't want to do it, but got to!* And so little by little I watched the light brighten the factory room through the crack in the fabric, and then some of the Iraqis like walk outside to take a piss. And then they like went back to hanging in their chairs and smoking butts and looking sour. And when I looked back Tommy Trang was like looking at me, and I gave him a quick nod, and made a signal with my thumb like to push down the clacker. And he looked at me like: *you sure, man?* And I nodded again. And he quietly touched his shoulder where he had the tattoo that said: DIE A HERO! And I did the same to my shoulder, and then he like moved to me and whispered in my ear: *you are a Captain Shakespear approved dude, Cody Carmichael!*

So then the Iraqi brass started to arrive, and each one like bustles around giving the sorry Iraqi dudes in the room a busload of crap. And it was clear all these Iraqi generals were pretty nervous, and that made me think Saddam was really coming. And so then the Iraqi dudes start to like take their chairs, until there were like twenty rows of various Iraqi officers. The back rows were filled with enlisted men. And some more time passed, and the Iraqi officers just stared straight at the stage like they could see us, but I guess they had their eyes on the empty royal chairs above. And I thought that the two who *really* belonged in royal chairs were Lulu and Trang. And right then I looked back and my man Trang and Lulu were like both looking down at the pearl in Trang's open palm, and then they were hugging, and Lulu and Trang both had serious tears rolling down their cheeks. And although I knew it to be true, it showed me these two kids knew what they were giving up here on Earth. I mean they were both pretty damn crazy I have to admit, but I bet they were both thinking about how sweet it would be to be sailing away on the old *barghala* right now! And looking at the pearl right then in Trang's open palm I was like forever shot—I mean I just totally knew the pearl rules and will someday conquer all.

And then it happened. There was the sound of like a couple of big cars pulling up outside and everyone in the room got dead silent. And I slithered across to the side to another crack in the fabric. And when I glanced back I saw Lulu and Trang breaking off their embrace and Trang taking up the clacker. And so I was able to see the door to the factory, and man, whoever was out there took their time. And then a bunch of real nasty-looking Iraqis in black glasses came into the room that must of been some of those superbad Iraqi dudes the Mukharabat, *and then there was Saddam Hussein!* He was standing in the door of the factory. And I like raised my fist with a thumb up to Trang, Lulu, and Ali to *let them know the badass dude had arrived!*

And right as I see the eyes of Saddam Hussein like seem to burn with evil right into mine, *the whole room just seemed to be blown sky-high!* And my first thought was: *shit! the plastic explosives blew too early!* And

I even thought: *I'm exploding into bits in slow motion!* It was that big a shuddering explosion. There was total chaos in the room, Iraqis like screaming and firing their weapons for some reason. And I like look back at Trang and Lulu and Ali and we are all like: *what the hell just happened?* And I peek out again and *the room is just bailing of Iraqis like rats leaving a sinking ship!* And soon enough the damn room is empty of Iraqis and you can hear shots and screaming in the streets where there seems to be total chaos!

And all Trang kept whispering over and over during this total mad chaos was: *We had Saddam by the balls, man! We had Saddam by the balls, man! We had Saddam by the balls, man!* Even when we had crawled out from under the stage, Trang kept saying: *We had Saddam, man!* You know, I think if we hadn't come so close to nailing Saddam my man Trang *might* have chilled right then, and we four *might* have all hit the *barghala* and sailed away into the Persian Gulf sunset with time to spare.

Anyway, we went over to the blown-in windows on one side of the factory, and kind of dragged over some chairs and snuck a look out a window. And what we saw was this: the huge factory *right next to this* one had been totally *flattened!* And as there were no planes that we heard in the sky it was clear this factory had been flattened by United States cruise missiles launched from somewhere in the Persian Gulf. So then we knew: *somehow through their satellites they had seen all these vehicles converge around here and knew it was a meeting, but when it came down to plugging the coordinates into the computer they had like screwed up and nailed the factory like a hundred yards away!* And that factory was like obliterated, *there was nothing left but like smoking dust and rubble!*

And then I looked at Lulu's face. And what Trang never grabbed on to was like the experience with almost getting blown up to rid the world of Saddam was like *it* for Lulu. I mean we first linked up with Lulu trying to drown herself to avoid marriage with Colonel Fawwaz, and she had been fired up to die for her Kuwaiti people since then, but something about this last experience of like *lying in Trang's arms waiting for the plastic explosives to blow*—she was like now *done with dying,* is what I'm saying. She didn't come right out and say *screw that inshallah crap, I got a major reason to live!* right then, but it would kind of quickly become clear that what Lulu *really* wanted from here on in was to keep her and her man Trang *alive*. Which seemed reasonable to me—as I had been ready to hit the *barghala* for weeks—but of course not so much to Tommy Trang, who was higher than ever on heroism having come so close to nailing Saddam.

So we are looking out a window at the flattened building. And the Iraqi brass and enlisted dudes are out there like staring at it like they are in shock too. Some are like kicking the rubble and like looking nervously at the sky through all the concrete dust. But Trang was just totally riding the rocket rush of coming so close to nailing Saddam, because as we headed to the vehicle later he was like totally shaking with stoke as he said: *we got just one last thing to try and do in Kuwait, man. We got to try and bust out the resistance and bring some democracy to these desert folks!* And there was like no human way to calm down Trang on this topic of democracy for Kuwait, because he was now just a man totally burning up with his final mission of like bringing American-style freedom to the locals. He waved his M16 like he was spraying a clip and yelled: *we'll write* DEMOCRACY *with bullets, man!*